Tree-House Comix Proudly Presents

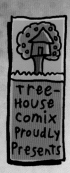

DOG MAN

A Tale of Two Kitties

WRITTEN AND ILLUSTRATED BY DAV PILKEY
AS GEORGE BEARD AND HAROLD HUTCHINS
WITH COLOR BY JOSE GARIBALDI

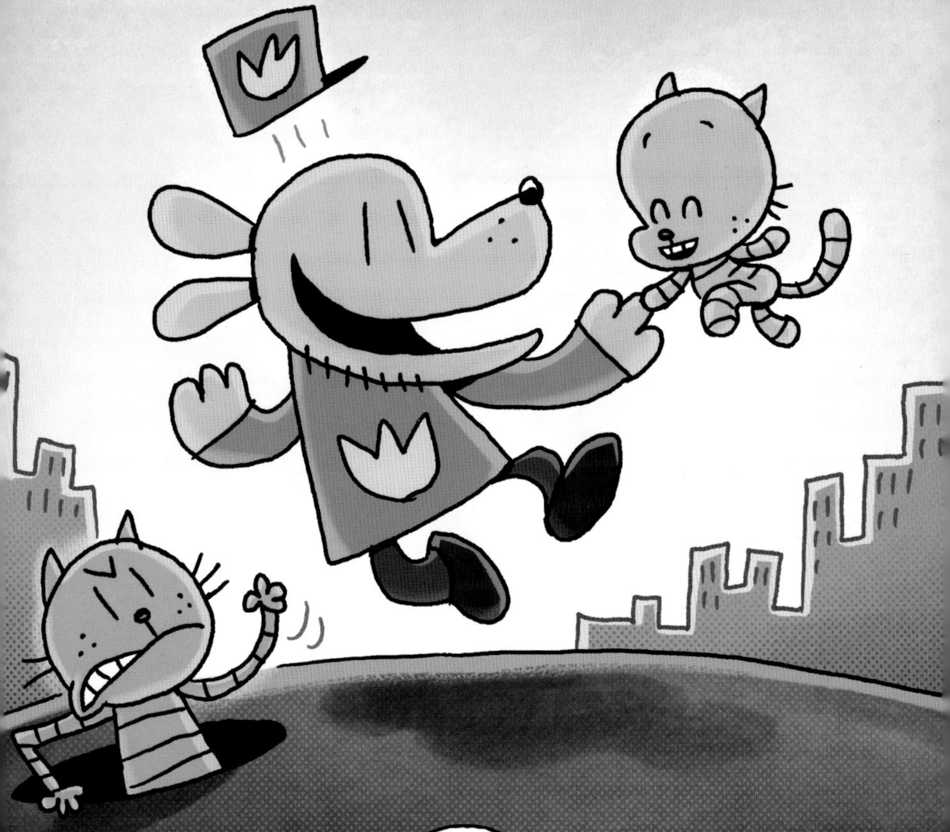

graphix
AN IMPRINT OF
SCHOLASTIC

HERE'S TO YOU, MR. ROBINSON!
(THANK YOU, DICK.)

With thanks to Charles Dickens, whose novels, particularly A Tale of Two Cities, still resonate with readers today.

Library of Congress Control Number 2016961907

ISBN 978-0-545-93521-0

10 9 8 7 6 5 4 3 2 1 17 18 19 20 21

Printed in China 62
First edition, September 2017

Edited by Anamika Bhatnagar
Book design by Dav Pilkey and Phil Falco
Color by Jose Garibaldi
Creative Director: David Saylor

Chapters

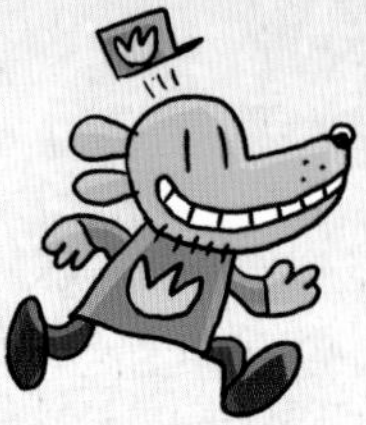

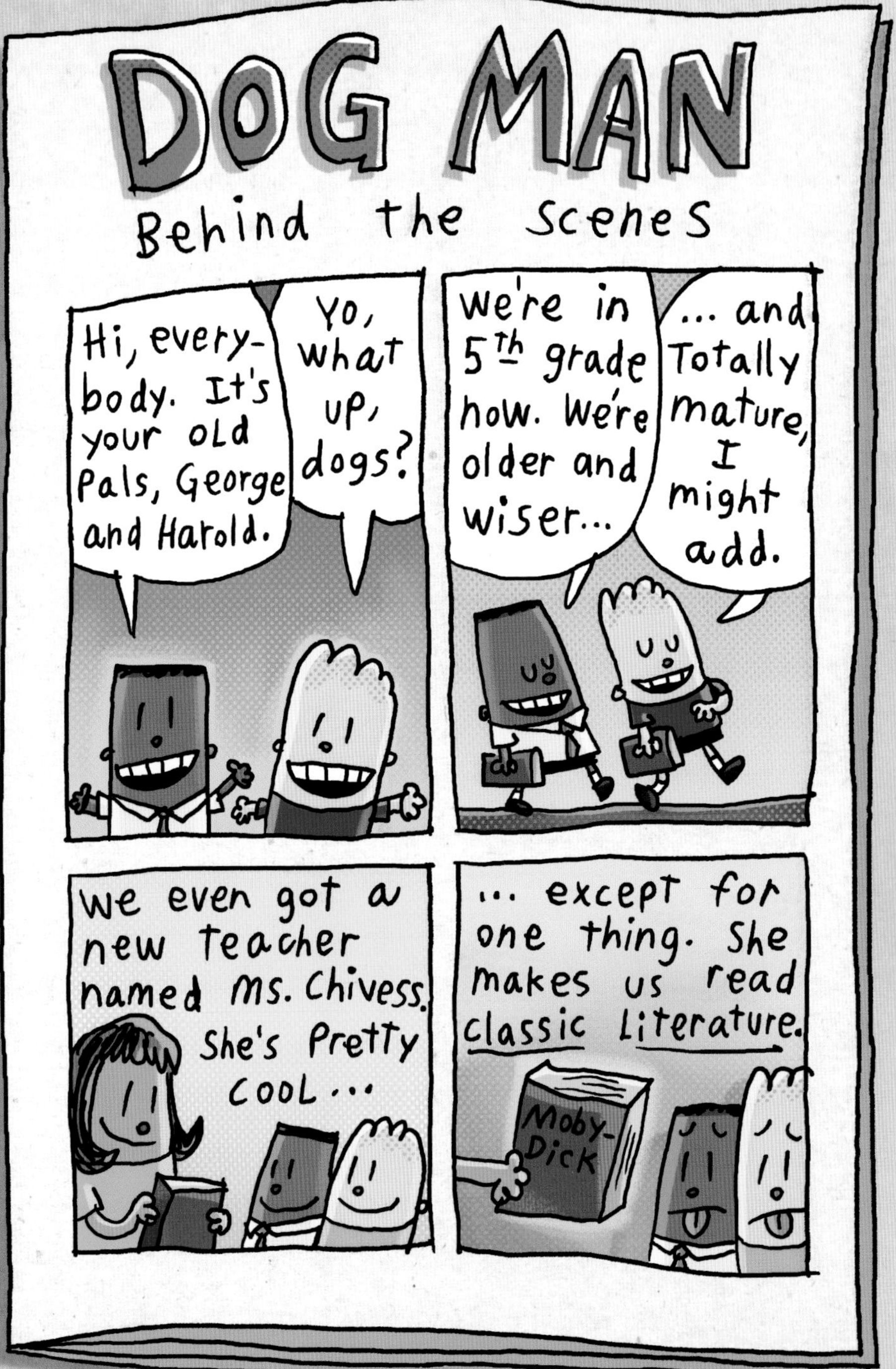
DOG MAN
Behind the Scenes
Hi, every-body. It's your old pals, George and Harold.
Yo, what up, dogs?
We're in 5th grade now. We're older and wiser...
... and totally mature, I might add.
We even got a new teacher named Ms. Chivess.
She's pretty cool...
... except for one thing. She makes us read classic literature.
Moby-Dick

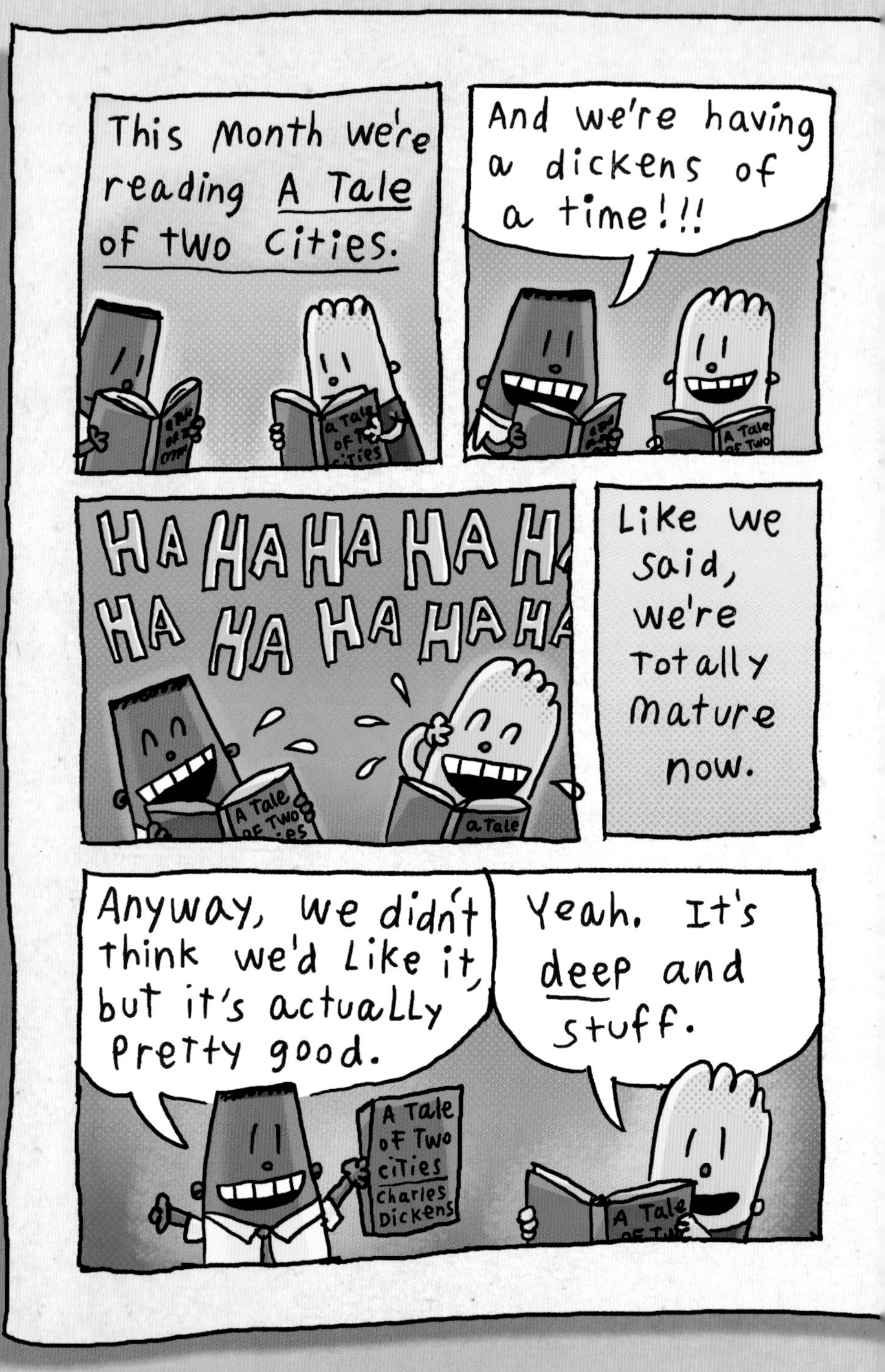

This Month we're reading A Tale of Two Cities.
And we're having a dickens of a time!!!
HA HA HA HA HA H
HA HA HA HA HA
Like we said, we're Totally mature now.
Anyway, we didn't think we'd Like it, but it's actually pretty good.
Yeah. It's deep and stuff.

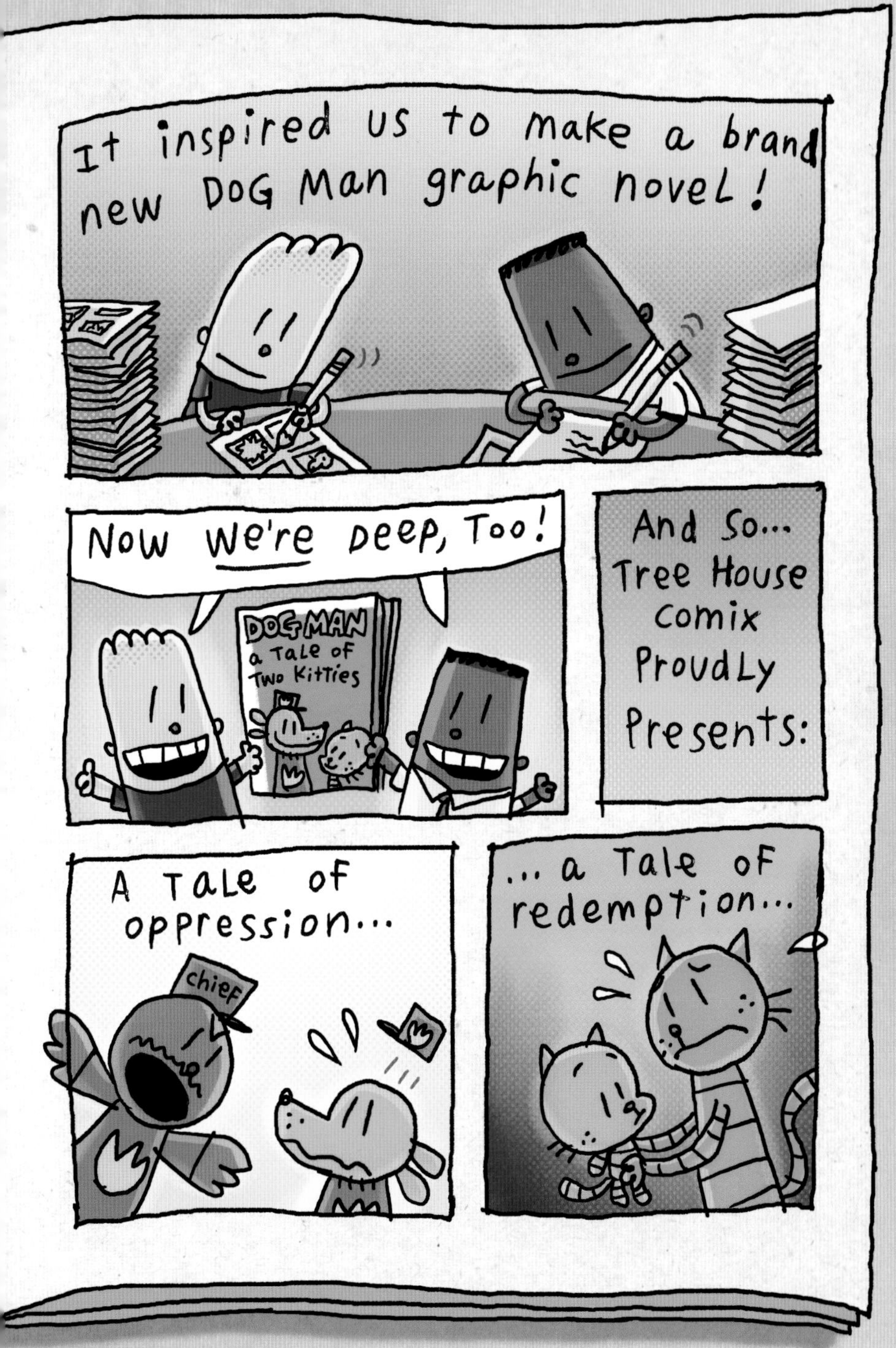
It inspired us to make a brand new DOG MAN graphic novel!
Now we're deep, too!
DOG MAN
a Tale of Two Kitties
And so... Tree House Comix Proudly Presents:
A Tale of oppression...
chief
... a Tale of redemption...

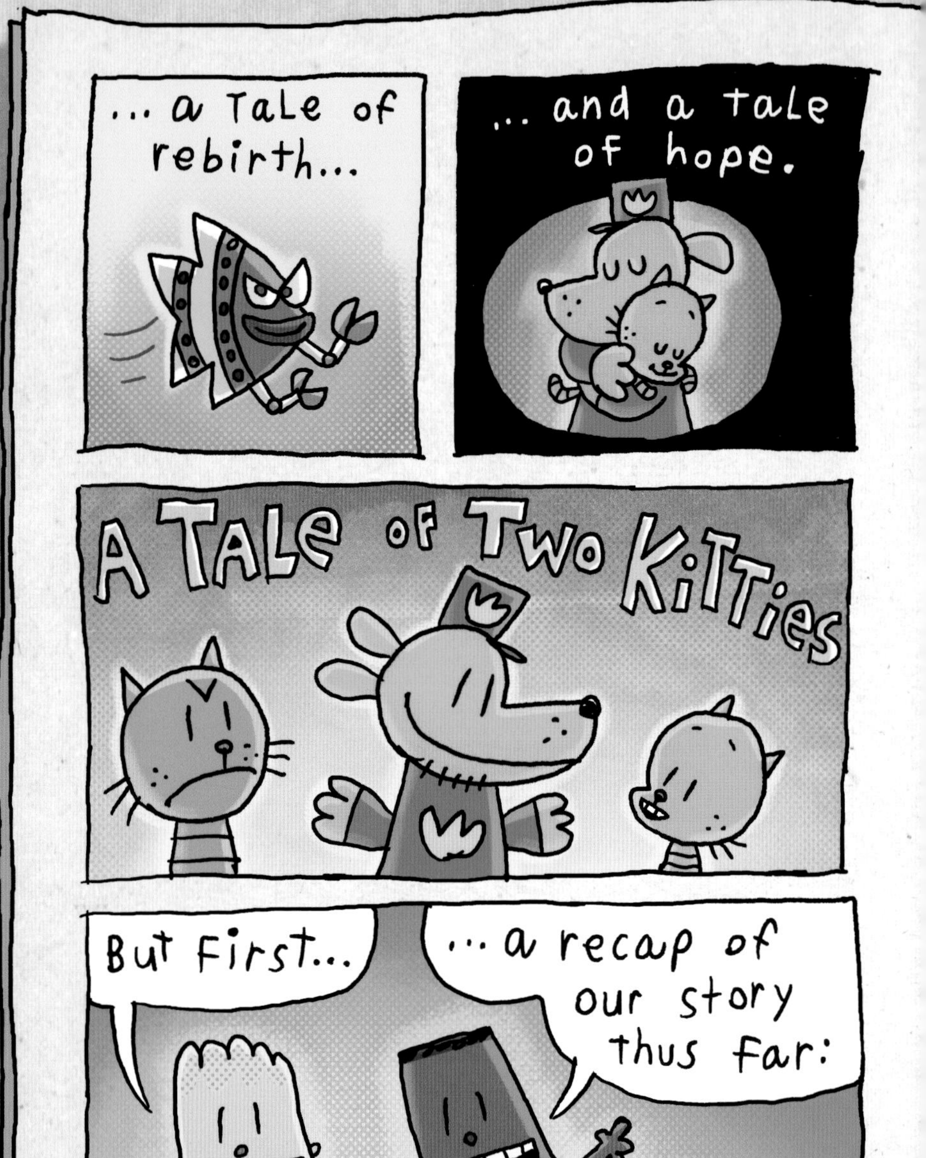
... a TaLe of rebirth...
... and a tale of hope.
A TALE OF TWO KITTIES
But First...
... a recap of our story thus Far:

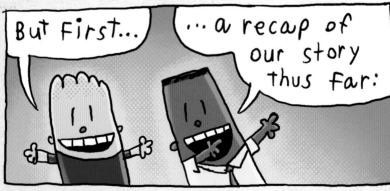

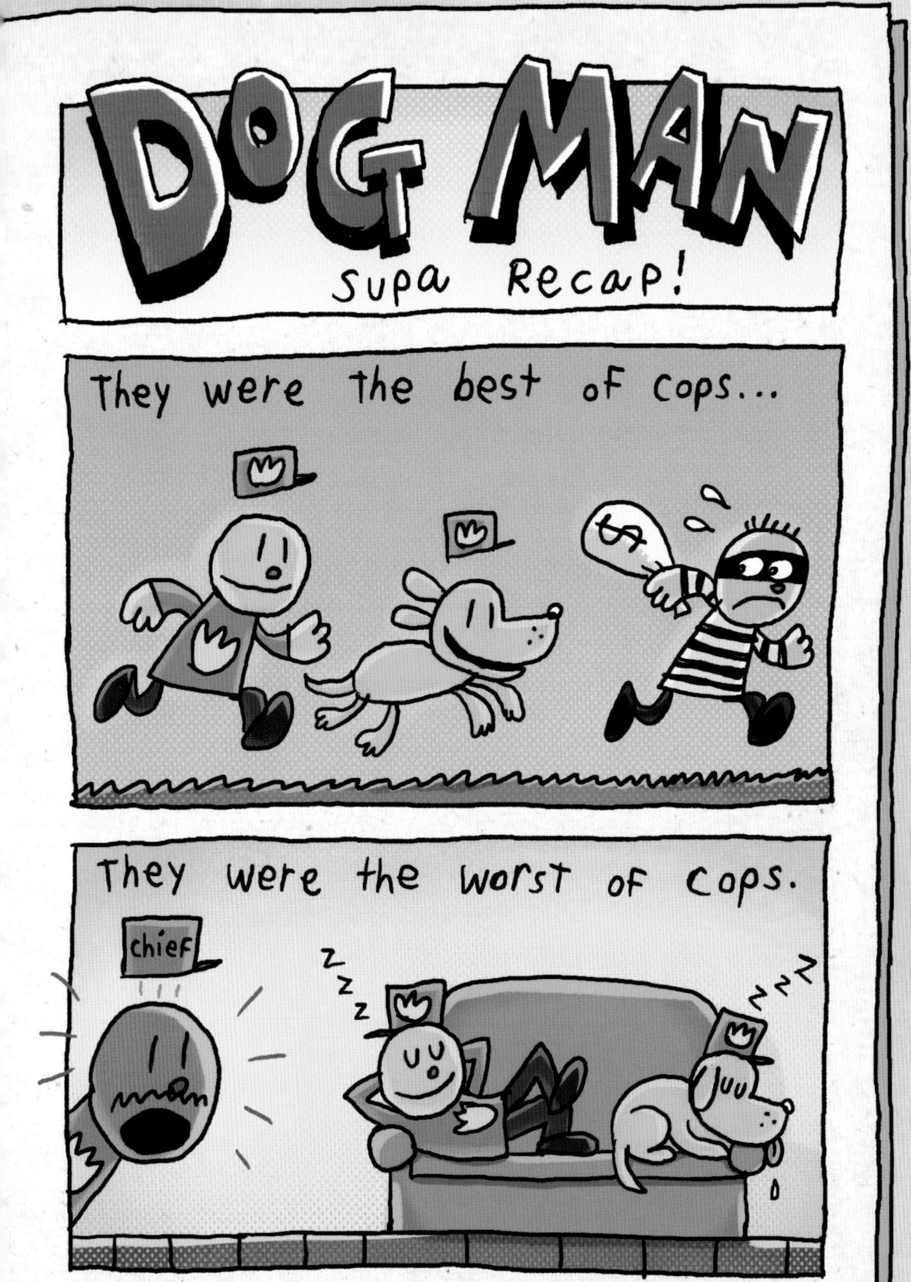
DOG MAN
Supa Recap!
They were the best of cops...
$
They were the worst of cops.
chief
Z Z Z
Z Z Z

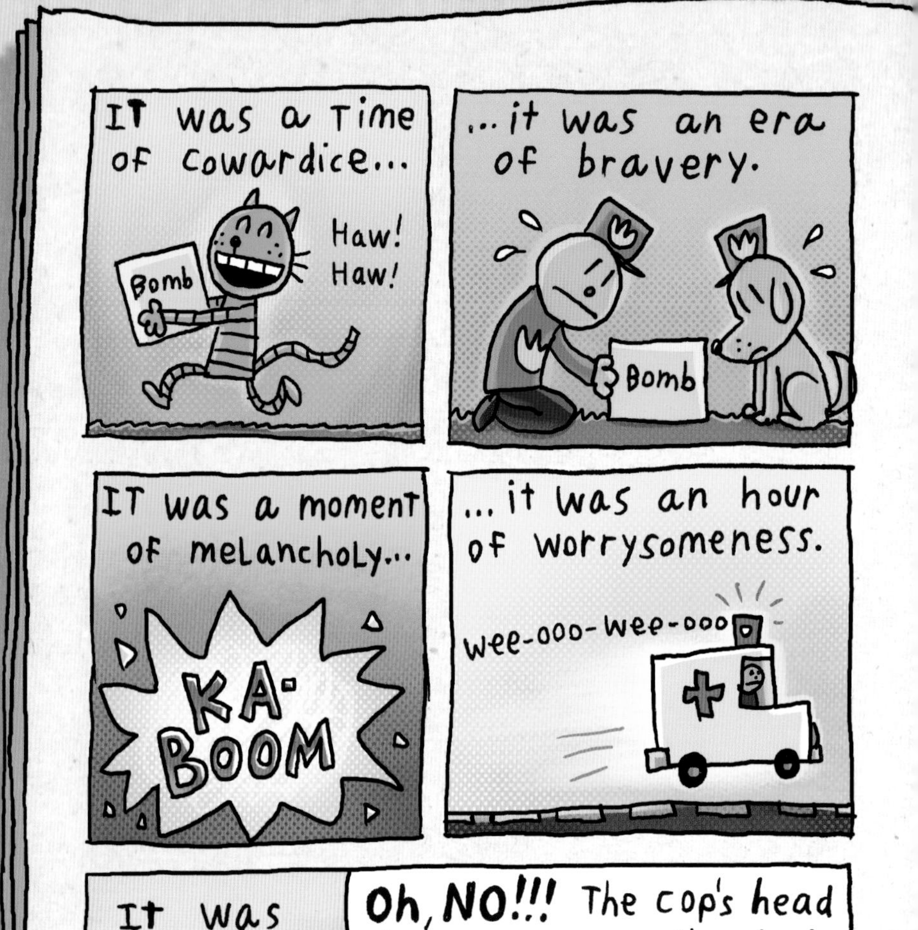
IT was a Time of cowardice...
Haw! Haw!
Bomb
... it was an era of bravery.
Bomb
IT was a moment of melancholy...
KA-BOOM
... it was an hour of worrysomeness.
wee-ooo-wee-ooo
It was a day of despair...
Oh, NO!!! The cop's head is dying, and the dog's body is dying!!!

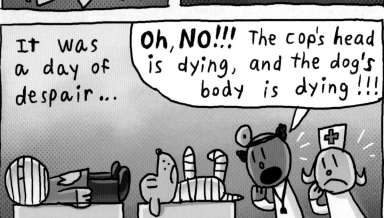

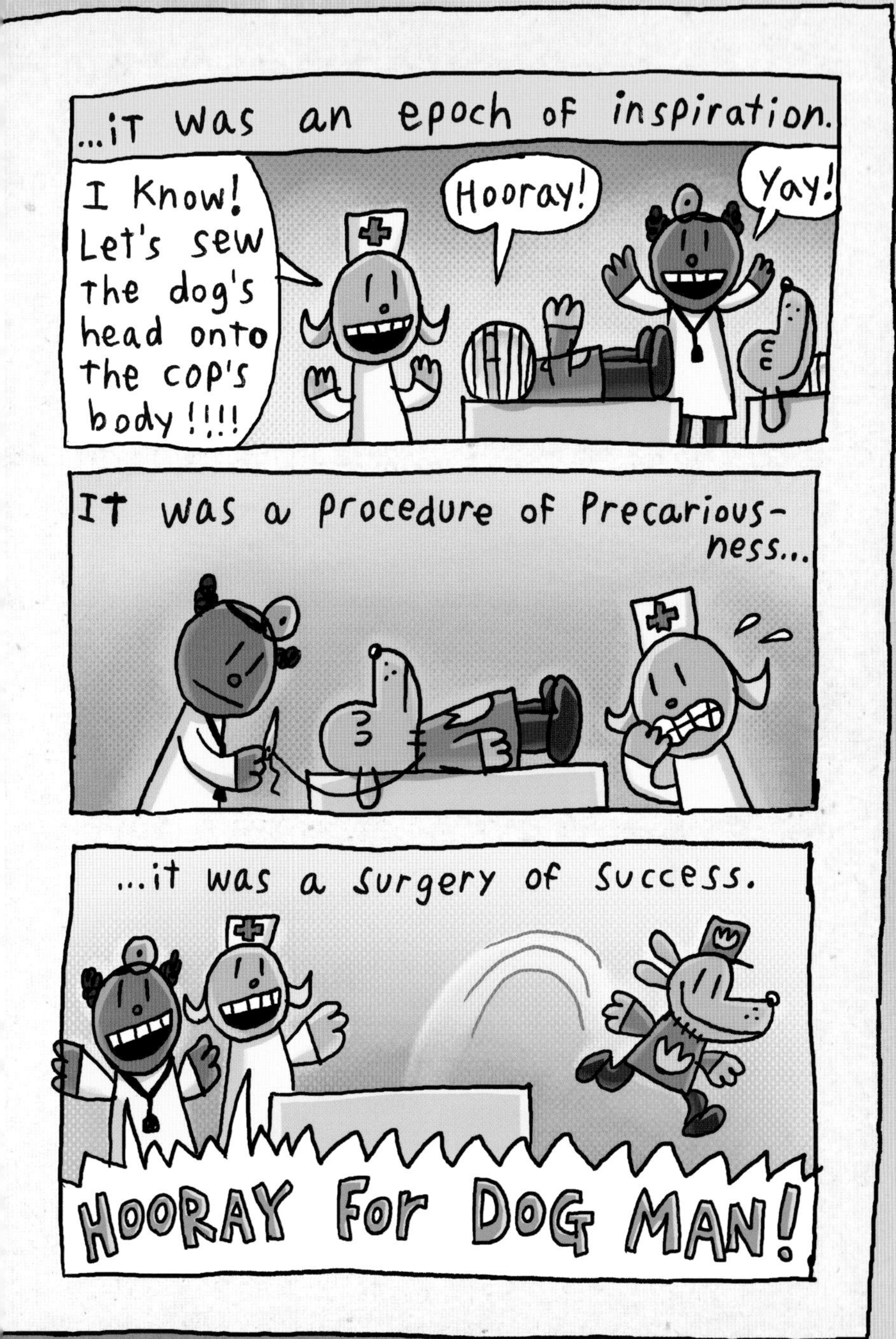
...iT was an epoch of inspiration.
I Know! Let's sew the dog's head onto the cop's body!!!!
Hooray!
Yay!
IT was a procedure of Precarious-ness...
...it was a surgery of success.
HOORAY For DOG MAN!

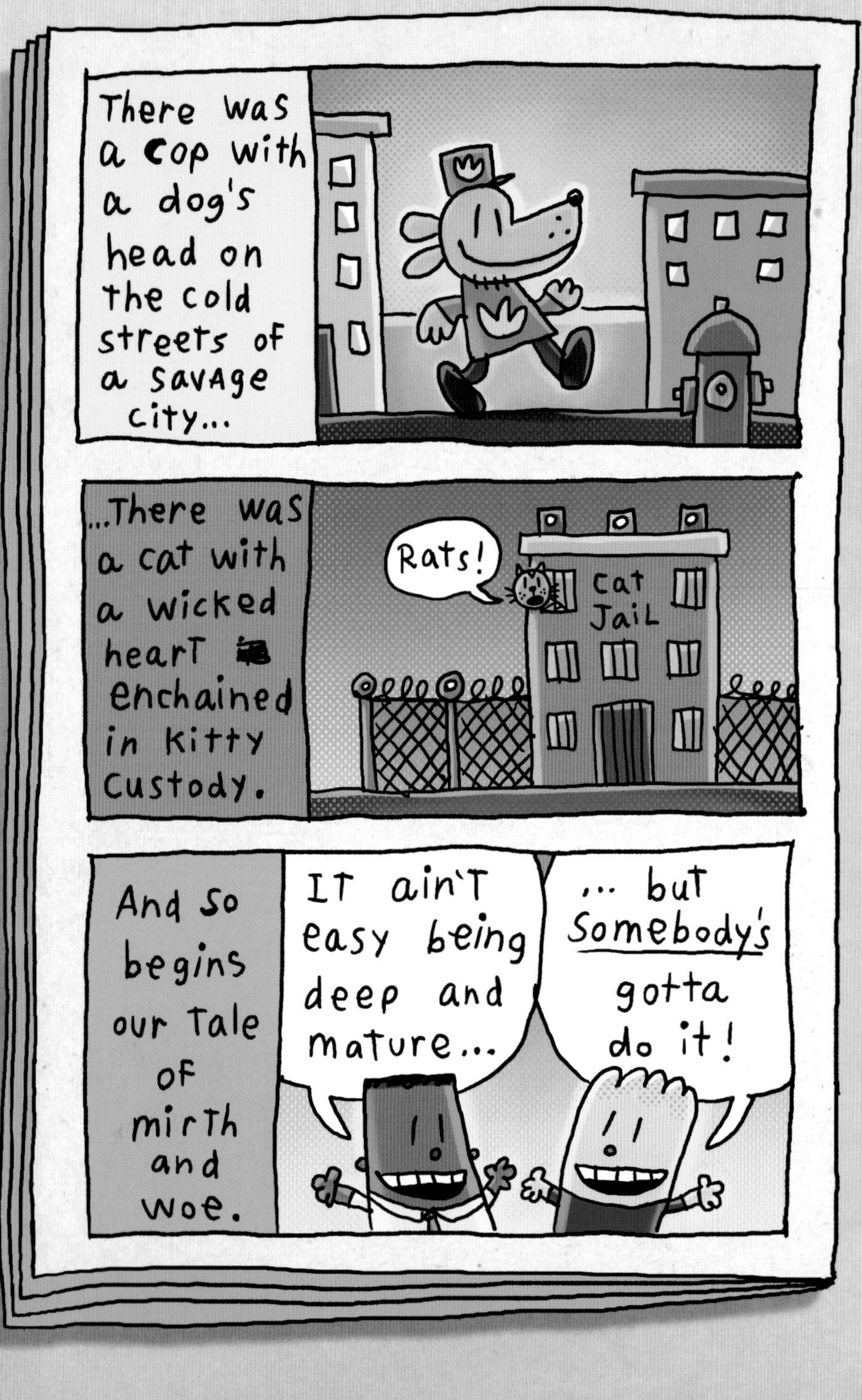
There was a cop with a dog's head on the cold streets of a savage city...
...There was a cat with a wicked heart enchained in kitty custody.
Rats!
Cat Jail
And so begins our tale of mirth and woe.
It ain't easy being deep and mature...
... but Somebody's gotta do it!

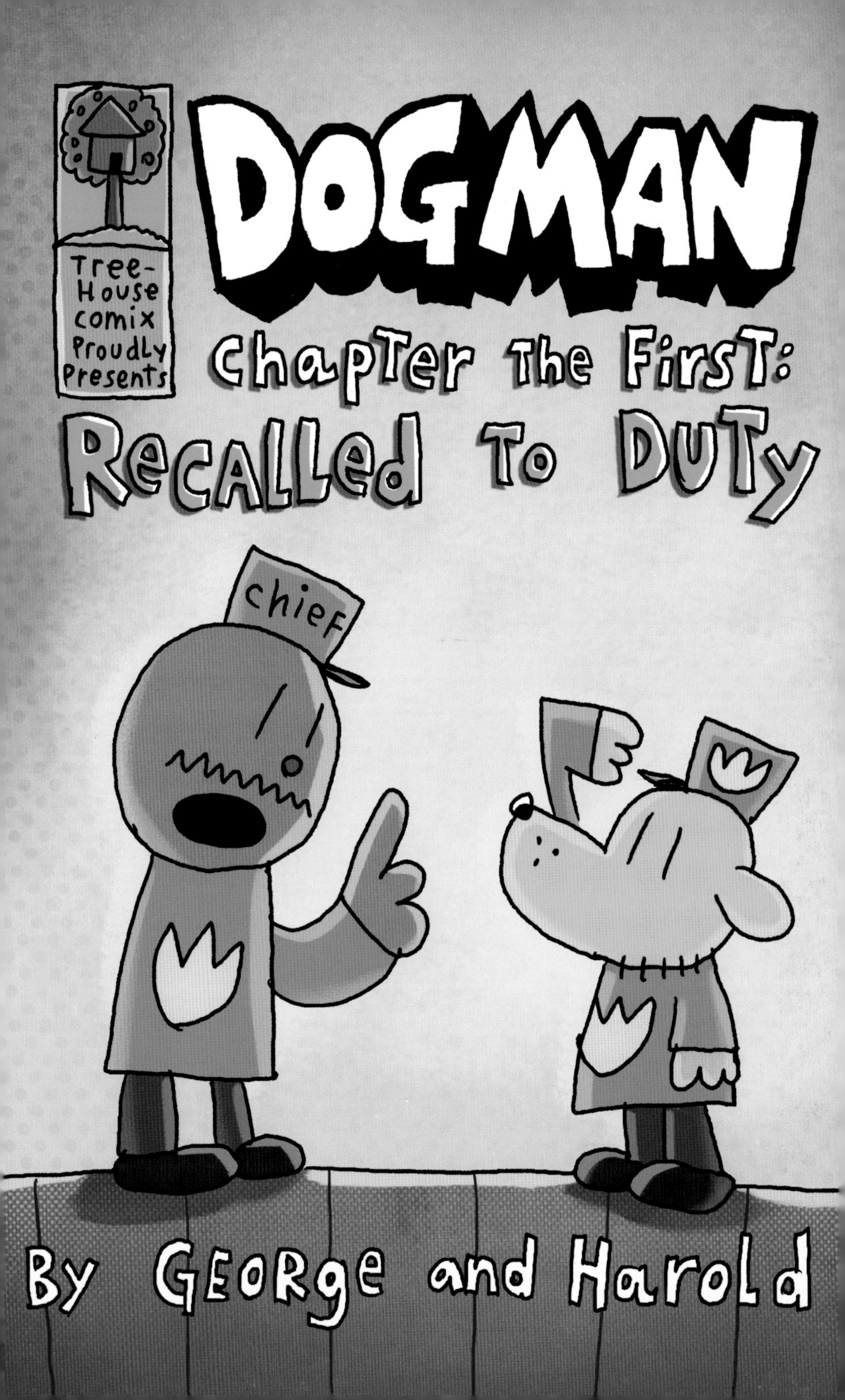

Tree-House comix Proudly Presents
DOG MAN
Chapter the First:
Recalled To Duty
chief
By George and Harold

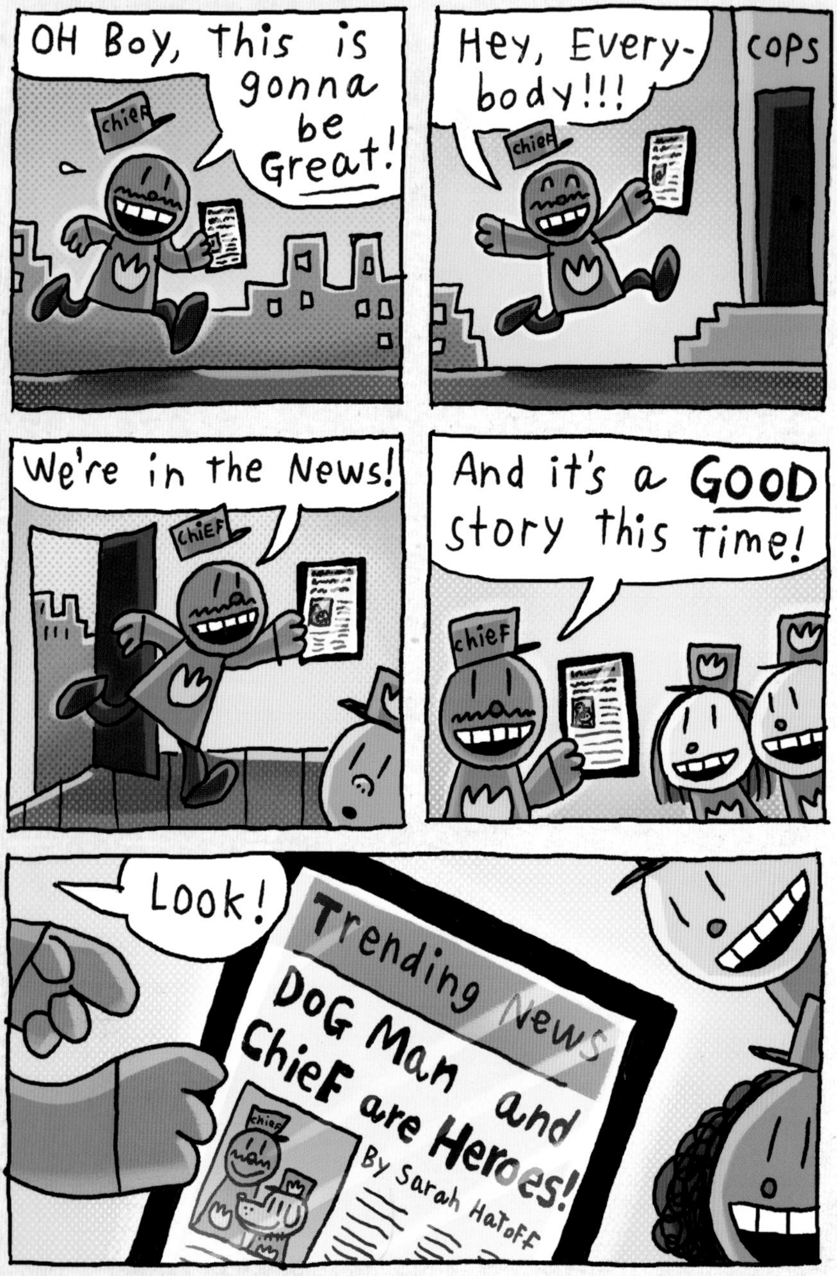

OH Boy, This is gonna be Great!
chieF
Hey, Every-body!!!
COPS
chieF
We're in the News!
ChiEF
And it's a GOOD story this Time!
chieF
Look!
Trending News
DoG Man and ChieF are Heroes!
By Sarah HaToFF
chieF

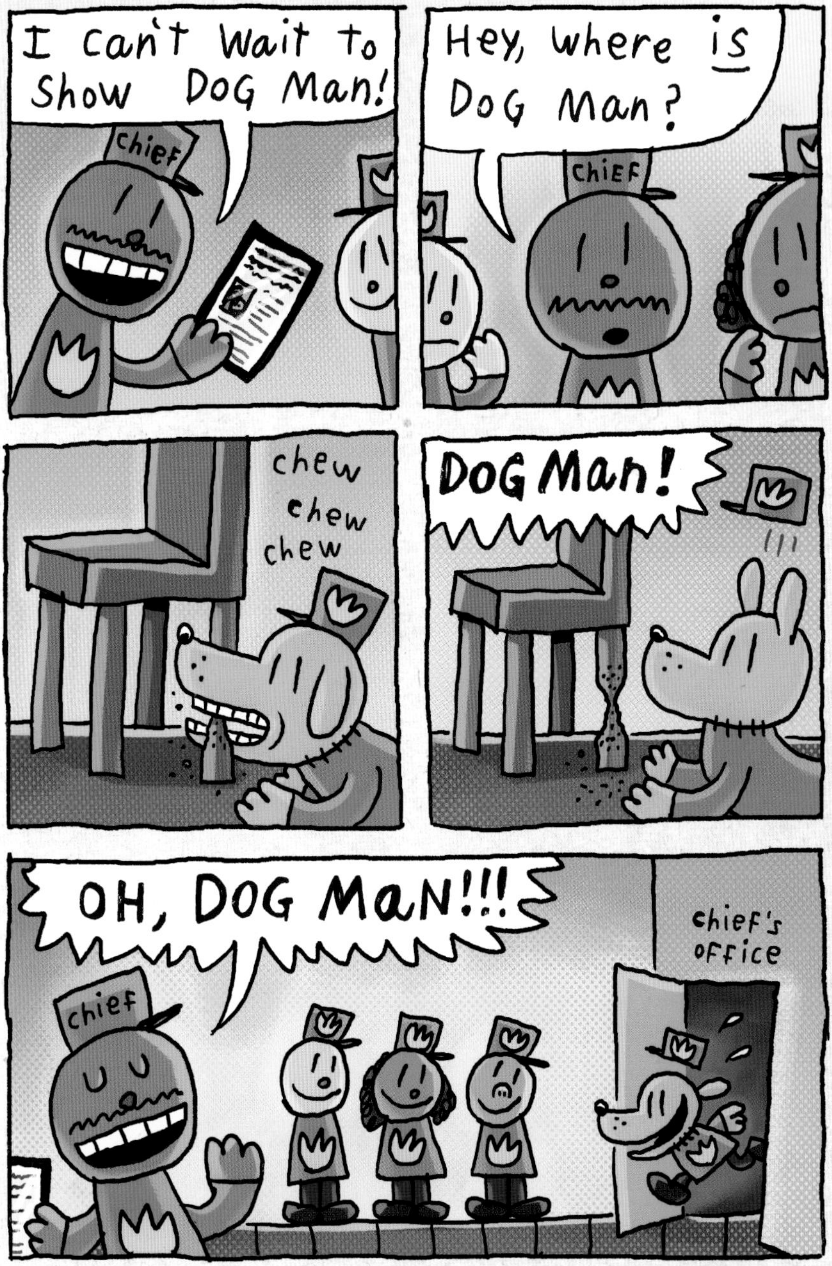
I can't wait to Show DOG Man!
chief
Hey, where is DoG Man?
CHIEF
chew
chew
chew
DOG Man!
OH, DOG MaN!!!
chief's office
chief

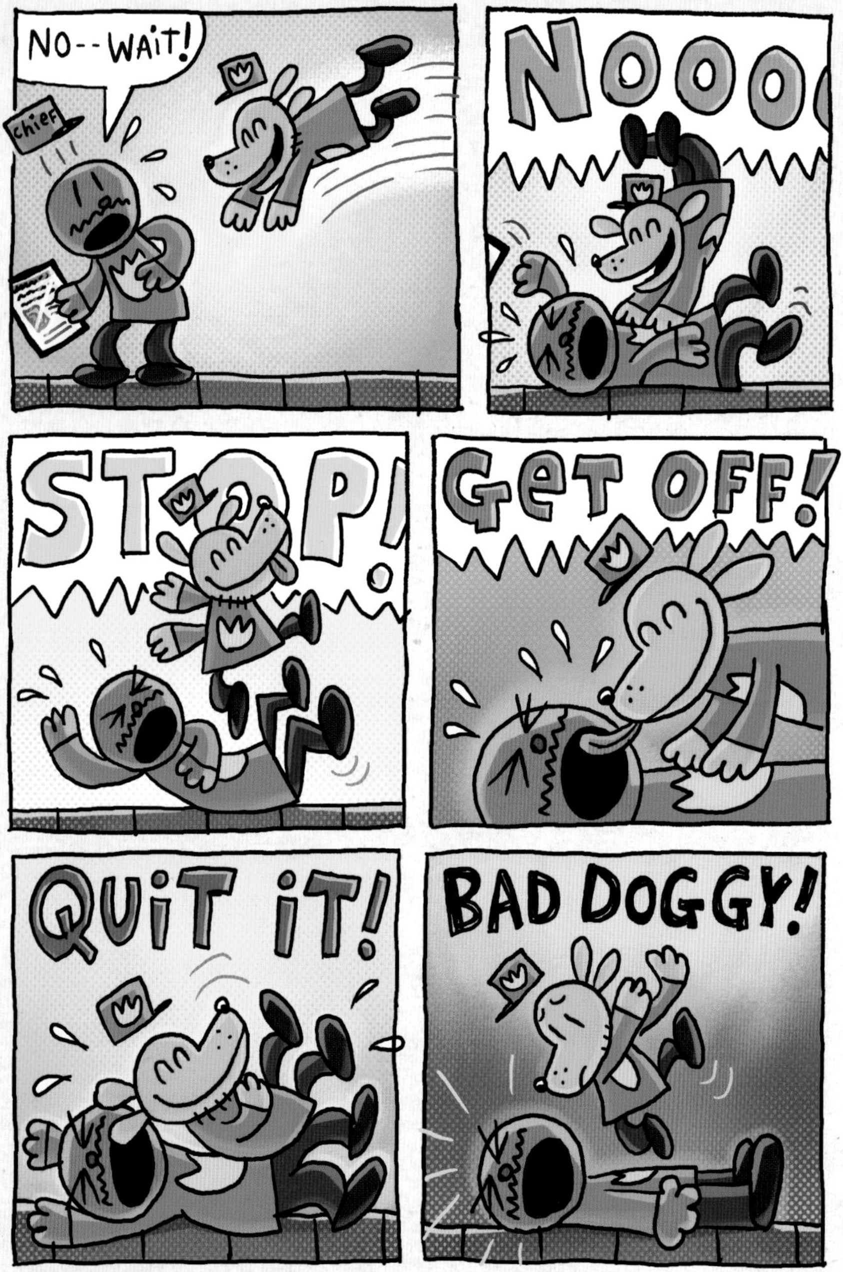
NO--WAIT!
chief
NOOOO
STOP!
GET OFF!
QUIT IT!
BAD DOGGY!

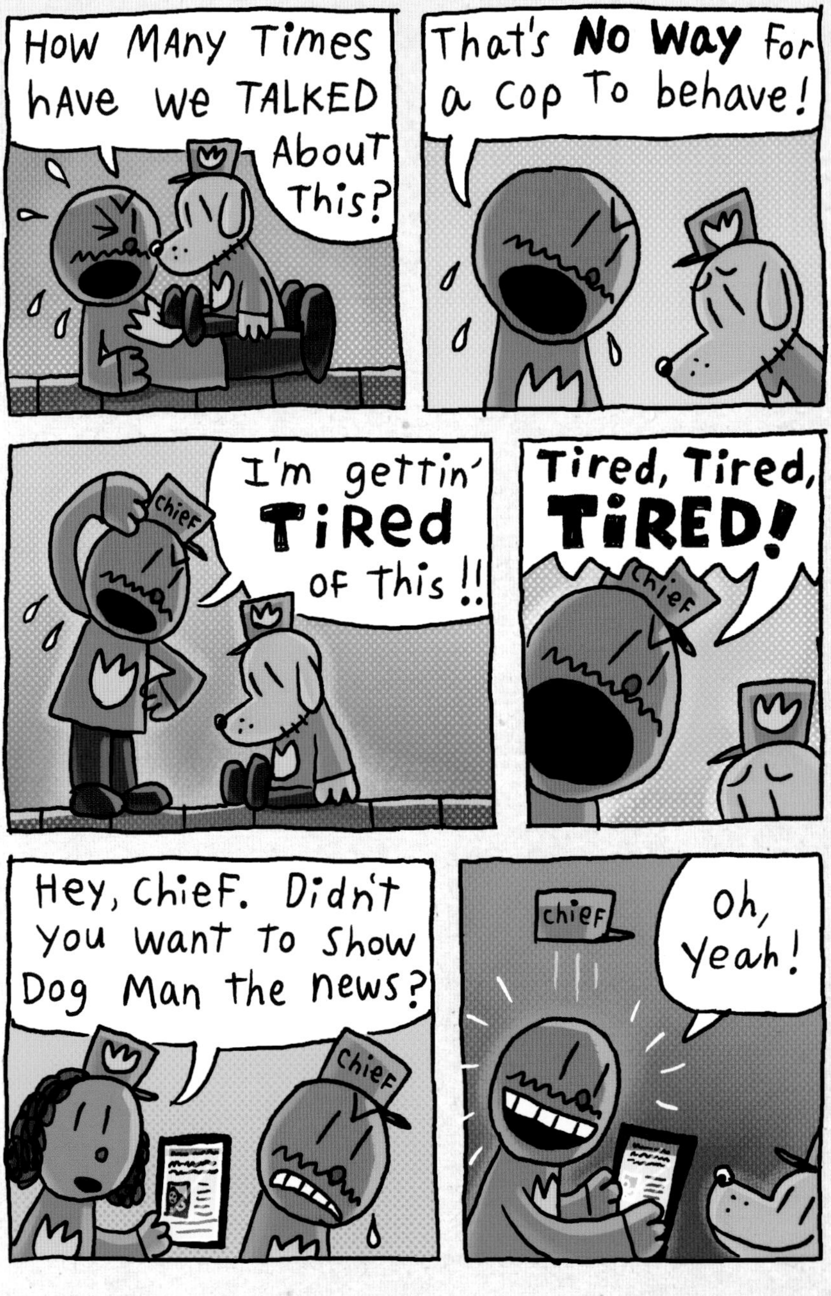
How MAny Times have we TALKED About This?
That's **No Way** For a cop To behave!
I'm gettin' TiRed of This !!
Tired, Tired, TiRED!
Chief
Hey, Chief. Didn't you want to Show Dog Man the news?
Chief
chief
Oh, Yeah!

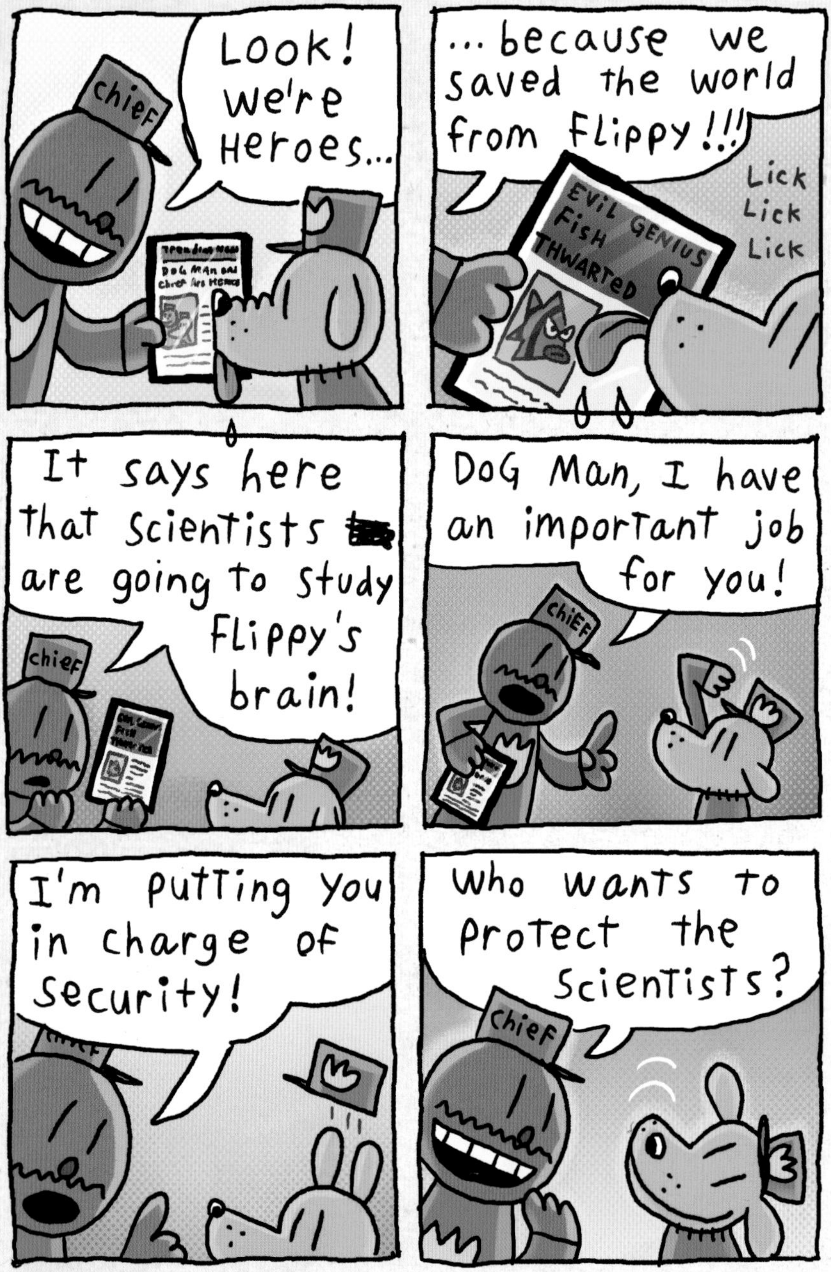
Look! We're Heroes...
... because we saved the world from Flippy!!!
EVIL GENIUS FISH THWARTED
Lick Lick Lick
It says here that scientists are going to study Flippy's brain!
Dog Man, I have an important job for you!
I'm putting you in charge of security!
Who wants to protect the scientists?

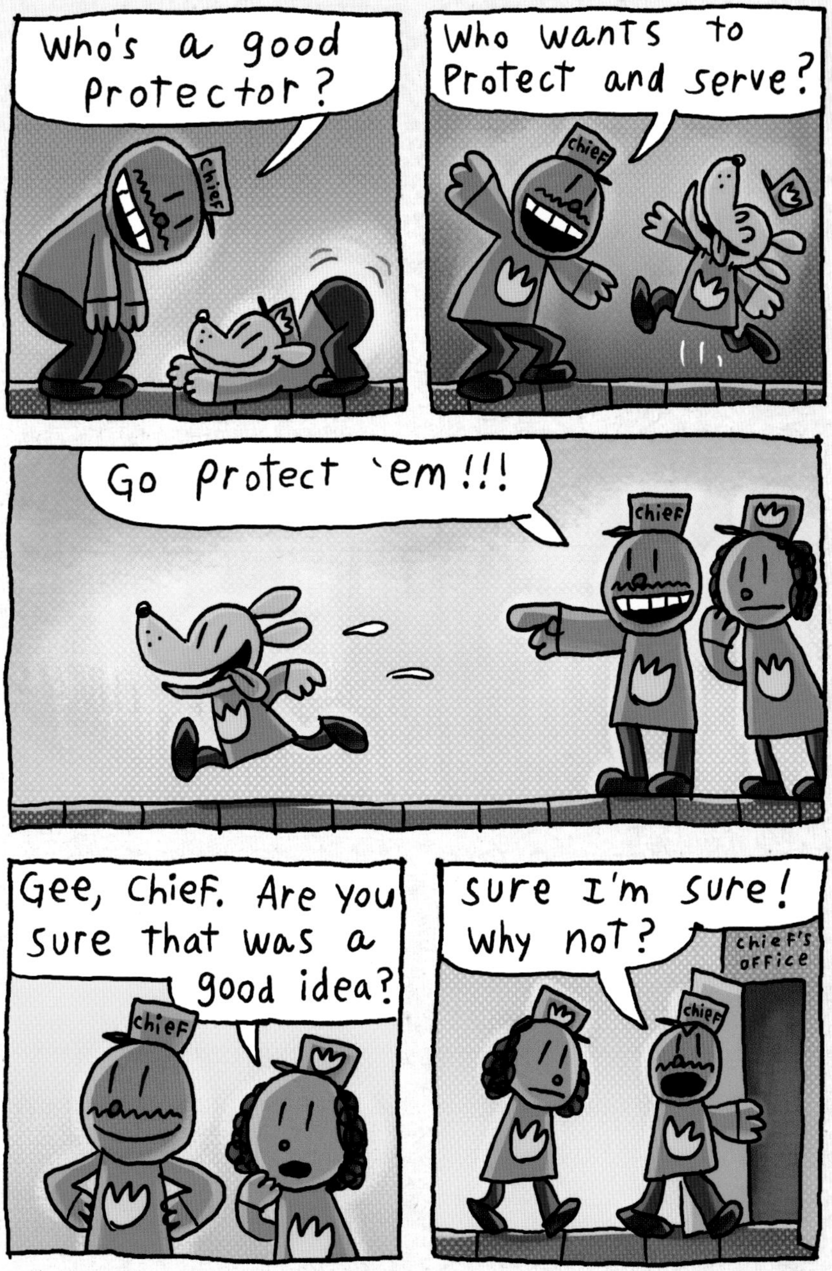
Who's a good protector?
Who wants to Protect and serve?
chief
Go protect 'em!!!
chief
Gee, Chief. Are you sure that was a good idea?
chief
Sure I'm sure! Why not?
chief's office
chief

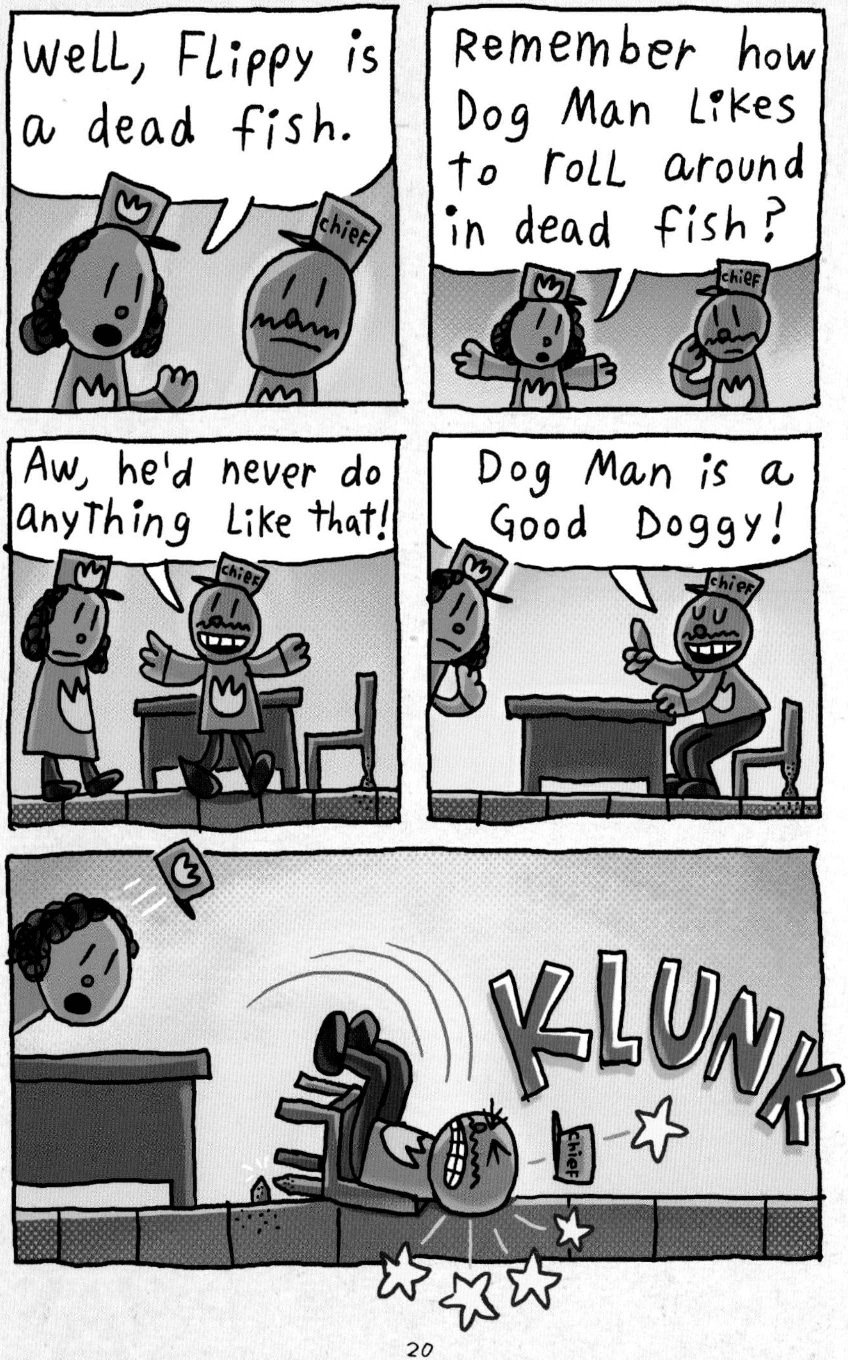
Well, Flippy is a dead fish.
Remember how Dog Man Likes to roll around in dead fish?
chief
Aw, he'd never do anything Like that!
Dog Man is a Good Doggy!
KLUNK
chief

Chapter the Second: You've Gotta Be Kitten Me!

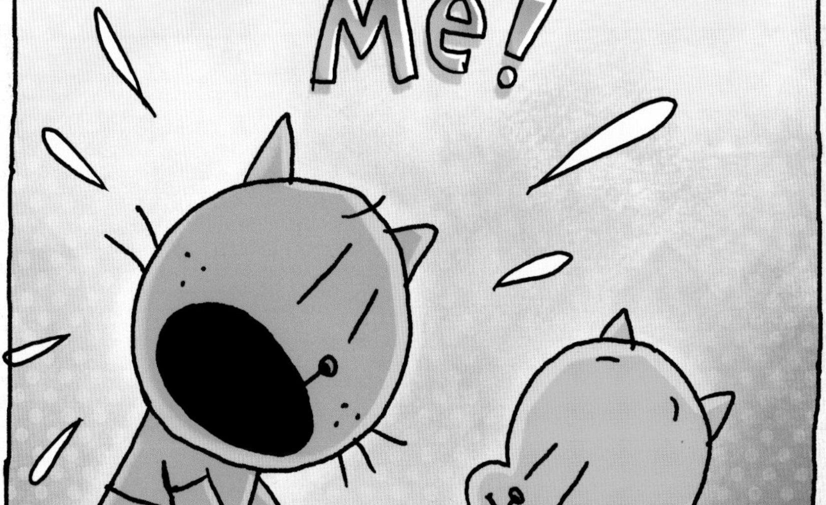

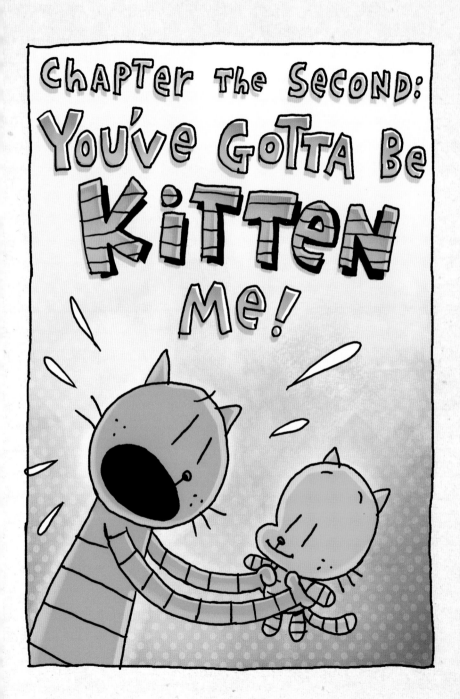

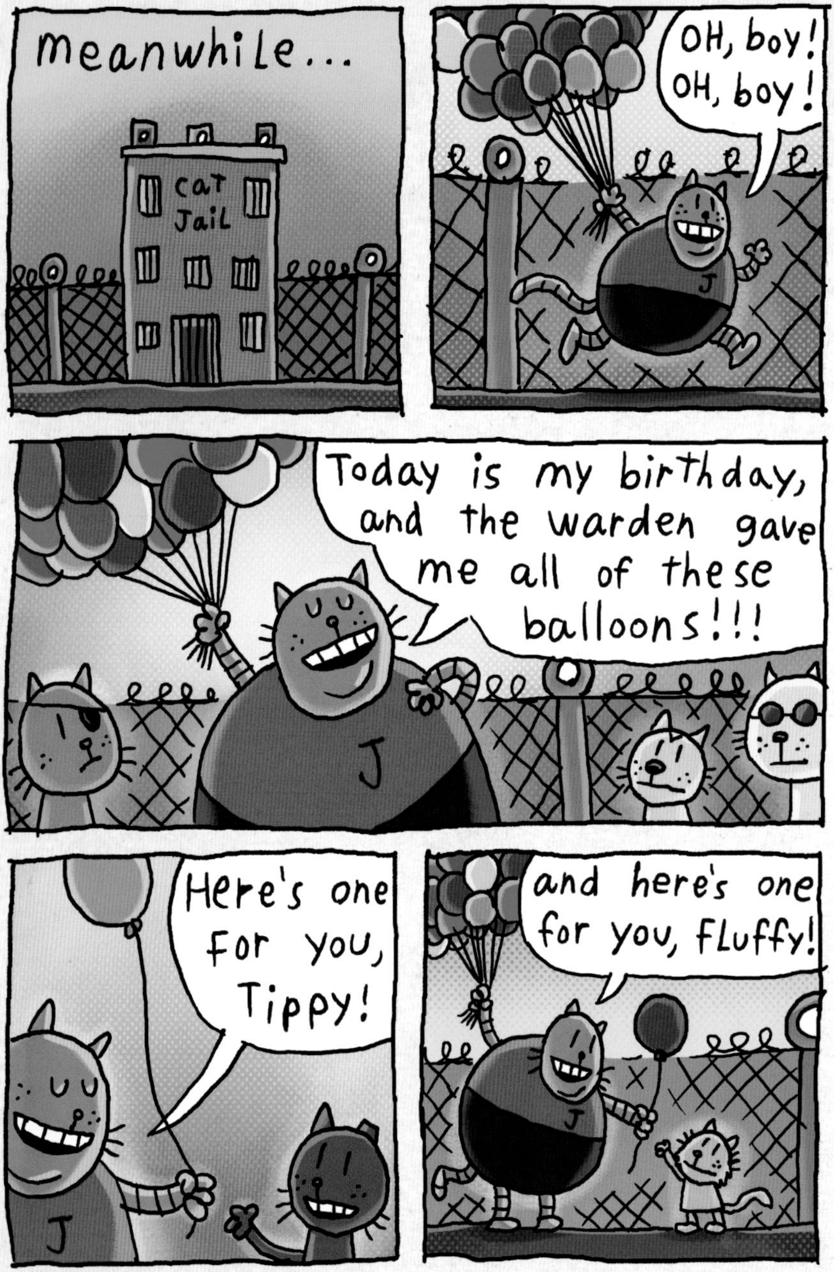
meanwhile...
CAT JAIL
OH, boy! OH, boy!
Today is my birthday, and the warden gave me all of these balloons!!!
Here's one for you, Tippy!
and here's one for you, Fluffy!

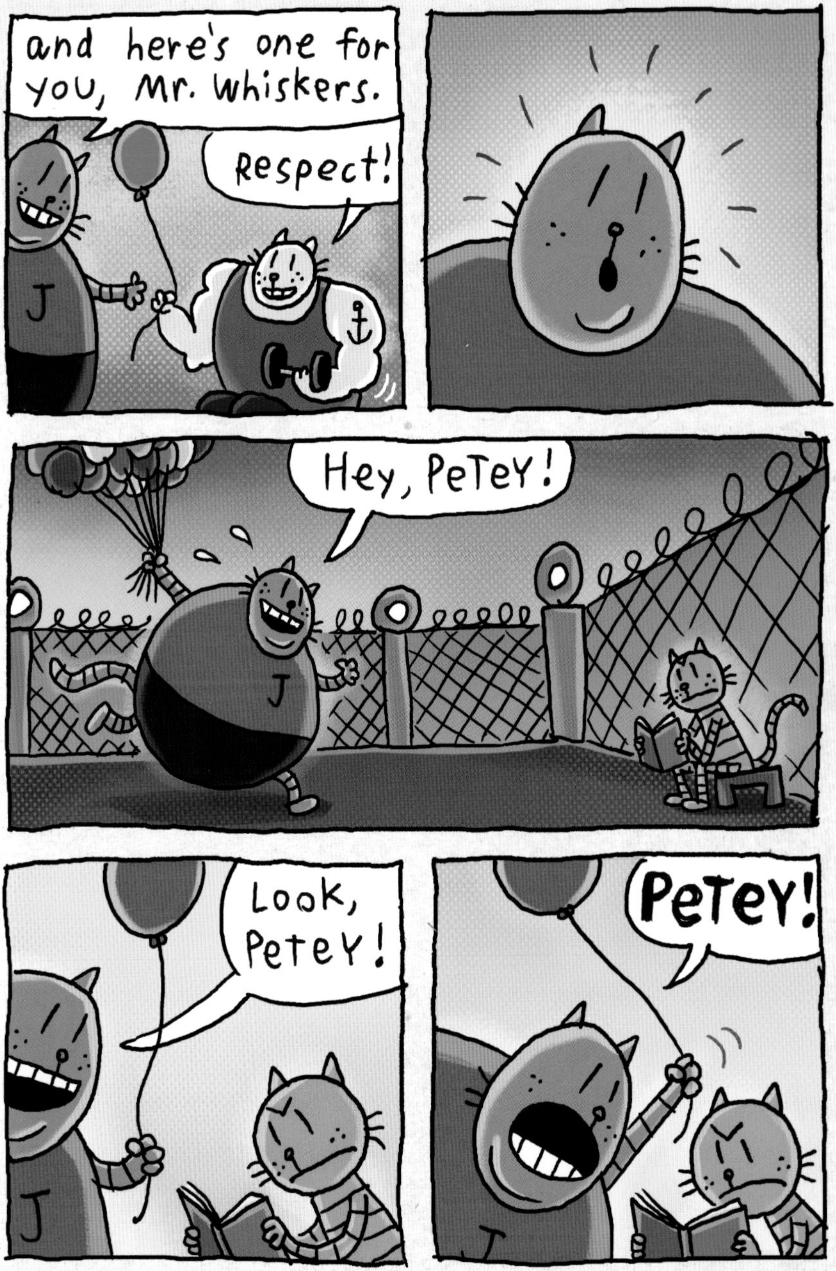
and here's one for you, Mr. Whiskers.
Respect!
Hey, PeTey!
Look, PeTeY!
PeTeY!

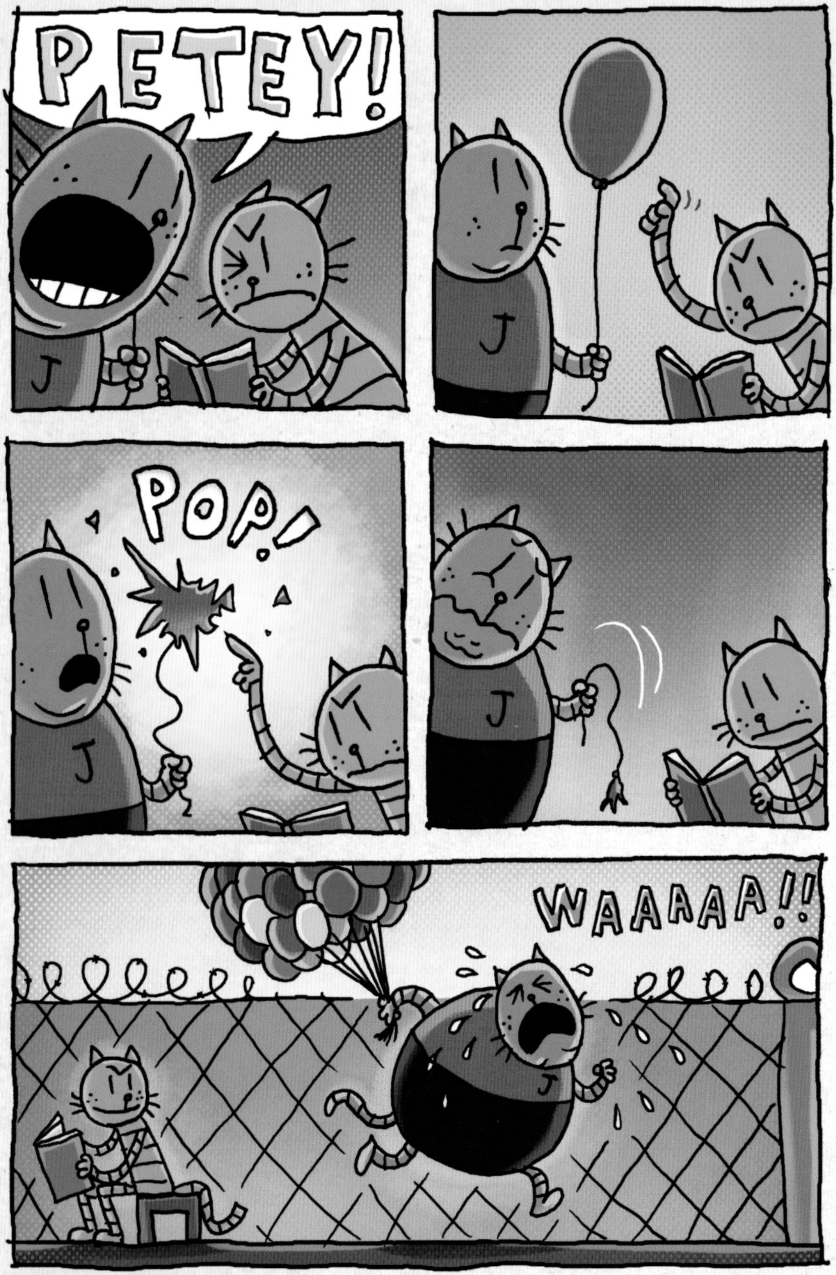
PETEY!
POP!
WAAAAA!!

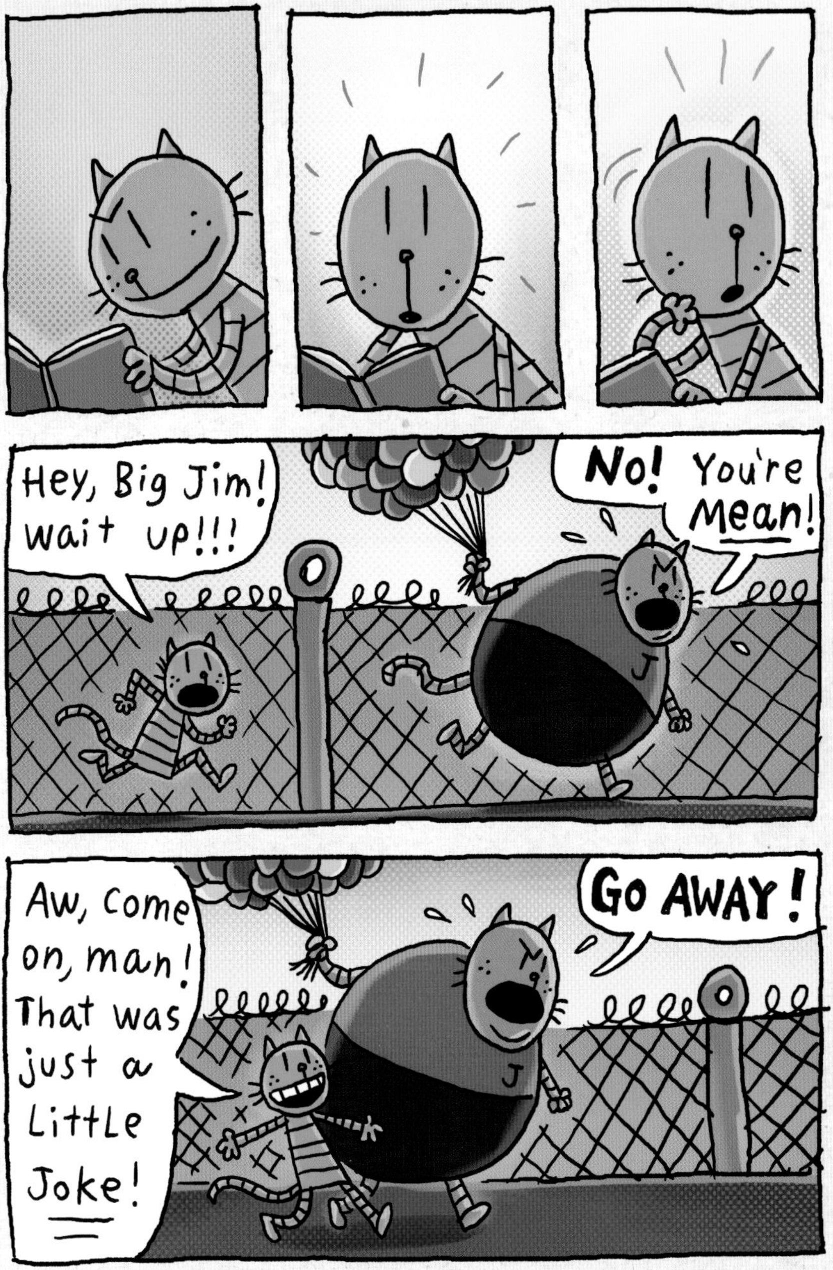
Hey, Big Jim! wait up!!!
No! You're Mean!
Aw, come on, man! That was just a Little Joke!
GO AWAY!

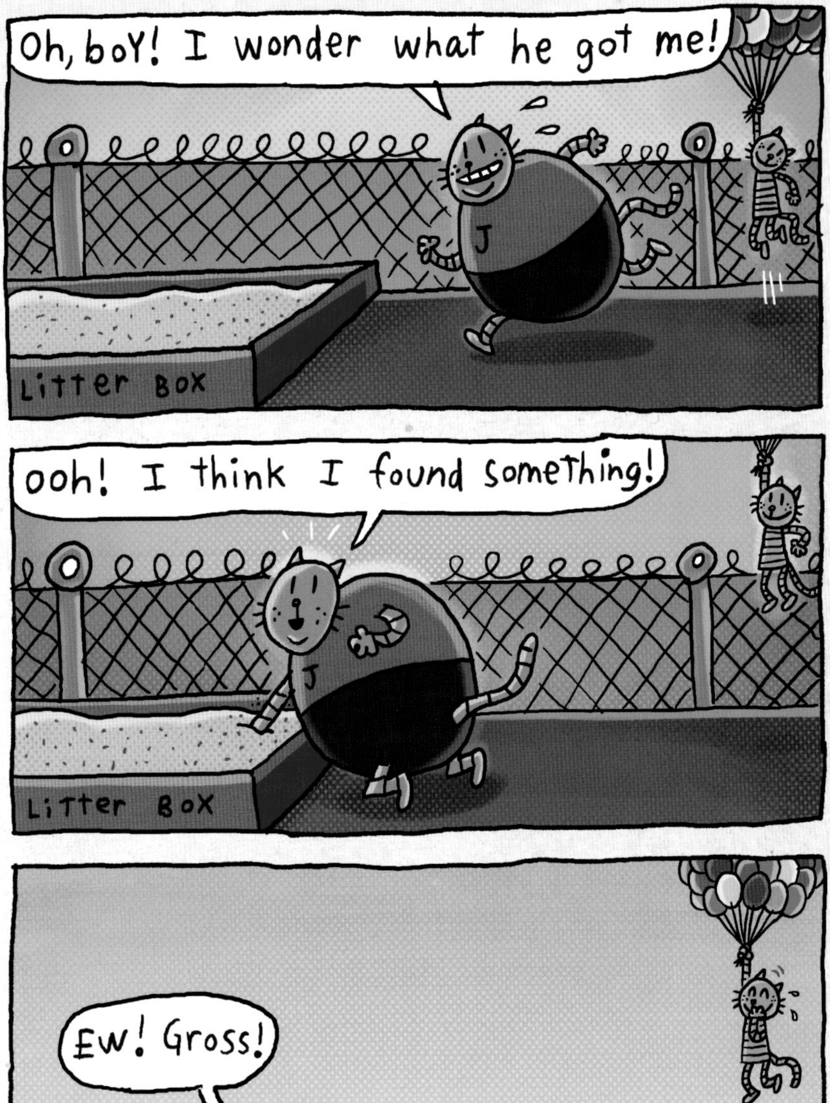
Oh, boY! I wonder what he got me!
LiTTer BOX
ooh! I think I found someThing!
LiTTer BOX
Ew! Gross!

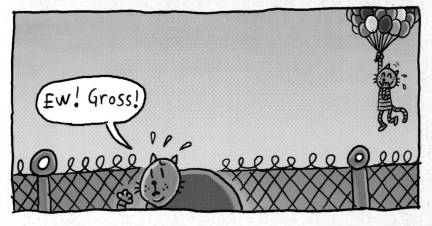

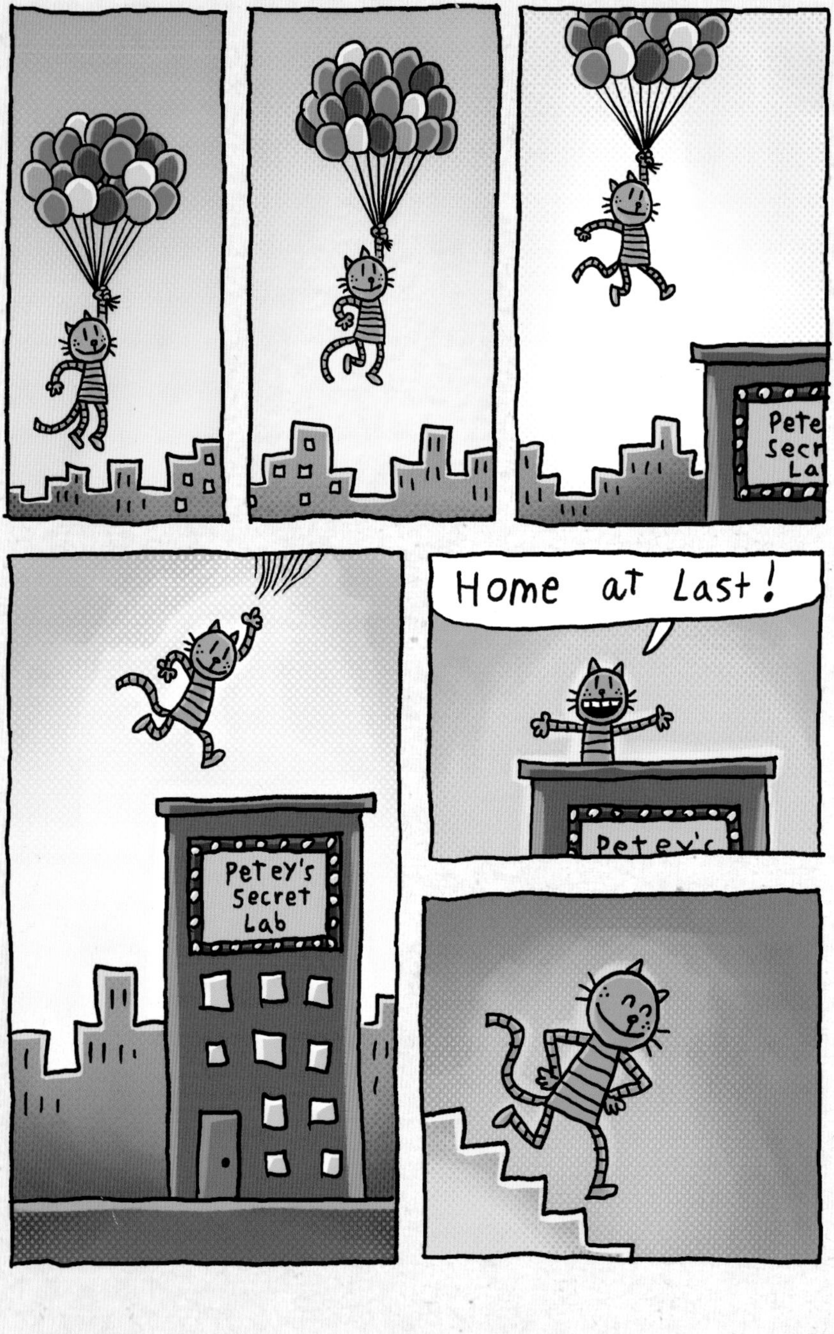
Pete
Secr
La
Petey's
Secret
Lab
Home at Last!
Petey's

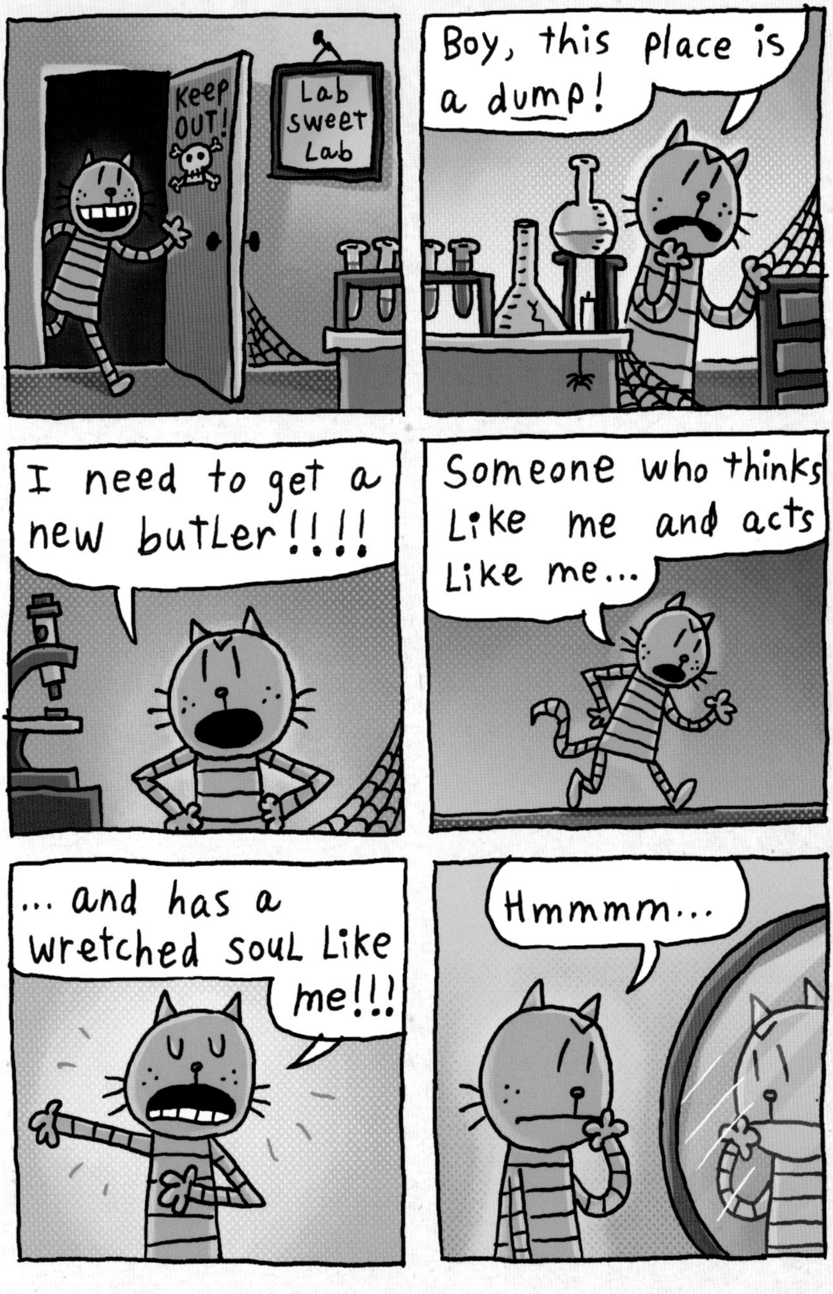
Keep OUT!
Lab Sweet Lab
Boy, this place is a dump!
I need to get a new butLer!!!!
Someone who thinks Like me and acts Like me...
... and has a wretched souL Like me!!!
Hmmmm...

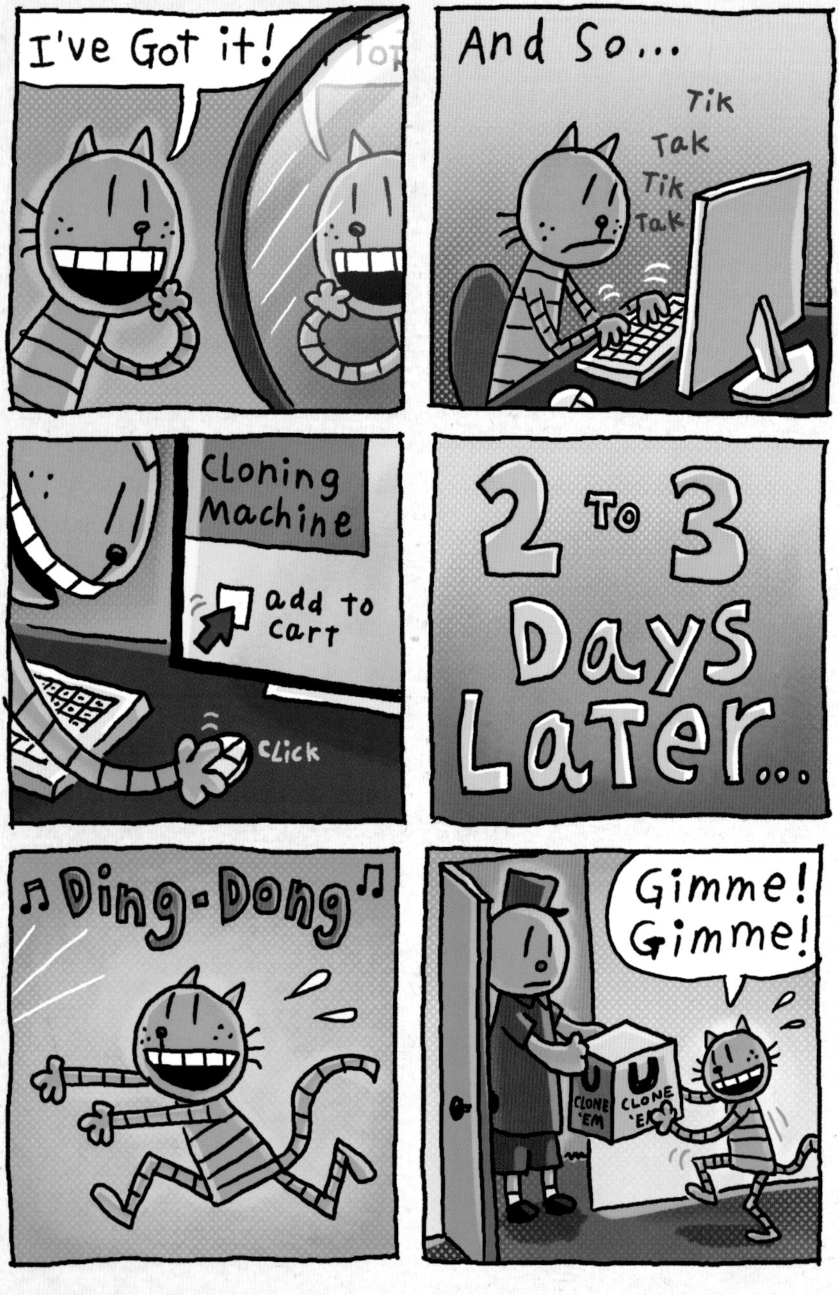
I've Got it!
And So...
Tik
Tak
Tik
Tak
Cloning Machine
add to cart
Click
2 To 3 Days Later...
Ding-Dong
Gimme! Gimme!
CLONE 'EM
CLONE 'EM

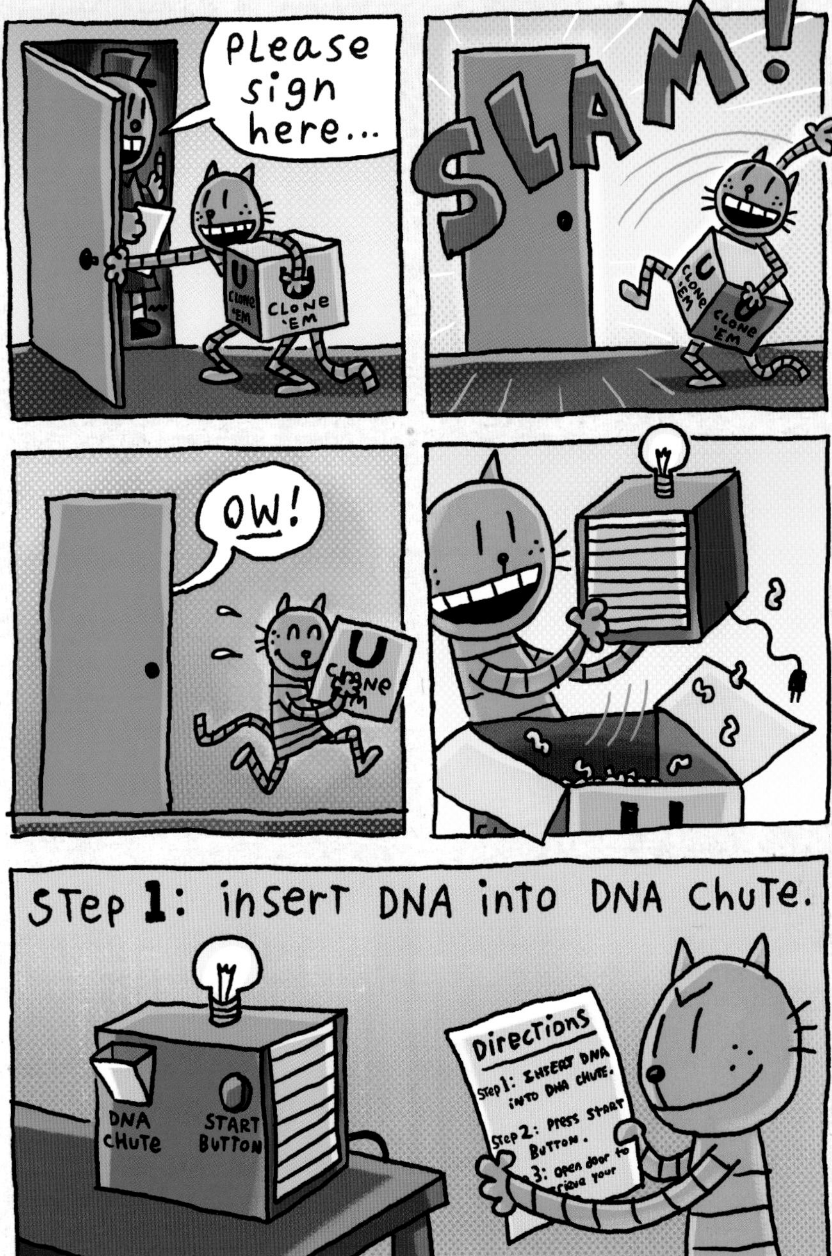
Please sign here...
CLONE 'EM
SLAM!
OW!
Step 1: insert DNA into DNA chute.
DNA CHUTE
START BUTTON
Directions
Step 1: INSERT DNA INTO DNA CHUTE.
Step 2: Press START BUTTON.
3: Open door to

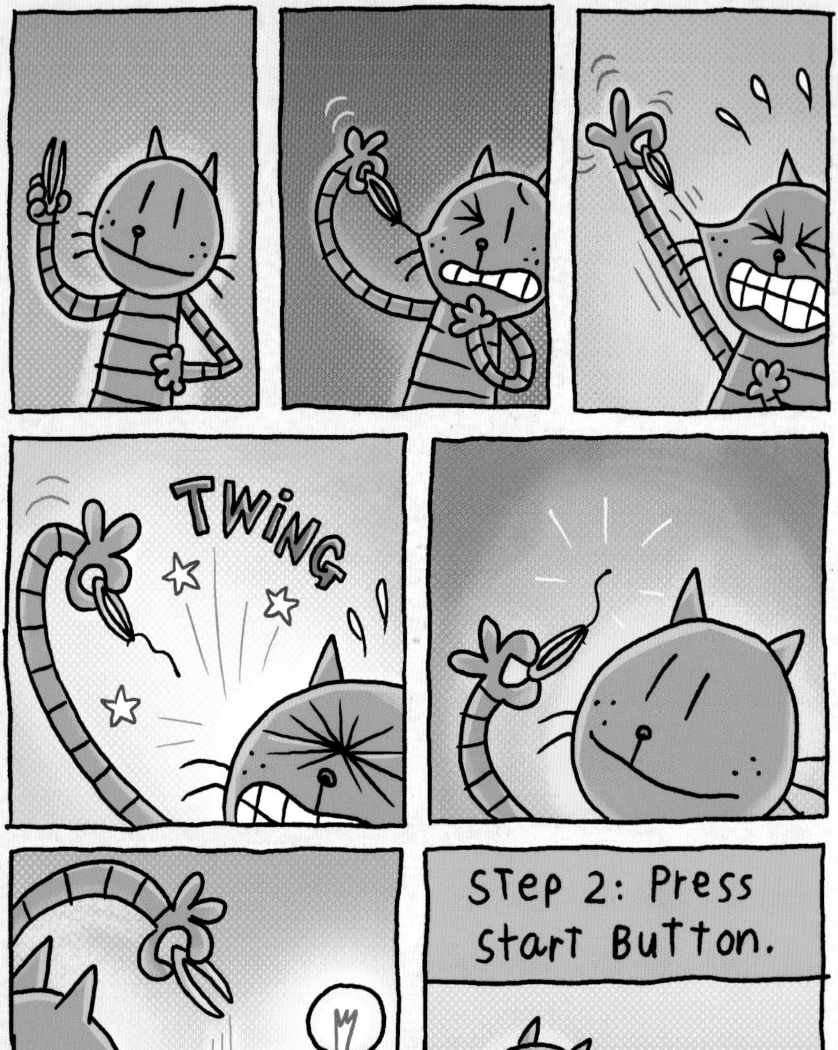
TWING
STEP 2: Press start Button.
DNA CHUTE
Directions

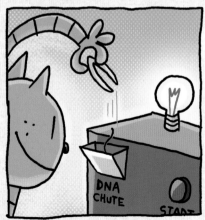

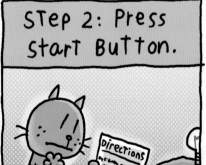

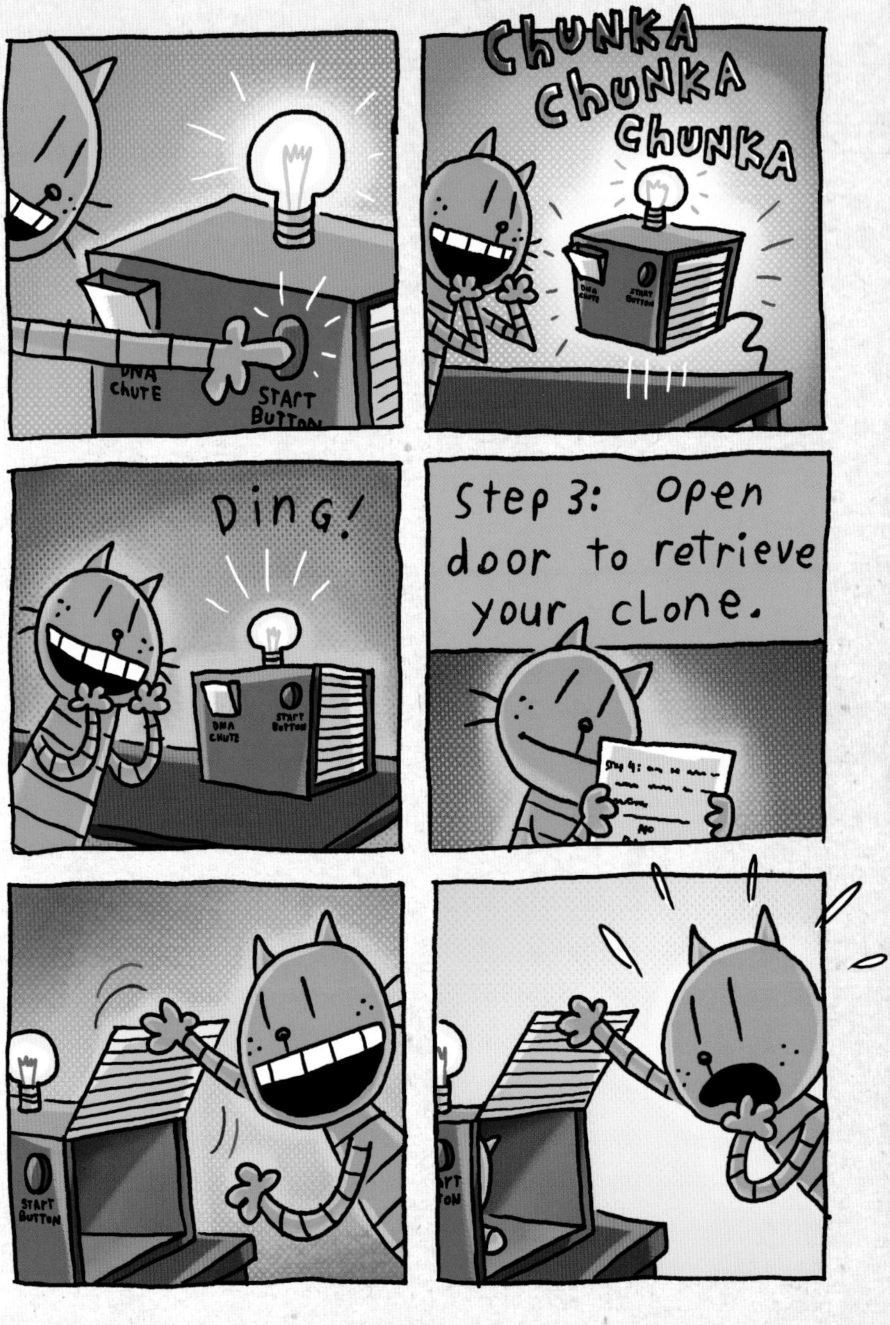
DNA CHUTE
START BUTTON
CHUNKA
CHUNKA
CHUNKA
DING!
Step 3: Open door to retrieve your clone.

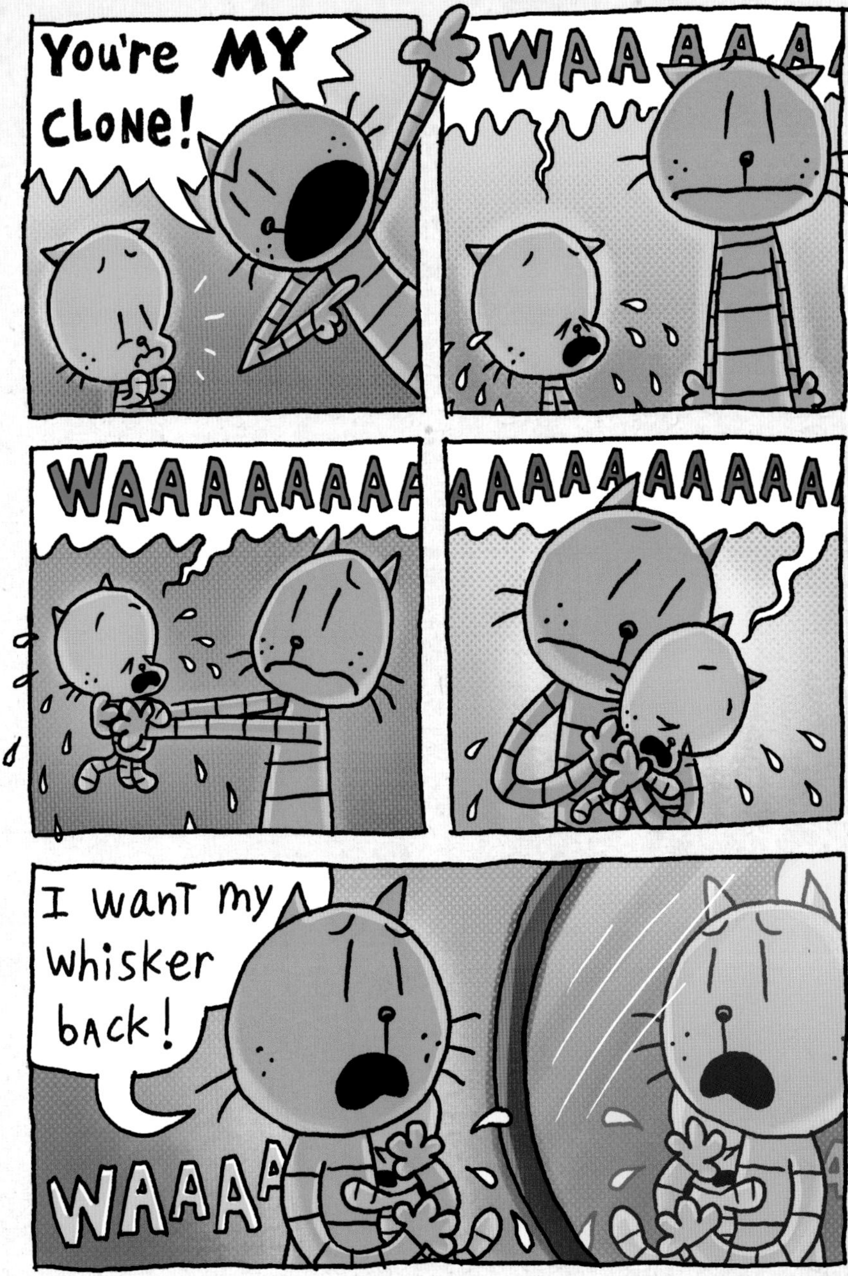
You're MY CLONE!
WAAAAAA
WAAAAAAAA
AAAAAAAAAA
I WANT my whisker bACK!
WAAAA

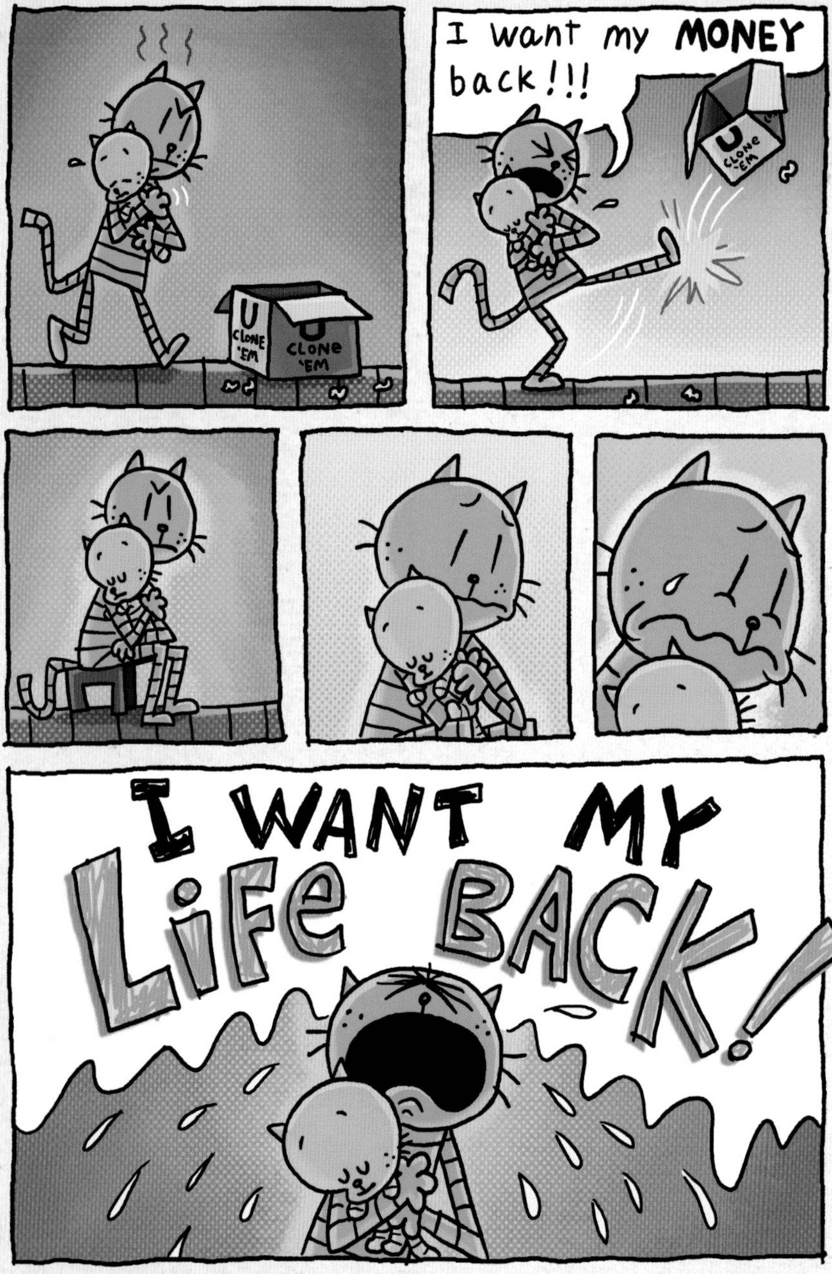
CLONE 'EM
CLONE 'EM
I want my MONEY back!!!
CLONE 'EM
I WANT MY LIFE BACK!

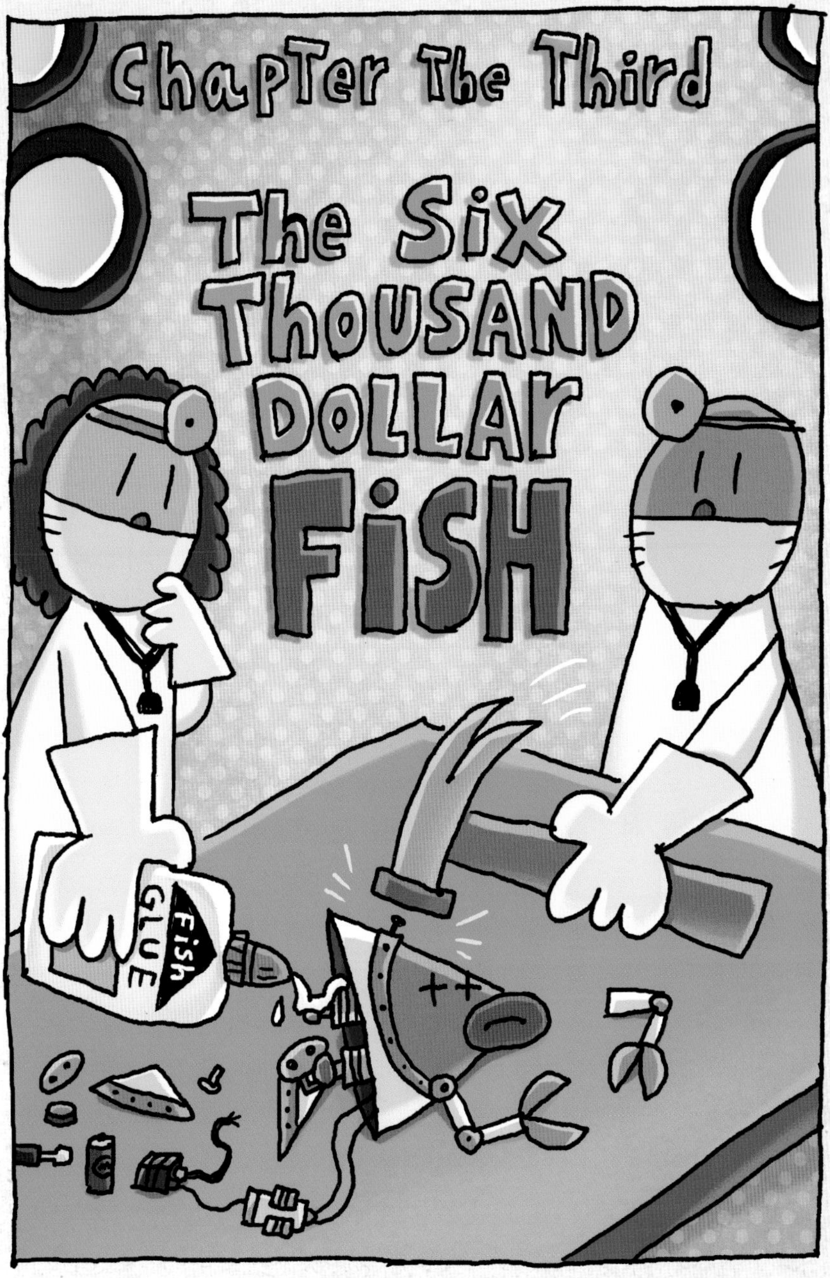
Chapter The Third
The Six Thousand Dollar Fish
Fish GLUE

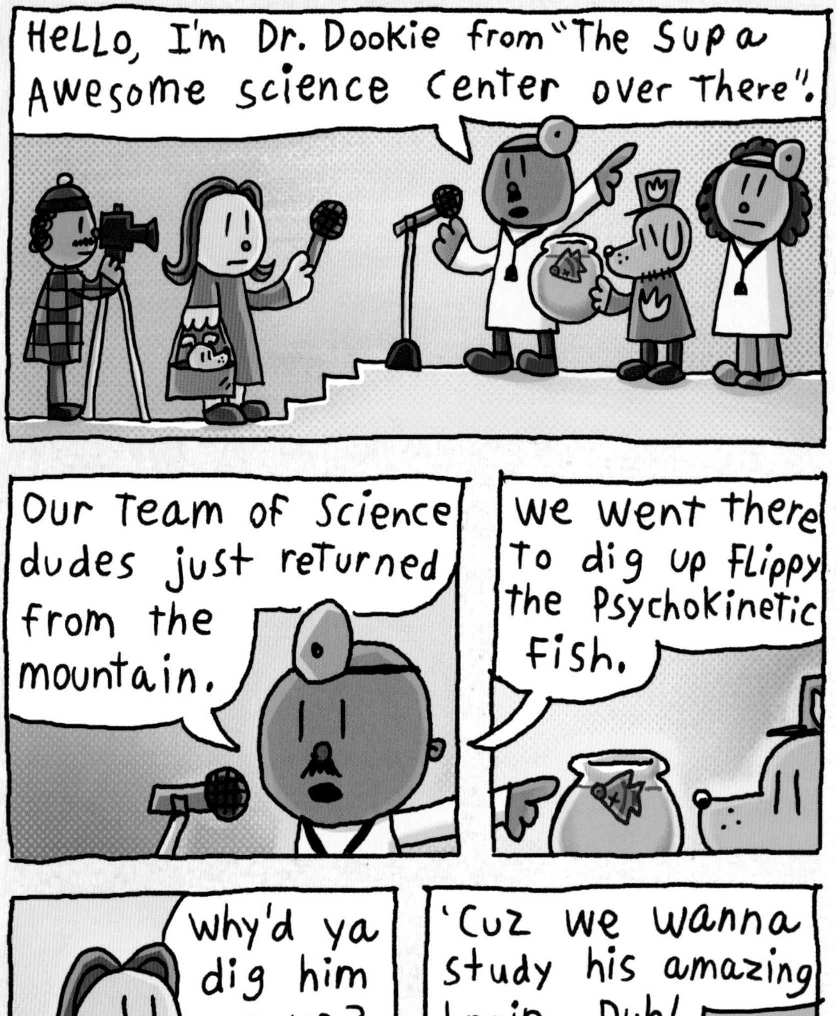

Hello, I'm Dr. Dookie from "The Supa Awesome science center over There".
Our Team of Science dudes just returned from the mountain.
We went there to dig up Flippy the Psychokinetic Fish.
Why'd ya dig him up?
'Cuz we wanna study his amazing brain. Duh!

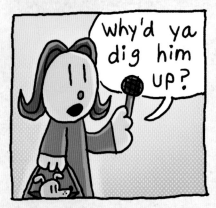

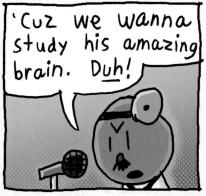

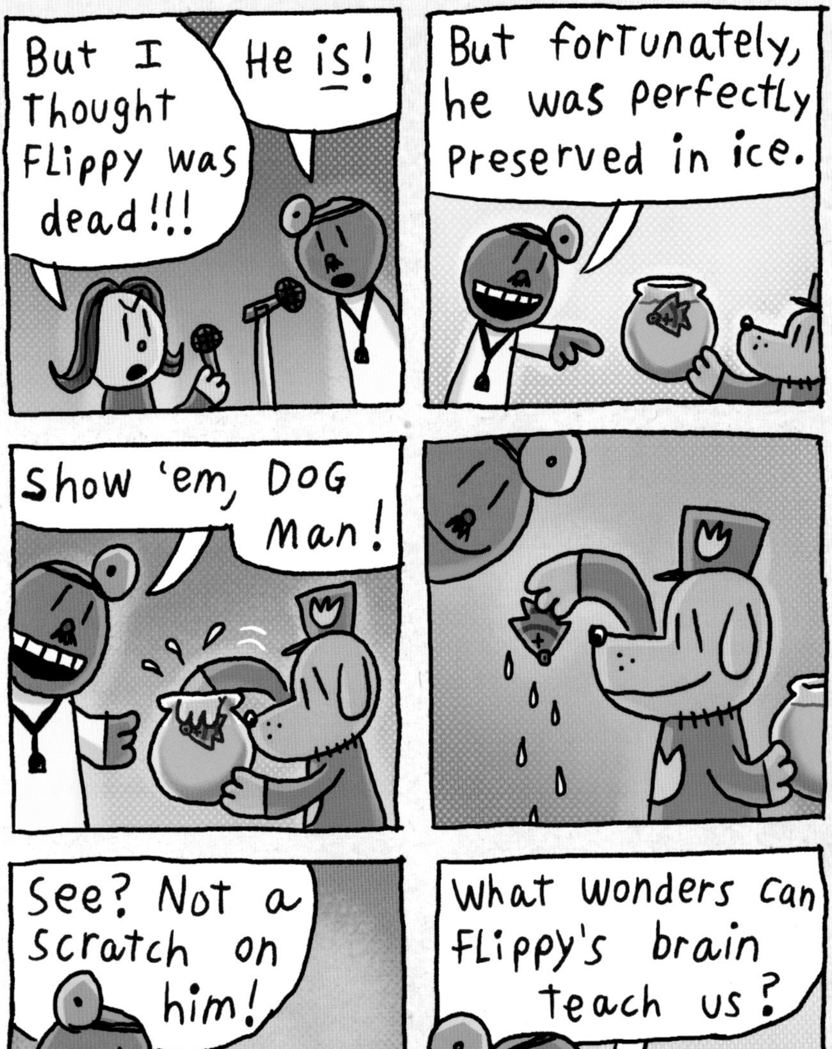
But I Thought Flippy was dead!!!
He is!
But fortunately, he was perfectly preserved in ice.
Show 'em, Dog Man!
See? Not a scratch on him!
What wonders can Flippy's brain teach us?

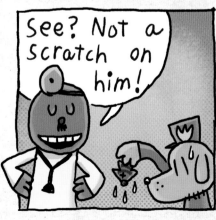

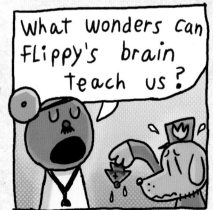

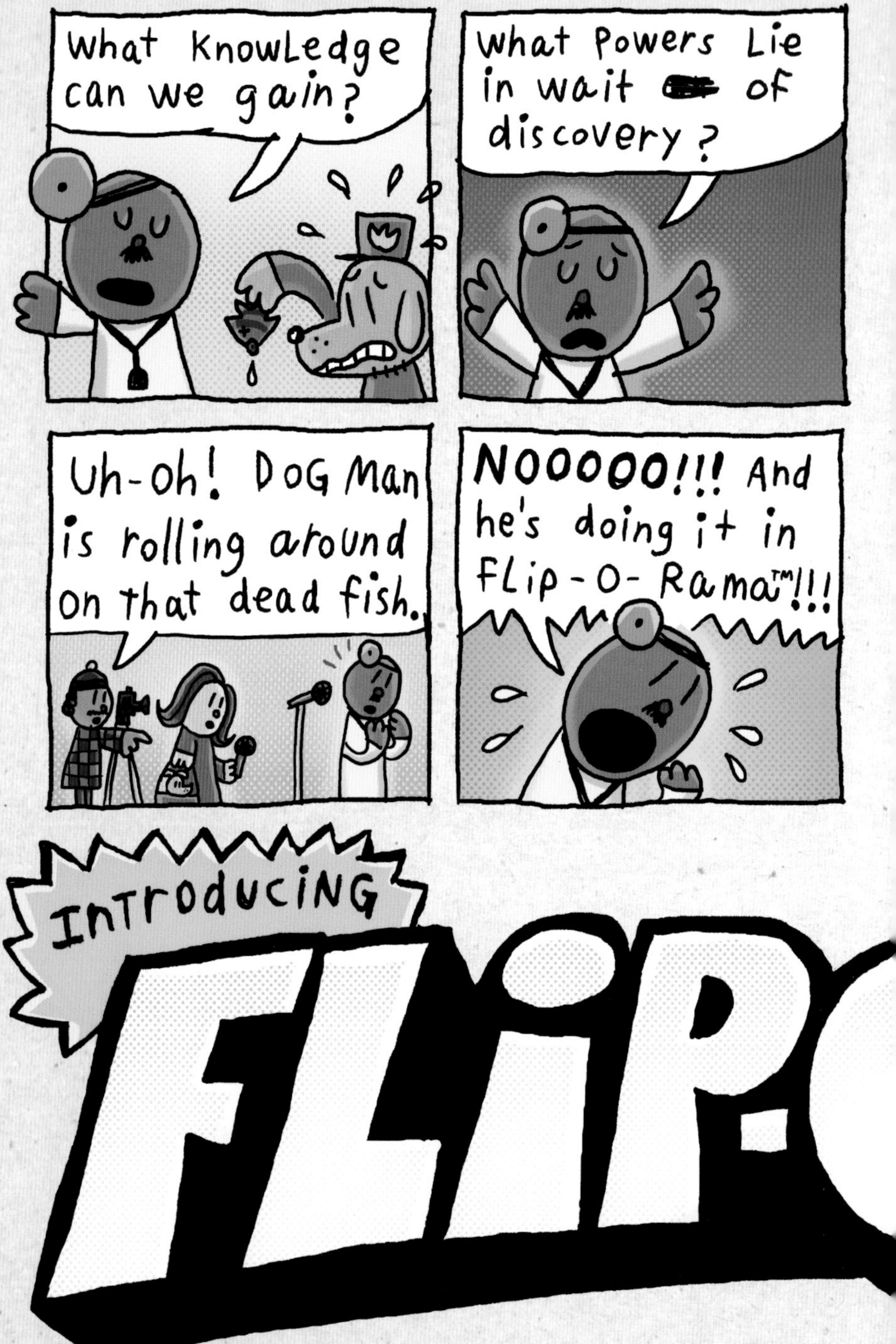
What knowledge can we gain?
What powers lie in wait of discovery?
Uh-oh! Dog Man is rolling around on that dead fish.
NOOOOO!!! And he's doing it in Flip-O-Rama™!!!
Introducing
FLIP-

STEP 1.
First, Place your Left hand inside the dotted Lines marked "Left hand here". Hold The book open FLAT!

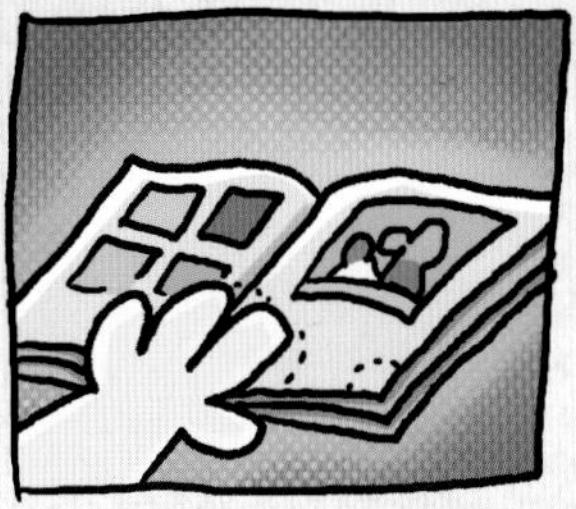

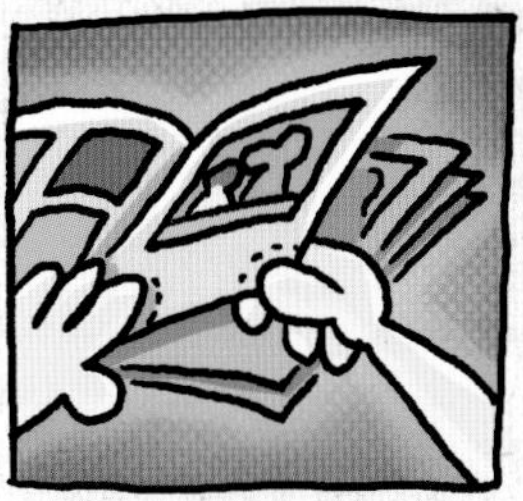

STEP 2:
Grasp the right-hand Page with your Thumb and index finger (inside the dotted Lines marked "Right Thumb Here").

STEP 3:
Now QUICKLY flip the right-hand page back and forth until the Picture appears to be Animated.

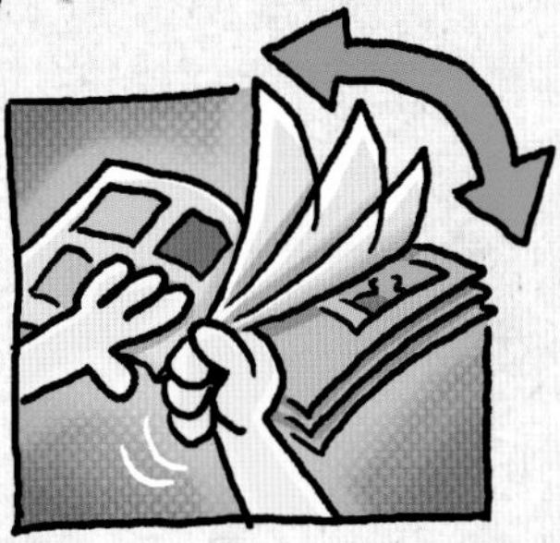

(For extra fun, try adding your own sound-effects!)

RAMA

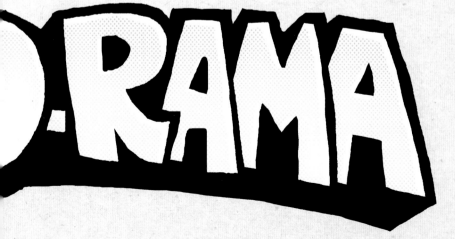

Remember,

while you are flipping,
be sure you can see
the image on page **43**
AND the image on page **45.**

If you flip quickly,
the two pictures will
start to look like
one **ANimated** cartoon!

Don't forget to
add your own
sound-effects!

Left
hand here.

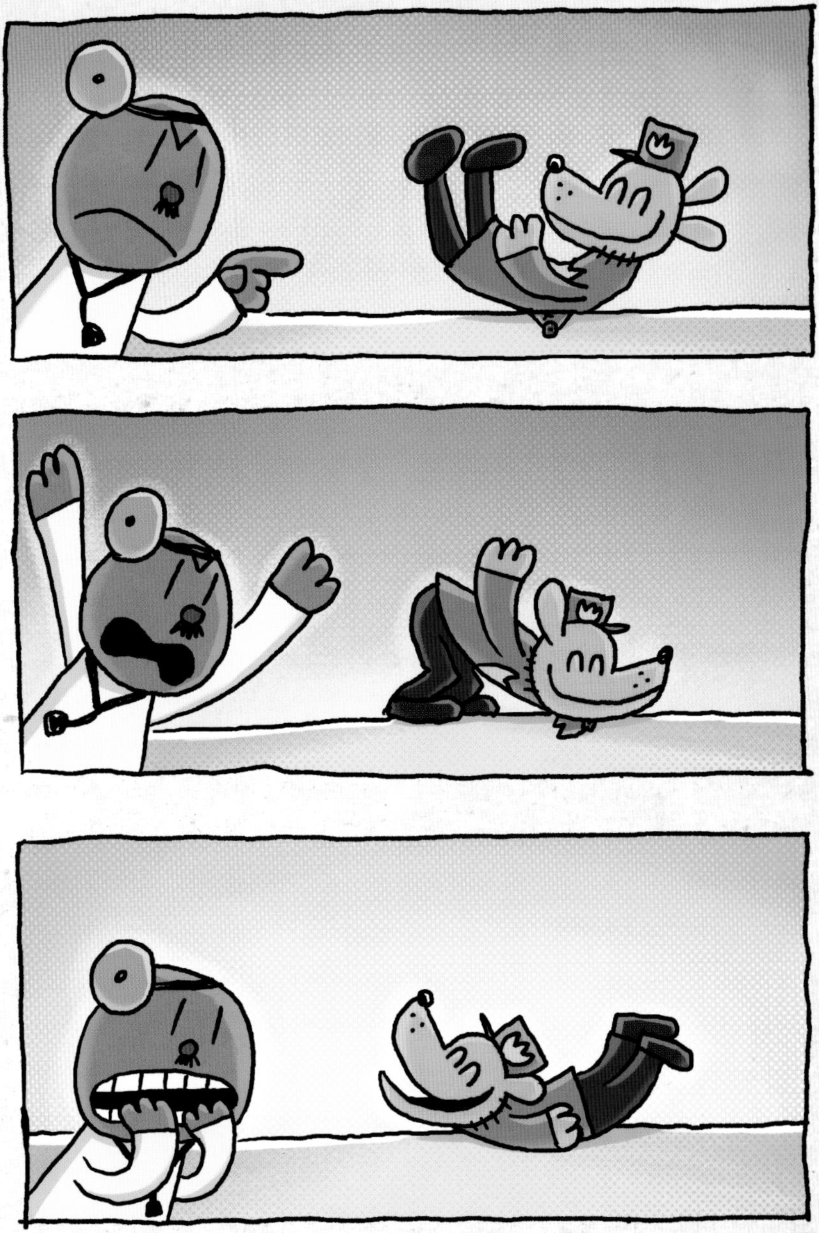

Right Thumb here.

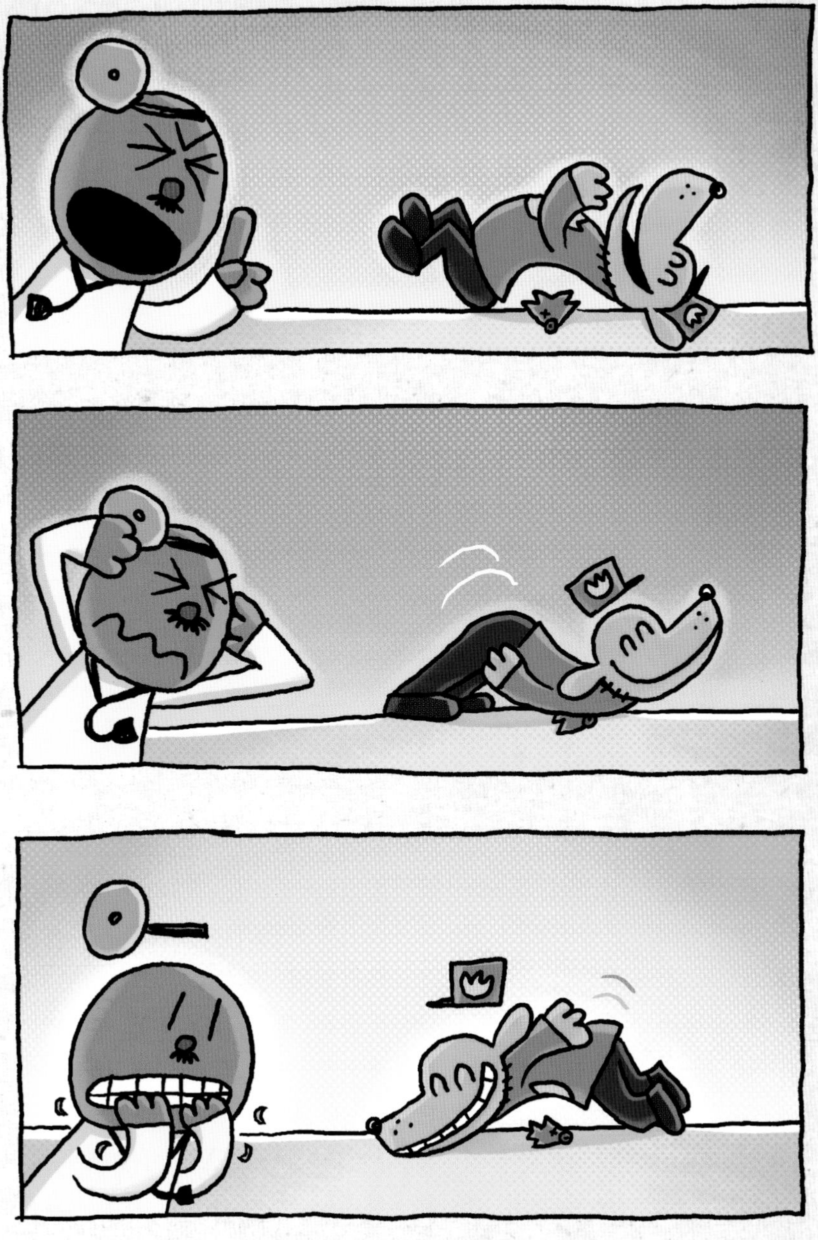

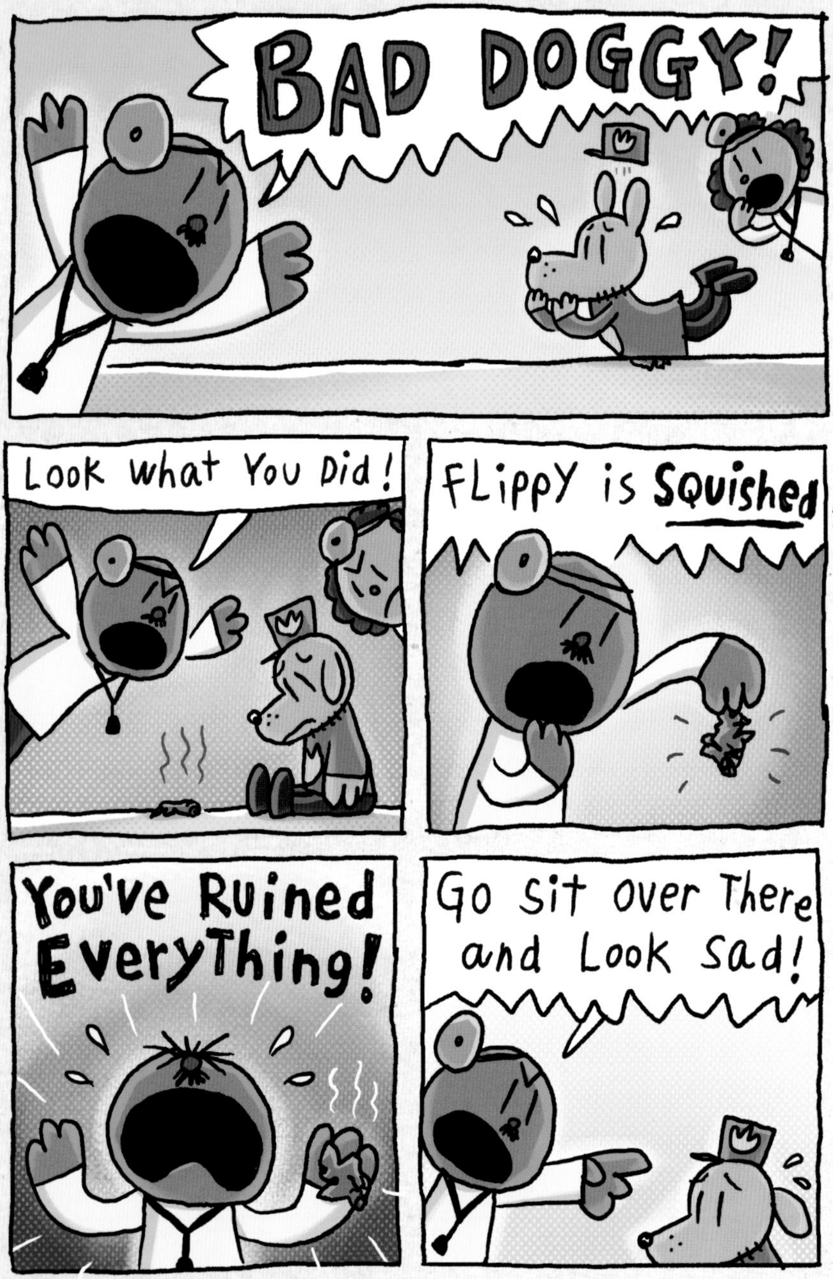
BAD DOGGY!
Look What You Did!
FLippY is Squished!
You've Ruined EveryThing!
Go sit over There and Look sad!

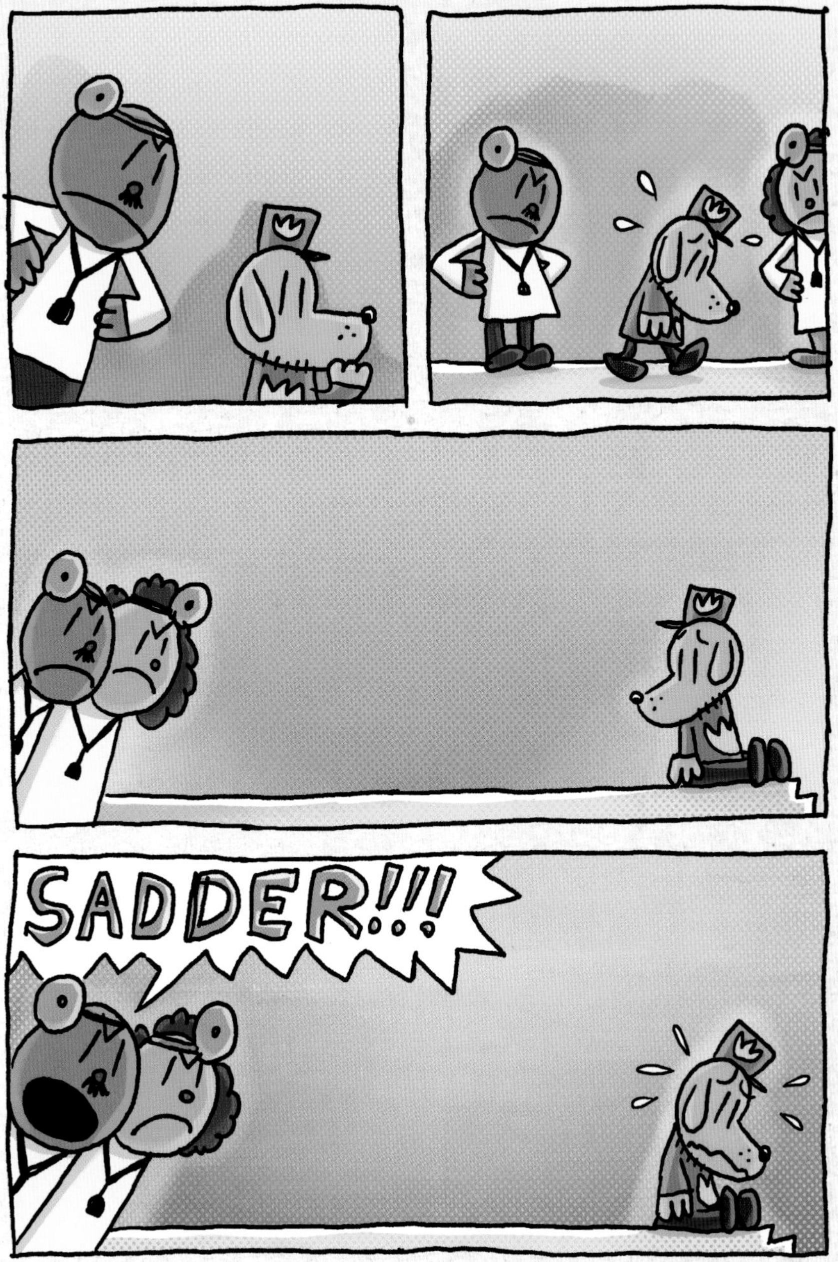
SADDER!!!

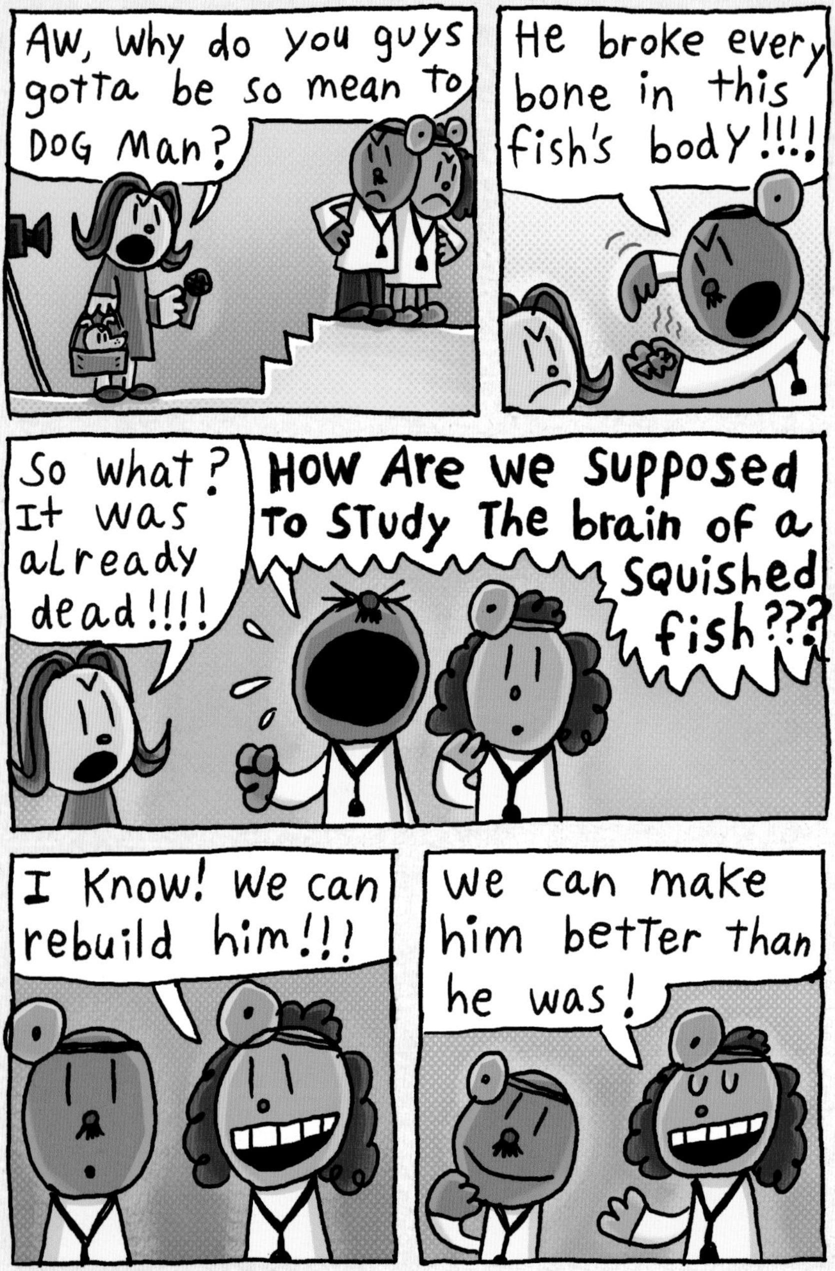
Aw, Why do you guys gotta be so mean to DOG Man?
He broke every bone in this fish's body!!!!
So what? It was already dead!!!!
HOW Are we supposed to STudy The brain of a squished fish???
I Know! We can rebuild him!!!
We can make him better than he was!

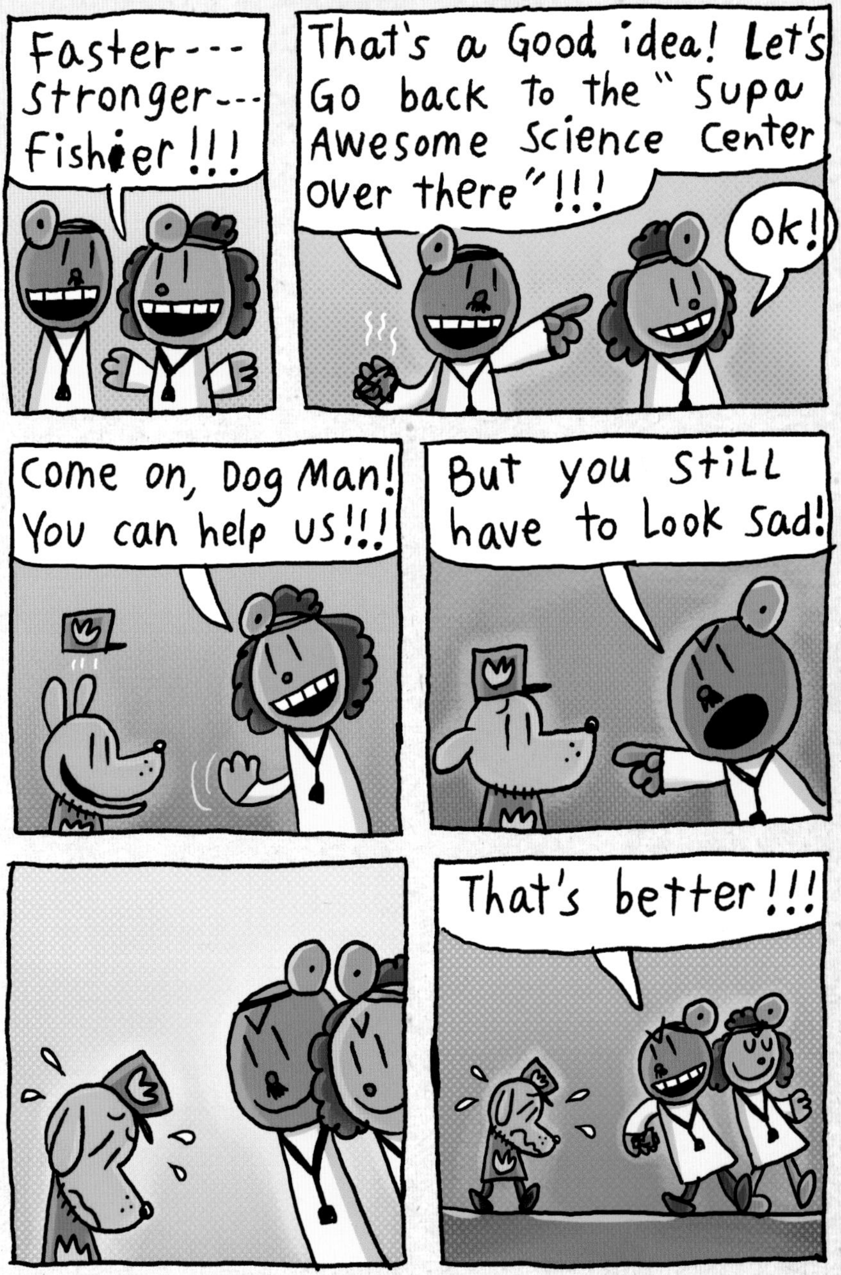

Faster--- Stronger--- Fishier!!!
That's a Good idea! Let's Go back to the "Supa Awesome Science Center over there"!!!
Ok!
Come on, Dog Man! You can help us!!!
But you STILL have to Look sad!
That's better!!!

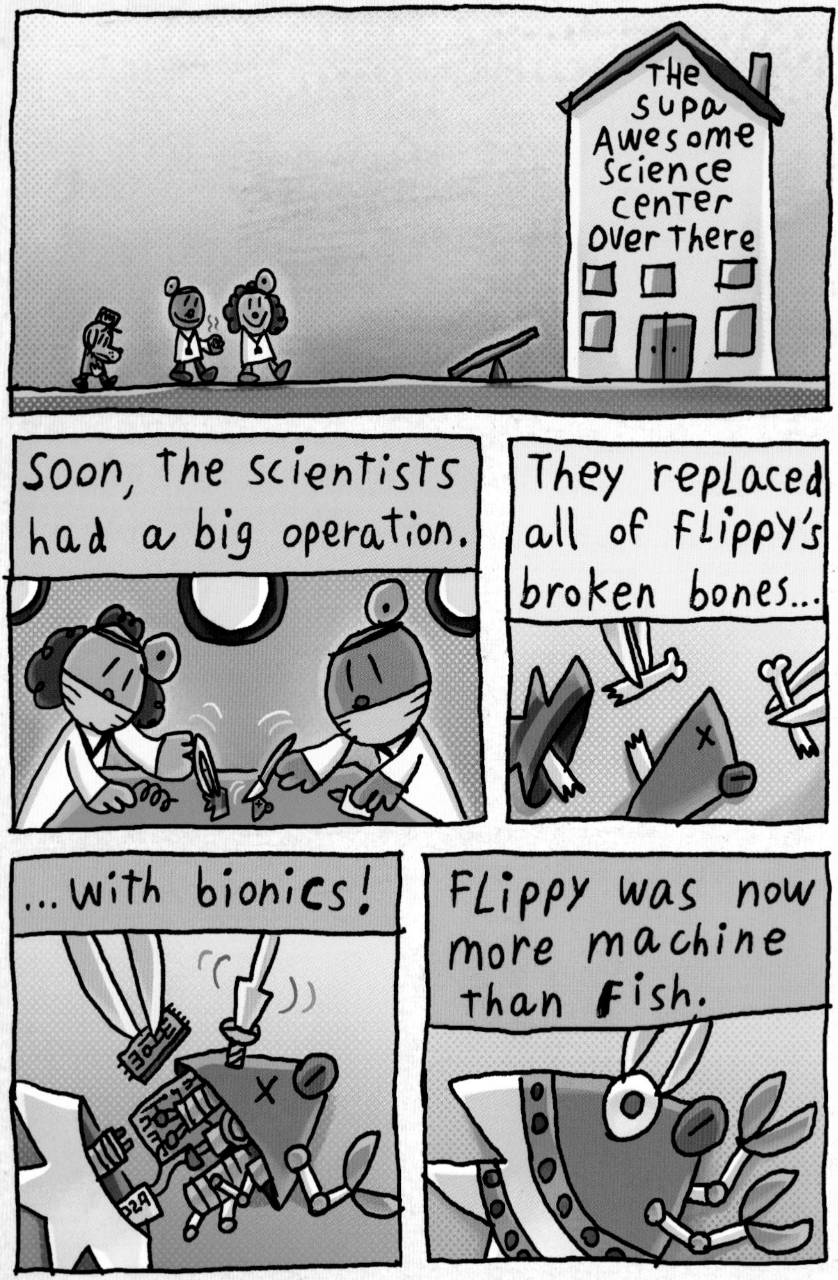
THE SUPA Awesome Science center over There
Soon, the scientists had a big operation.
They replaced all of Flippy's broken bones...
...with bionics!
Flippy was now more machine than fish.

Boy, it's a good thing Flippy is dead!

I know! He'd be _so_ Dangerous if he ever came back to Life!!!

Yeah--- with his telekinetic brain AND bionic super strength? He'd be **unstoppable**!!!

Well, I'm glad we don't have to worry about that!

Me too! With Dog Man guarding him, what could go wrong?

Let's go home and get some rest! good idea!

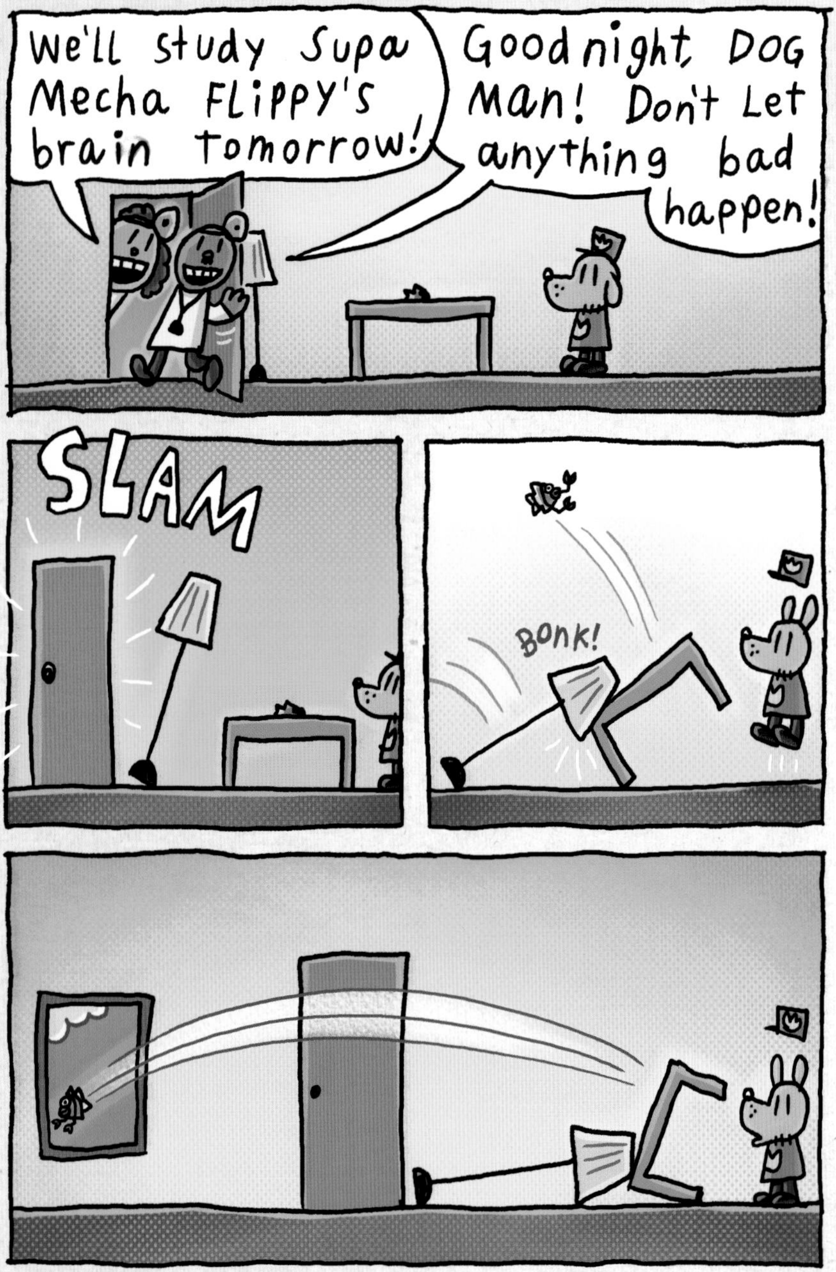
We'll study Supa Mecha Flippy's brain tomorrow!
Goodnight, DOG MAN! Don't let anything bad happen!
SLAM
BONK!

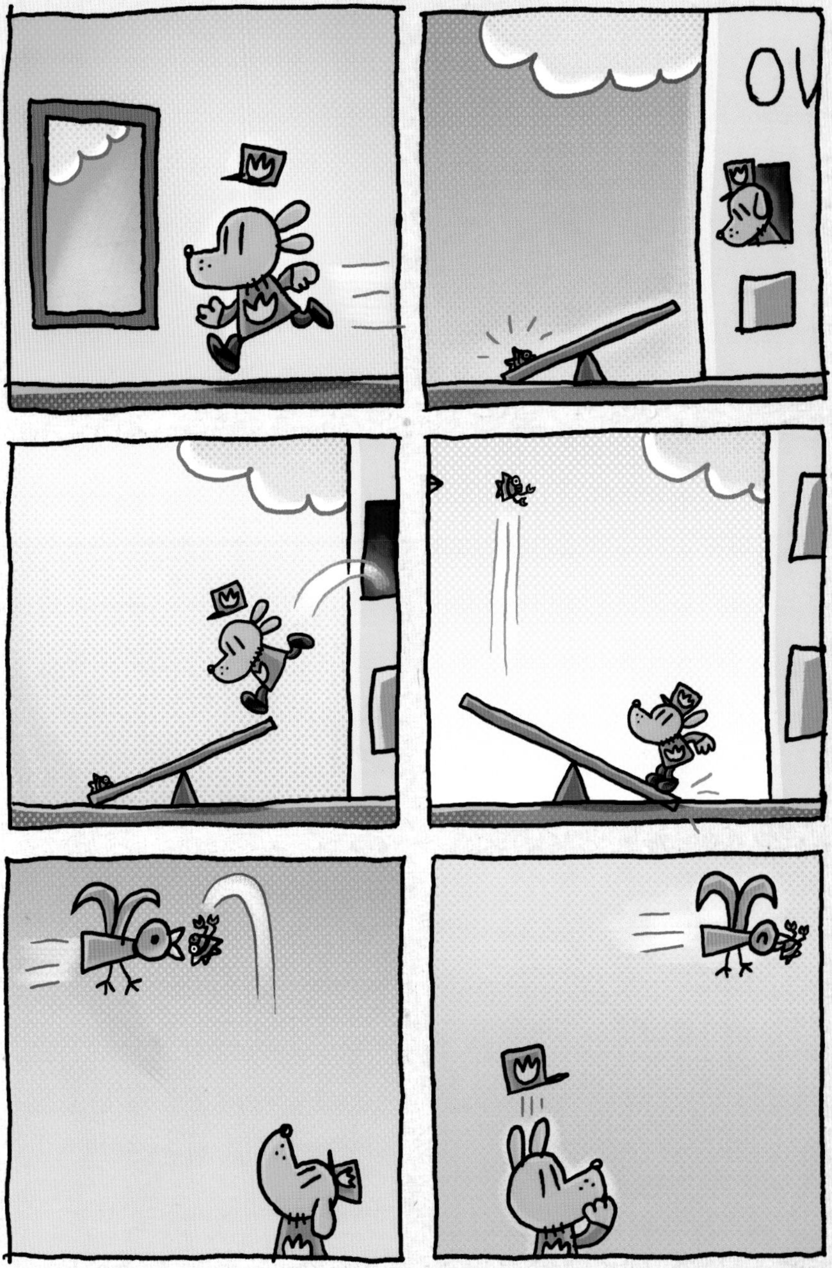
OV

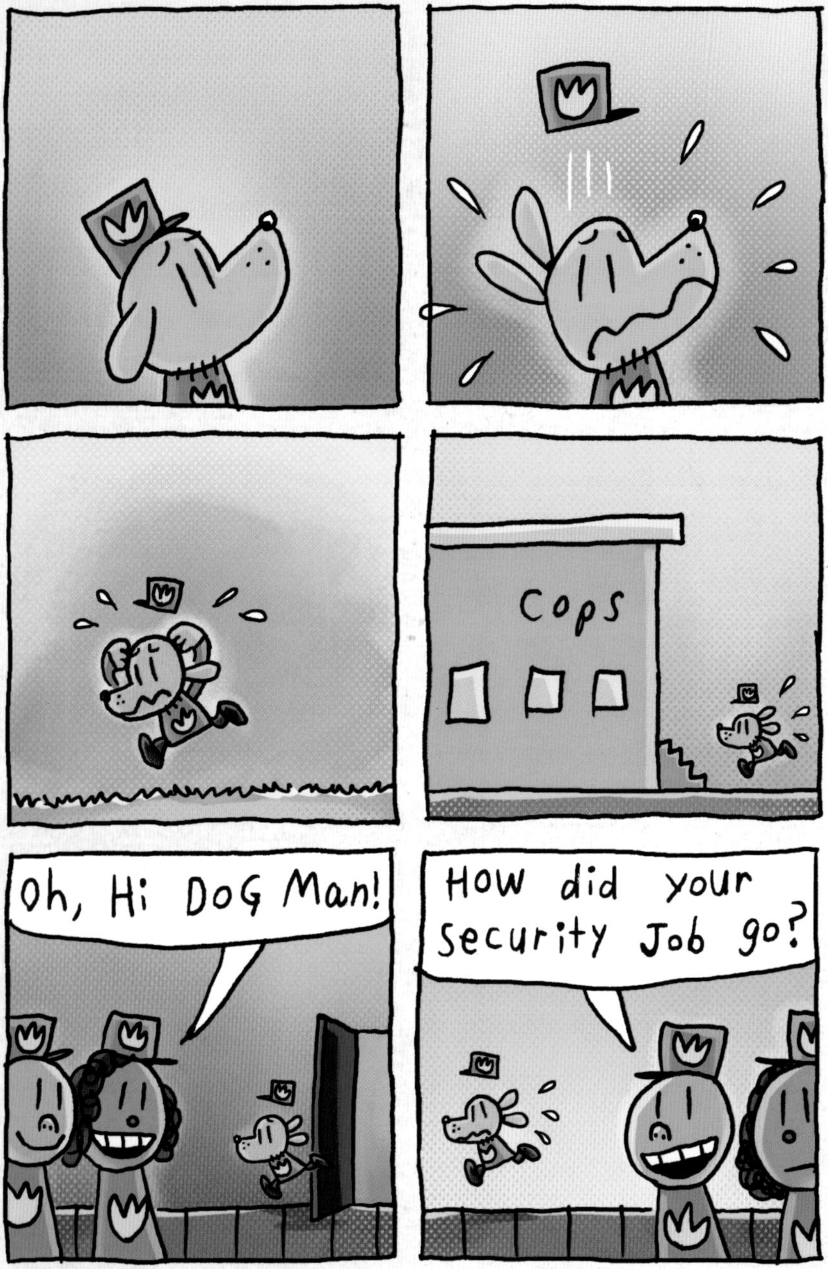
Cops
Oh, Hi DOG Man!
HOW did your security Job go?

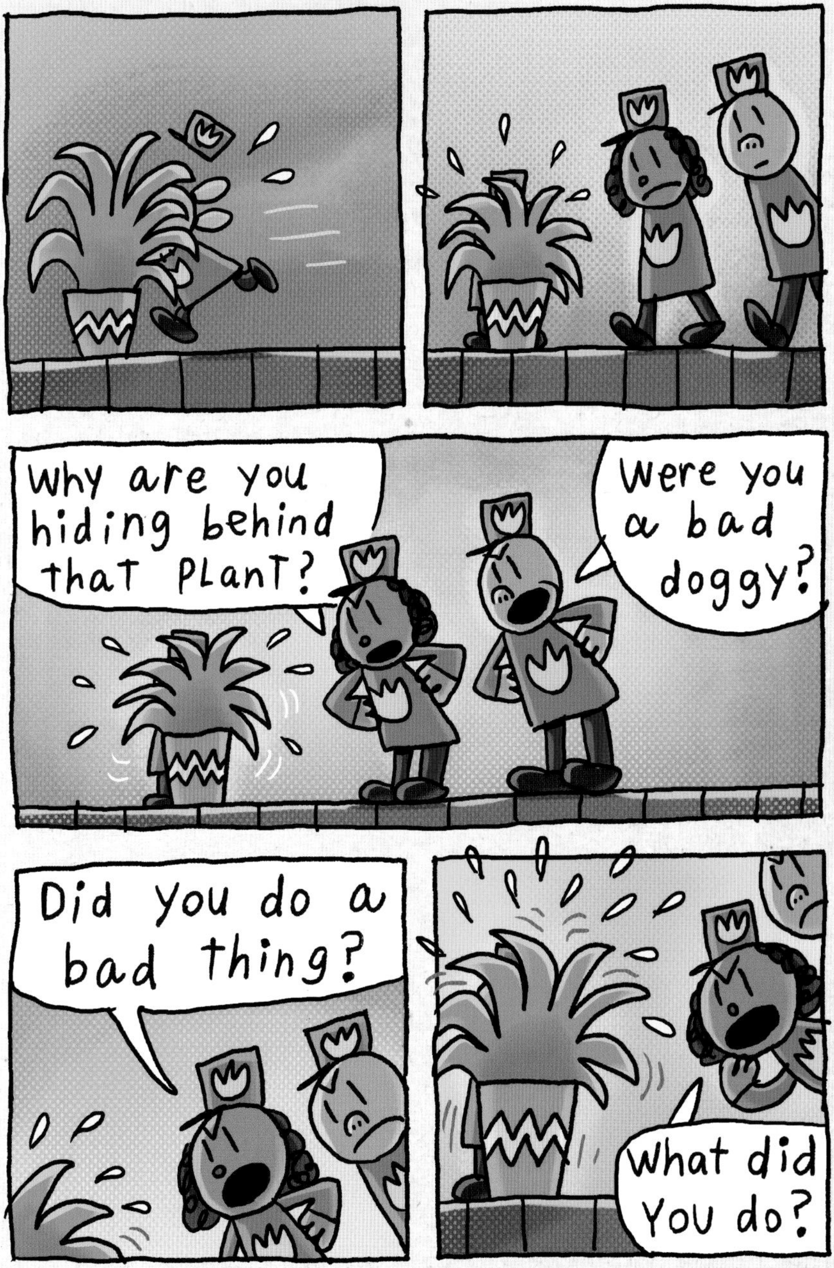
Why are you hiding behind that PLanT?
Were you a bad doggy?
Did you do a bad thing?
What did You do?

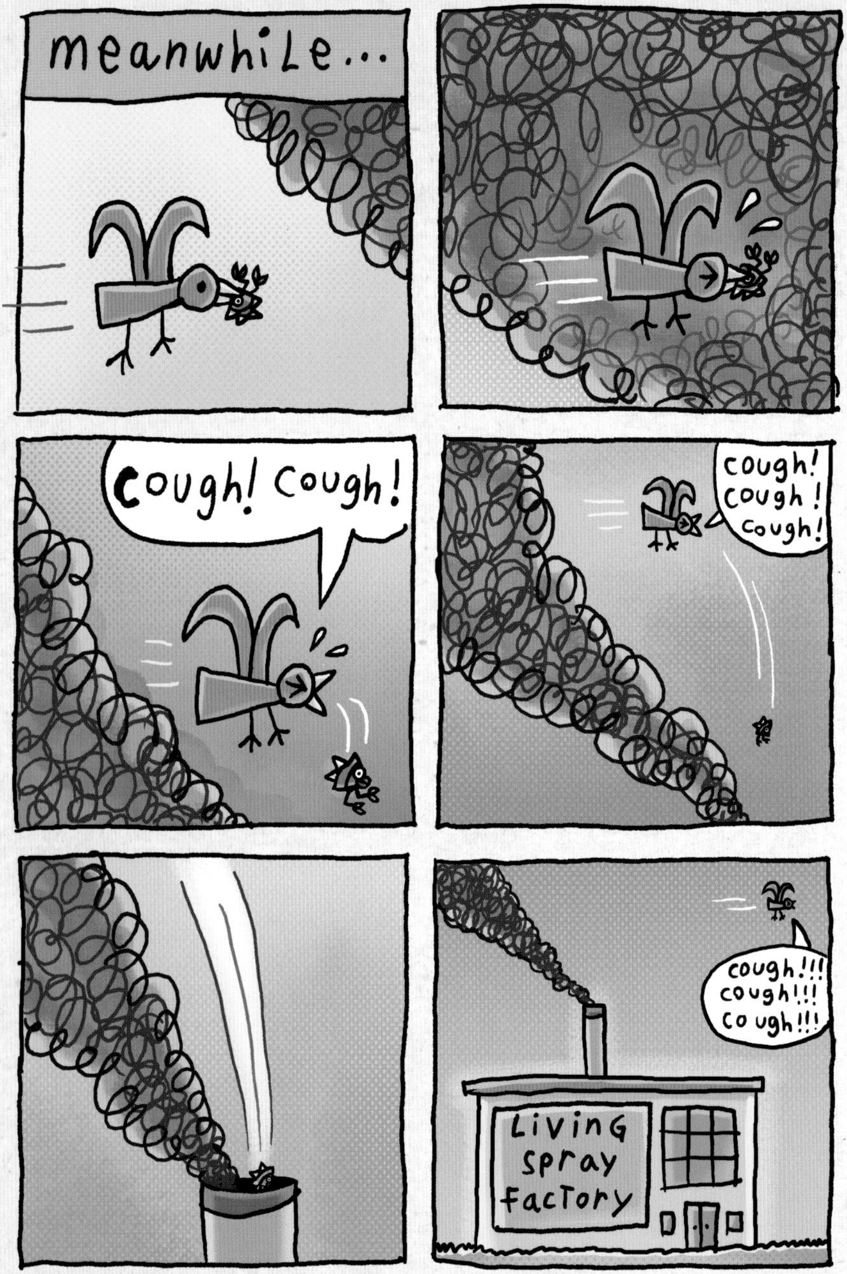
meanwhiLe...
Cough! Cough!
cough!
cough!
cough!
cough!!!
cough!!!
cough!!!
Living
spray
Factory

Chapter the Fourth

No More Kitten Around!

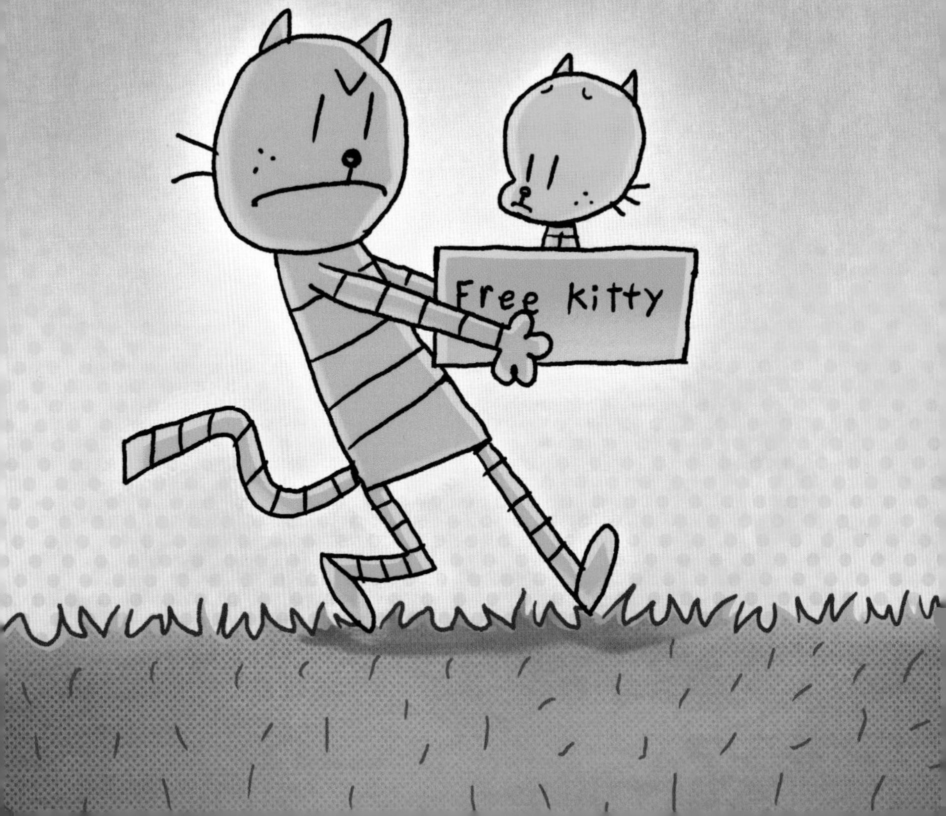
Free kitty

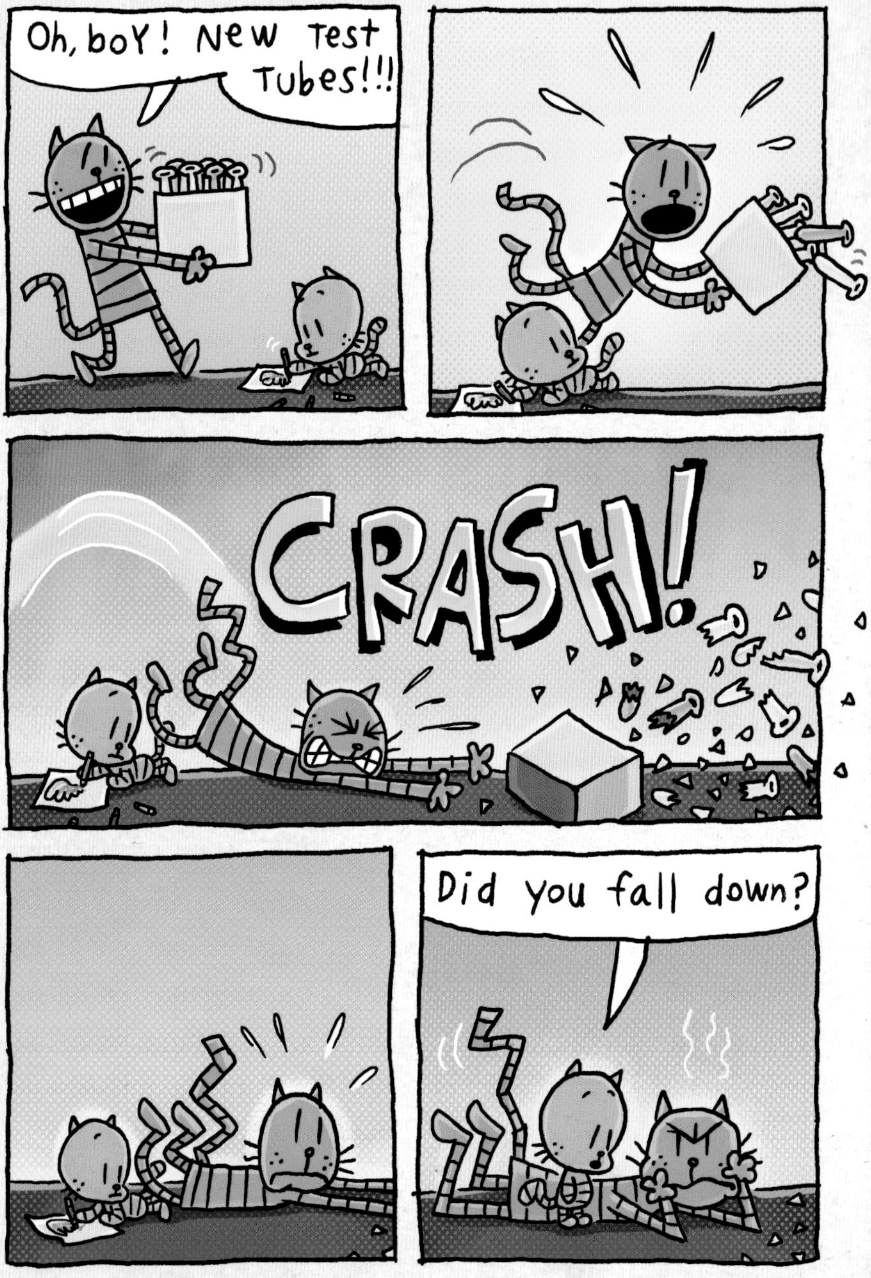
Oh, boY! New Test Tubes!!!
CRASH!
Did you fall down?

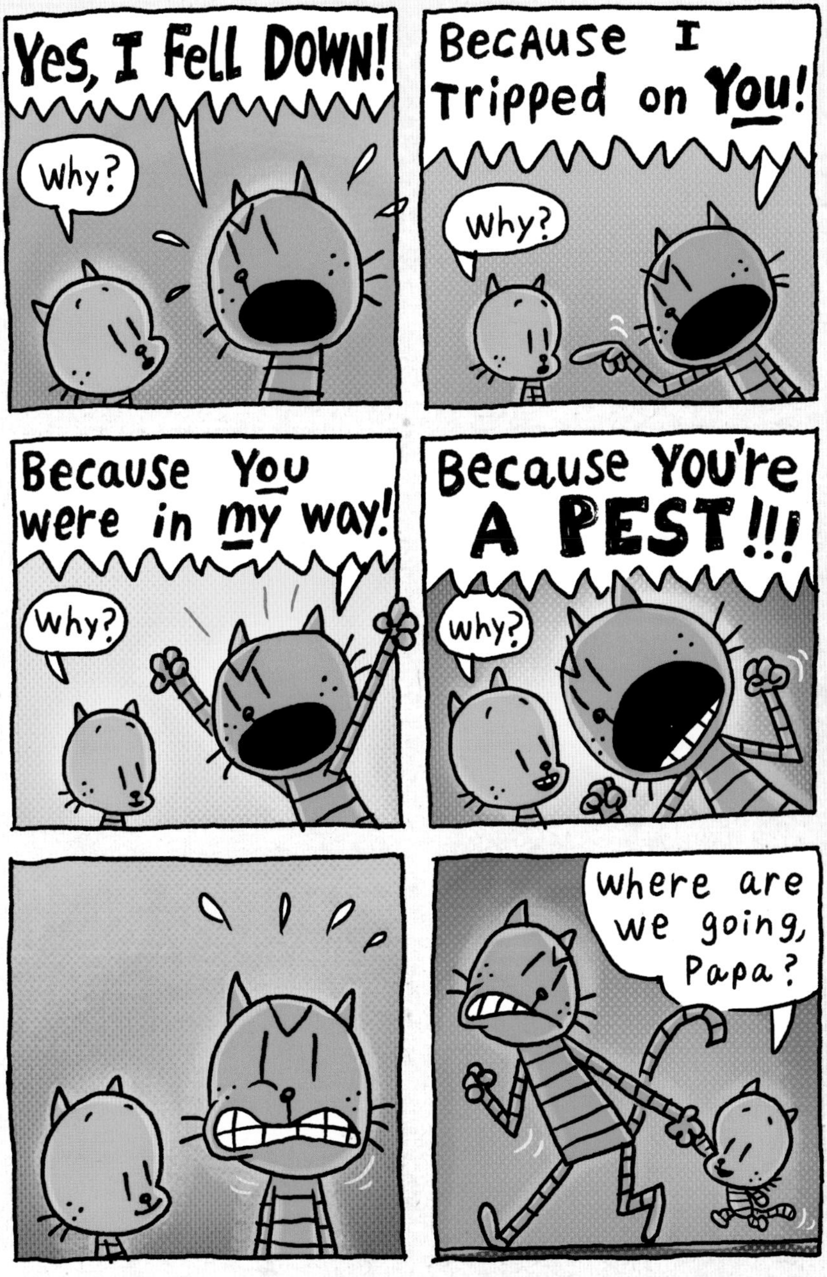
Yes, I Fell DOWN!
Why?
Because I Tripped on You!
Why?
Because You were in my way!
Why?
Because You're A PEST!!!
Why?
Where are we going, Papa?

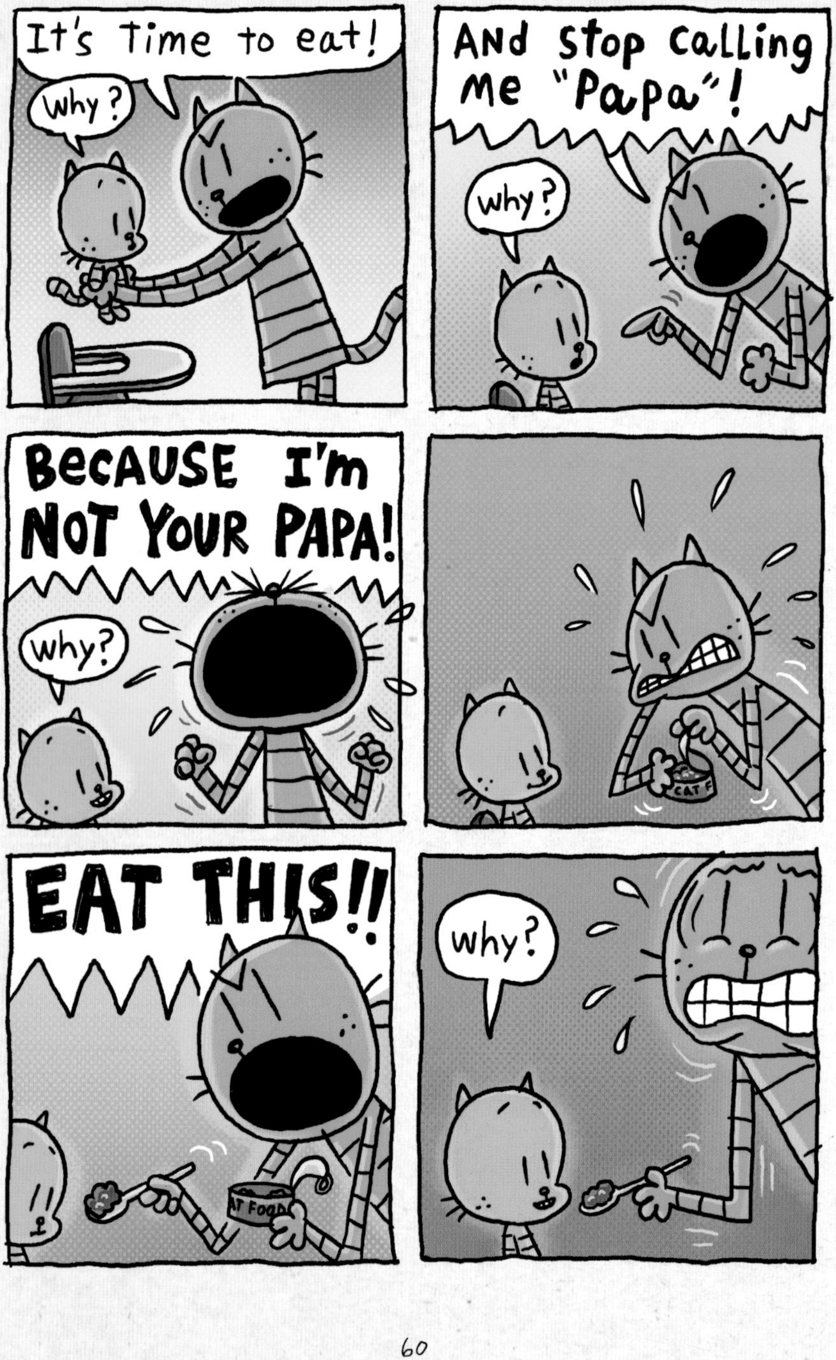
It's time to eat!
Why?
AND stop calling me "Papa"!
why?
BECAUSE I'm NOT YOUR PAPA!
why?
CAT F
EAT THIS!!
AT FOOD
why?

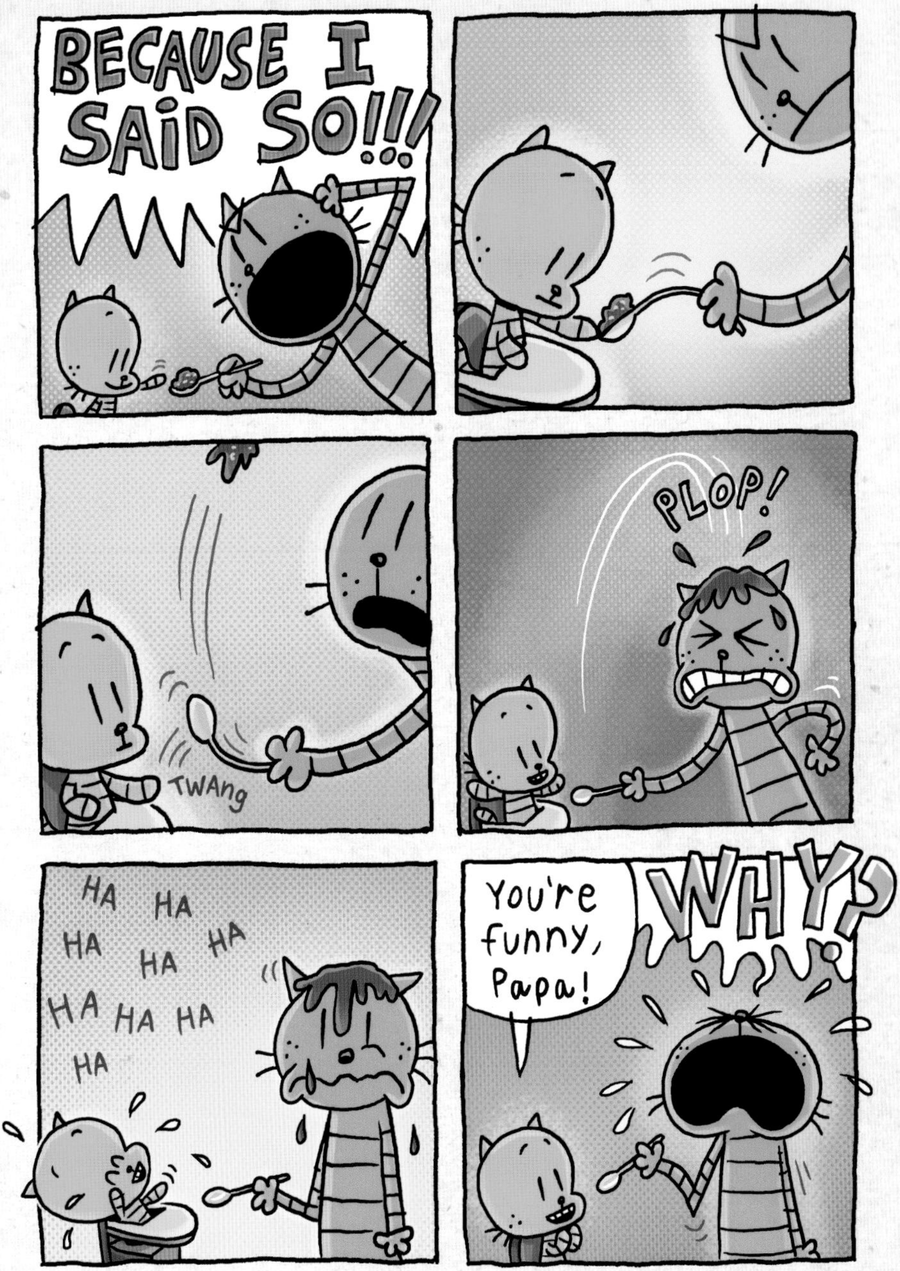
BECAUSE I SAID SO!!!
TWAng
PLOP!
HA HA HA HA HA HA HA HA HA HA
You're funny, Papa!
WHY?

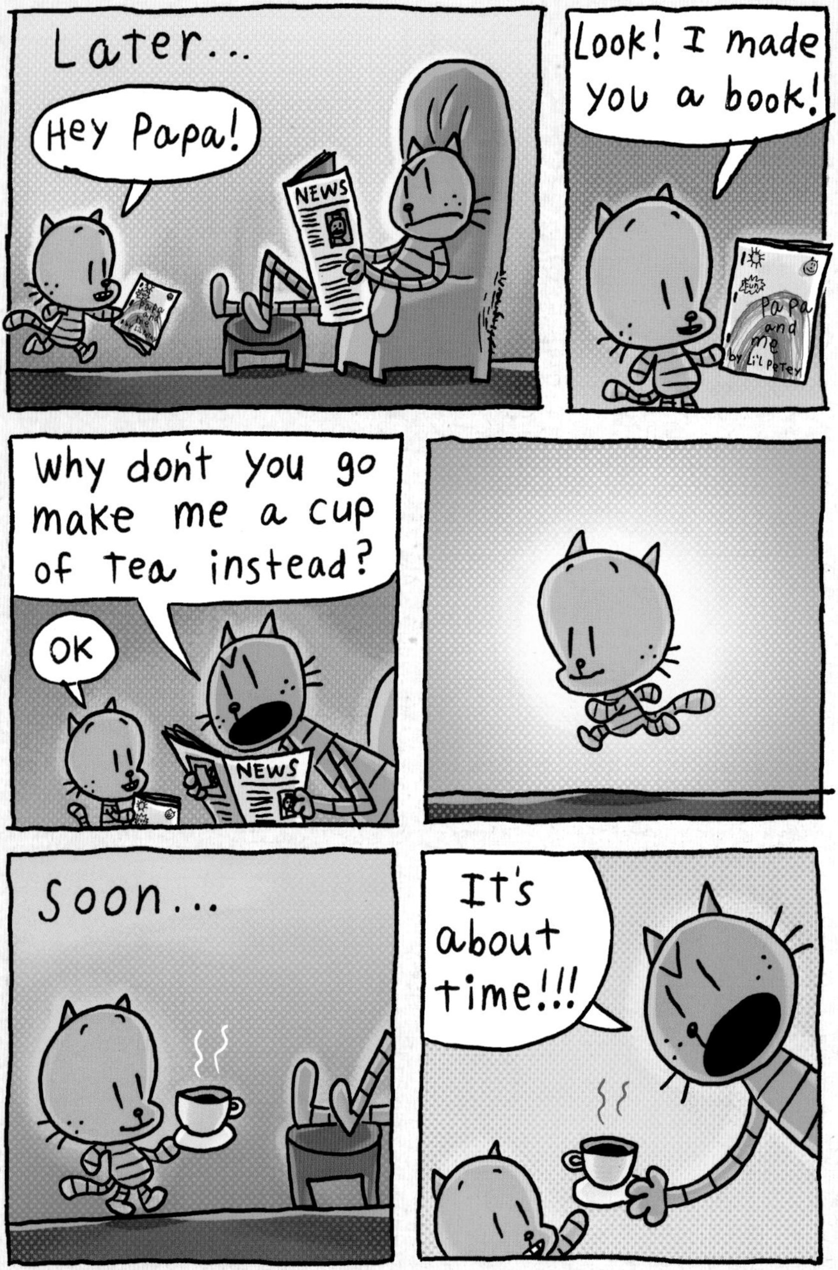
Later...
Hey Papa!
NEWS
Papa and me by Li'l Petey
Look! I made you a book!
Papa and me by Li'l Petey
Why don't you go make me a cup of tea instead?
OK
NEWS
Soon...
It's about time!!!

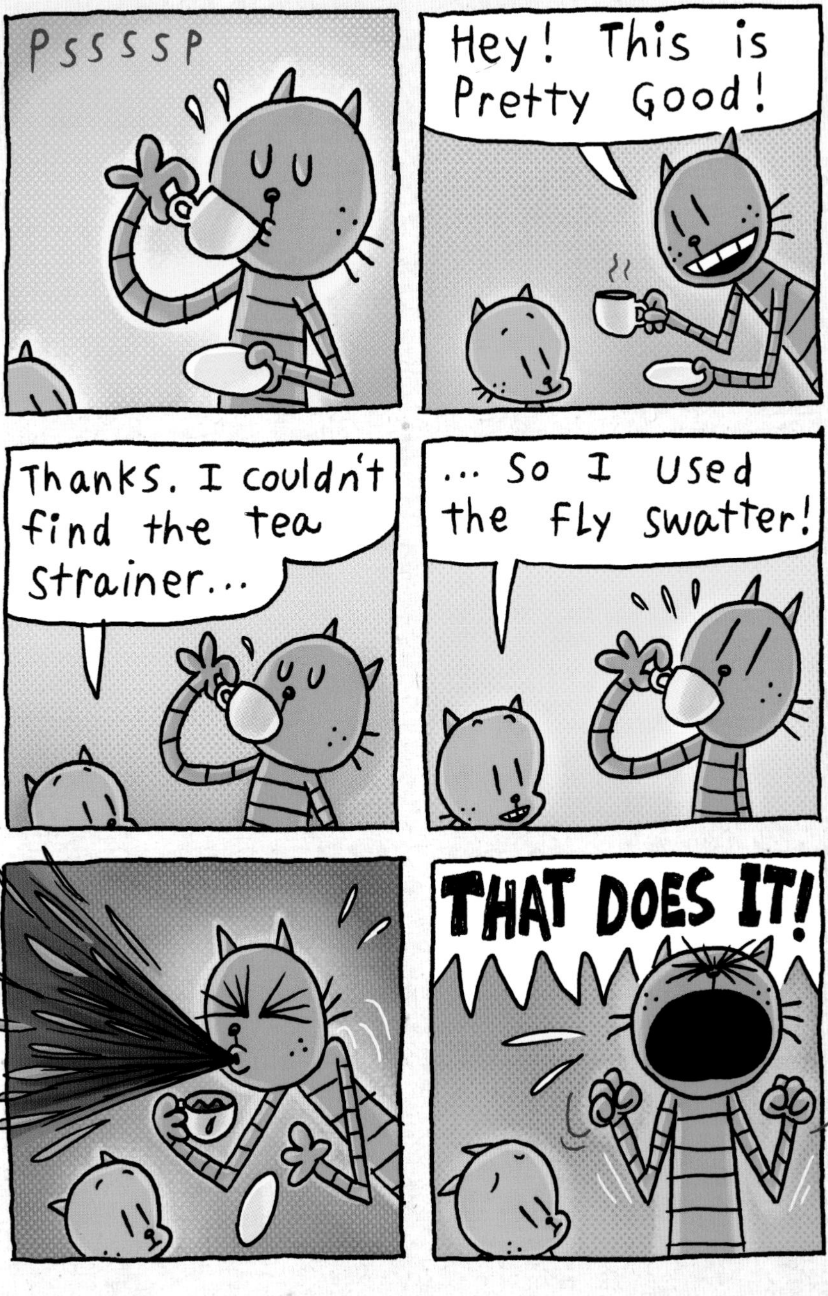
PSSSSP
Hey! This is Pretty Good!
Thanks. I couldn't find the tea strainer...
... So I used the fly swatter!
THAT DOES IT!

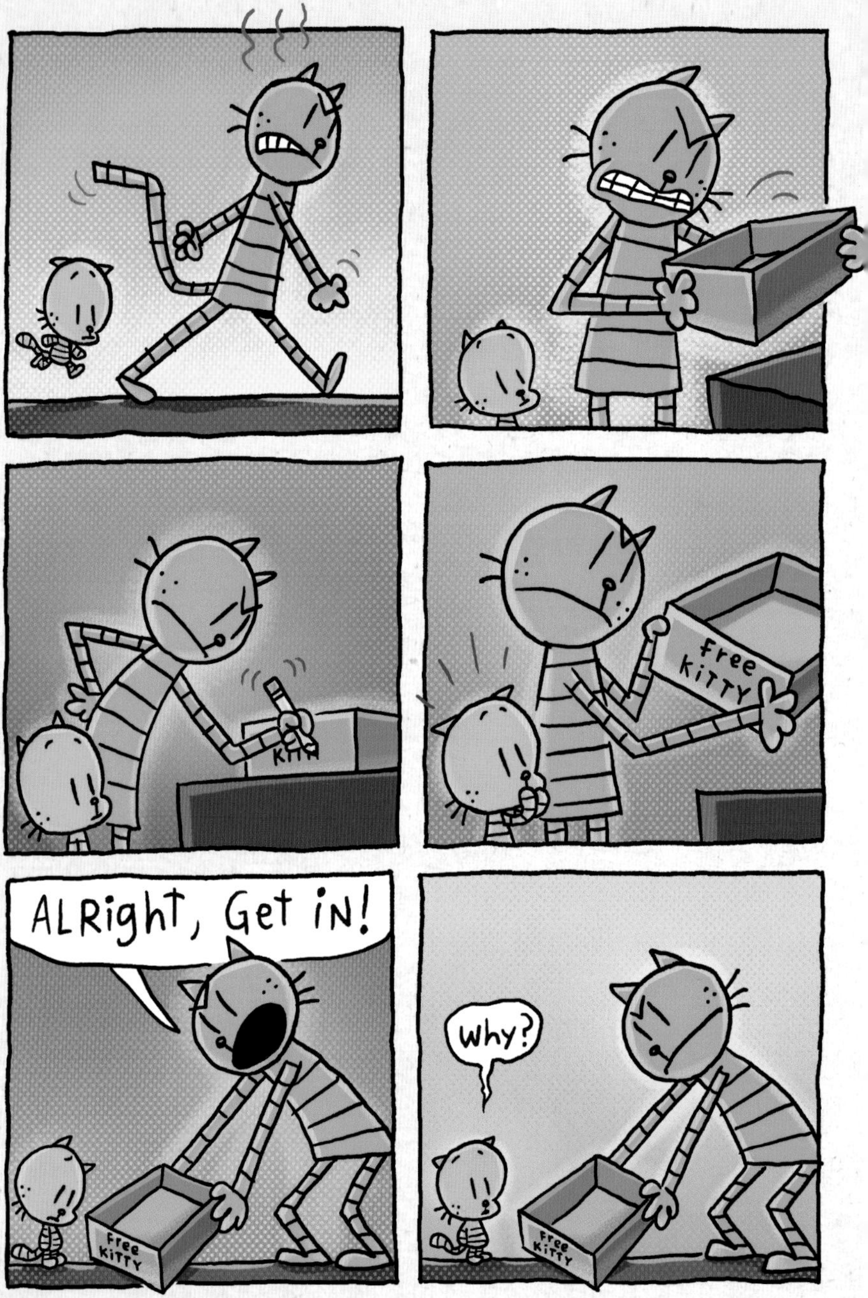
KITTY
Free KITTY
ALRight, Get iN!
Free KITTY
Why?
Free KITTY

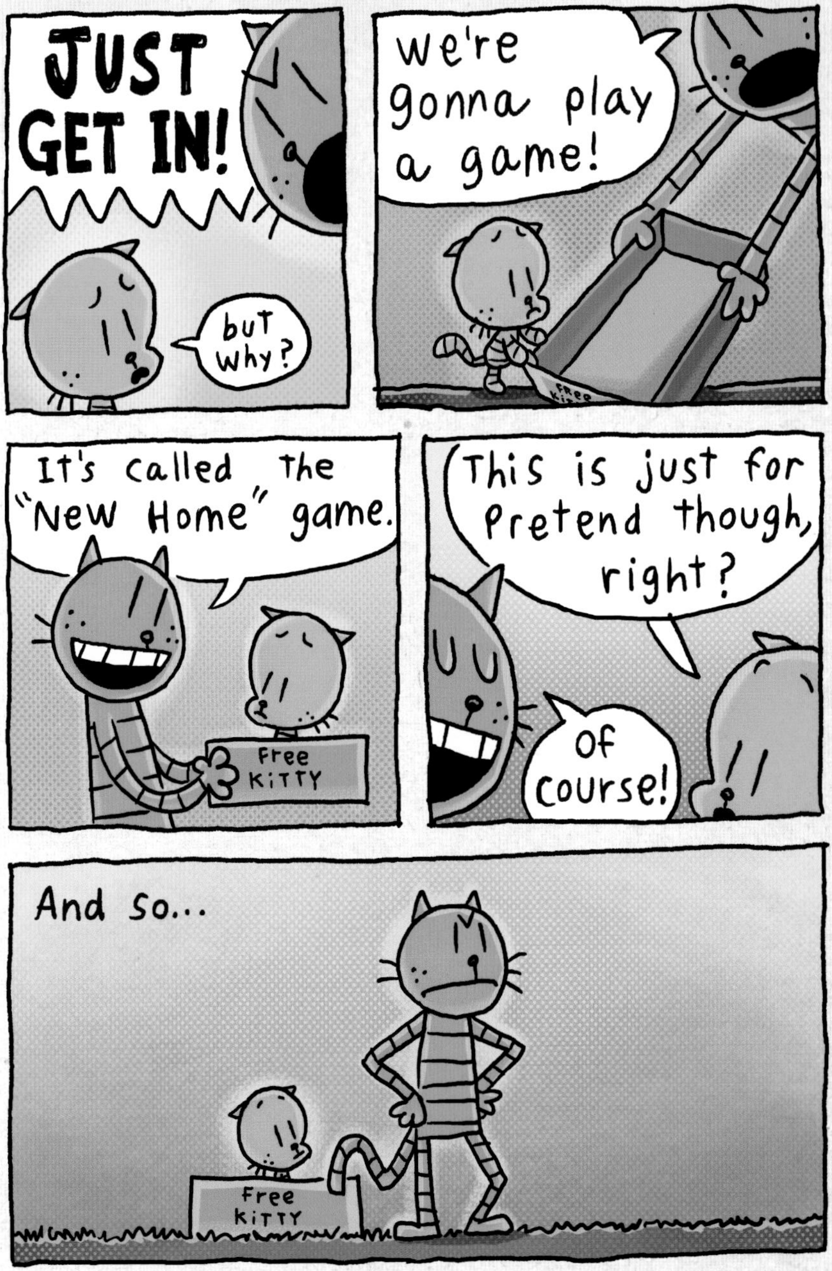
JUST GET IN!
but why?
we're gonna play a game!
Free Kitty
It's called the "New Home" game.
Free Kitty
This is just for pretend though, right?
Of course!
And so...
Free Kitty

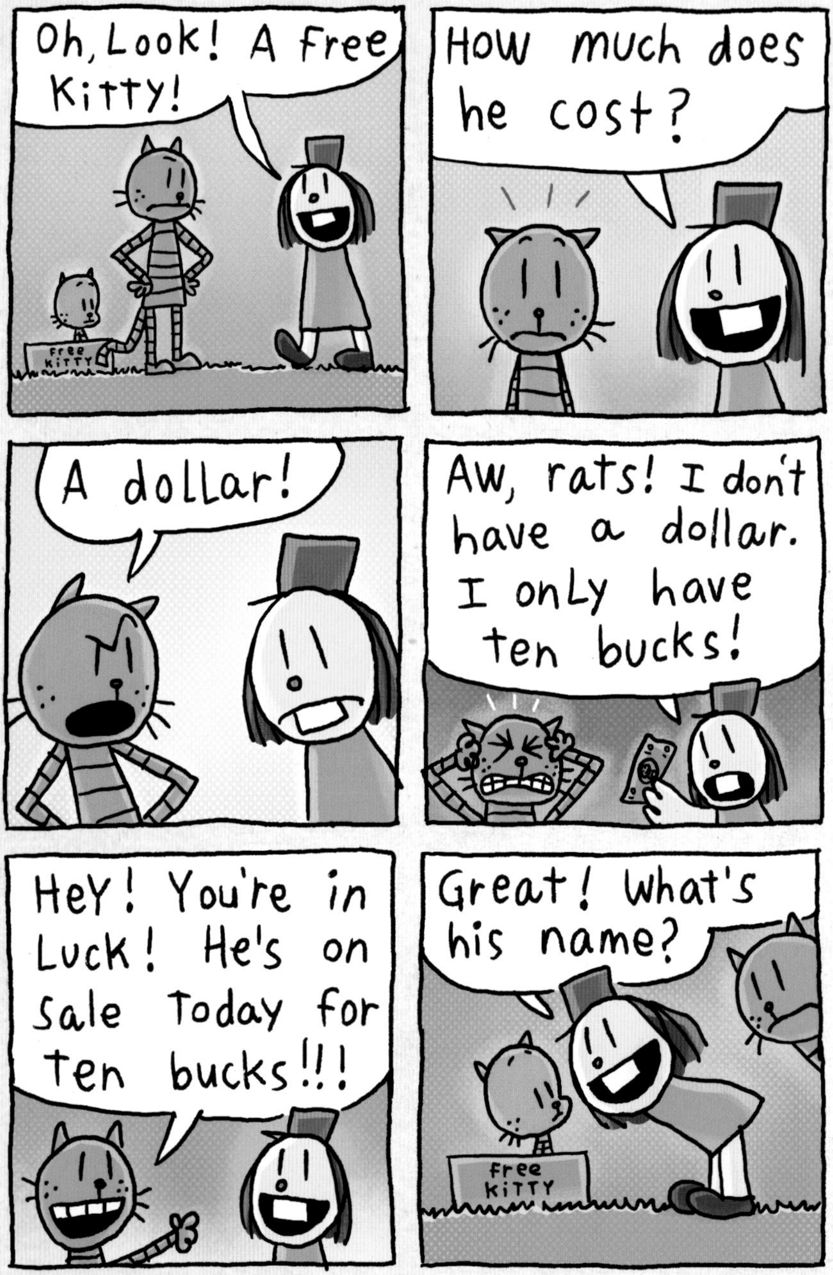
Oh, Look! A Free Kitty!
How much does he cost?
A dollar!
Aw, rats! I don't have a dollar. I only have ten bucks!
Hey! You're in Luck! He's on Sale Today for ten bucks!!!
Great! What's his name?
Free Kitty
Free Kitty
Free Kitty

Gee **Whiz!** What is **WRONG** with everybody these days?

It makes ya worry about the future!

"Duh, how much does he cost?"

WHAT AN IDIOT!!

I mean, The sign **CLEARLY** says...

Free KiTTY

Free KiTTY

Free KiTTY

69

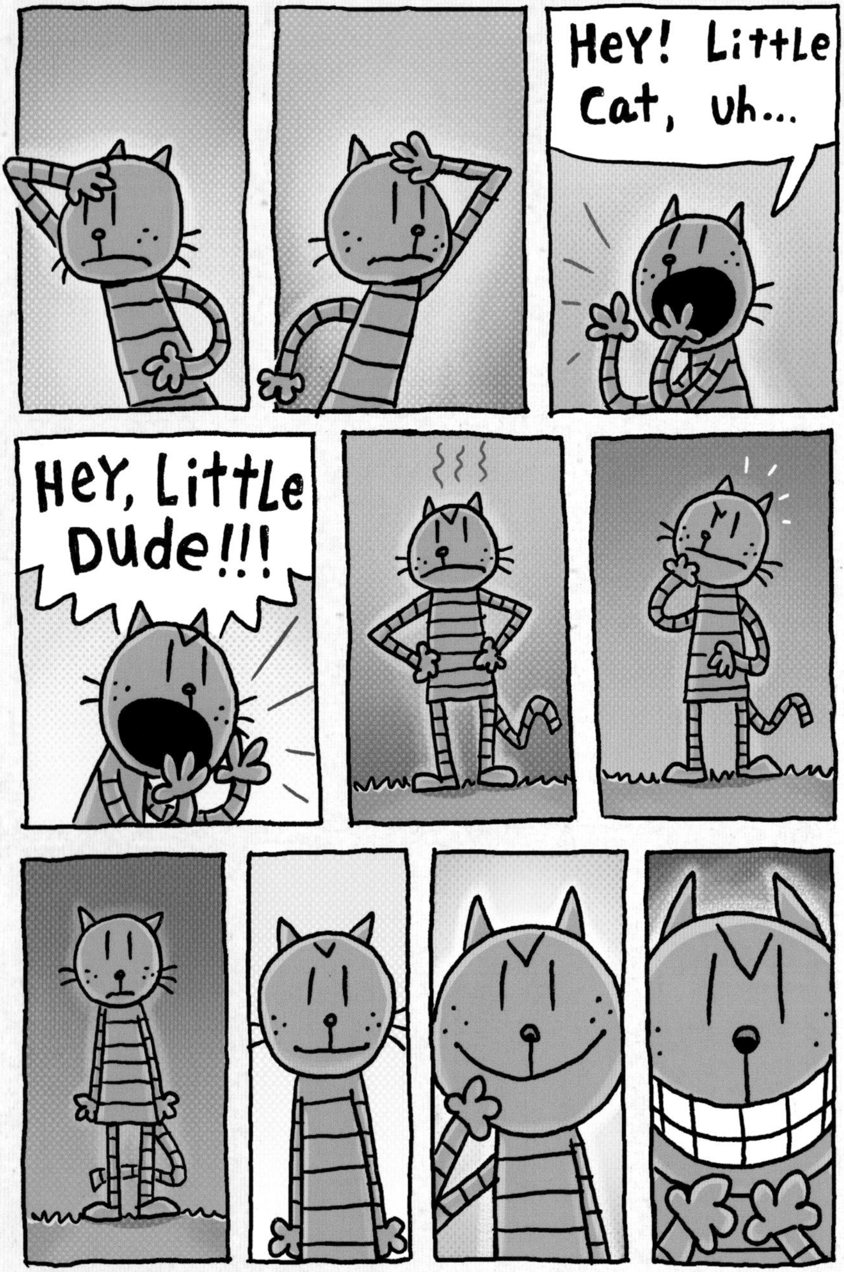
HEY! Little Cat, uh...
HEY, Little Dude!!!

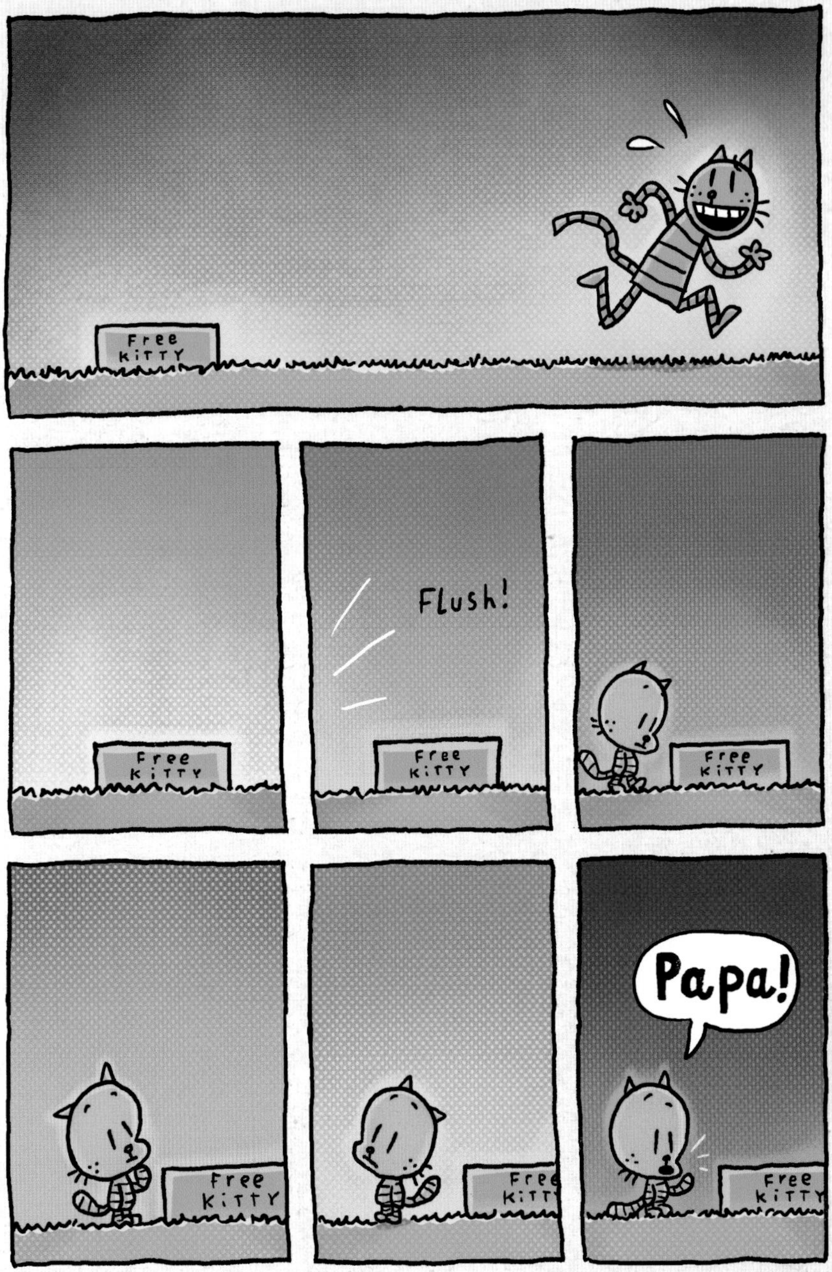
Free KiTTY
Free KiTTY
Flush!
Free KiTTY
Free KiTTY
Free KiTTY
Free KiTTY
Fre KiTT
Papa!
Free KiTTY

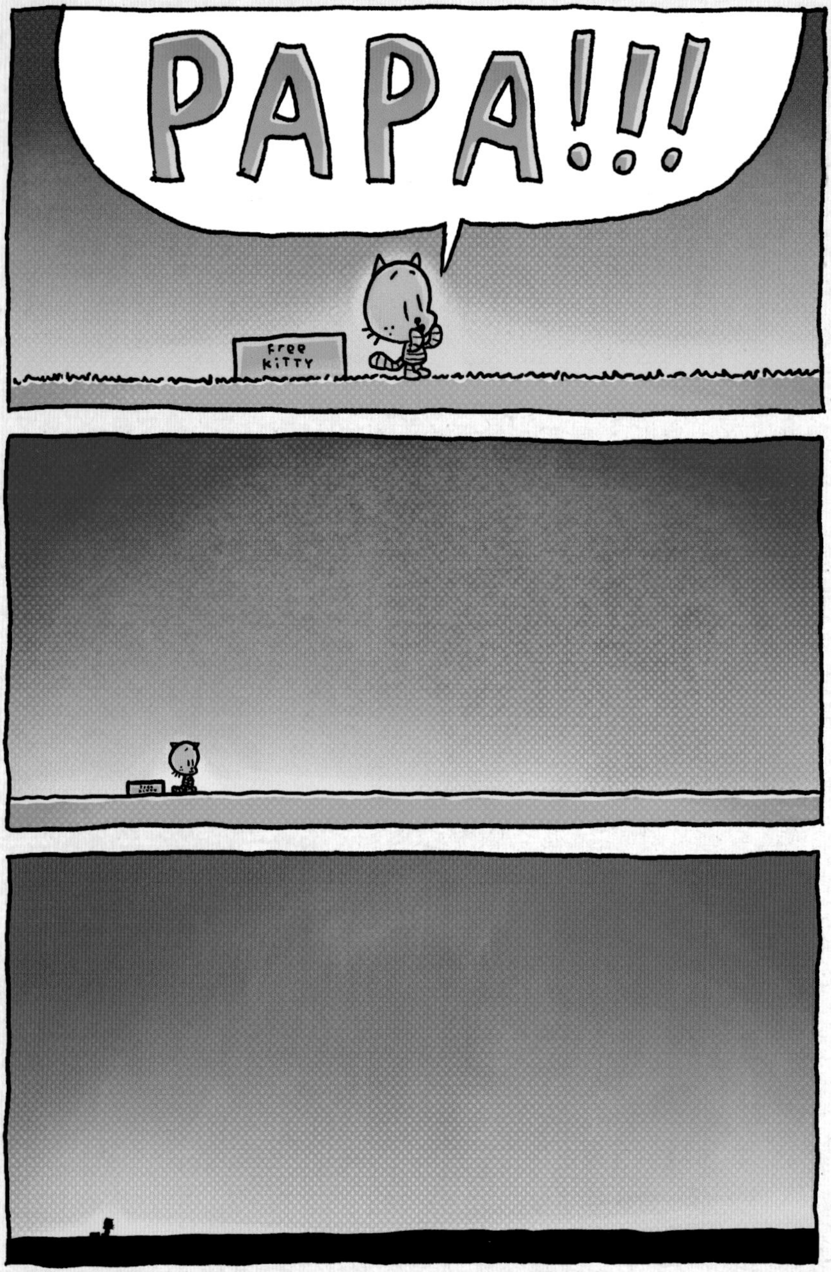
PAPA!!!
Free KiTTY

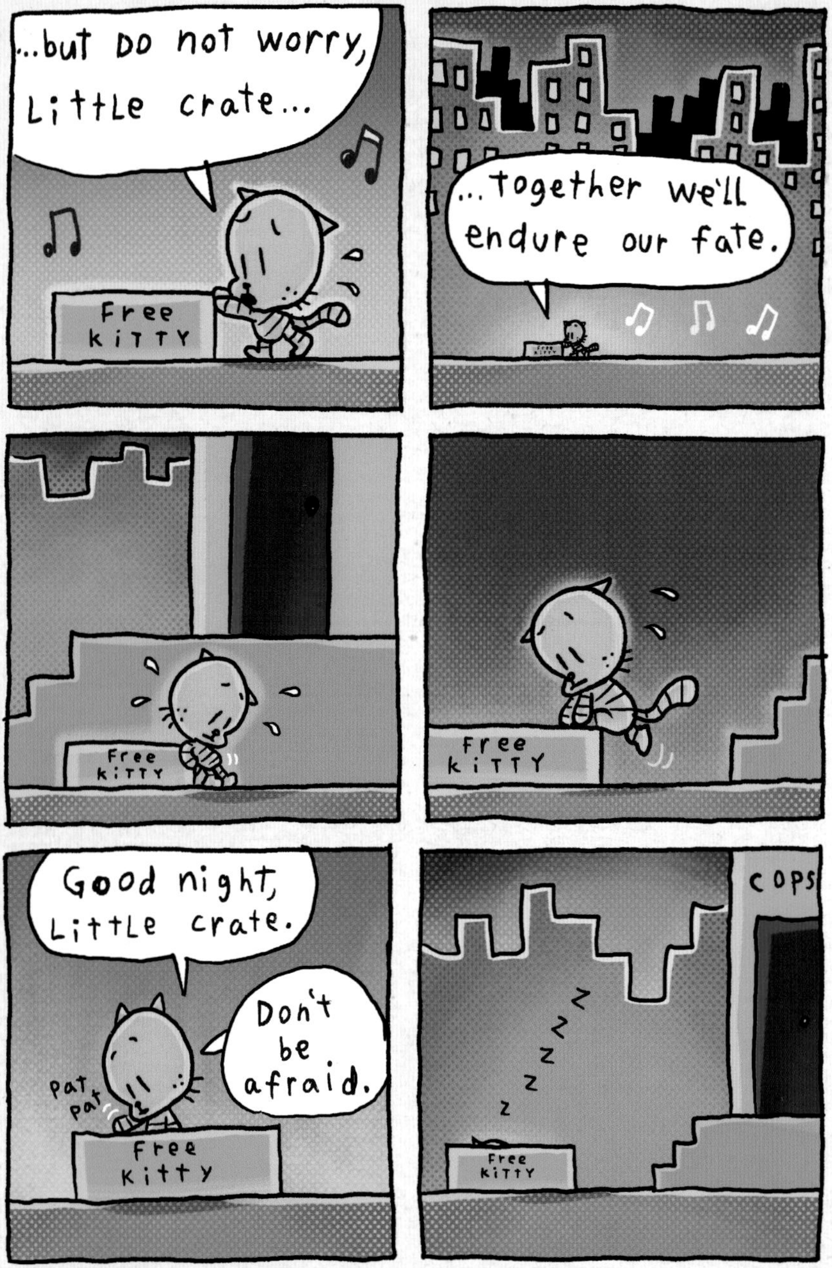
...but DO not worry, Little crate...
Free kitty
...together we'll endure our fate.
Free kitty
Free kitty
Free kitty
Good night, Little crate.
Don't be afraid.
pat pat
Free kitty
z z z z z
Free kitty
COPS

Chapter the Fifth

CRATE EXPECTATIONS

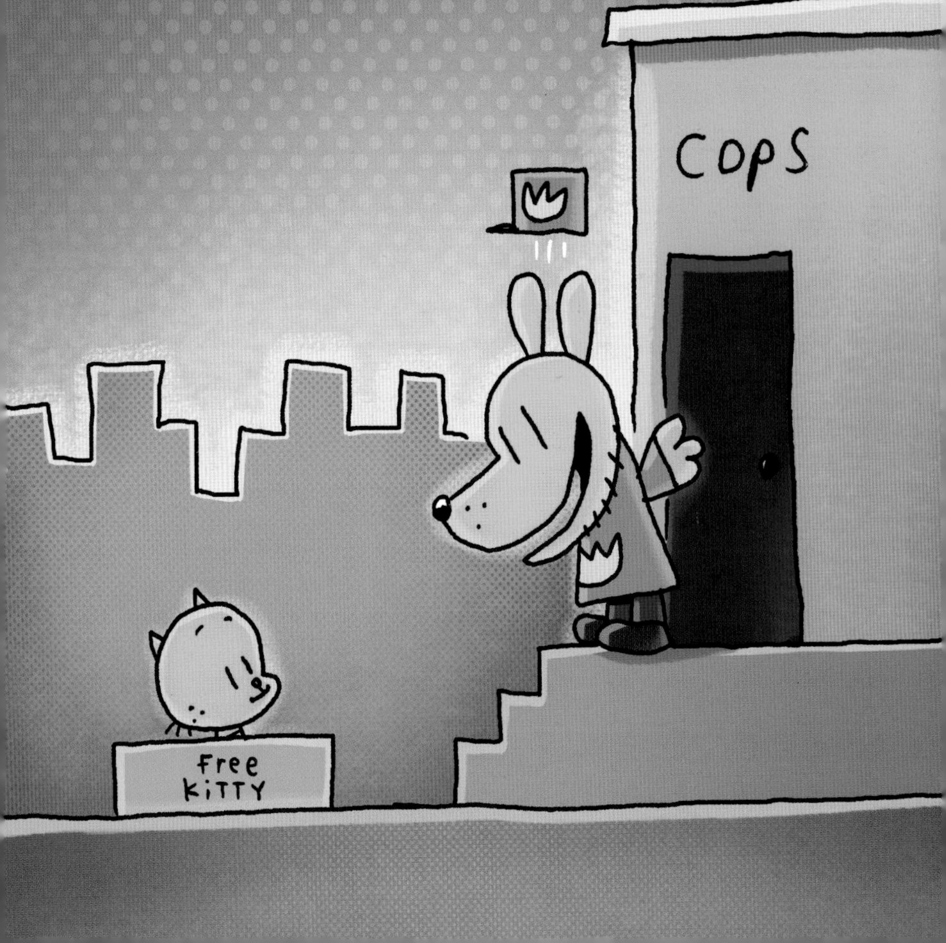
COPS
Free KITTY

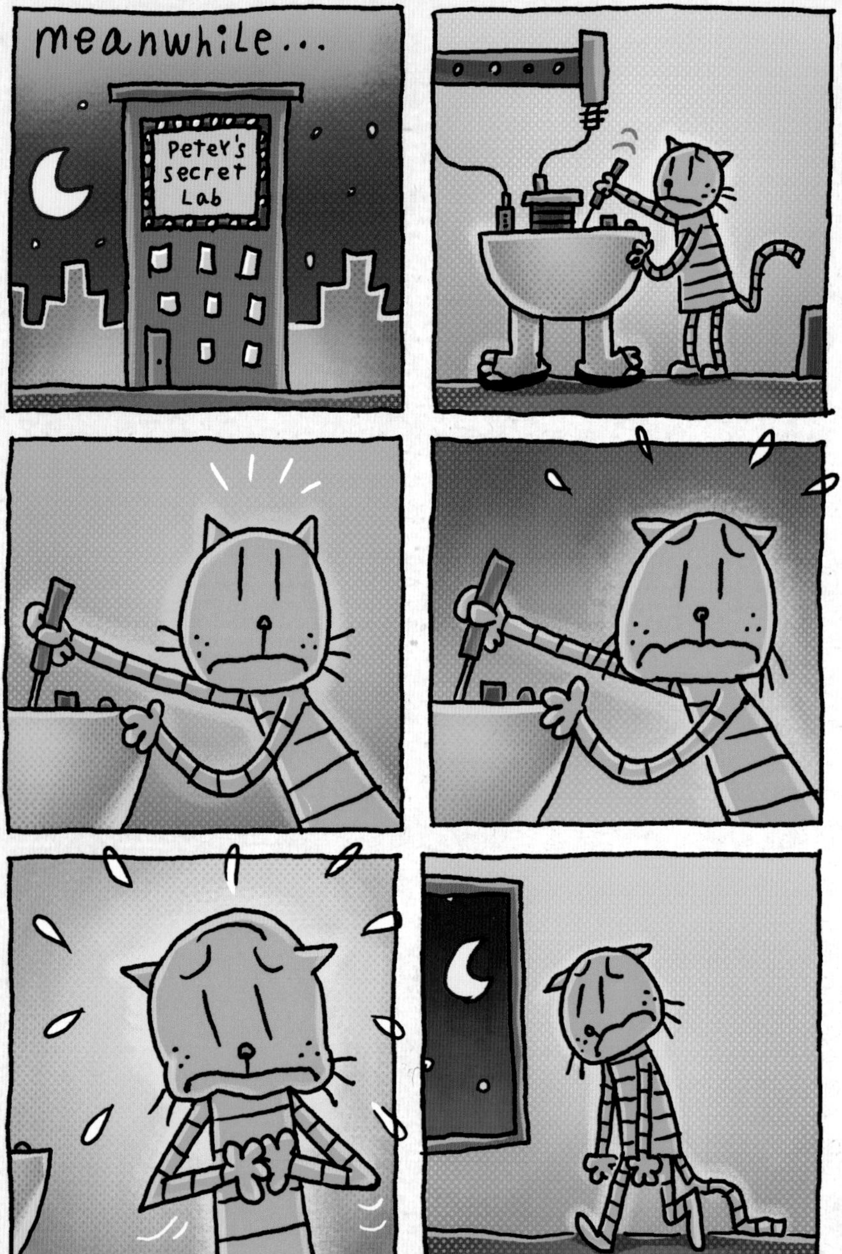
meanwhile...
Peter's secret Lab

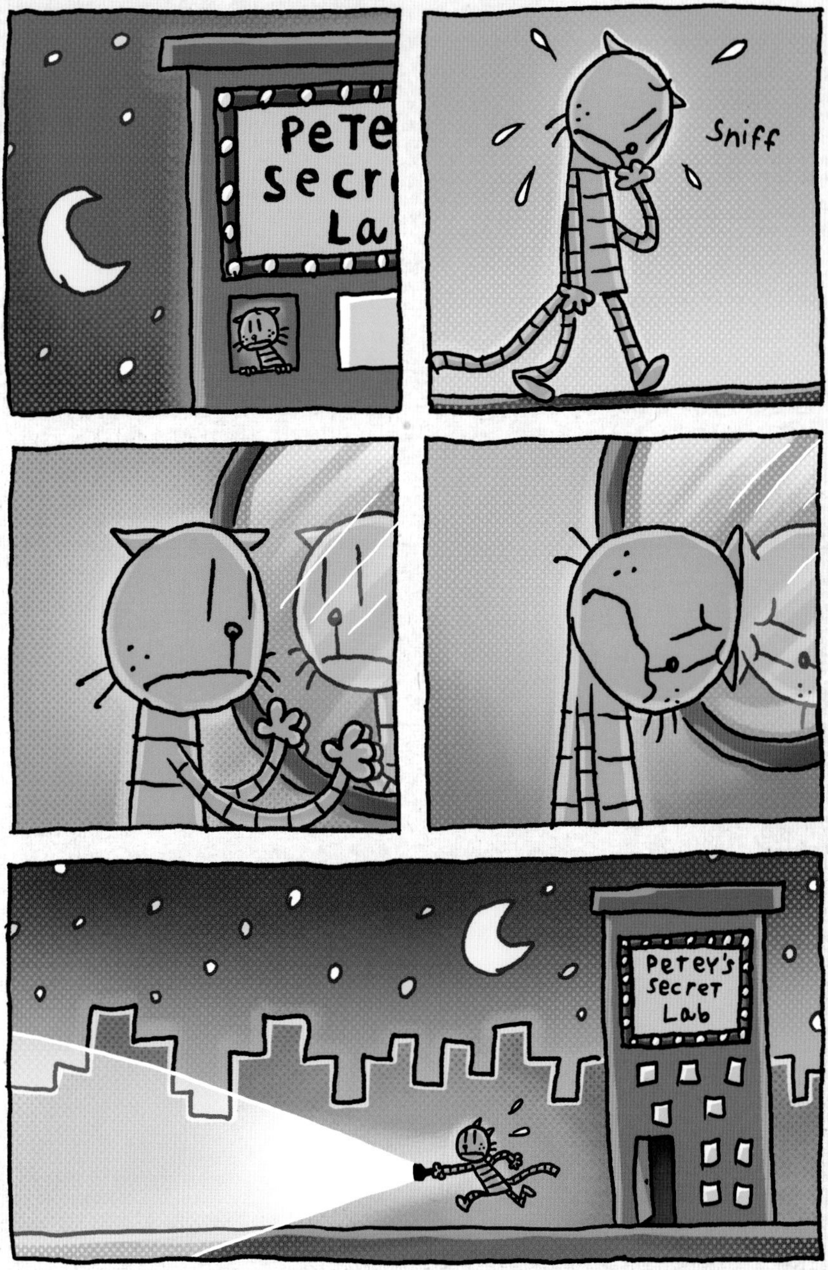

Sniff
Petey's Secret Lab

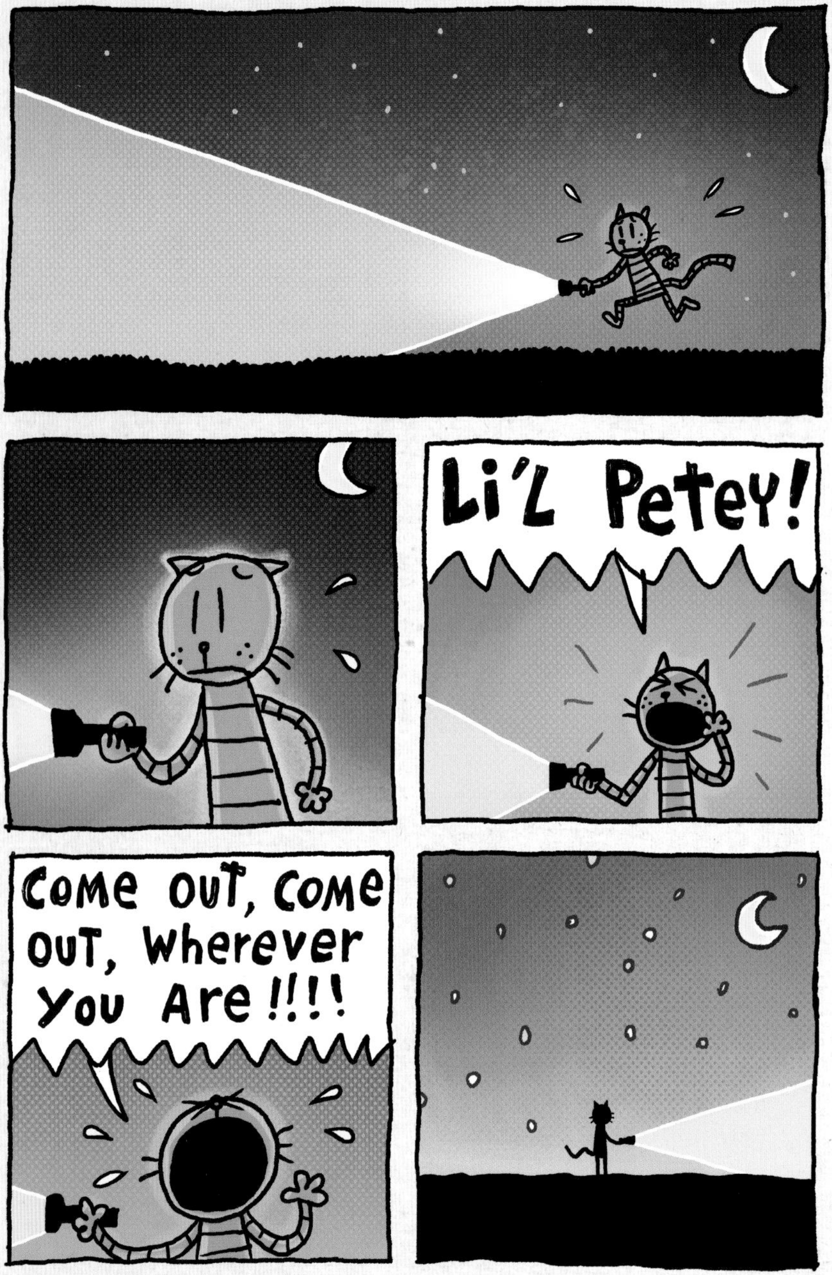
Li'L Petey!
Come out, come out, wherever you Are!!!!

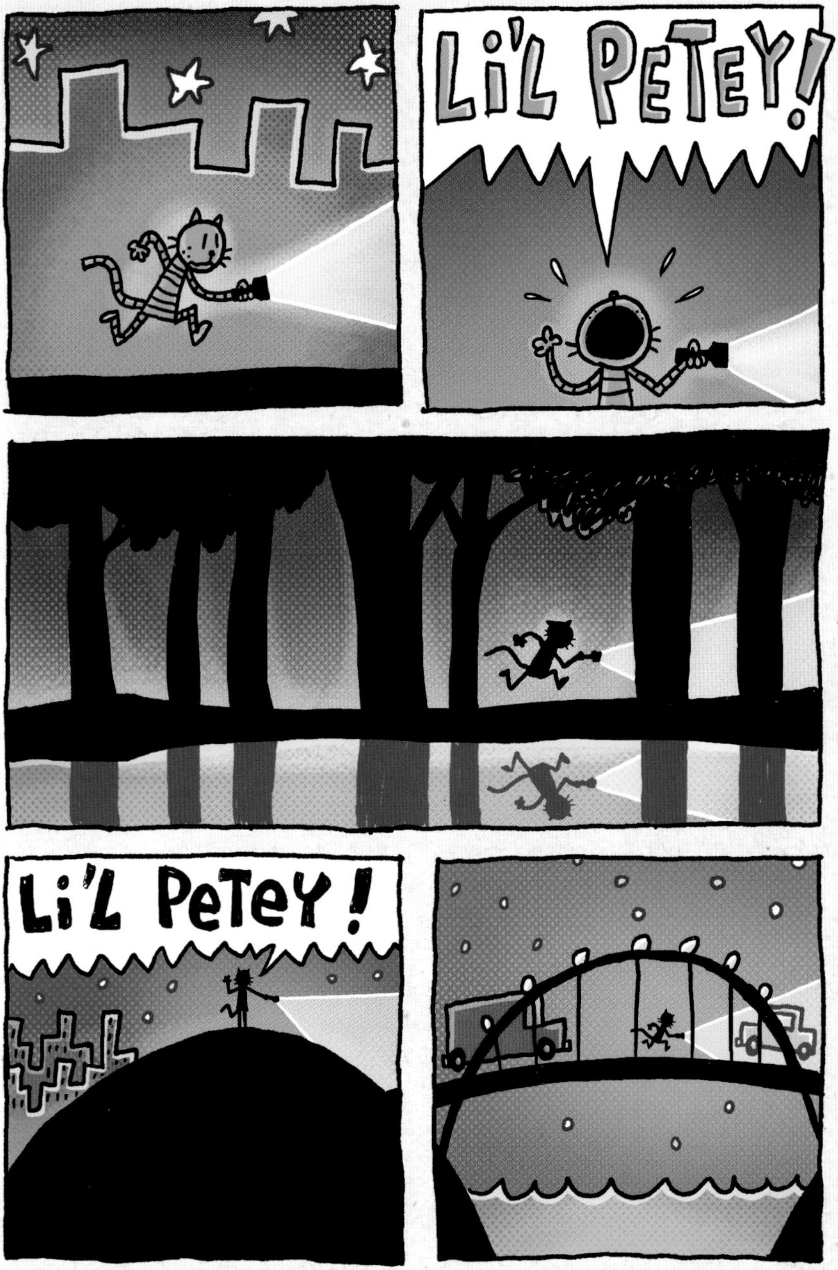
LI'L PETEY!
LI'L PETEY!

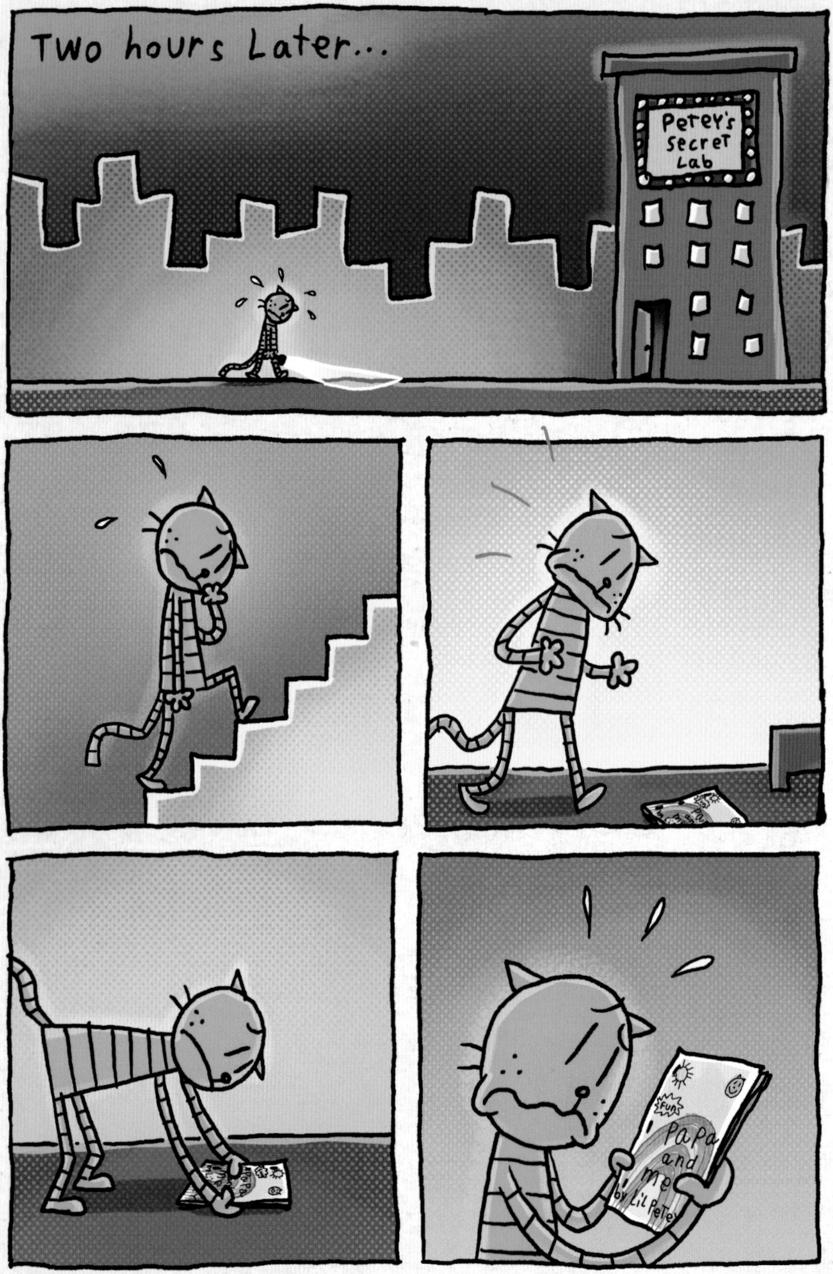
Two hours Later...
Petey's Secret Lab
Fun
Papa and me by Li'l Petey

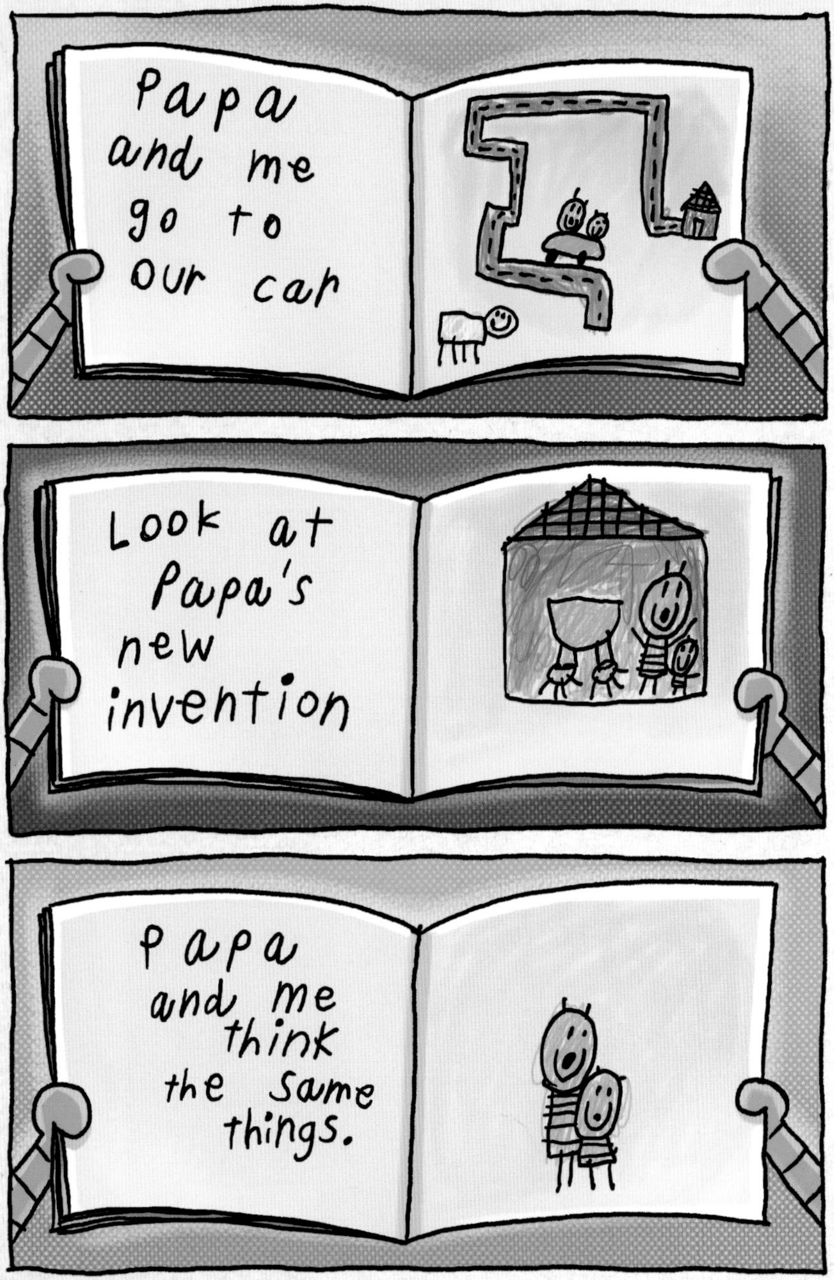
Papa and me go to our car
Look at Papa's new invention
Papa and me think the same things.

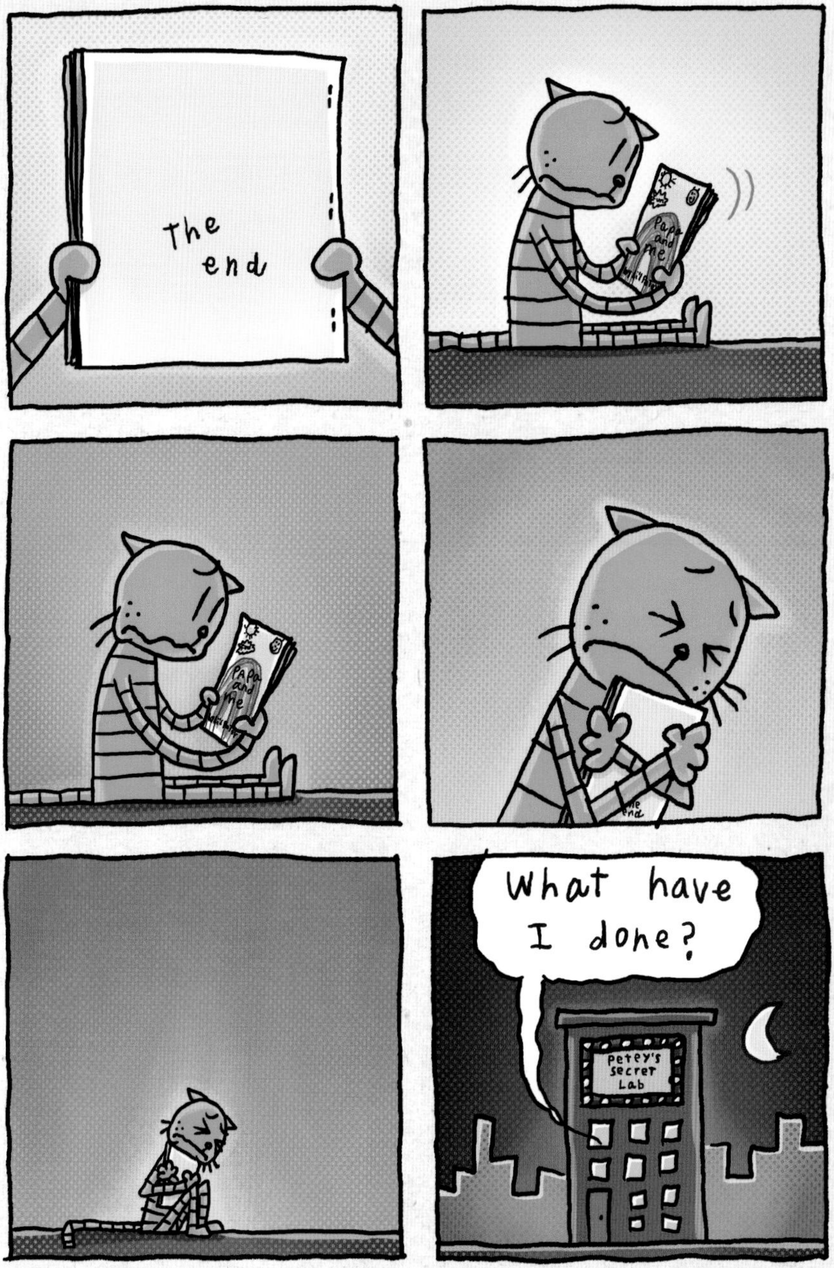
The end
Papa and me
What have I done?
Petey's Secret Lab

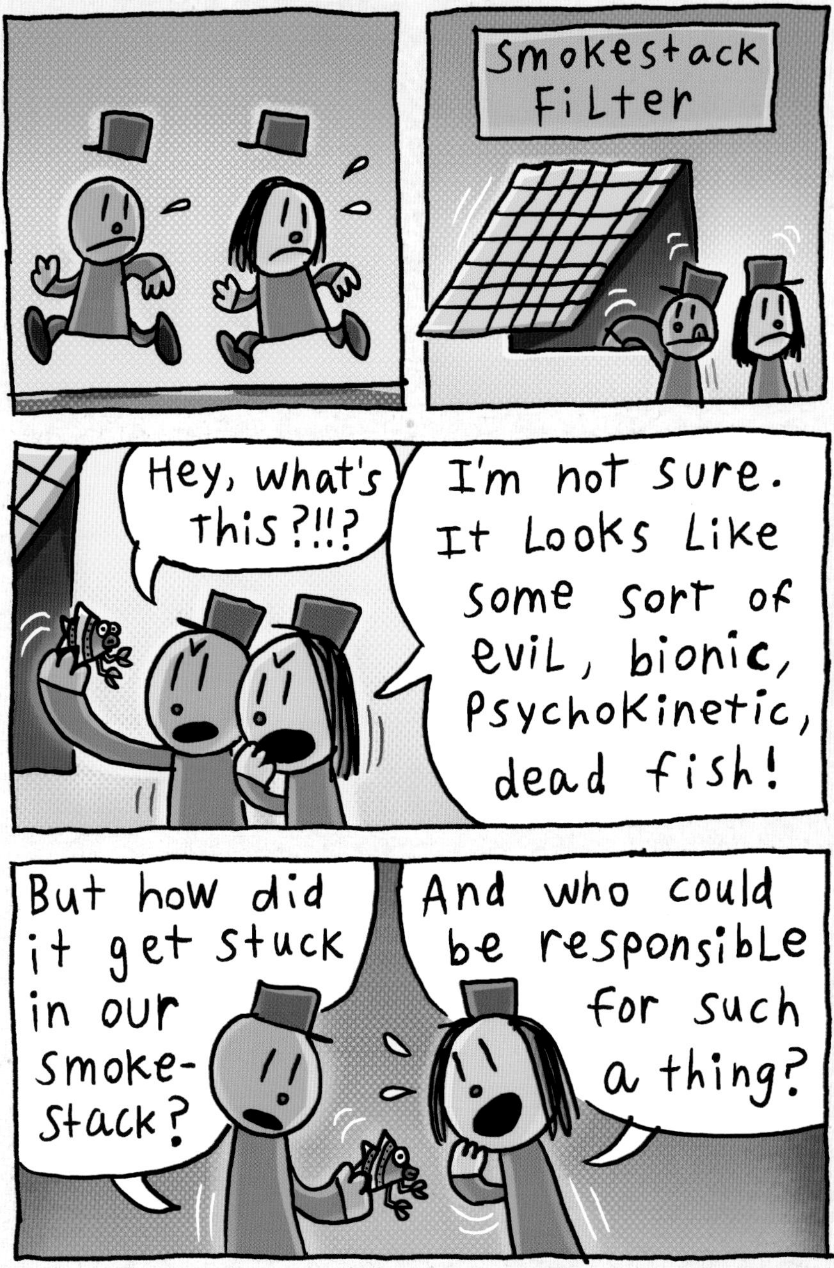
Smokestack Filter
Hey, what's this?!!?
I'm not sure. It looks like some sort of evil, bionic, psychokinetic, dead fish!
But how did it get stuck in our smoke-stack?
And who could be responsible for such a thing?

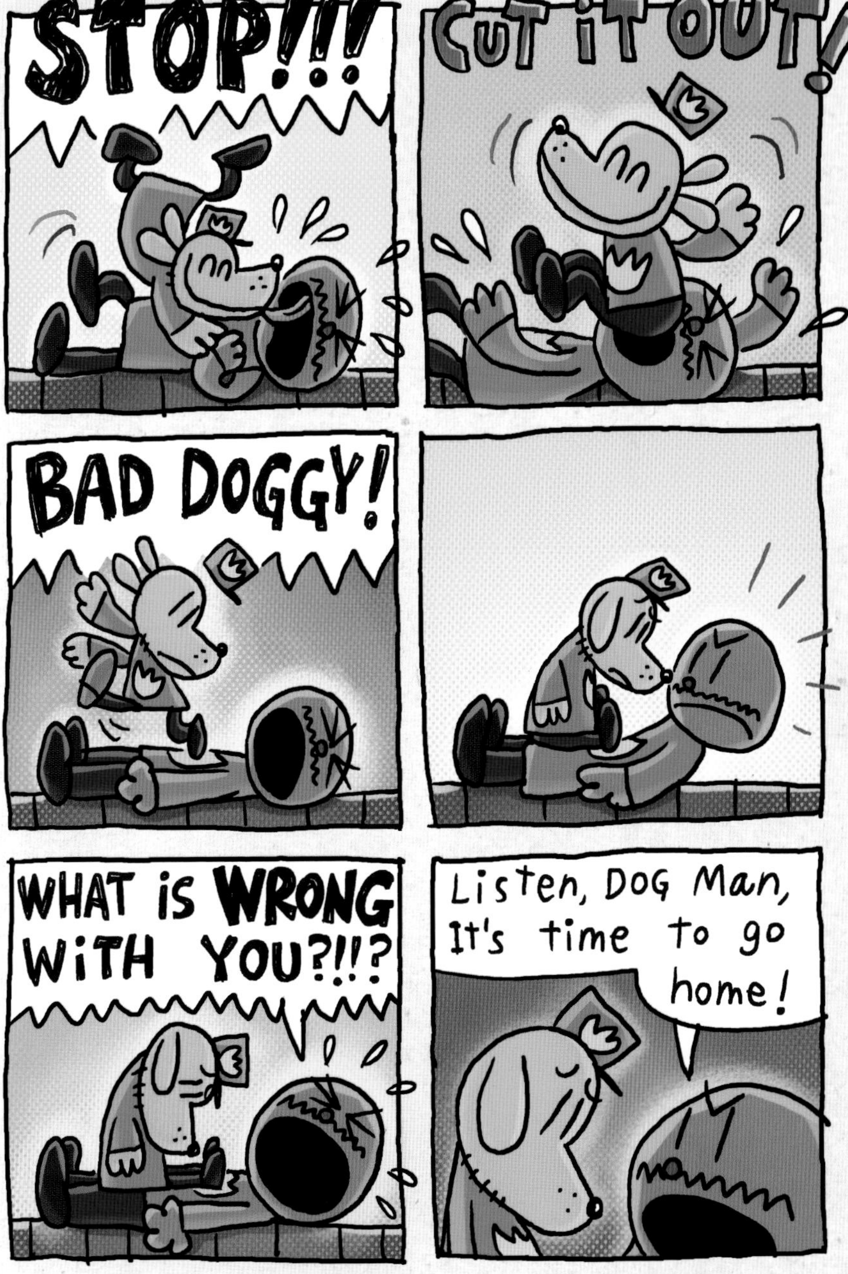
STOP!!!
CUT iT OUT!
BAD DOGGY!
WHAT is WRONG WiTH YOU?!!?
Listen, DOG Man, It's time to go home!

Hey, there's a cat out there, and---

NO! NO!

GET OFFA ME!

STOP!!

ENOUGH!!!

BAD DOGGY!!

I WAS ONLY GONE FOR TEN SECONDS!

DoG Man, there's a cat outside.

You need to get rid of him!

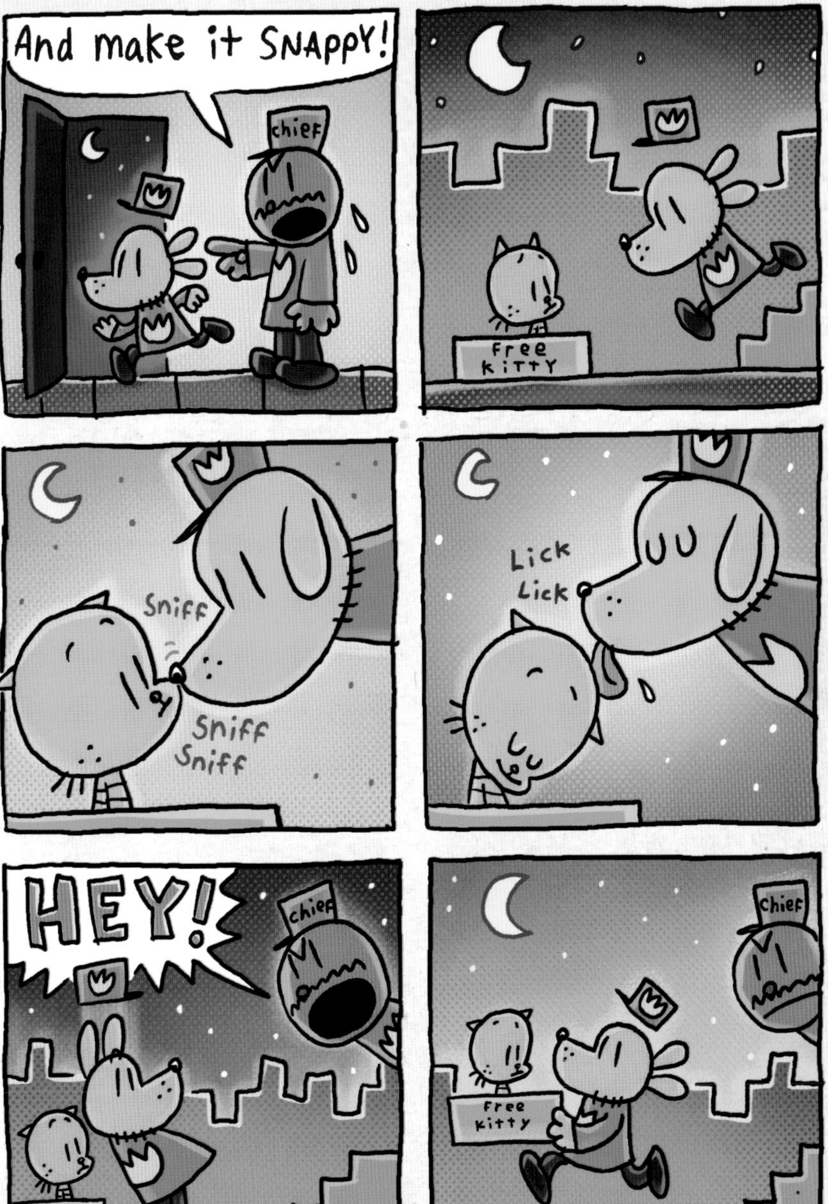

And make it SNAPPY!
chief
Free kitty
Sniff
Sniff
Sniff
Lick
Lick
HEY!
chief
Free kitty
Chief
Free kitty

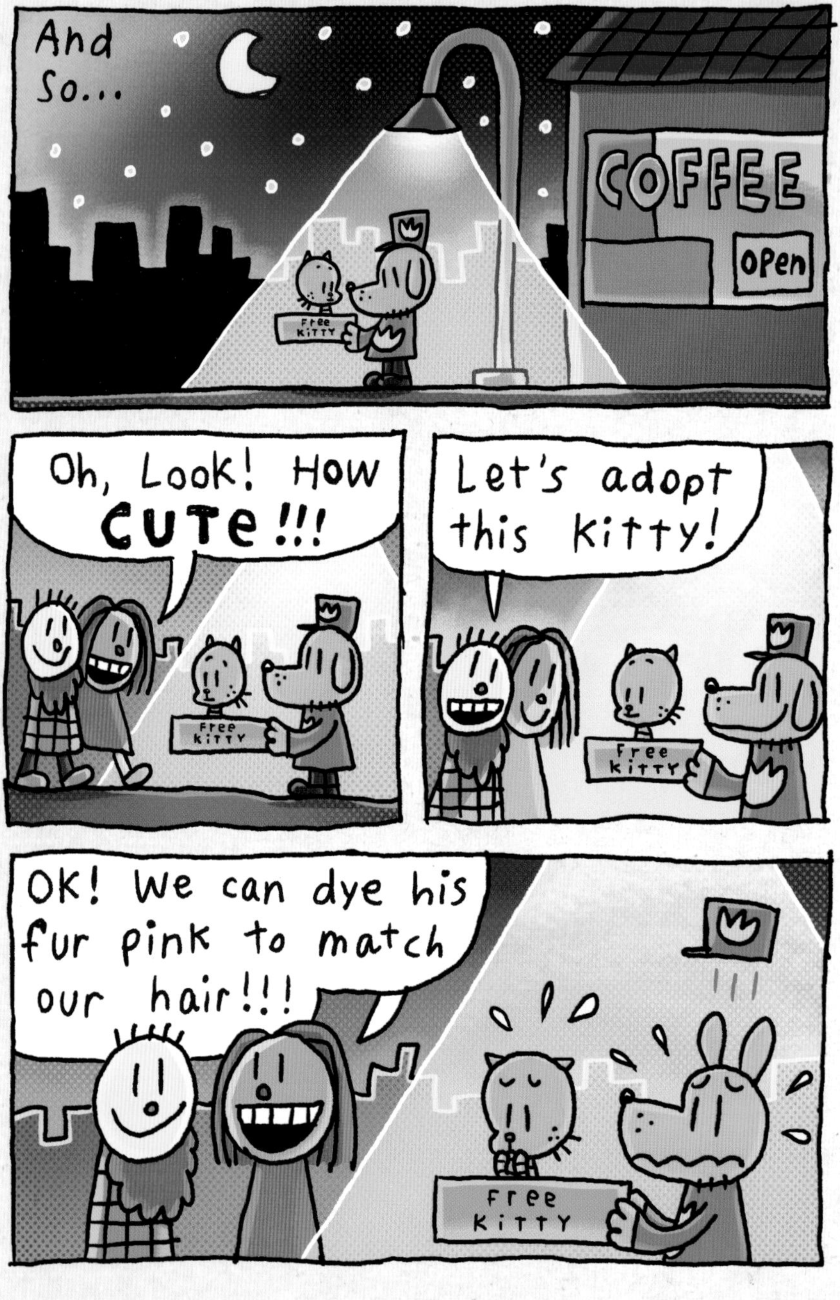
And So...
COFFEE
Open
Free KITTY
Oh, Look! How CUTE!!!
Free KITTY
Let's adopt this kitty!
Free KITTY
OK! We can dye his fur pink to match our hair!!!
Free KITTY

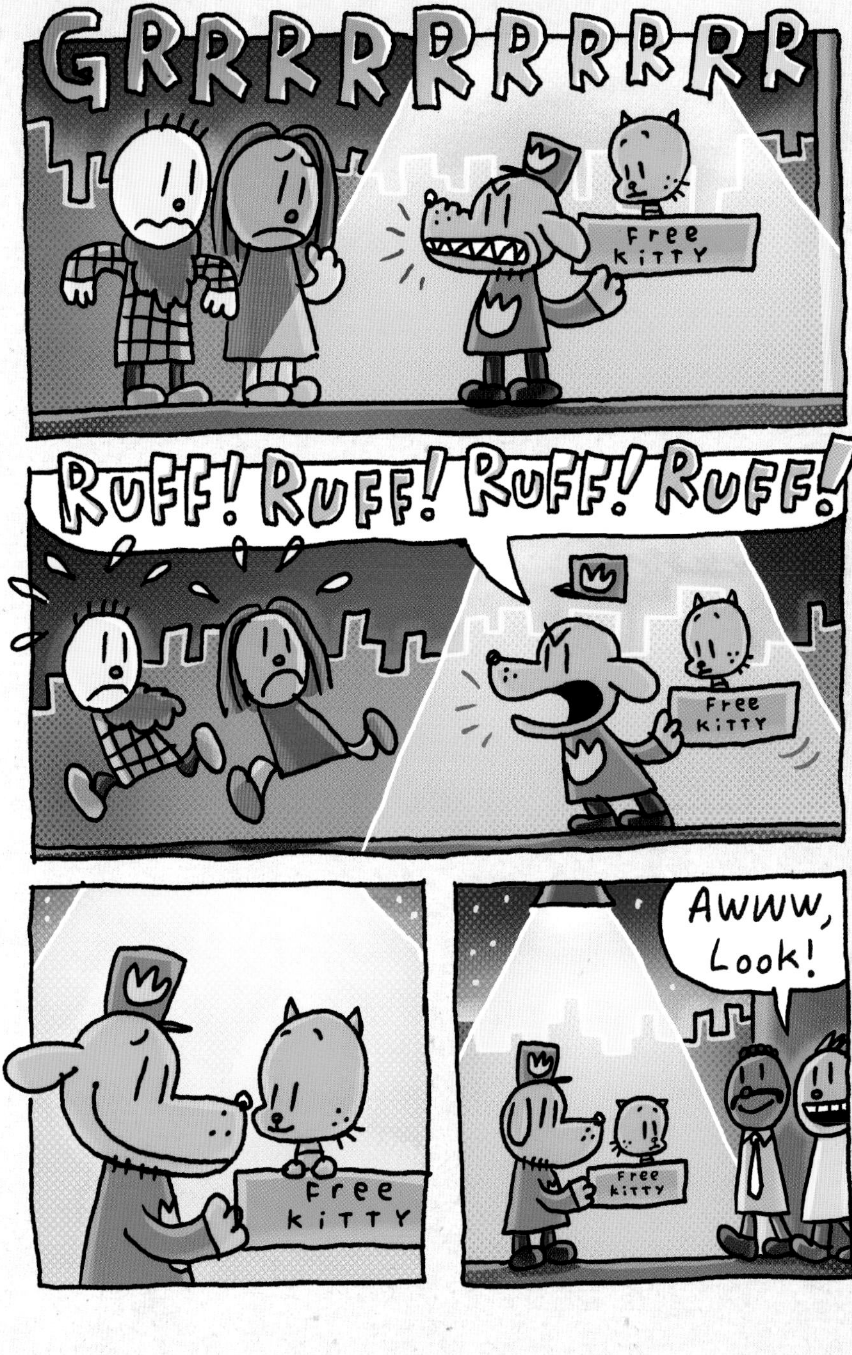
GRRRRRRRRRRR
Free kitty
RUFF! RUFF! RUFF! RUFF!
Free kitty
Free kitty
Free kitty
AWWW, Look!

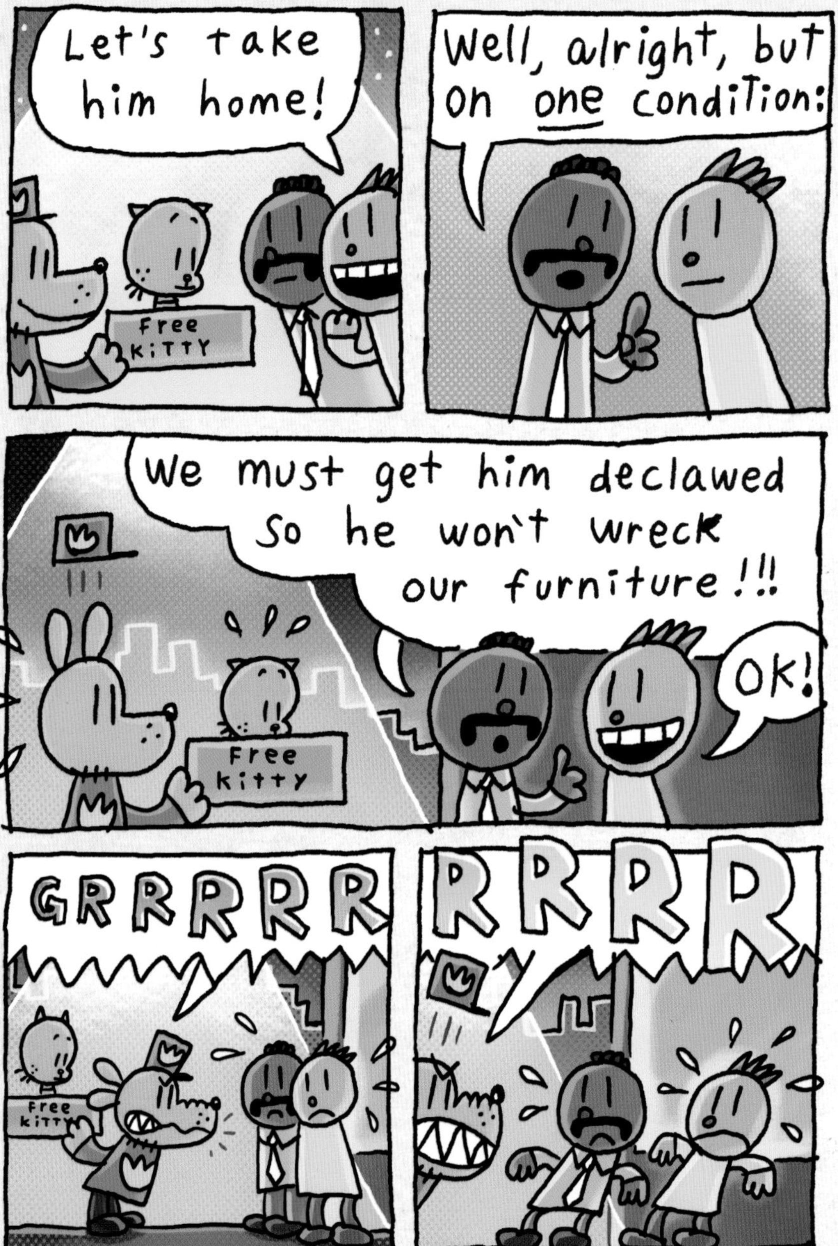
Let's take him home!
Free KITTY
Well, alright, but on one condition:
We must get him declawed So he won't wreck our furniture!!!
OK!
Free kitty
GRRRRR
RRRR
Free kitty

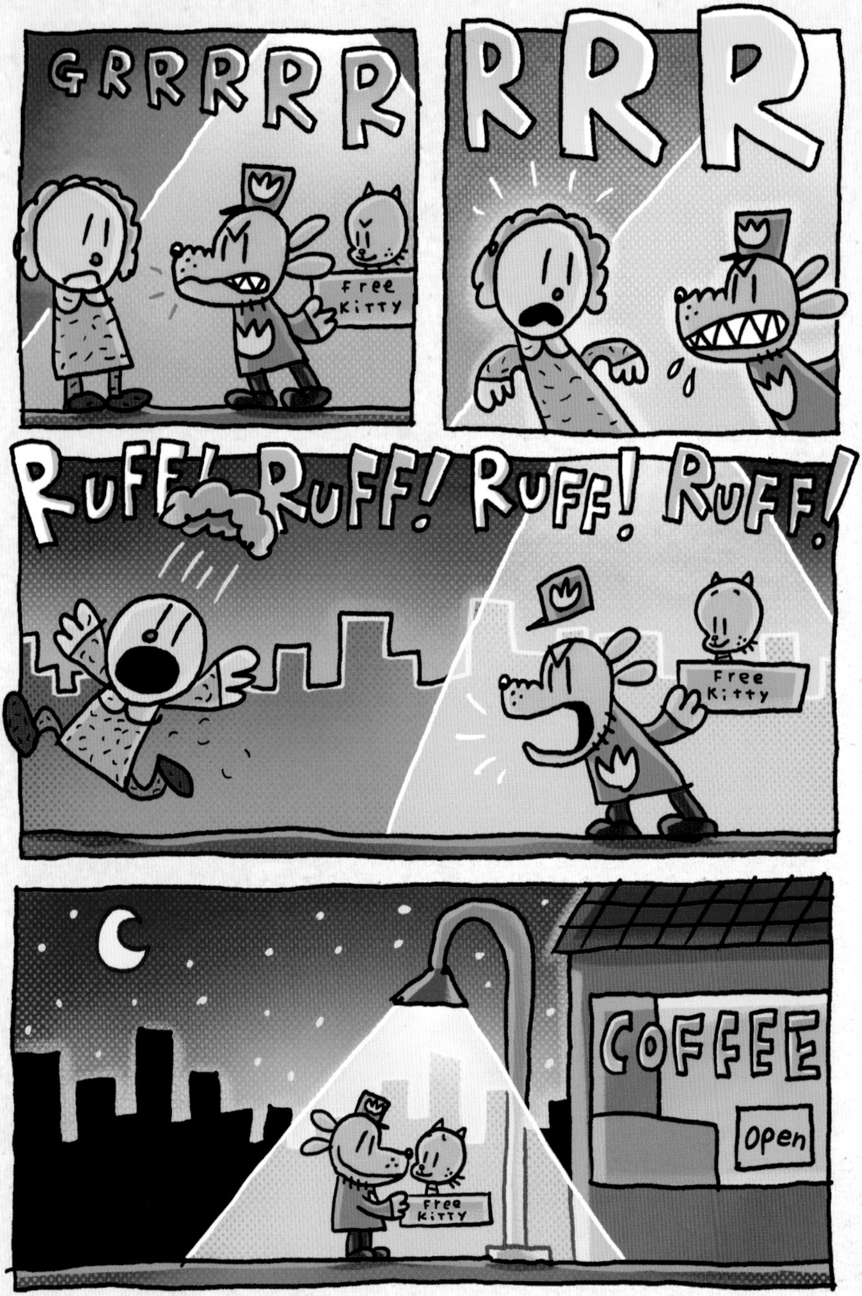

GRRRRRR
Free Kitty
RRR
RUFF! RUFF! RUFF! RUFF!
Free Kitty
COFFEE
Open
Free Kitty

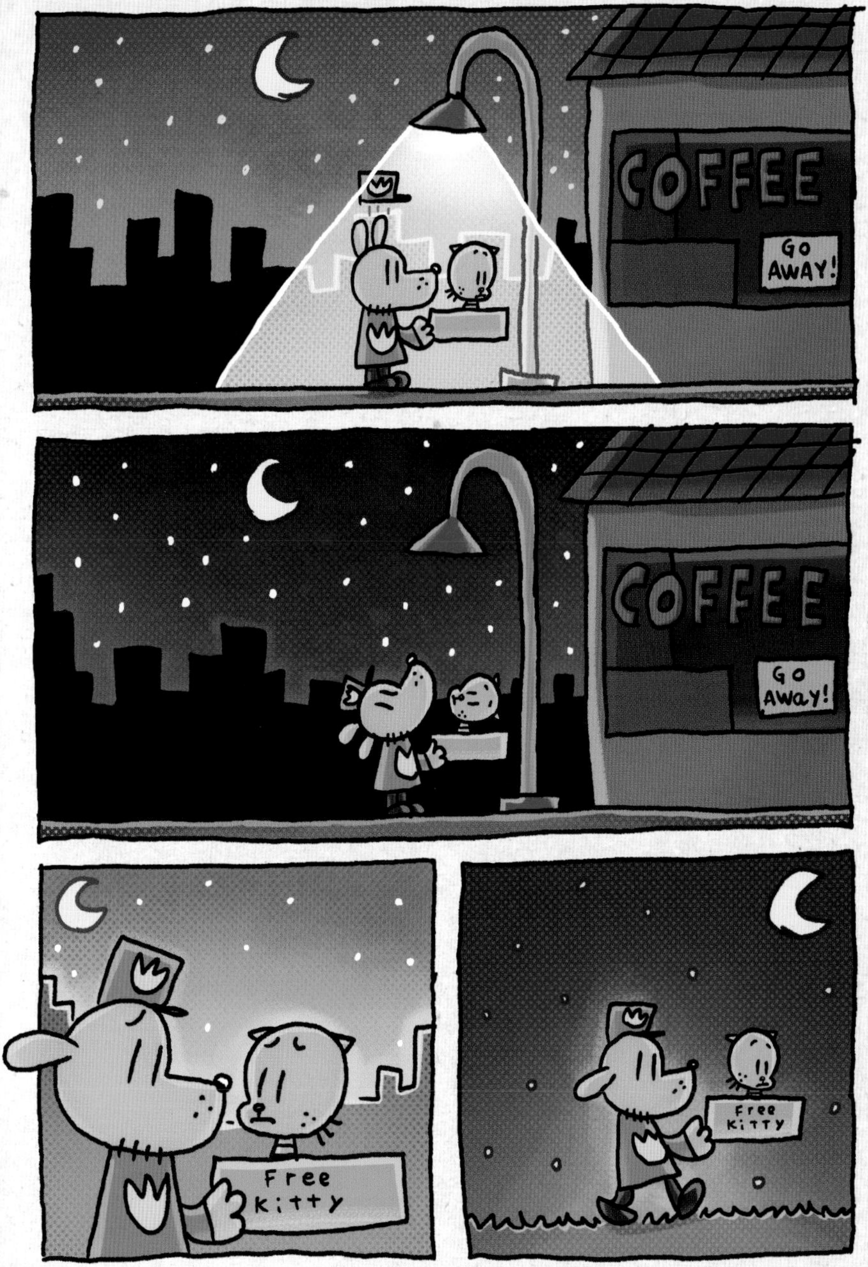
COFFEE
GO AWAY!
COFFEE
GO AWAY!
Free Kitty
Free Kitty

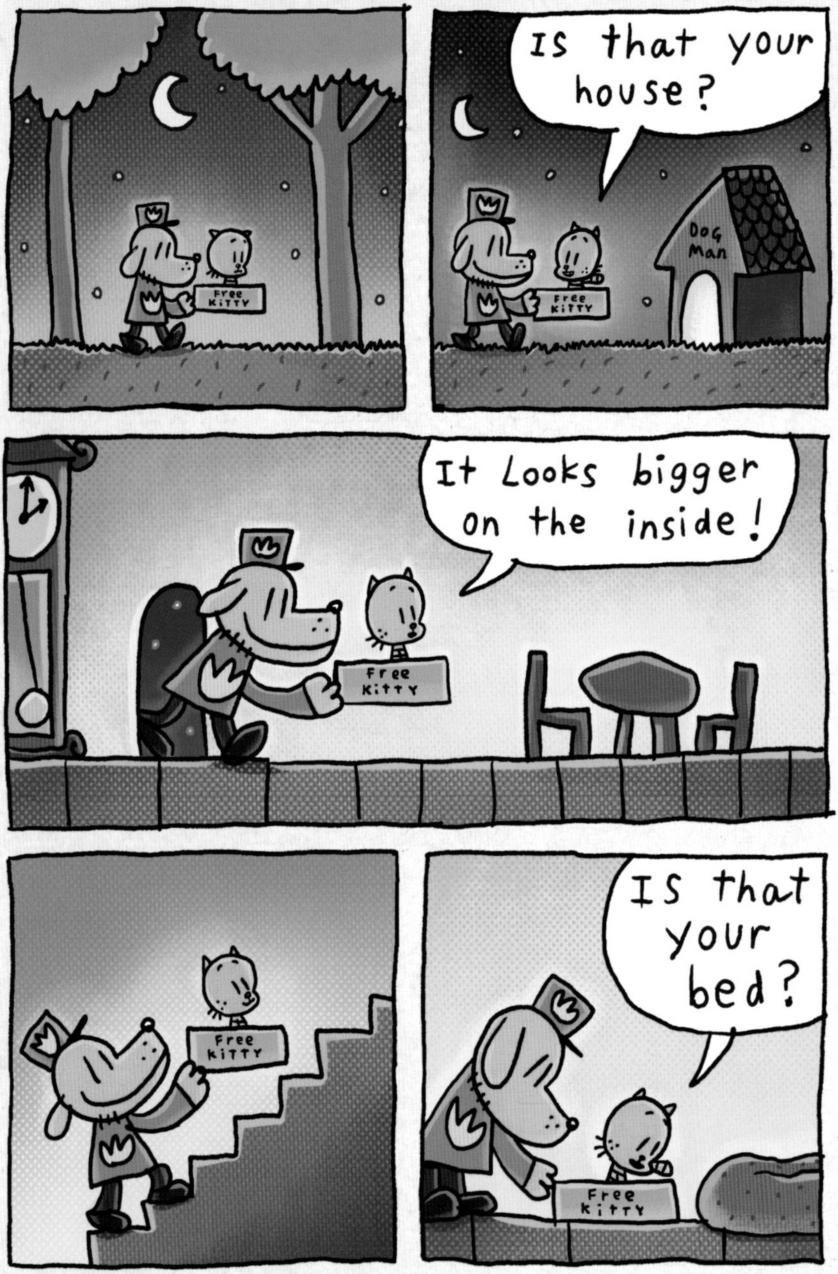
Free KITTY
Is that your house?
DOG Man
Free KITTY
It Looks bigger on the inside!
Free KITTY
Free KITTY
Is that your bed?
Free KITTY

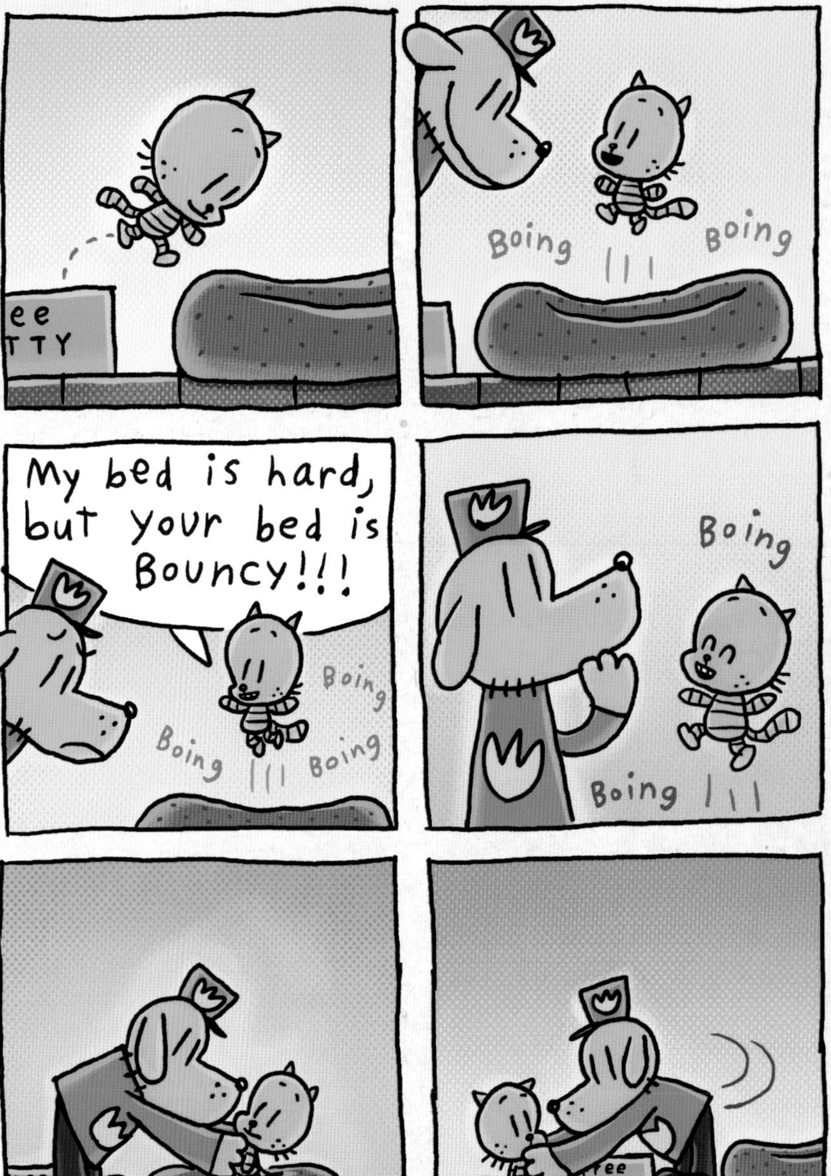
ee
TTY
Boing
Boing
My bed is hard, but your bed is Bouncy!!!
Boing
Boing
Boing
Boing
Boing
ree
ITTY
Free
KiTTY

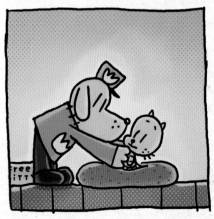

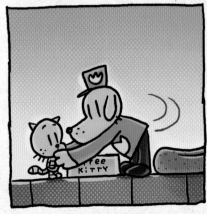

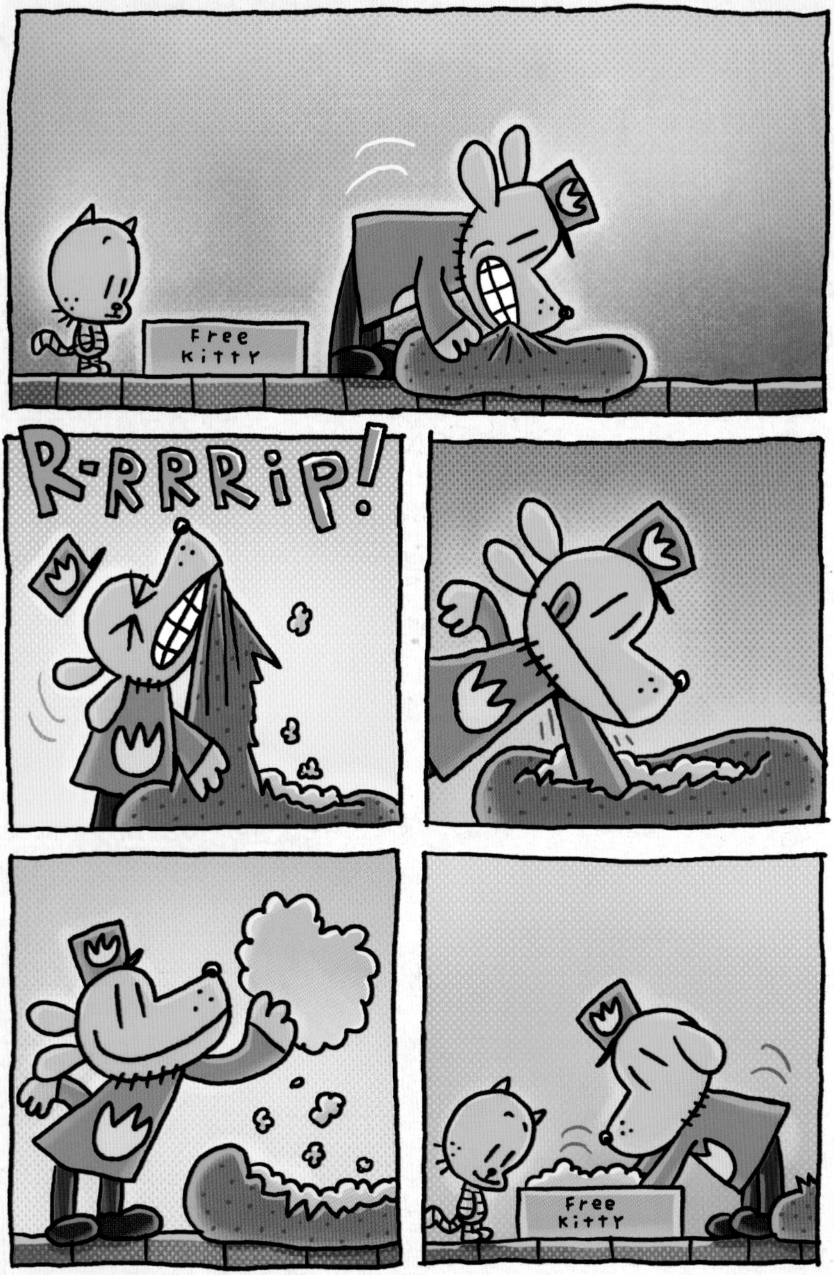
Free
kitty
R-RRRip!
Free
kitty

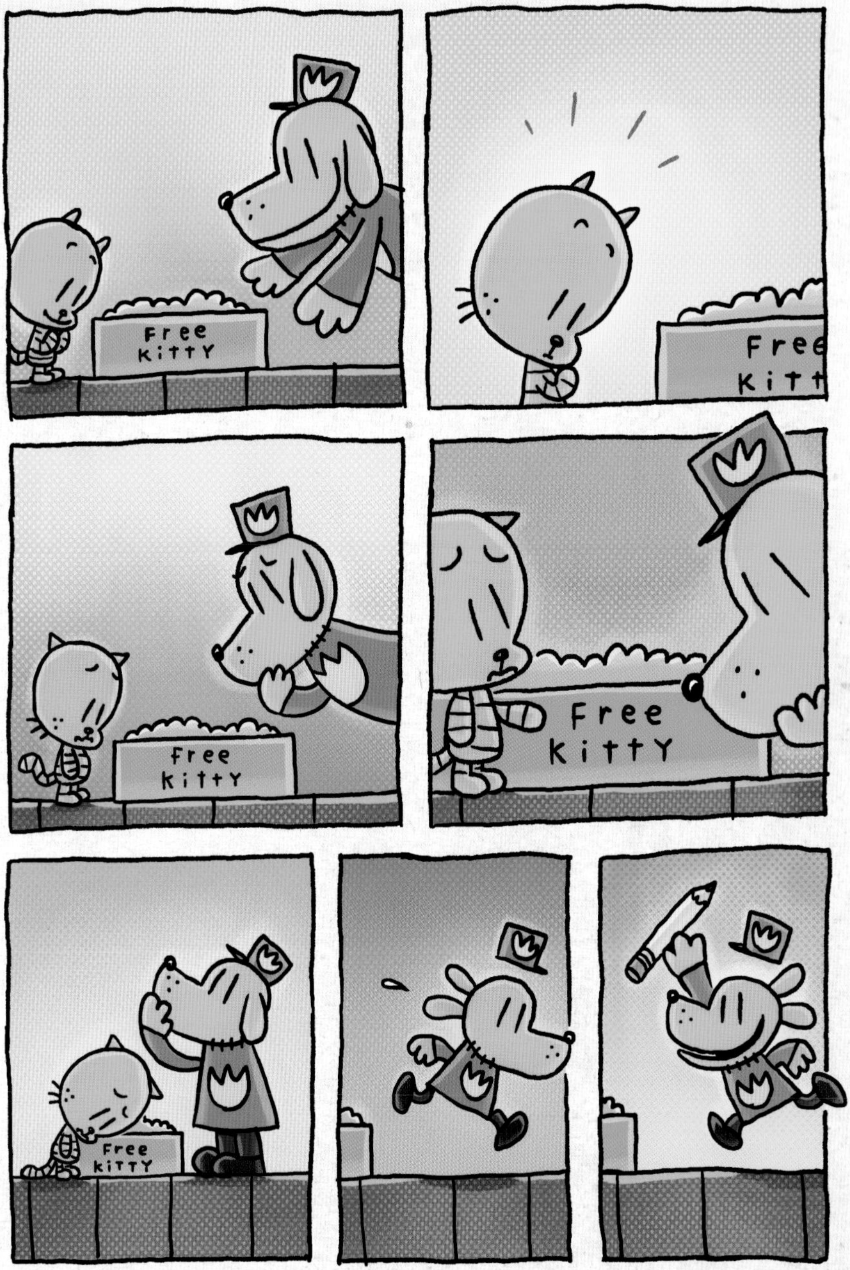
Free
Kitty
Free
Kitt
Free
Kitty
Free
Kitty
Free
Kitty

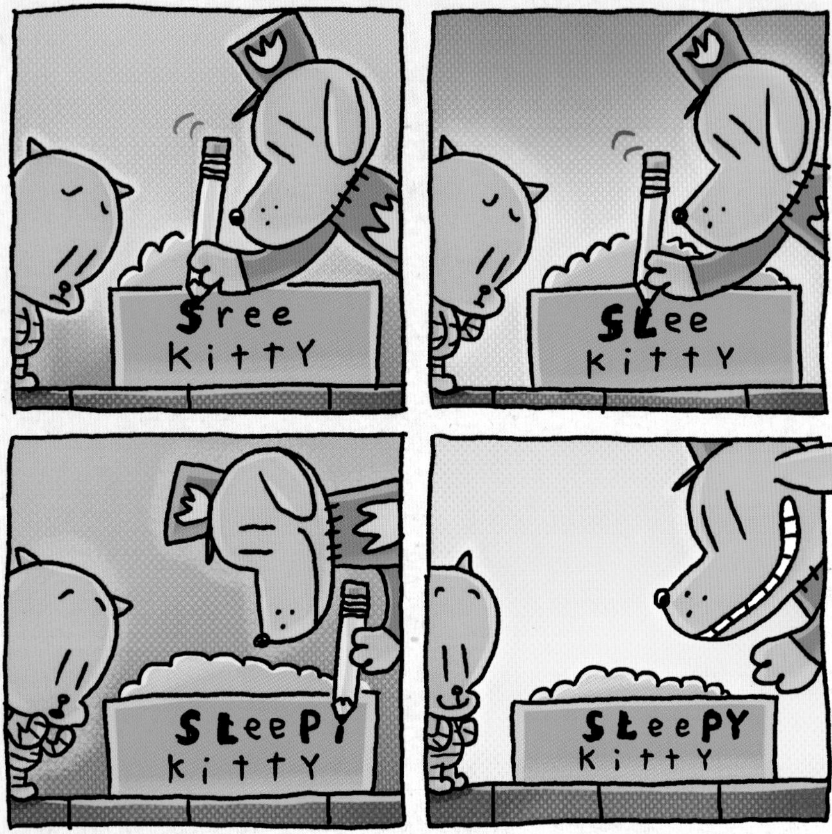
Sree
KittY
SLee
KittY
SLeePi
KittY
SLeePY
KittY

TRiPLe FLiP-O-RAMA

Left hand here.

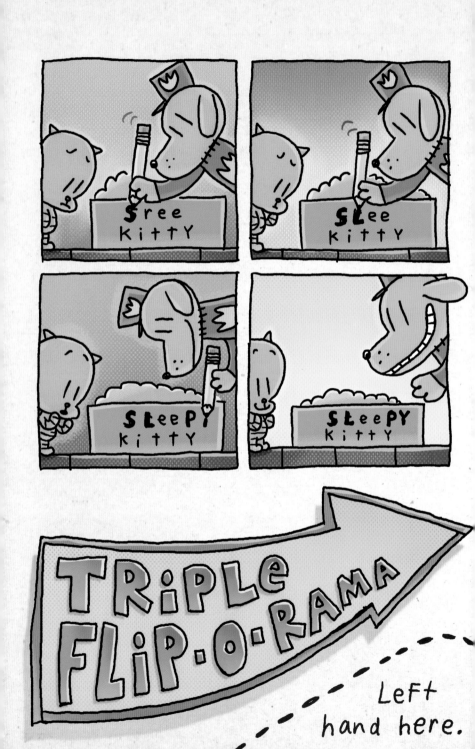

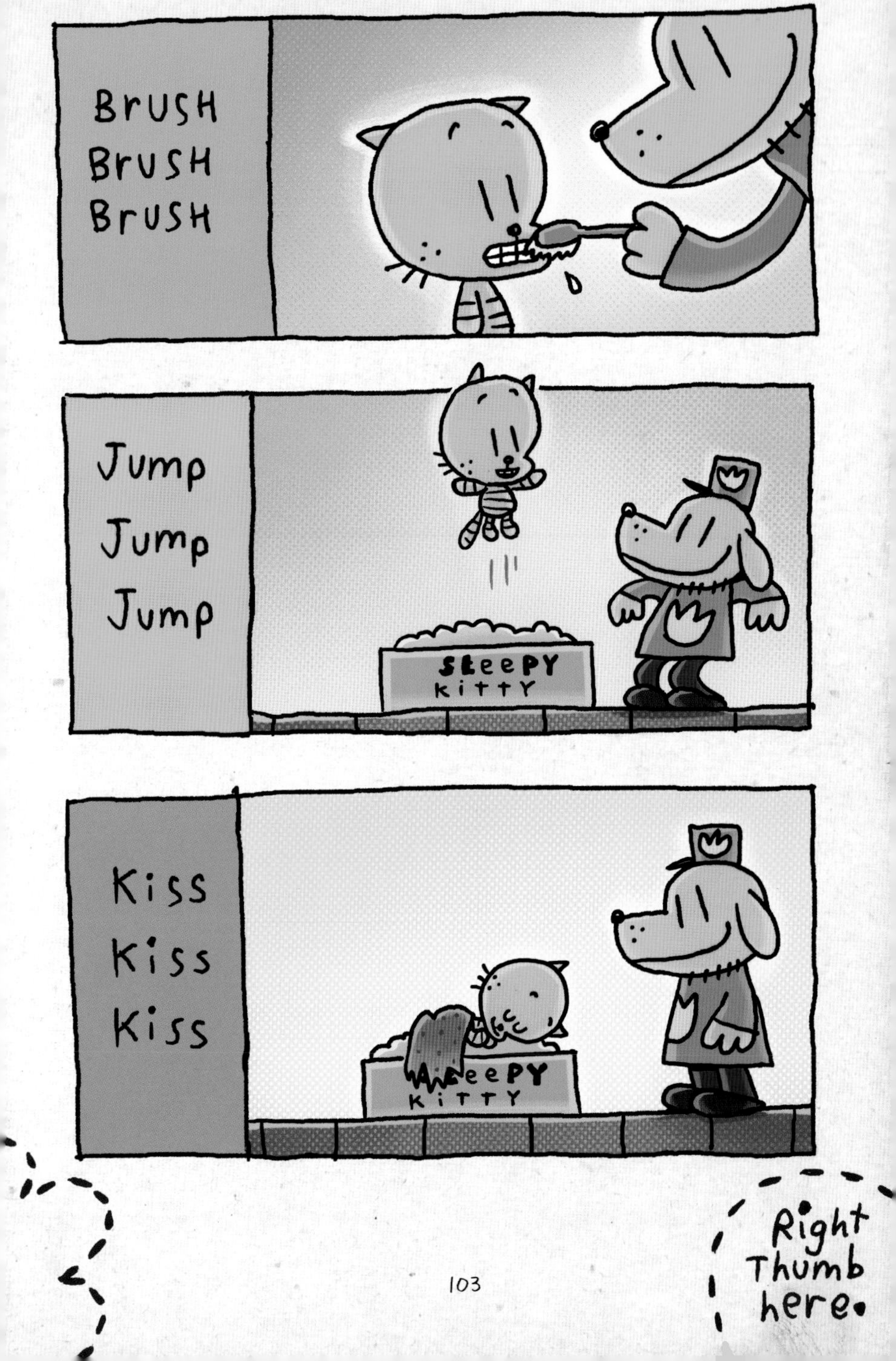
BrUSH
BrUSH
BrUSH
Jump
Jump
Jump
SLeePY
KiTTY
Kiss
Kiss
Kiss
eePY
KiTTY
Right
Thumb
here.

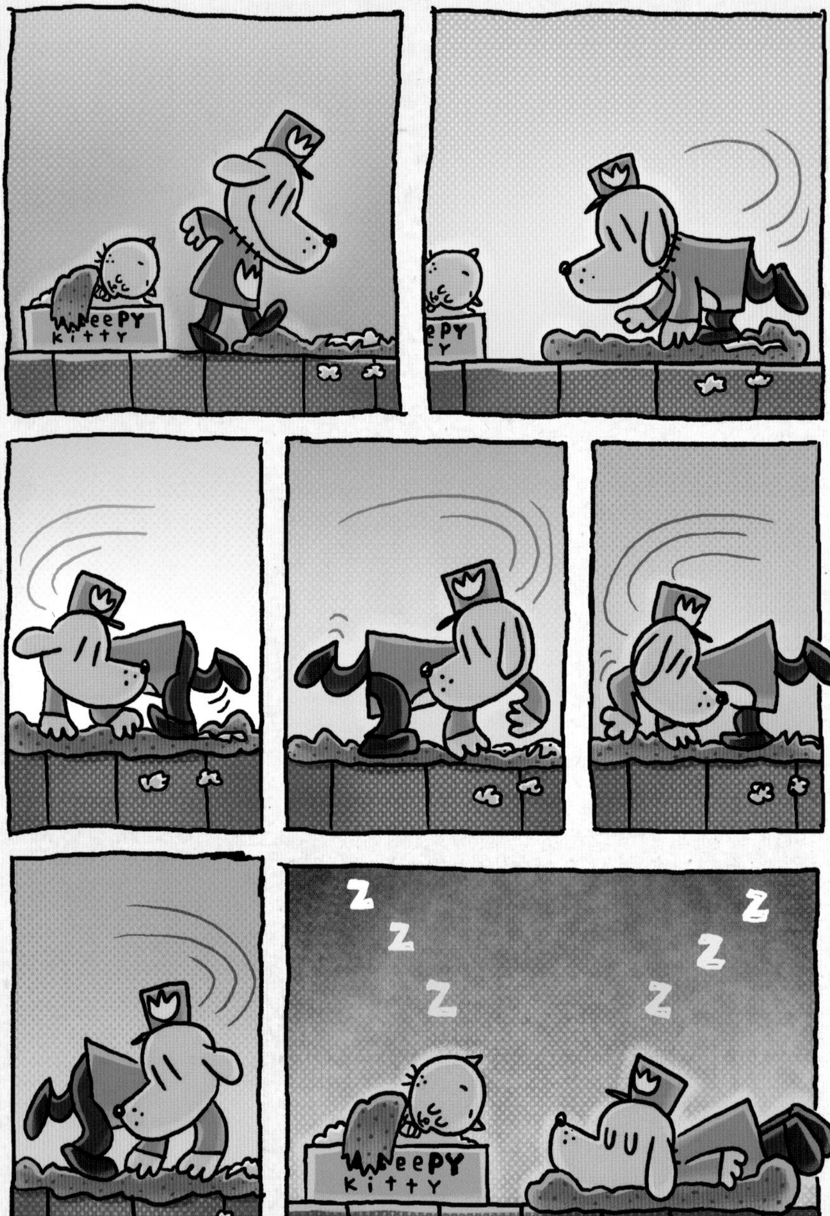
Z
Z
Z
Z
Z
Z

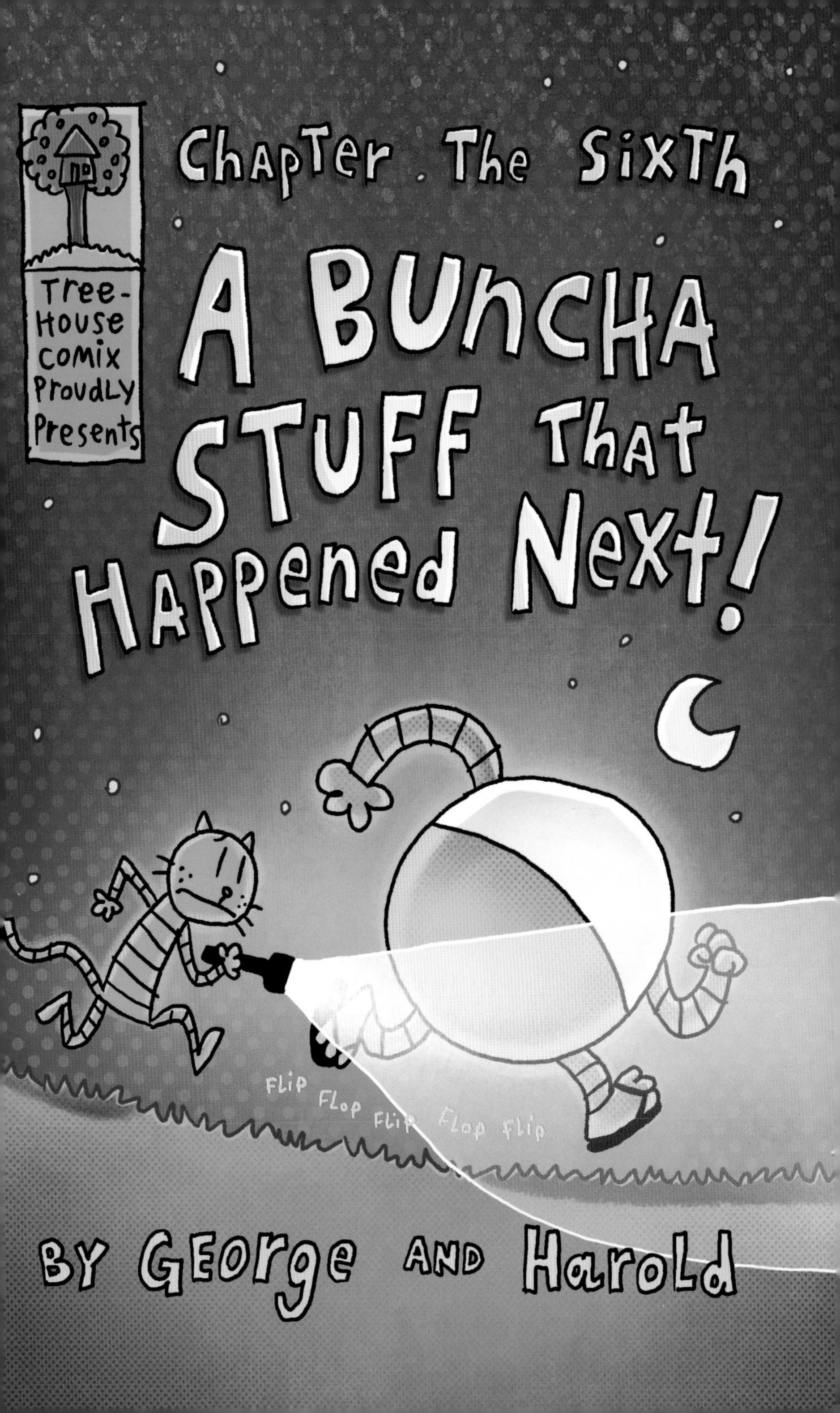
Tree-House Comix Proudly Presents
Chapter The Sixth
A BUNCHA STUFF That Happened Next!
FLIP FLOP FLIP FLOP FLIP
BY GEORGE AND HAROLD

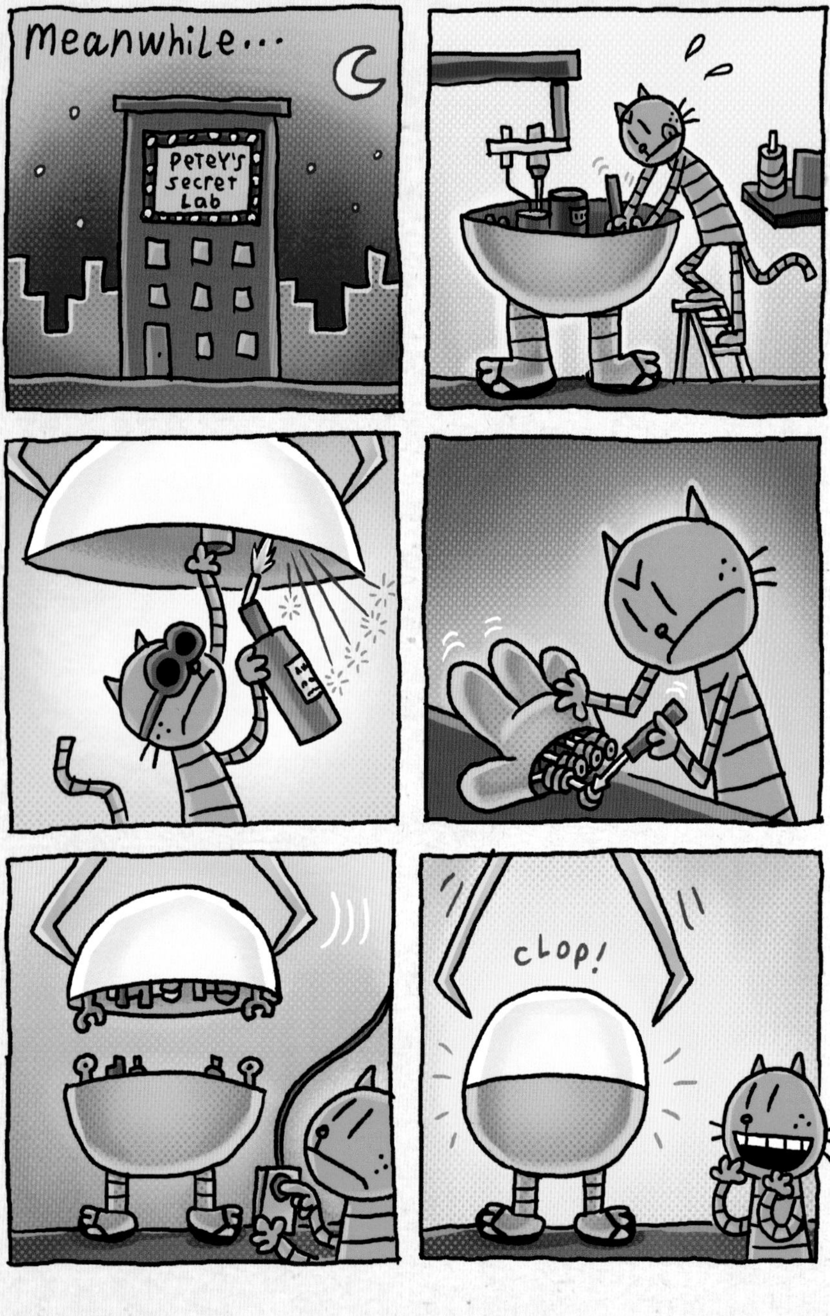
Meanwhile...
Petey's Secret Lab
CLOP!

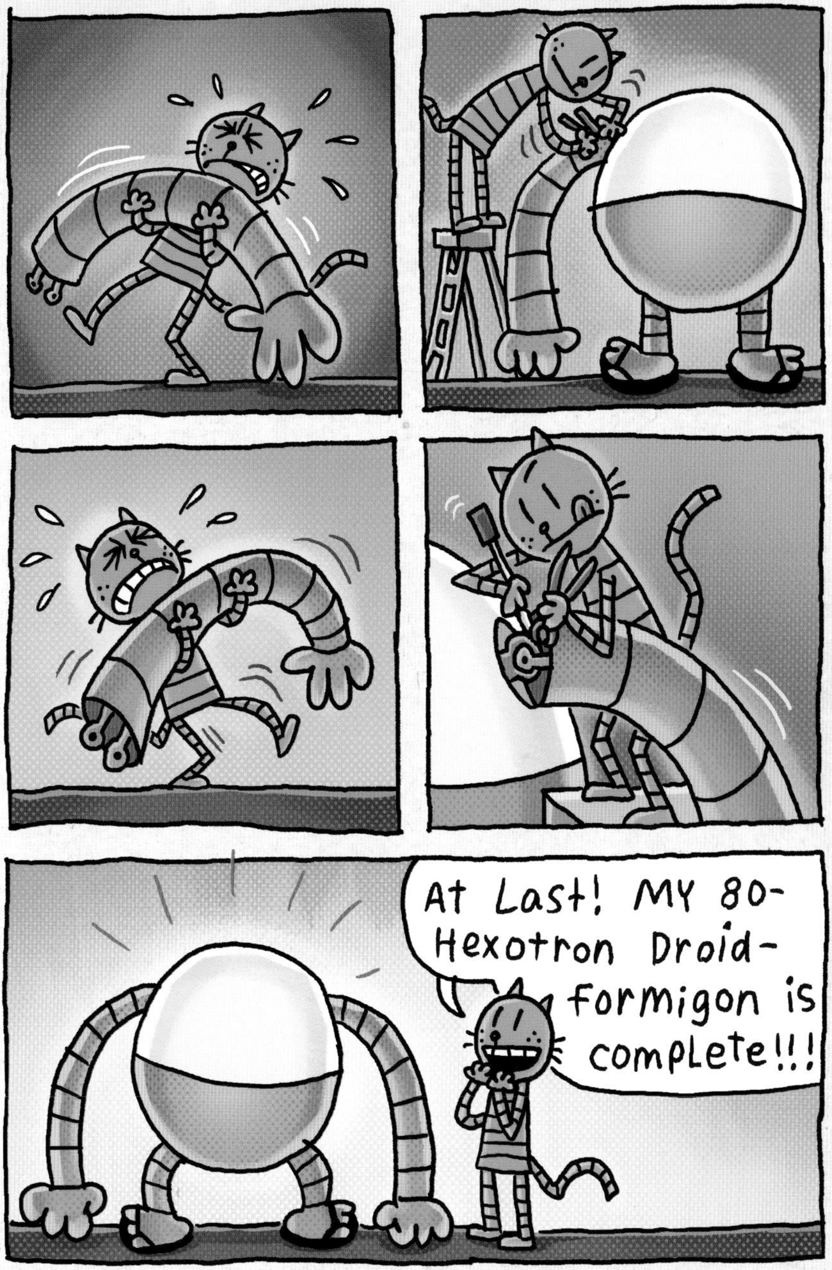
At Last! MY 80-Hexotron Droid-formigon is complete!!!

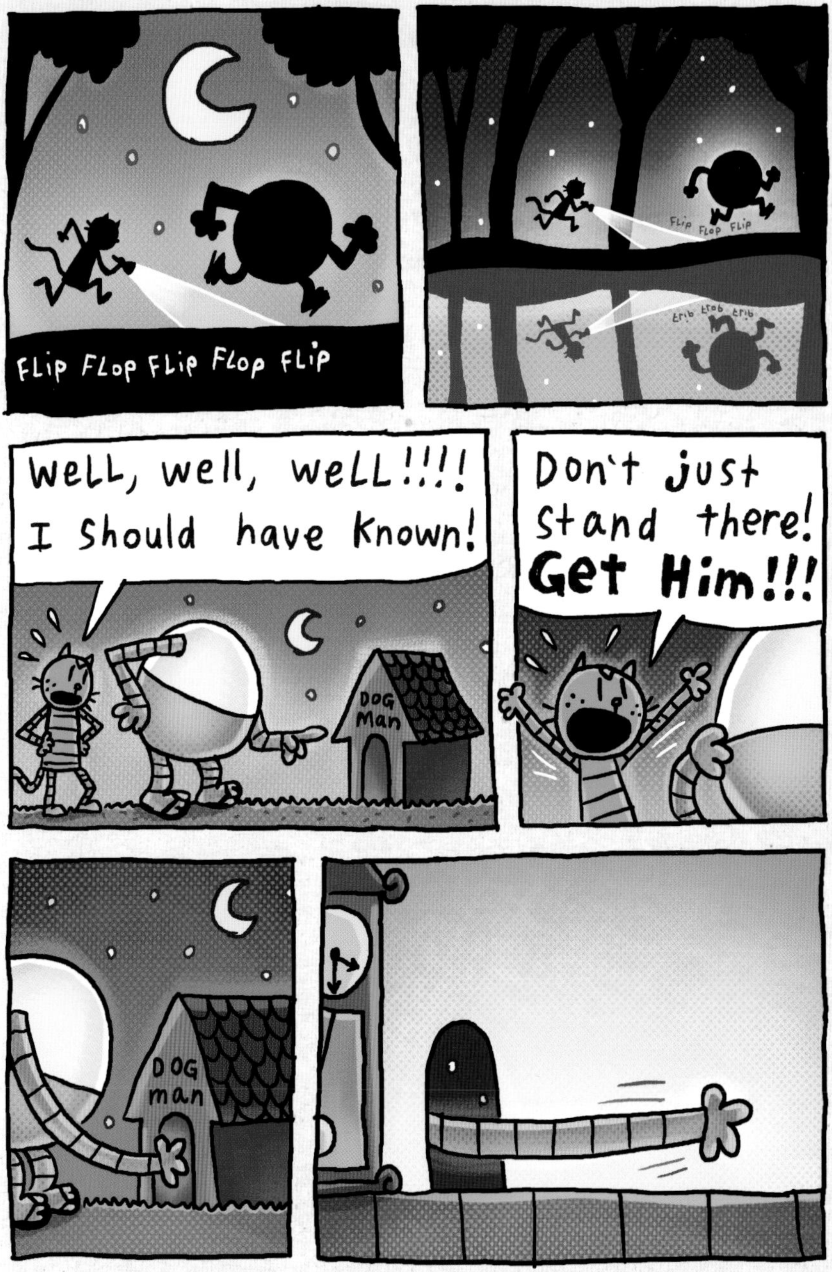
FLip FLop FLip FLop FLip
FLip FLop FLip
WeLL, well, weLL!!!! I Should have Known!
DOG Man
Don't just stand there! Get Him!!!
DOG man

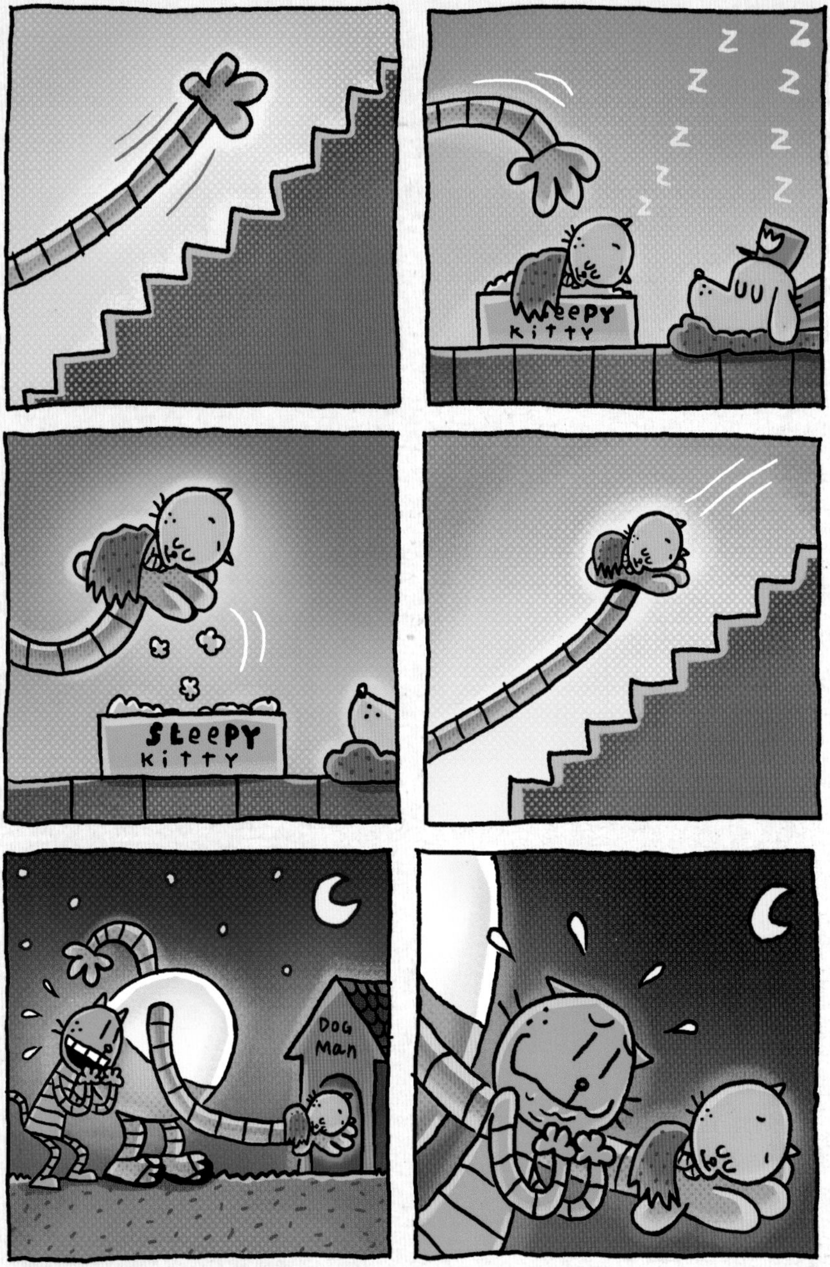
Z Z Z Z Z Z Z Z Z
Sleepy
kitty
Sleepy
kitty
DOG
Man

Peter's
Secret
Lab

FLIP FLOP FLIP FLOP!

FLIP FLOP F

And so...

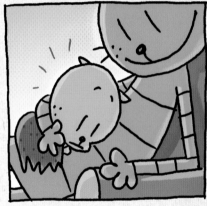

Oh, hi
Papa.

Don't call me
Papa!!!

Hey, where's
Dog Man?

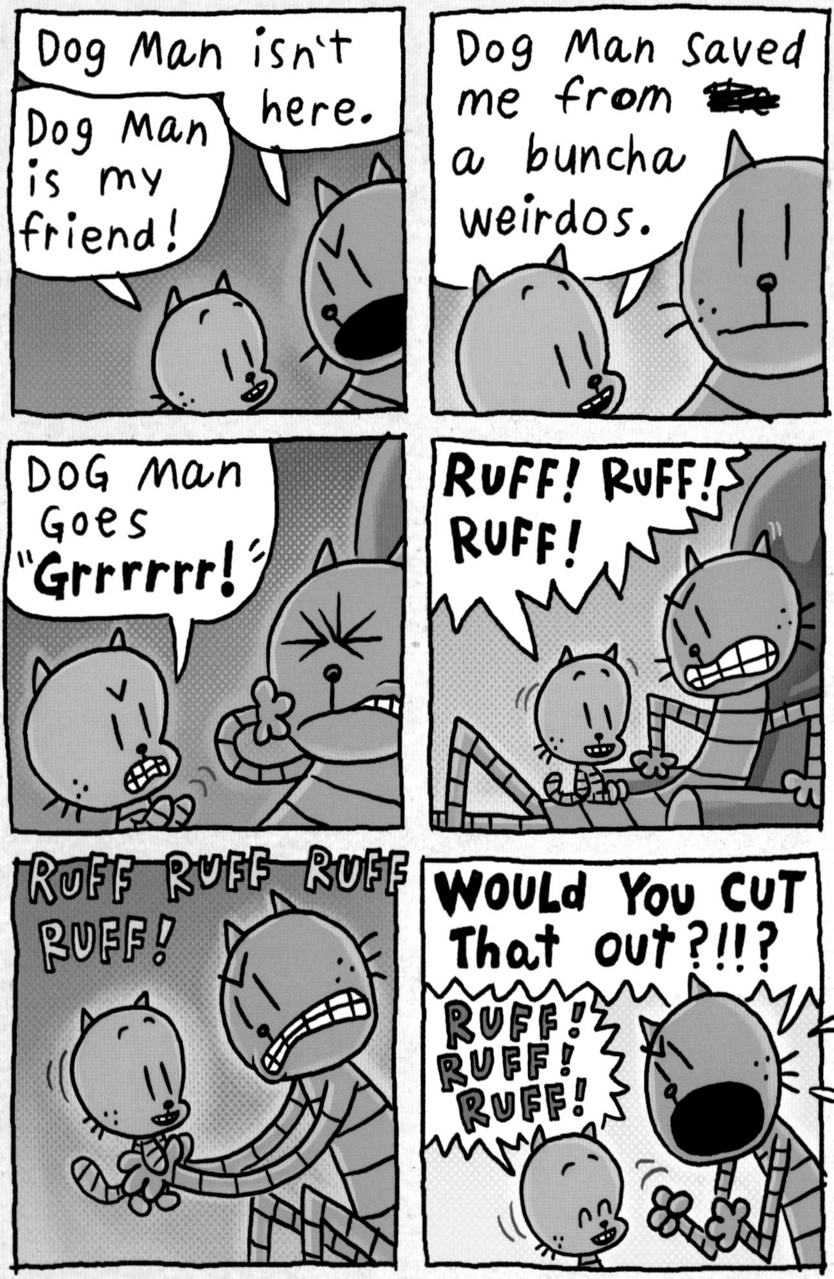
Dog Man isn't here.
Dog Man is my friend!
Dog Man saved me from a buncha weirdos.
DOG Man Goes "Grrrrrr!"
RUFF! RUFF! RUFF!
RUFF RUFF RUFF RUFF!
WOULd YOU CUT That OUT?!!?
RUFF! RUFF! RUFF!

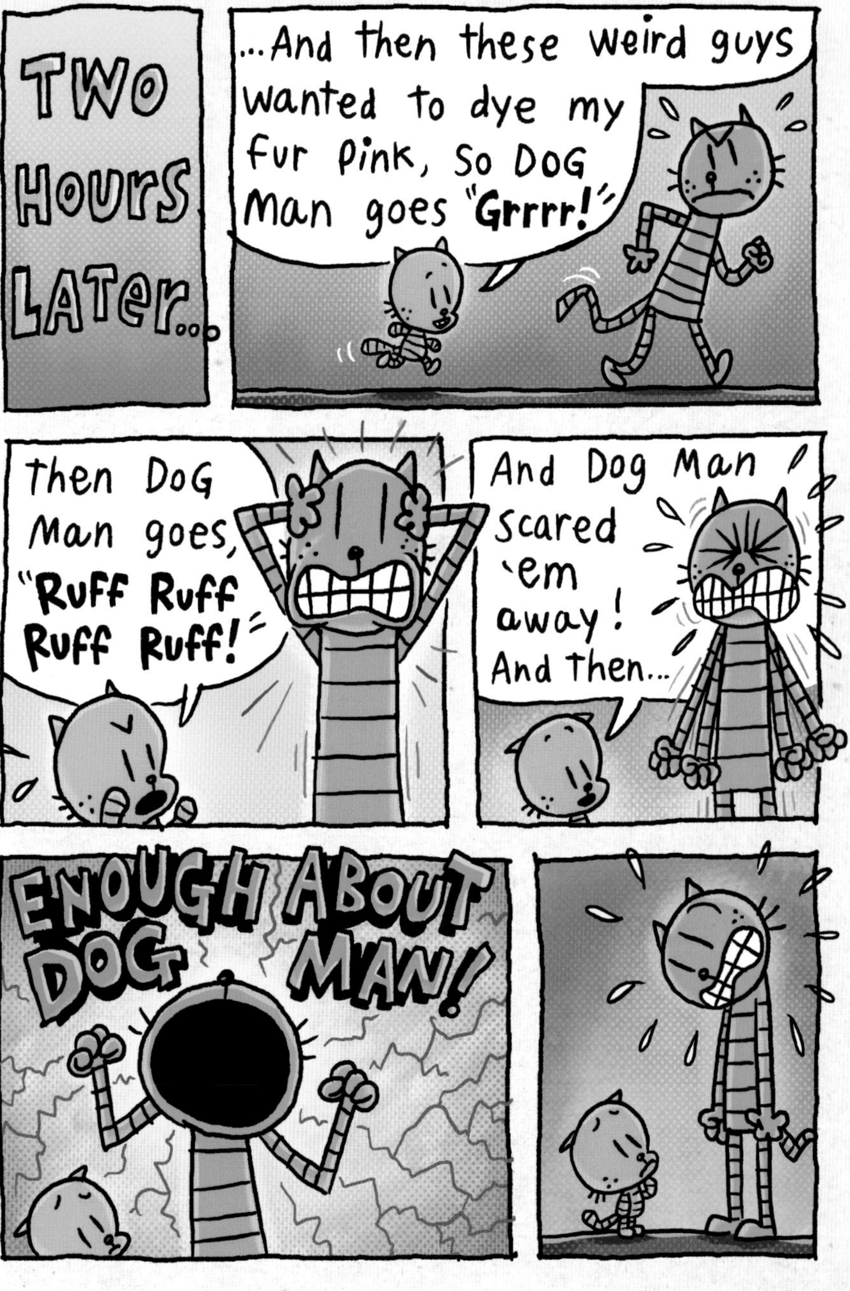

TWO HOURS LATER...
...And then these weird guys wanted to dye my fur pink, so DOG Man goes "Grrrr!"
Then DOG Man goes, "Ruff Ruff Ruff Ruff Ruff!"
And Dog Man scared 'em away! And then...
ENOUGH ABOUT DOG MAN!

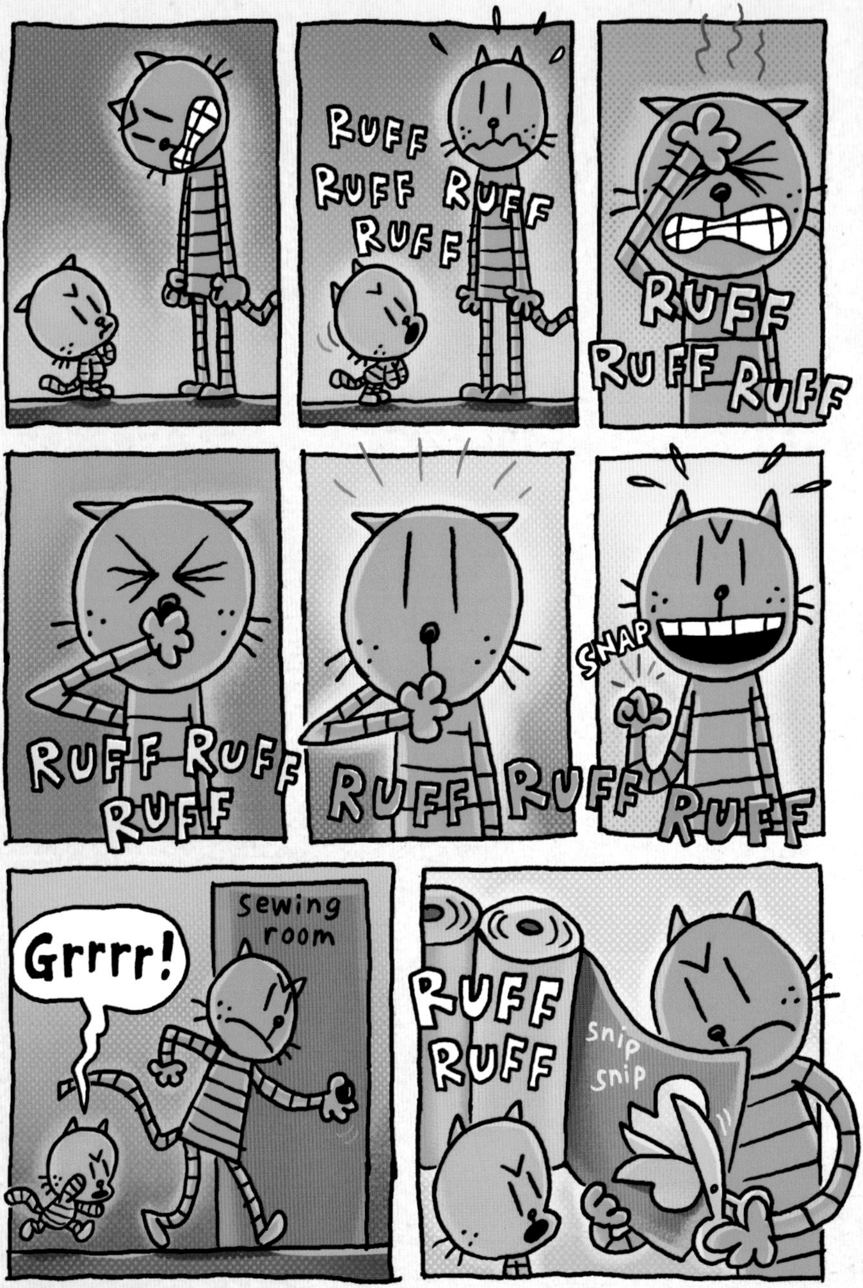
RUFF
RUFF RUFF
RUFF
RUFF
RUFF RUFF
RUFF RUFF
RUFF
RUFF RUFF
SNAP
RUFF
Grrrr!
sewing room
RUFF
RUFF
snip
snip

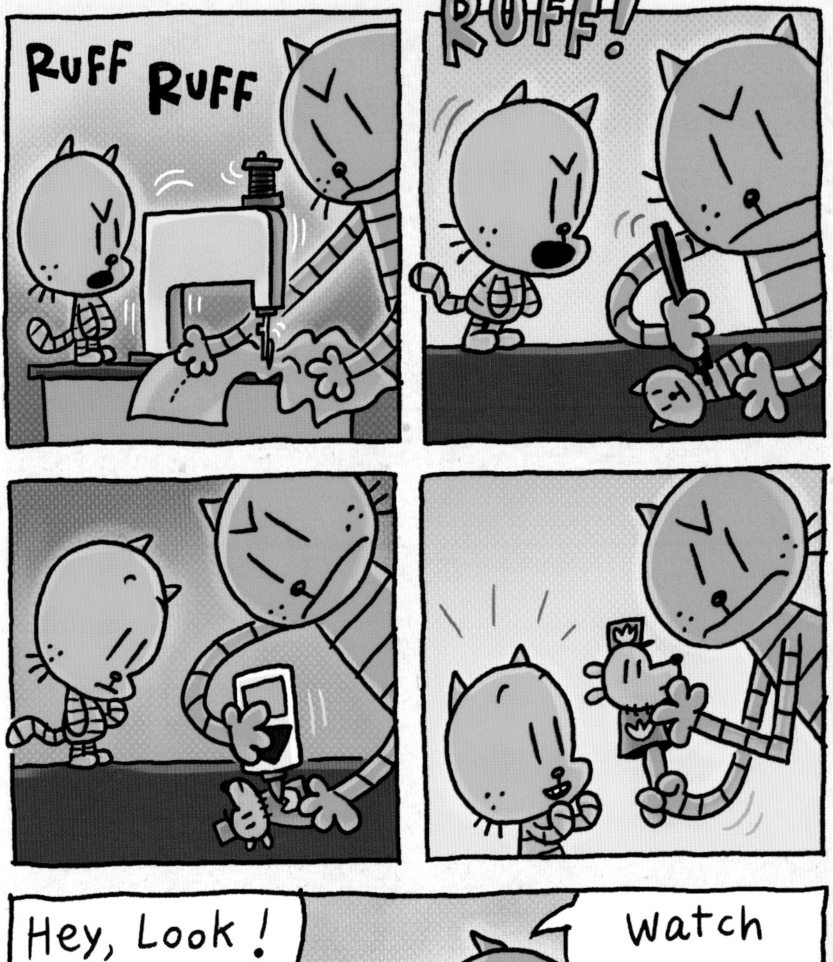
RUFF RUFF
RUFF!
Hey, Look! It's DOG Man!!!!
Watch and Learn, Kid!!!

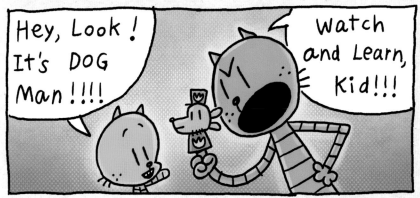

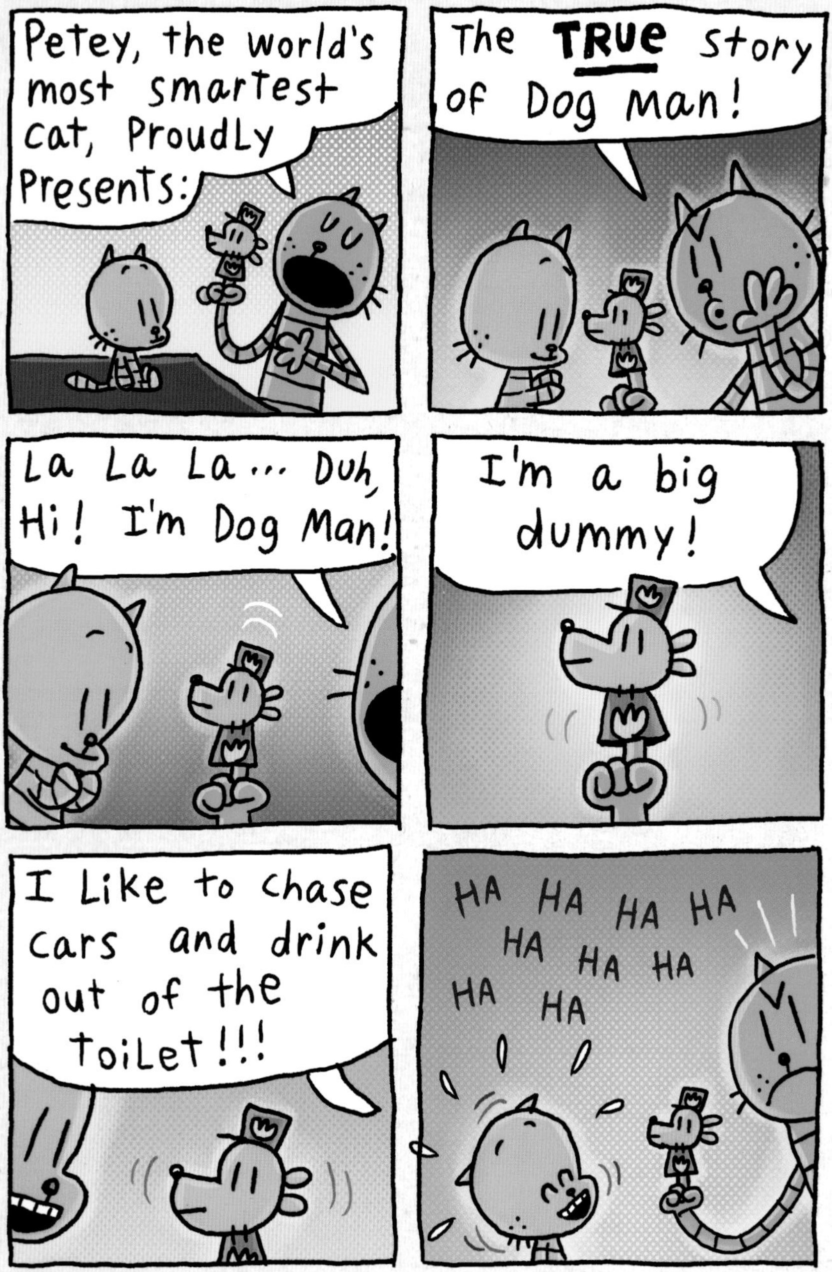
Petey, the world's most smartest cat, ProudLy Presents:
The TRUE story of Dog Man!
La La La... Duh, Hi! I'm Dog Man!
I'm a big dummy!
I Like to chase cars and drink out of the toiLet!!!
HA HA HA HA HA HA HA HA HA

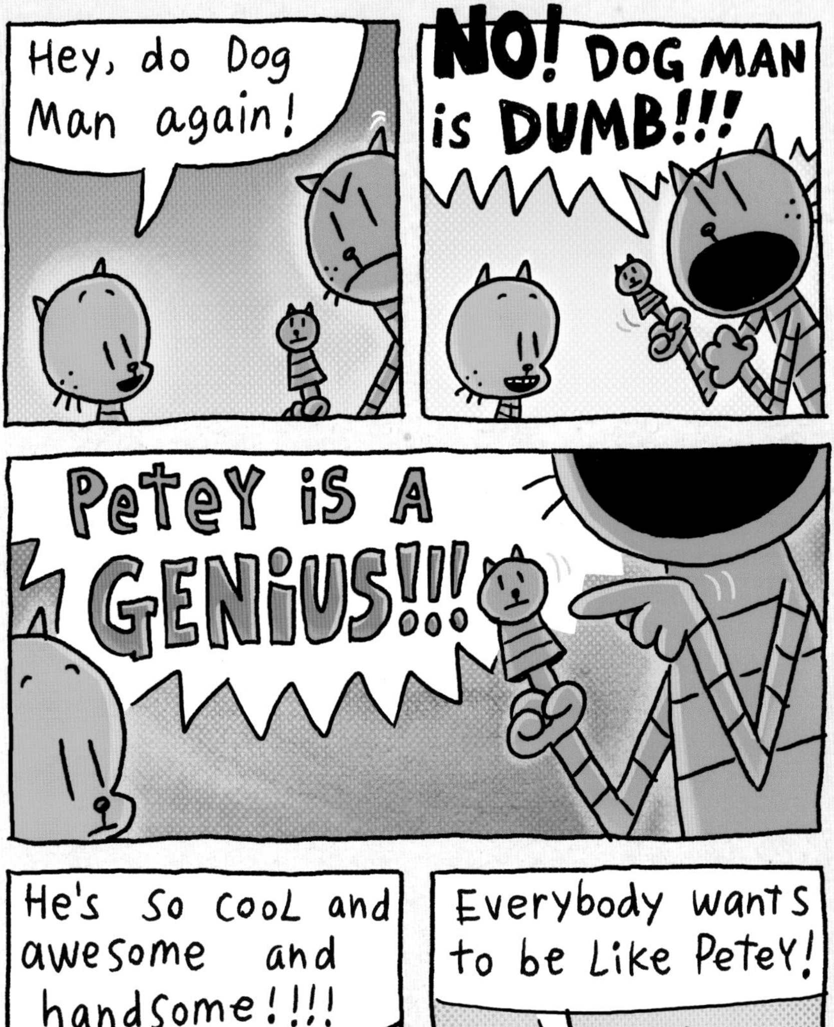
Hey, do Dog Man again!
NO! DOG MAN is DUMB!!!
Petey is a GENIUS!!!
He's so cool and awesome and handsome!!!!
Everybody wants to be like Petey!

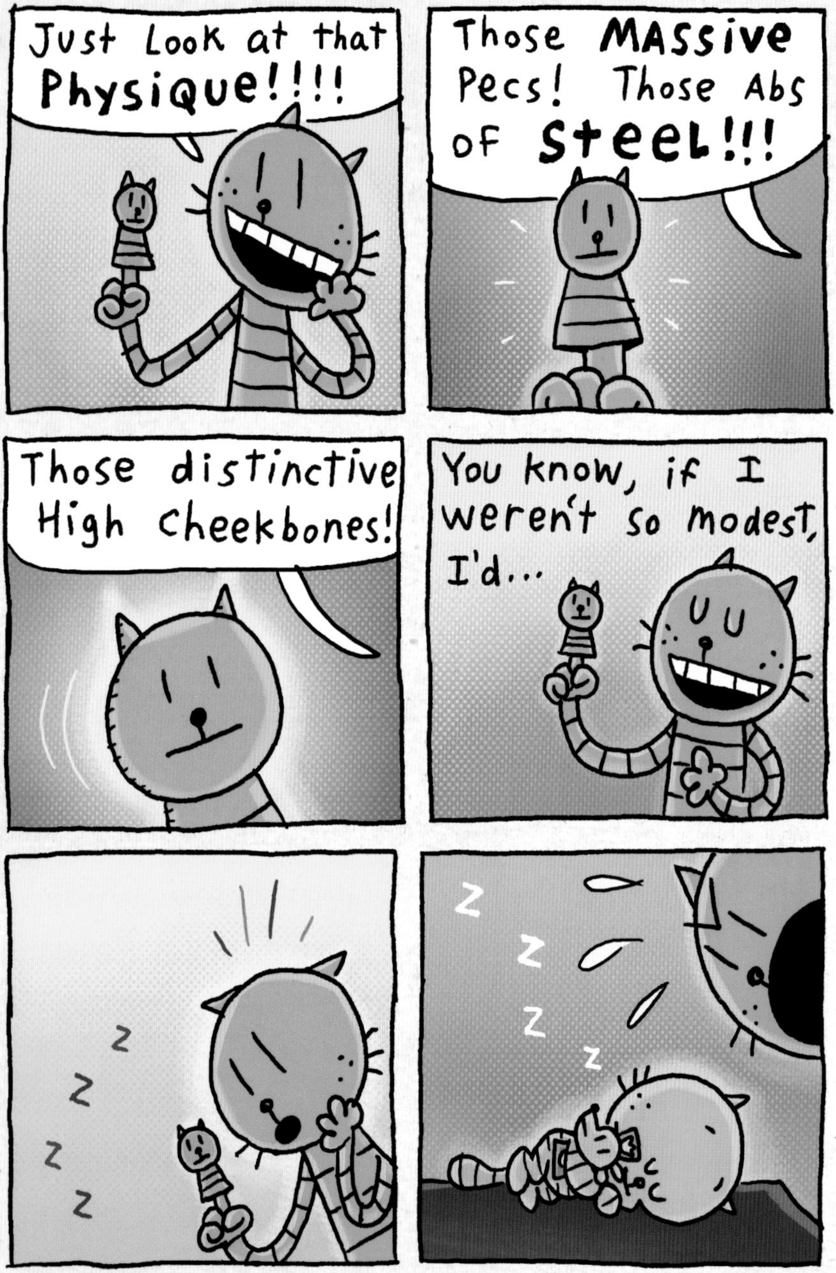
Just Look at that Physique!!!!
Those MASSIVE Pecs! Those Abs of STEEL!!!
Those distinctive High cheekbones!
You know, if I weren't so modest, I'd...
Z Z Z Z
Z Z Z Z

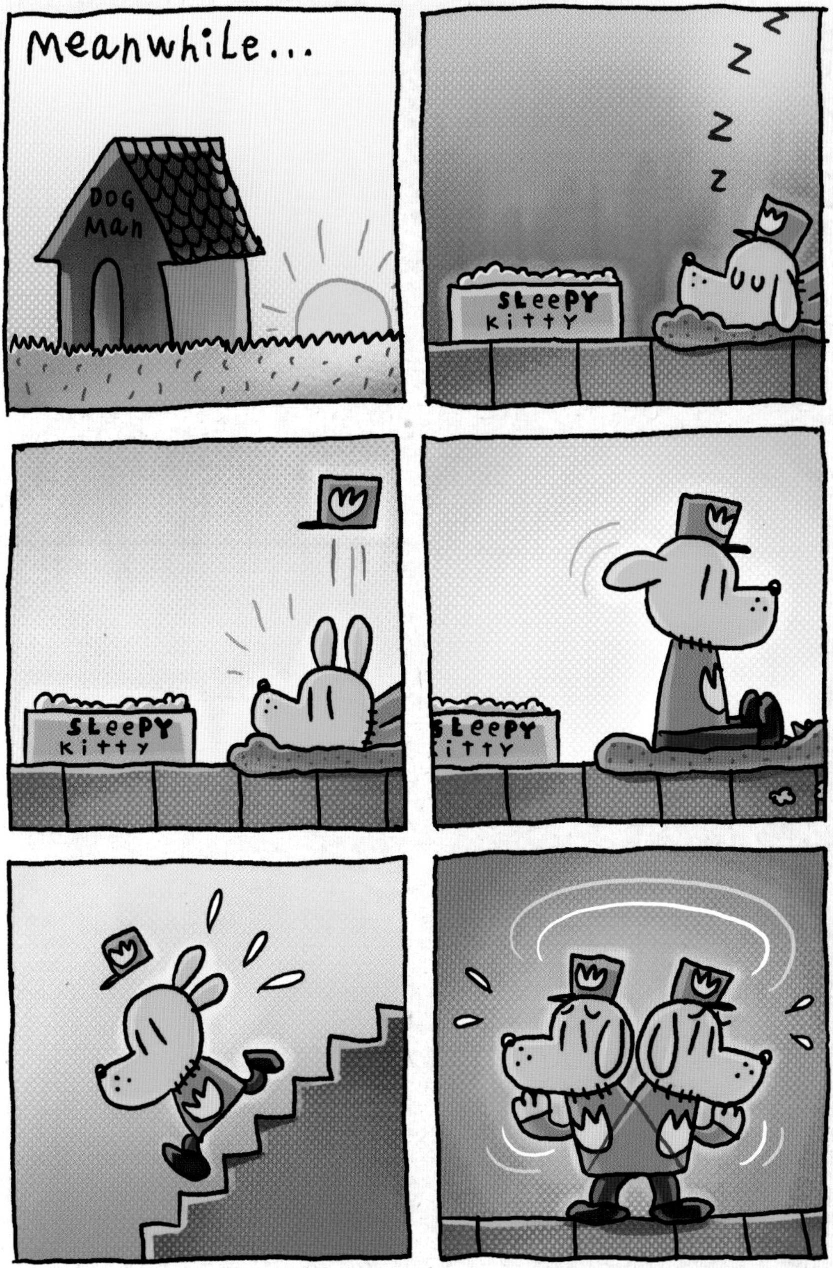
Meanwhile...
DOG
Man
Z
Z
Z
Z
SLEEPY
kitty
SLEEPY
kitty
SLEEPY
kitty

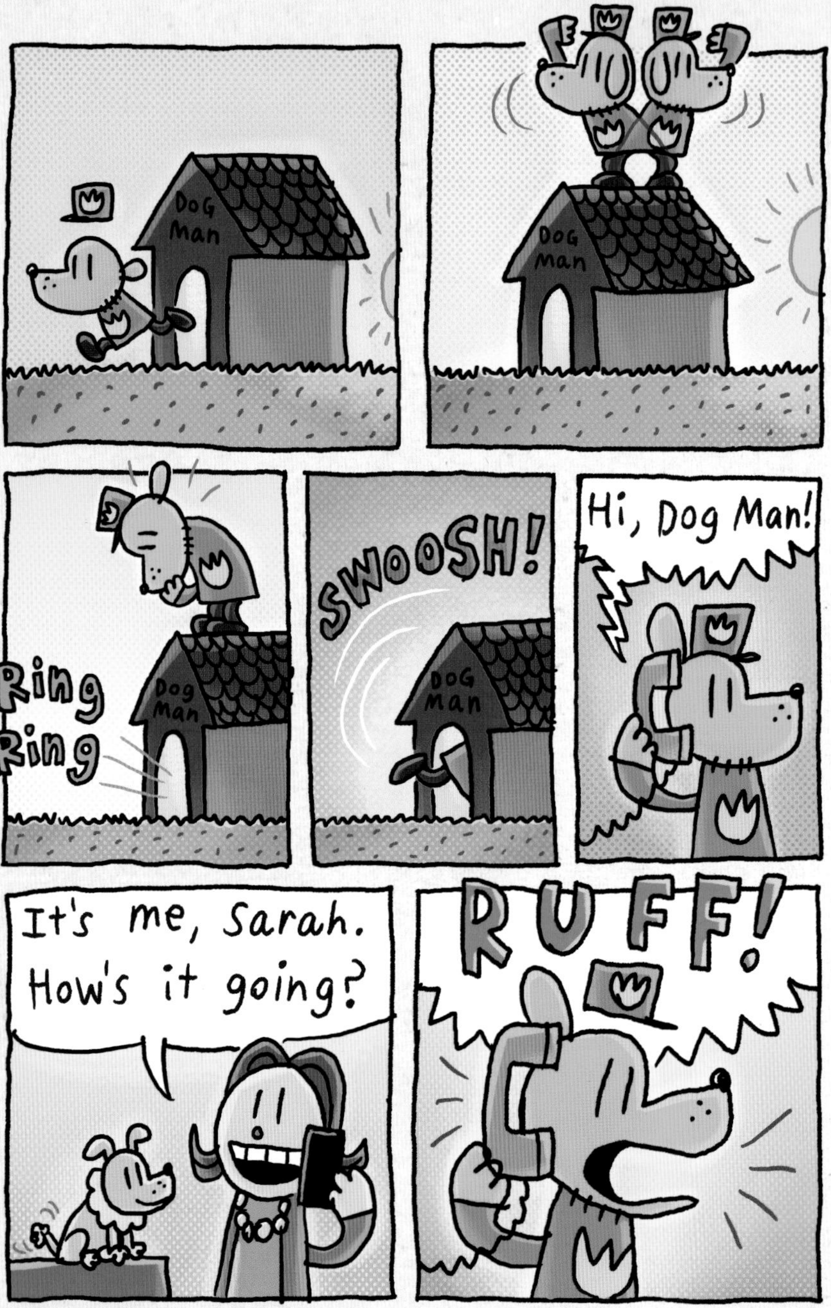
DOG
Man
DOG
Man
Ring
Ring
DOG
Man
SWOOSH!
DOG
Man
Hi, Dog Man!
It's me, Sarah.
How's it going?
RUFF!

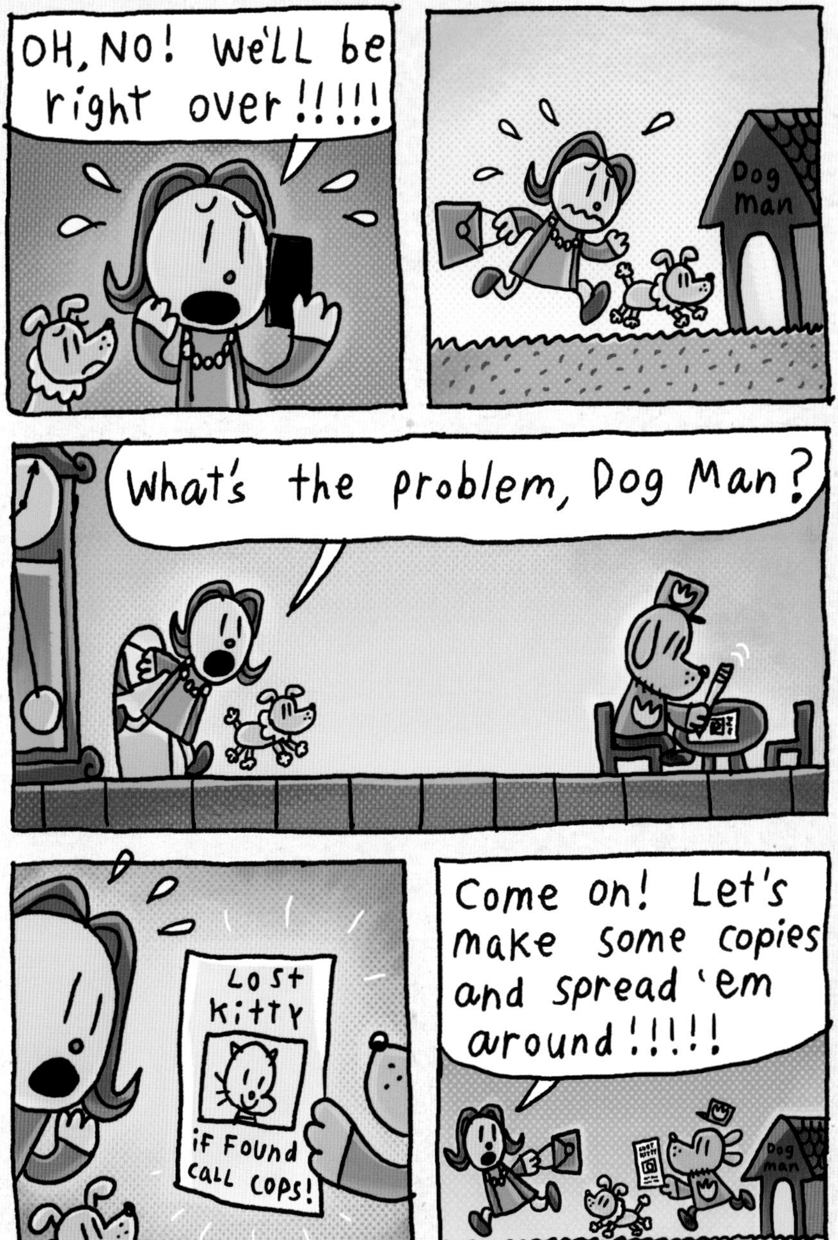
OH, NO! We'LL be right over!!!!!
Dog man
What's the problem, Dog Man?
Lost kitty
if Found call cops!
Come on! Let's make some copies and spread 'em around!!!!!
Dog man

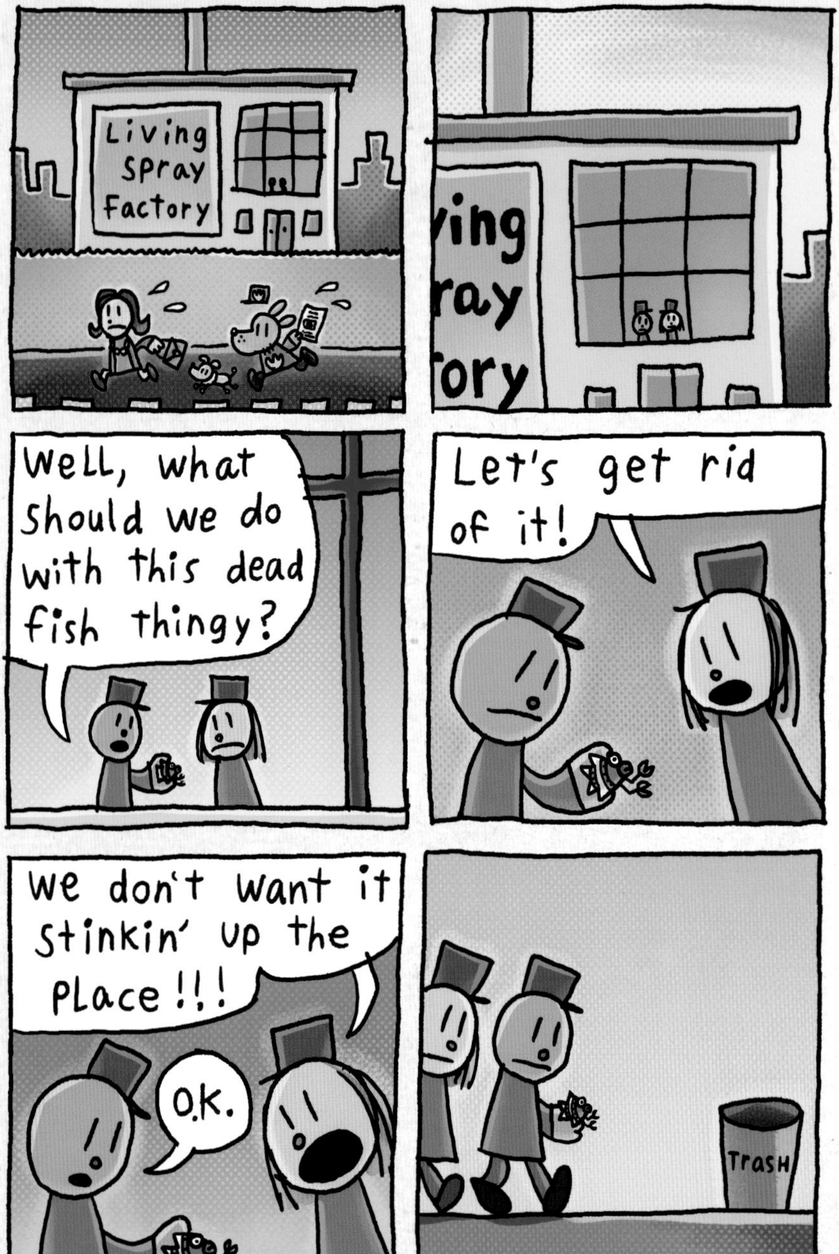
Living Spray Factory
ving ray tory
WeLL, what should we do with this dead fish thingy?
Let's get rid of it!
We don't want it stinkin' up the PLace!!!
O.K.
TrasH

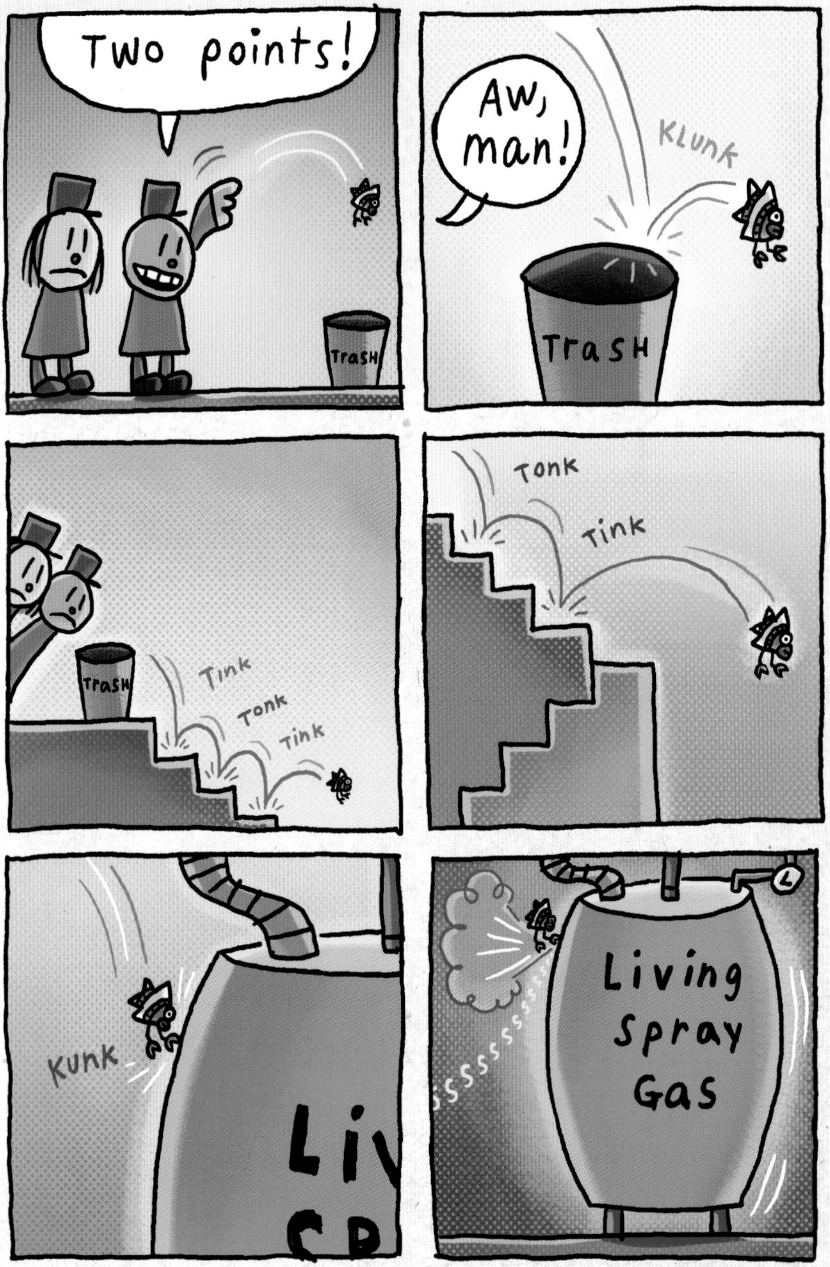
Two points!
TRASH
Aw, man!
KLUNK
TRASH
TRASH
TINK
TONK
TINK
TONK
TINK
KUNK
LIV
Living Spray Gas
SSSSSSSSSSSS

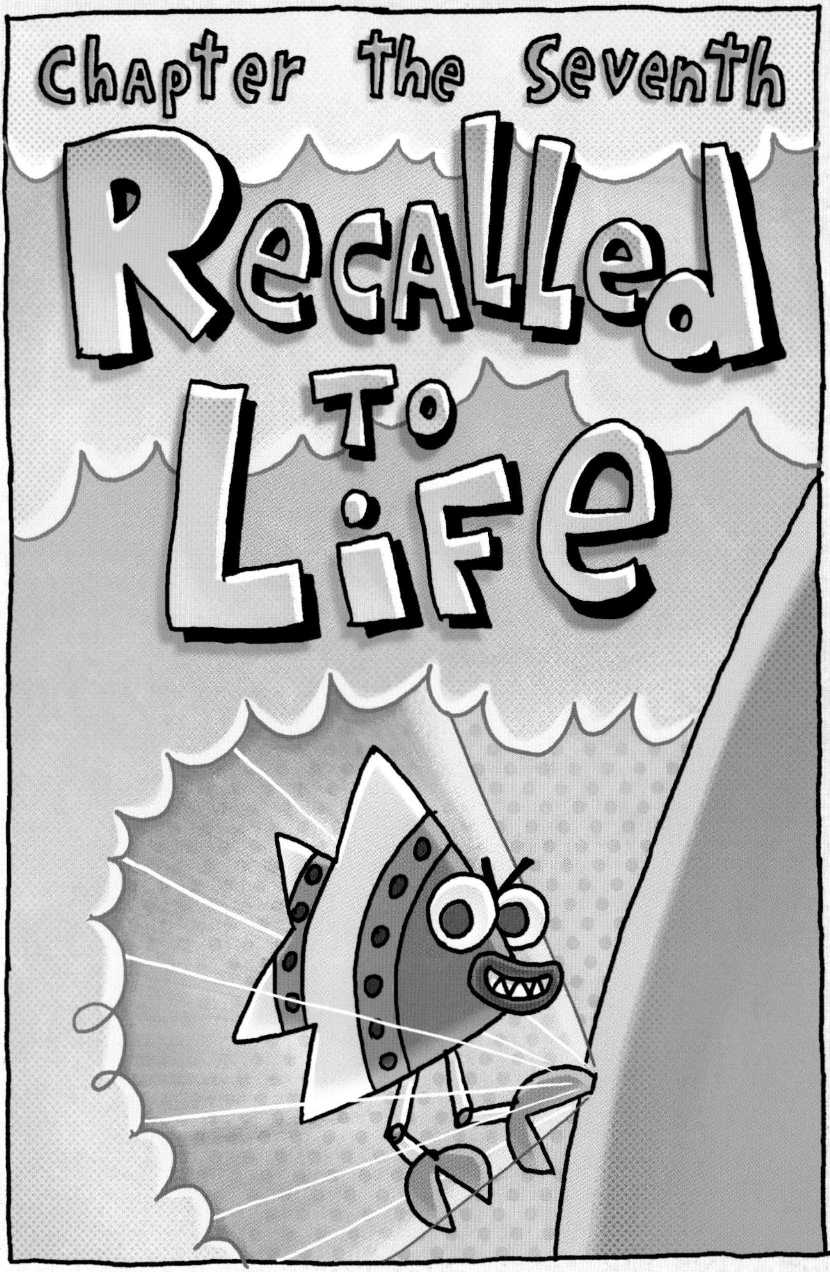
Chapter the Seventh
Recalled
To
Life

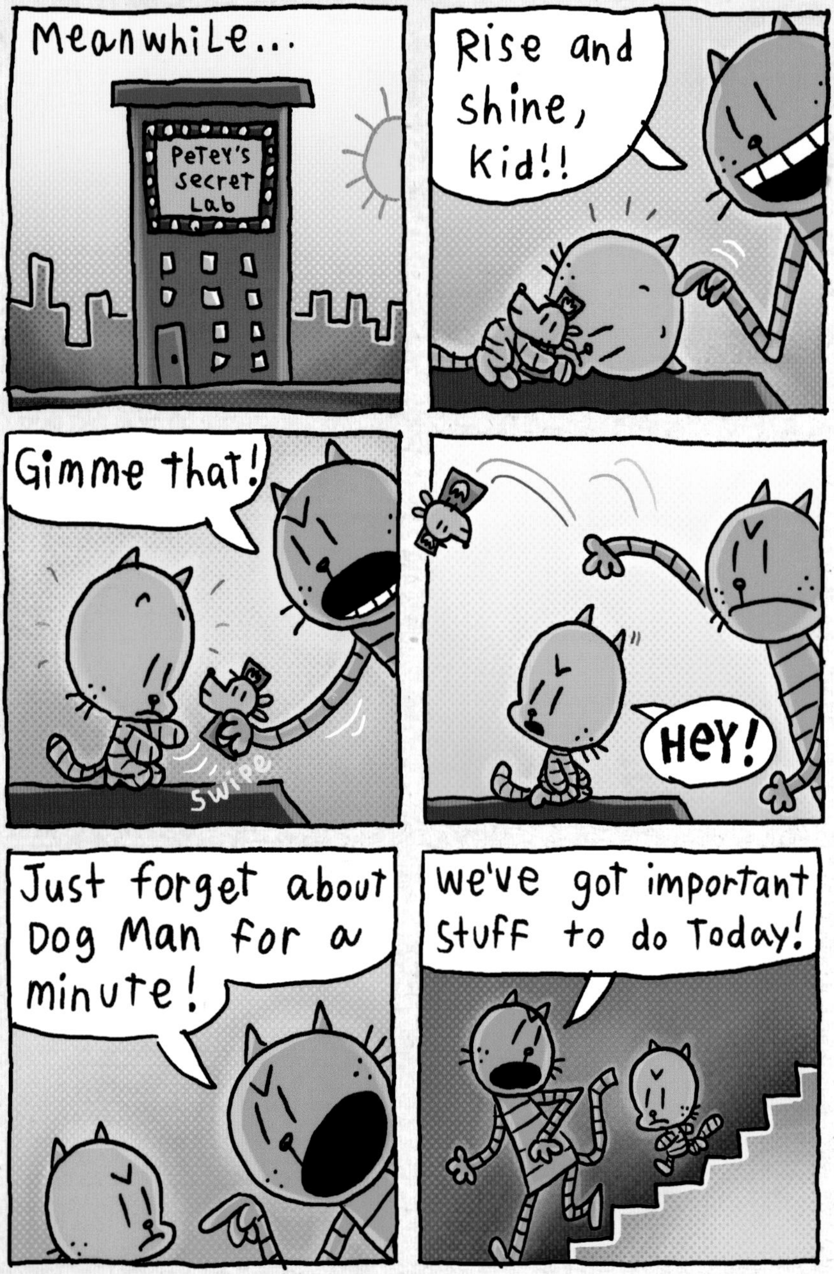
Meanwhile...
Petey's Secret Lab
Rise and shine, Kid!!
Gimme that!
SWIPE
HEY!
Just forget about Dog Man for a minute!
We've got important stuff to do today!

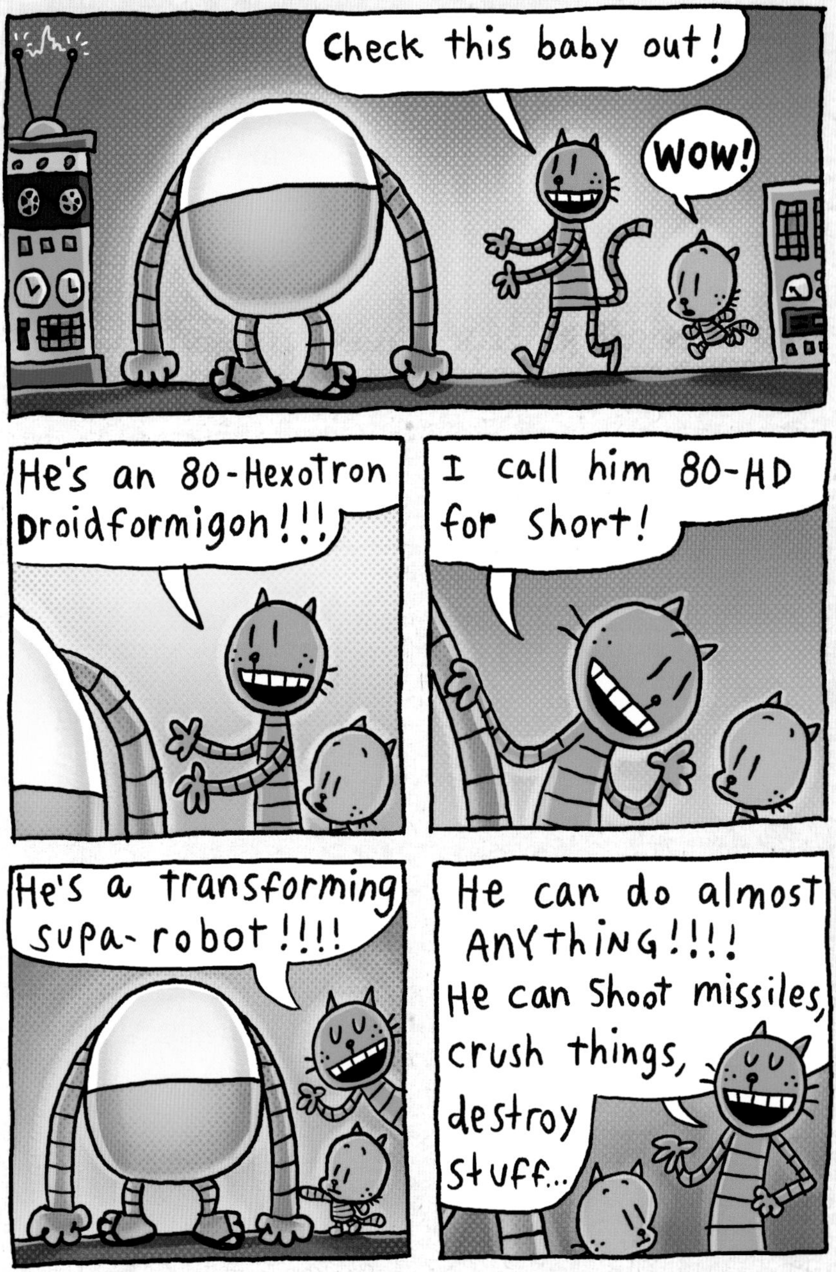
Check this baby out!
WOW!
He's an 80-Hexotron Droidformigon!!!
I call him 80-HD for Short!
He's a transforming supa-robot!!!!
He can do almost ANYTHING!!!!
He can Shoot missiles, crush things, destroy stuff...

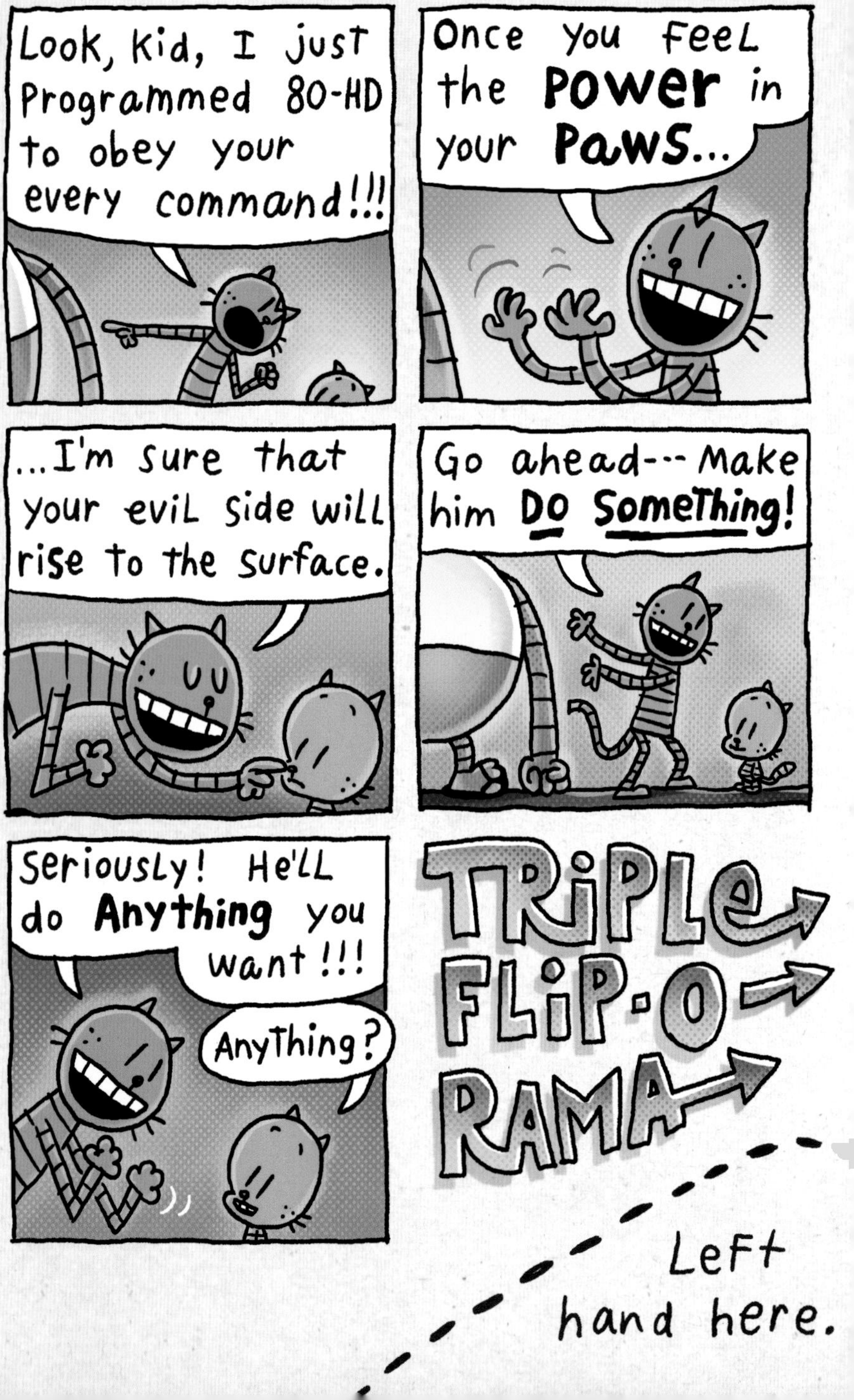

Look, Kid, I just Programmed 80-HD to obey your every command!!!
Once you Feel the POWER in your PAWS...
...I'm sure that your eviL Side wiLL rise to the surface.
Go ahead--- Make him DO SomeThing!
SeriousLy! He'LL do Anything you want!!!
AnyThing?
TRiPLe FLiP-O RAMA
LeFt hand here.

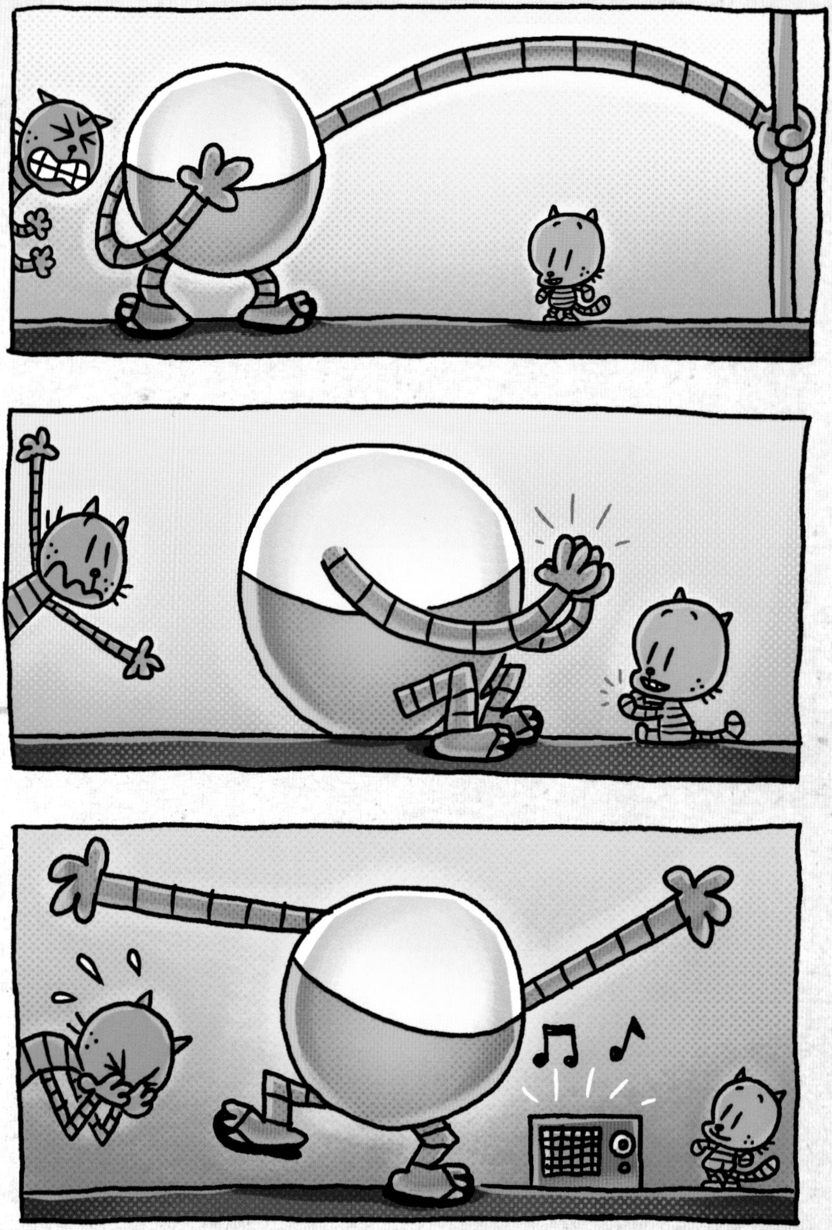

Right Thumb here.

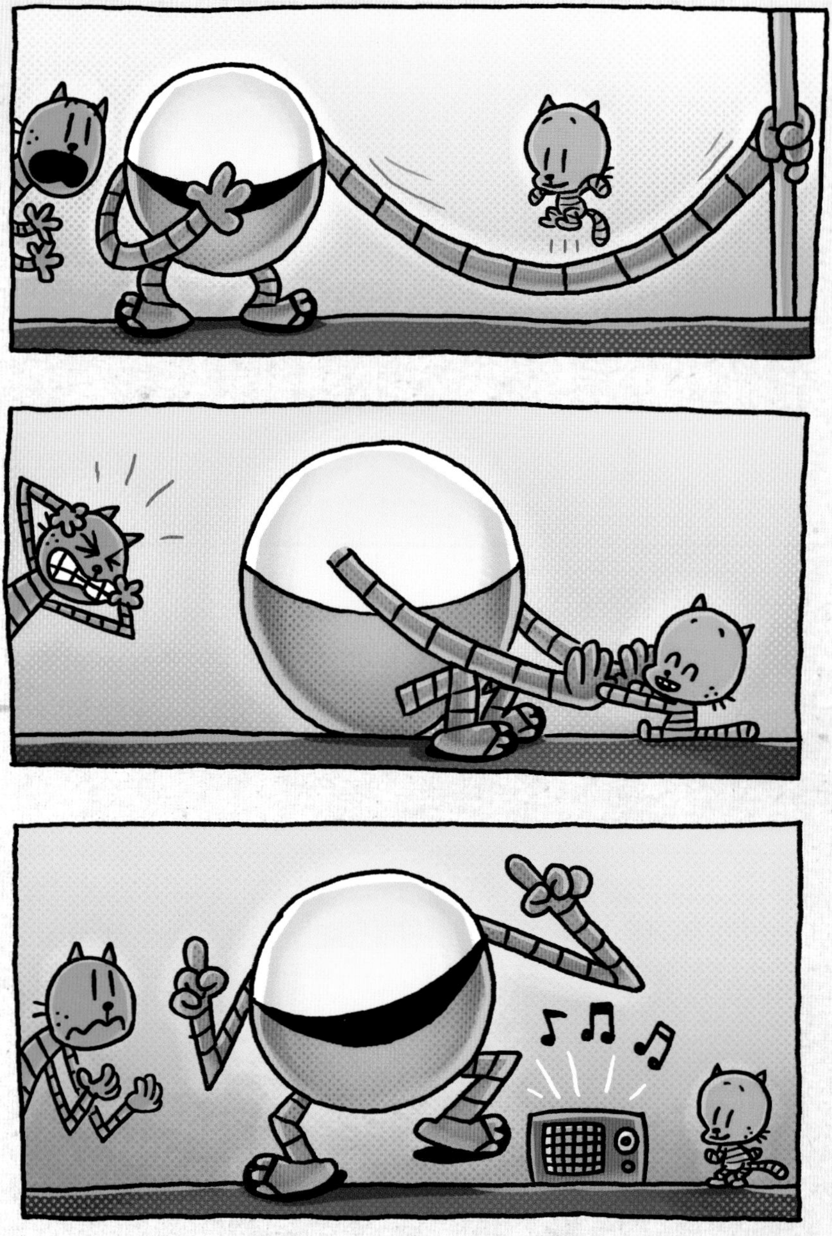

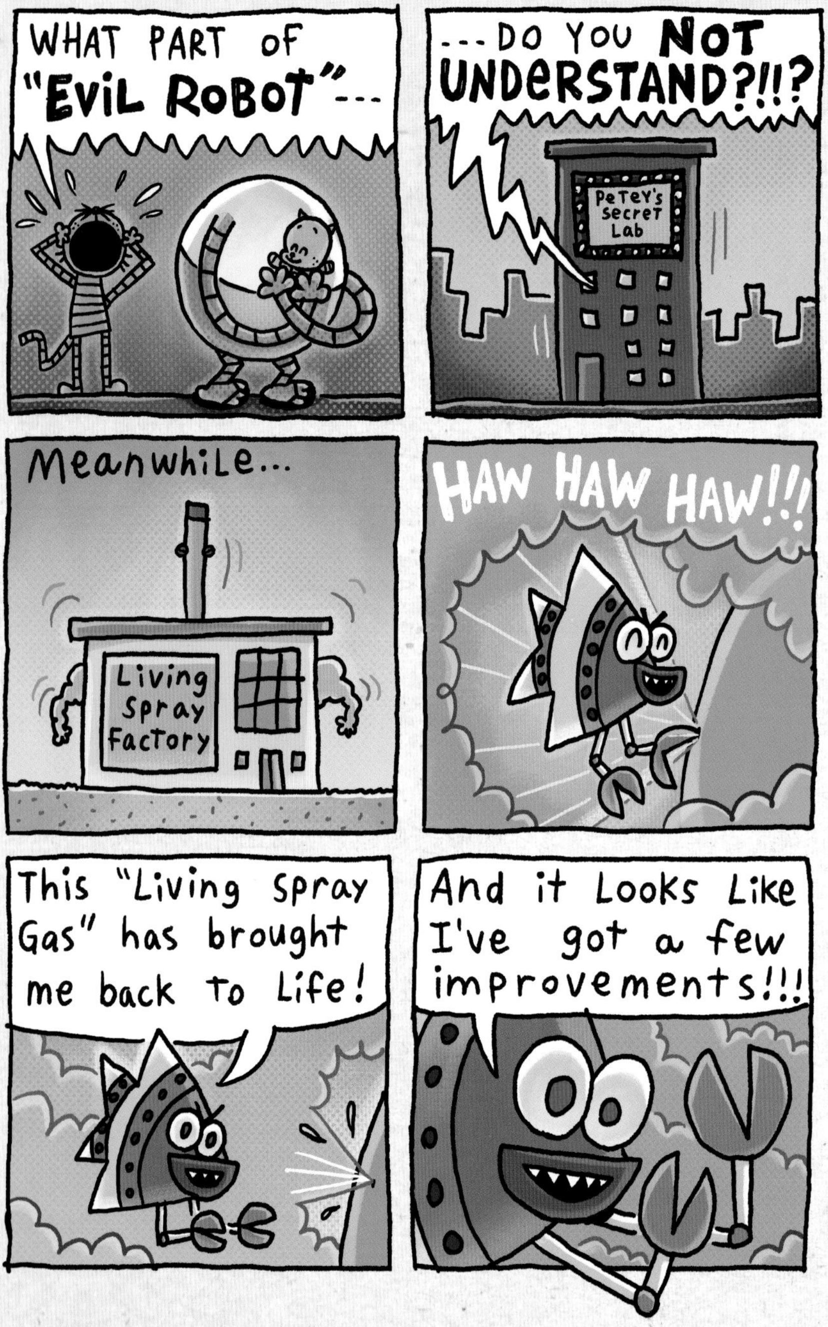
WHAT PART OF "EVIL ROBOT"...
...DO YOU NOT UNDERSTAND?!!?
PeTeY's SecreT Lab
Meanwhile...
Living Spray Factory
HAW HAW HAW!!!
This "Living Spray Gas" has brought me back to Life!
And it Looks Like I've got a few improvements!!!

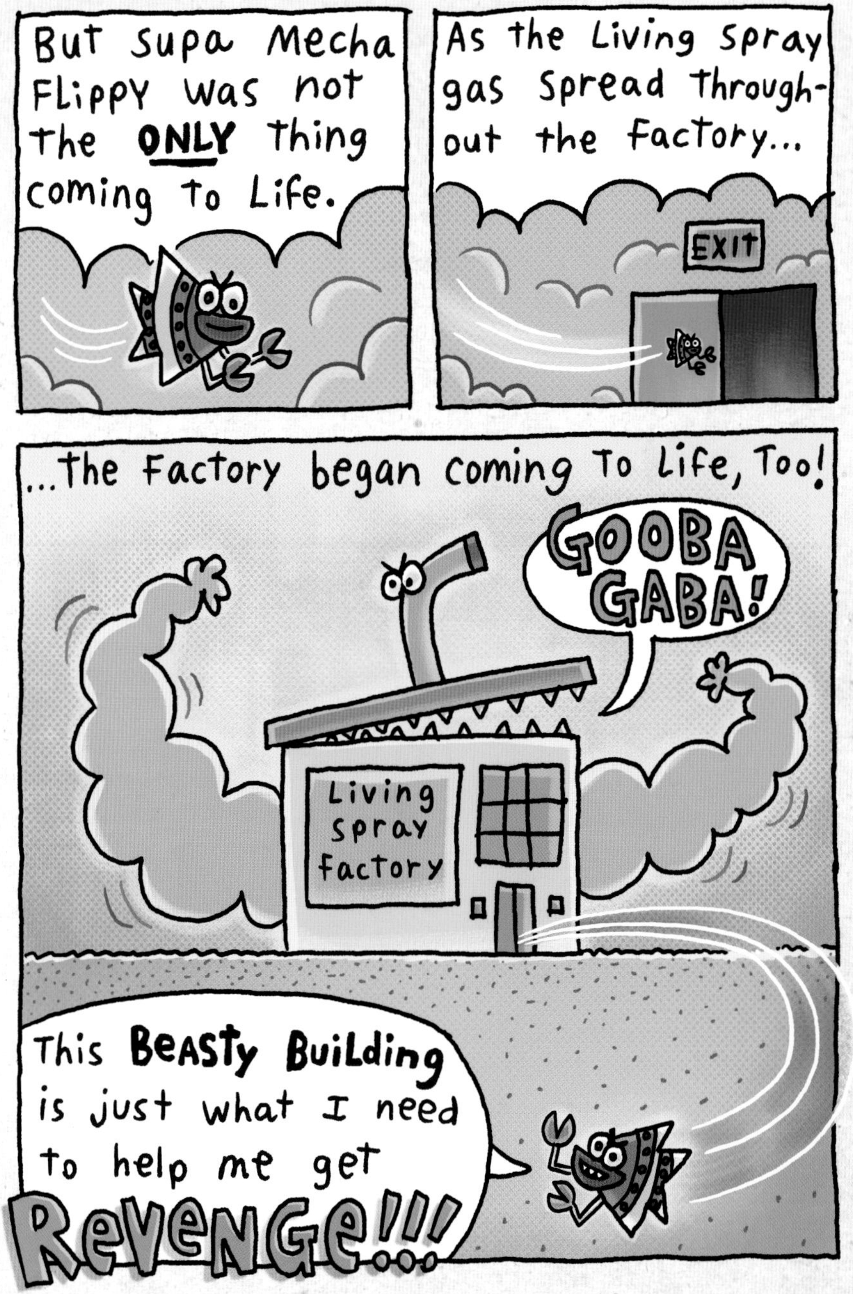
But Supa Mecha Flippy was not the ONLY thing coming to Life.
As the Living Spray gas Spread through-out the Factory...
EXIT
...the Factory began coming to Life, Too!
GOOBA GABA!
Living Spray Factory
This BEASTY BUILDING is just what I need to help me get REVENGE!!!

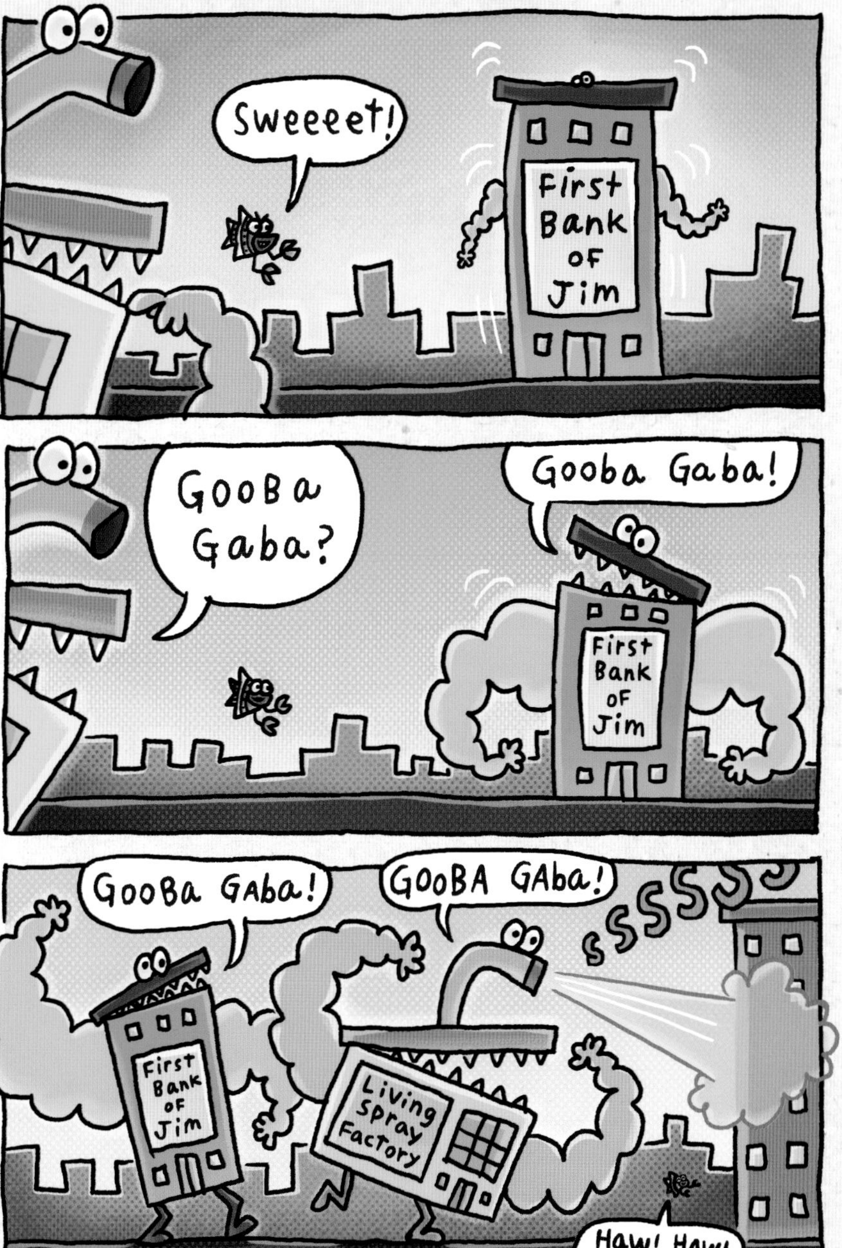
Sweeeet!
First Bank of Jim
GOOBa Gaba?
Gooba Gaba!
First Bank of Jim
GOOBa GAba!
GOOBA GAba!
First Bank of Jim
Living Spray Factory
HAW! HAW! HAW!!!

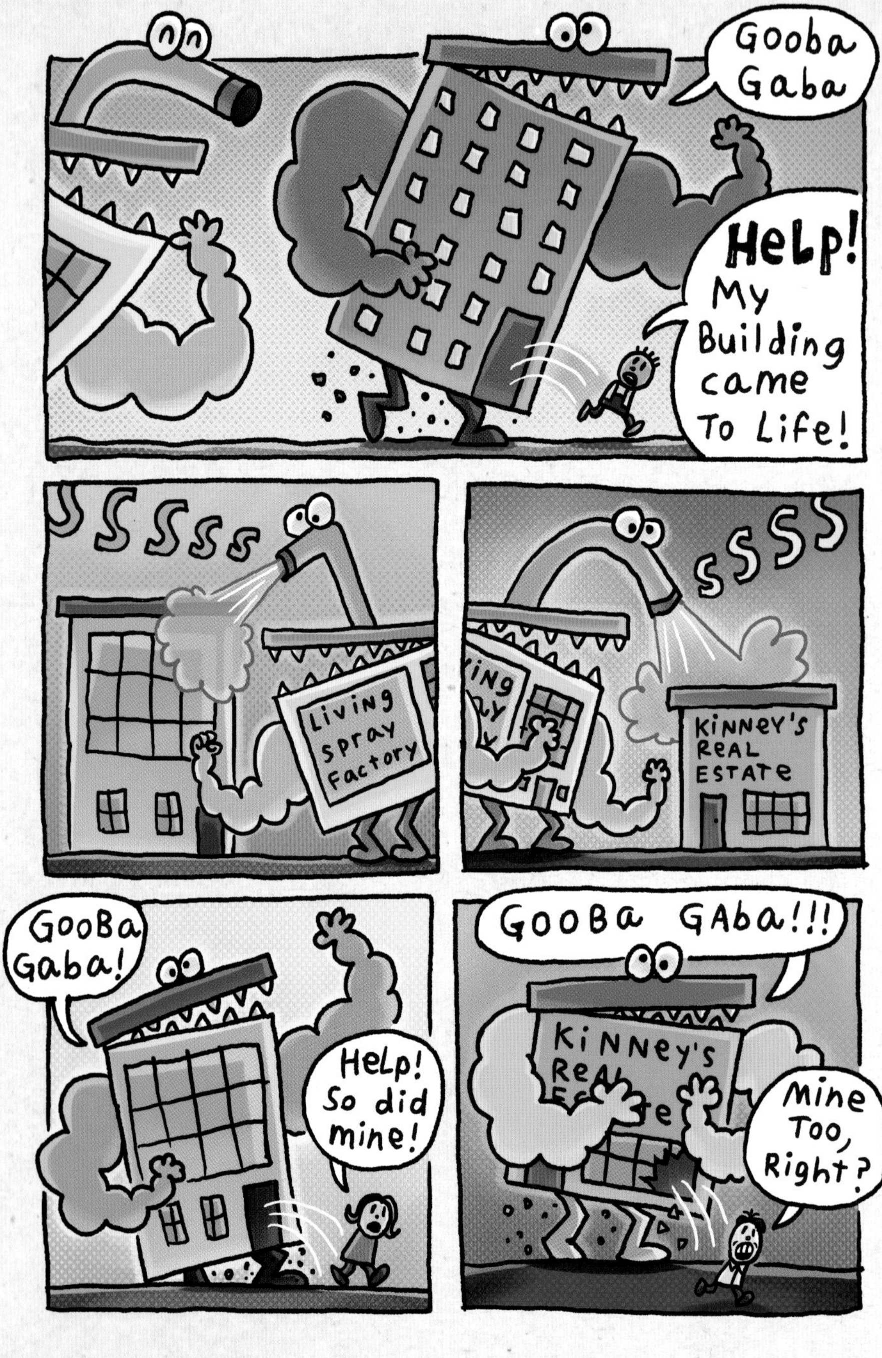
Gooba Gaba
HELP! My Building came To Life!
Living spray Factory
SSSSS
SSSSS
KINNEY'S REAL ESTATE
GooBa Gaba!
HeLp! So did mine!
GOOBA GABA!!!
KINNEY'S REAL
Mine Too, Right?

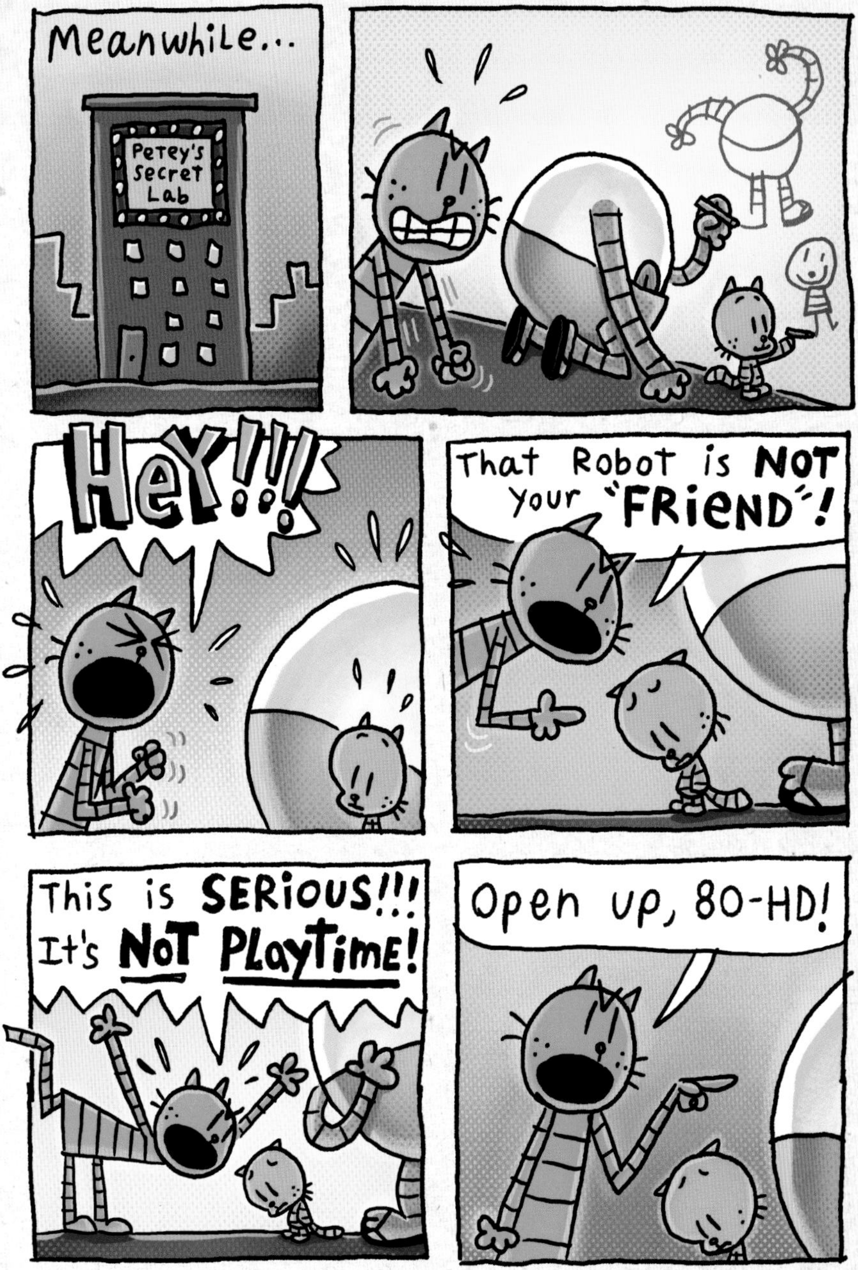
Meanwhile...
Petey's Secret Lab
HEY!!!
That Robot is NOT your "FRIEND"!
This is SERIOUS!!! It's NOT PLAYTIME!
Open up, 80-HD!

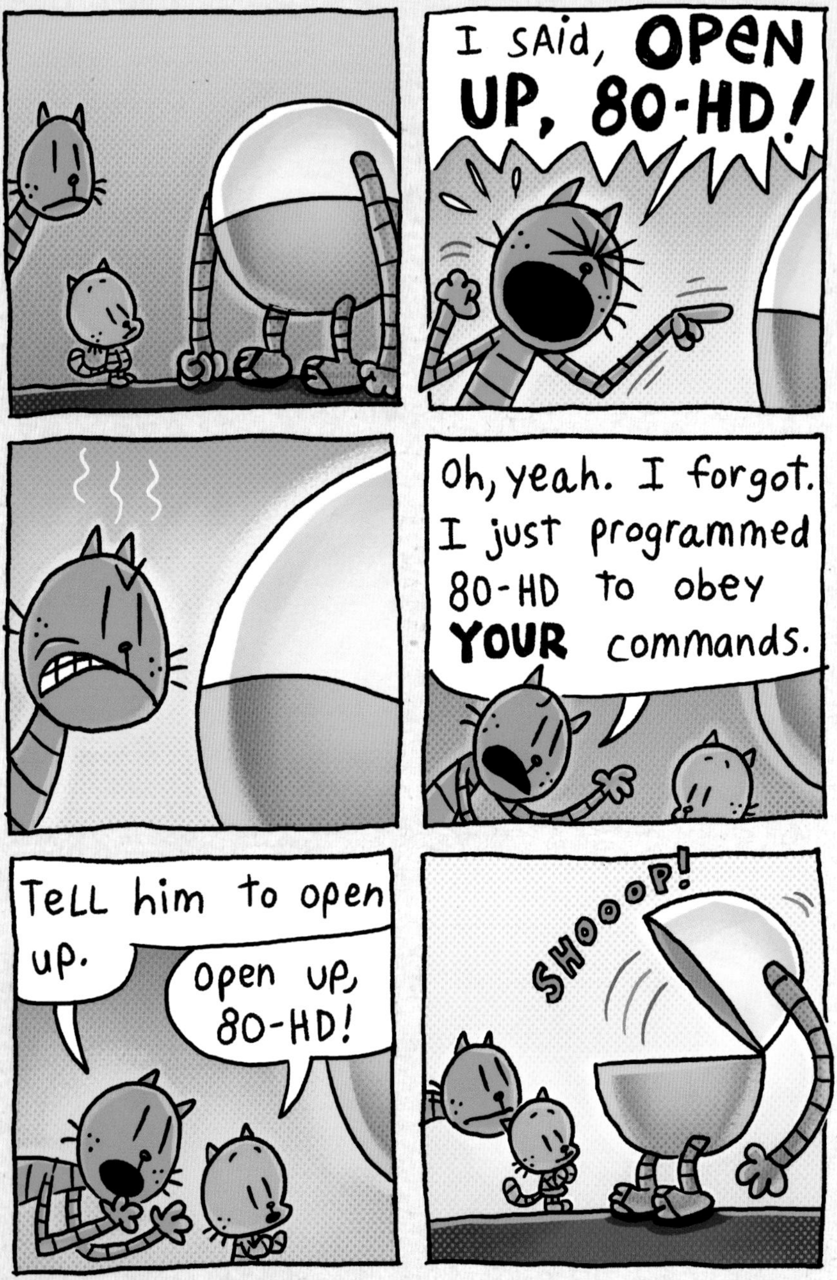
I SAID, OPEN UP, 80-HD!
Oh, yeah. I forgot. I just programmed 80-HD to obey YOUR commands.
TELL him to open up.
Open up, 80-HD!
SHOOOOP!

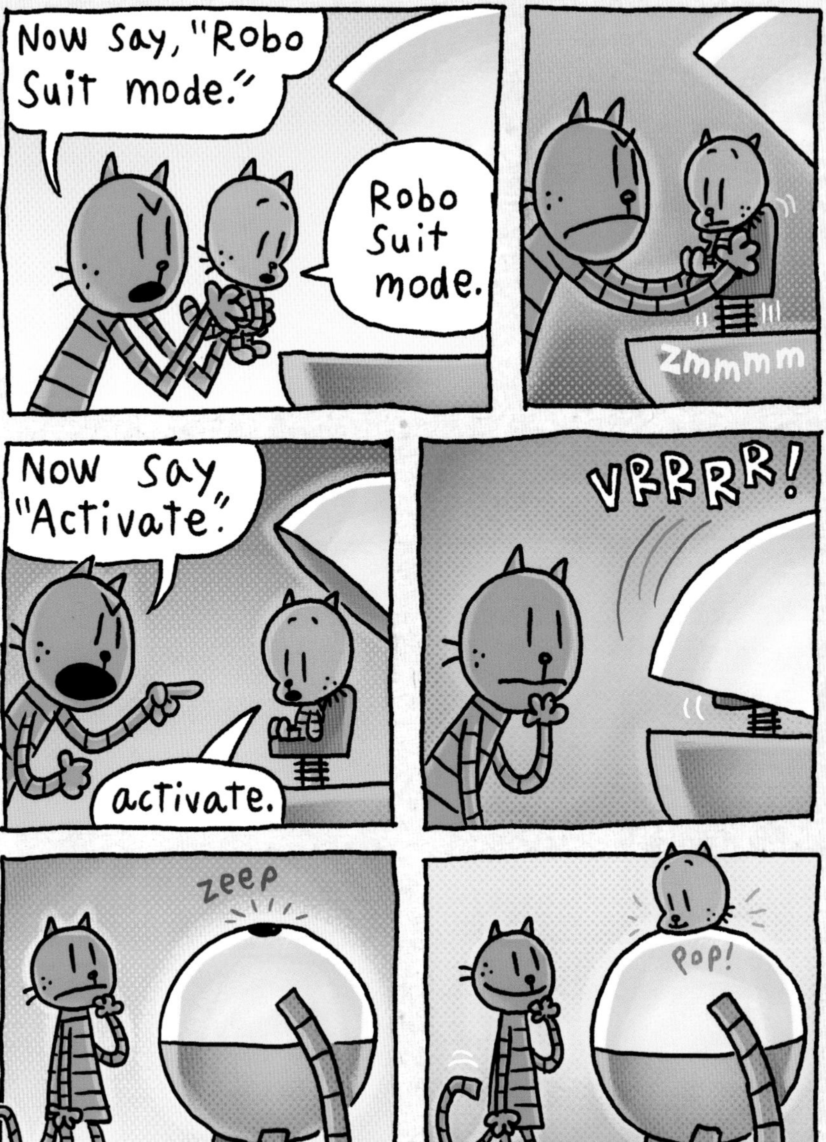
Now say, "Robo Suit mode."
Robo Suit mode.
zmmmm
Now say "Activate."
activate.
VRRRR!
zeep
POP!

Left hand here.

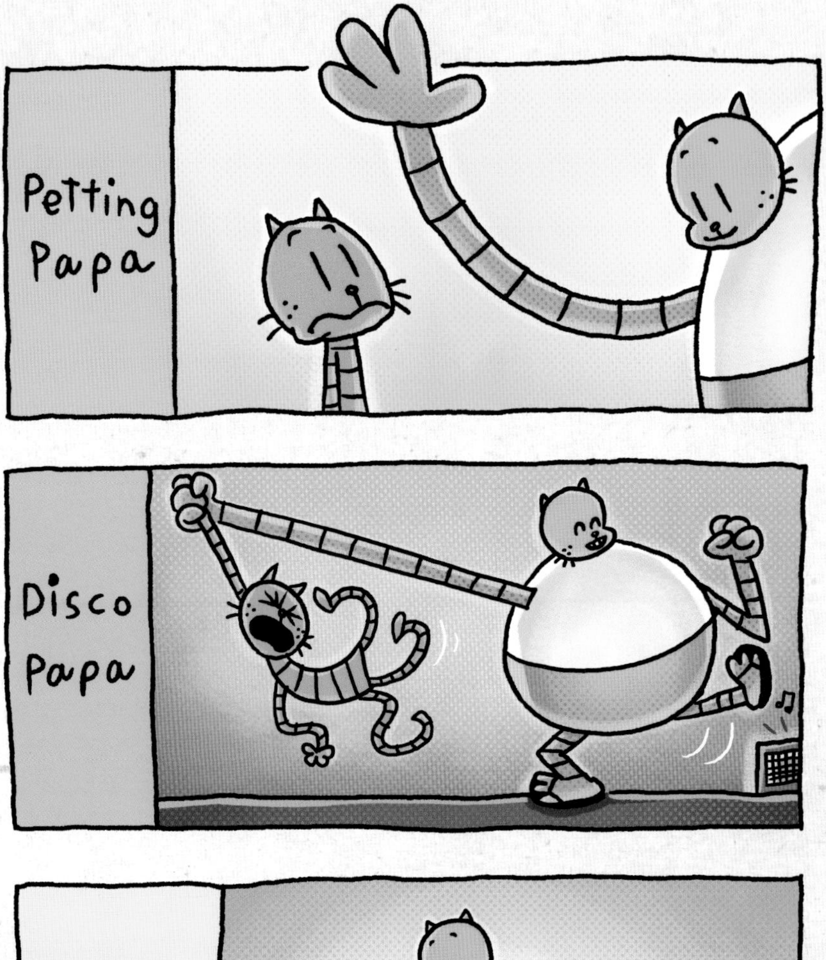
Petting Papa
Disco Papa
Rock-a-Bye Papa

Right Thumb here.

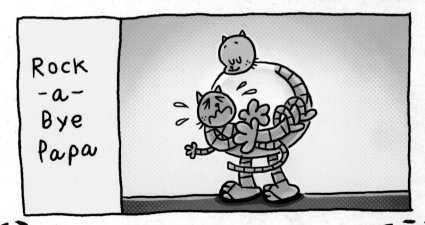

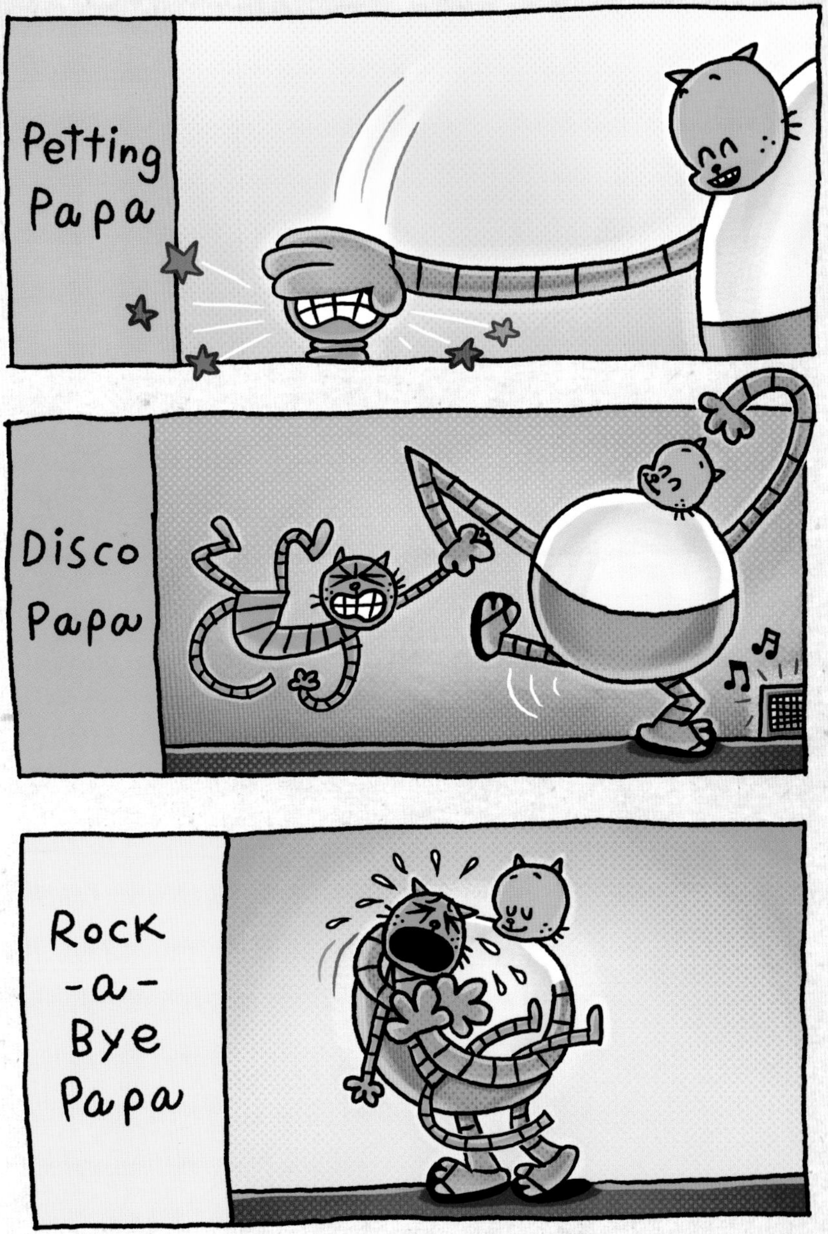
Petting Papa
Disco Papa
Rock -a- Bye Papa

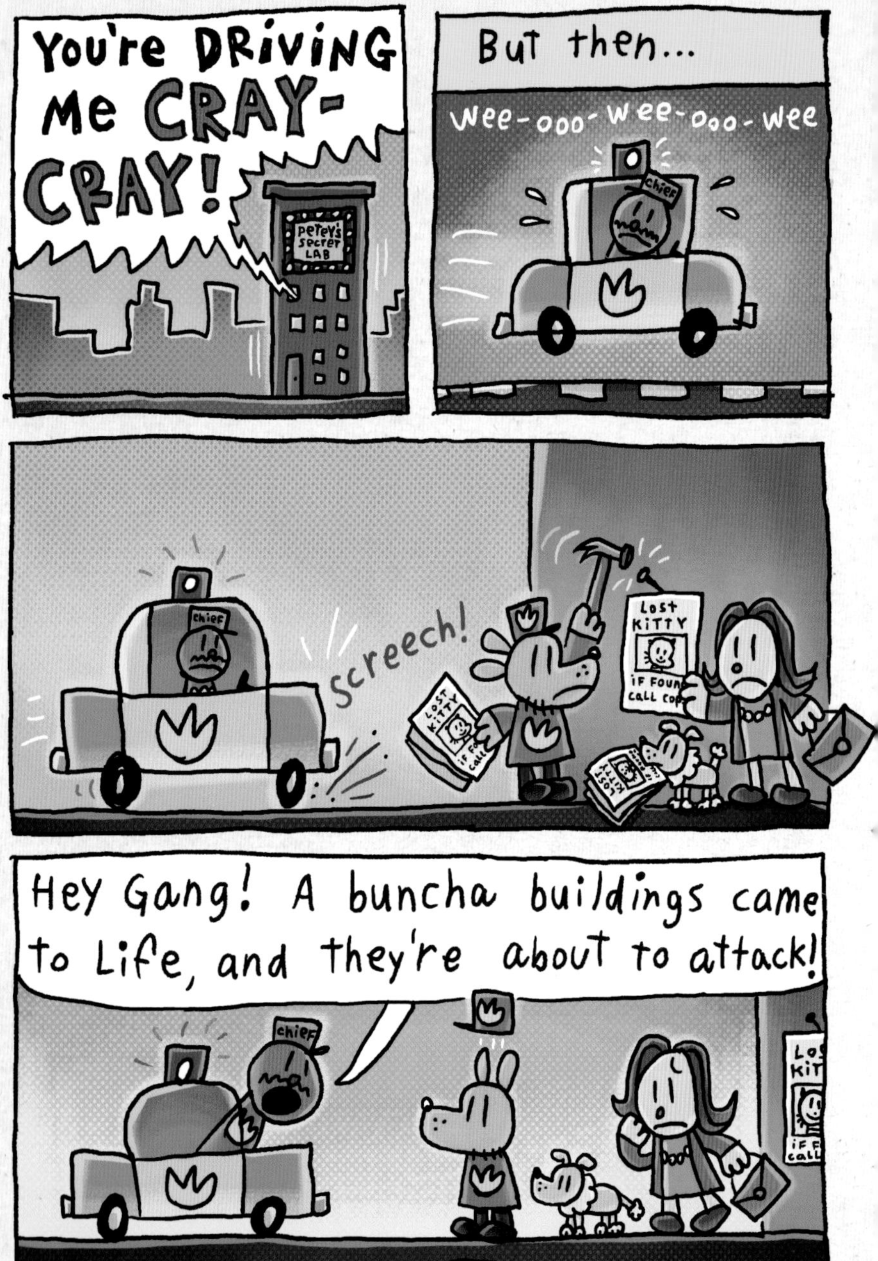
You're DRIVING Me CRAY-CRAY!
Petey's Secret LAB
But then...
Wee-ooo-Wee-ooo-Wee
Chief
Chief
Screech!
Lost Kitty
Lost Kitty If Found Call Cops
Hey Gang! A buncha buildings came to Life, and they're about to attack!
Chief

Quick, Chief. Grab the end of this dental floss...

... and tie it around that sign across the street.

TRIP

CRASH

FrencH
SaLad
Dressing

DoG Man and ZuZu
watched the action...

Slippery
When
wet

...then they got an
idea of their own!

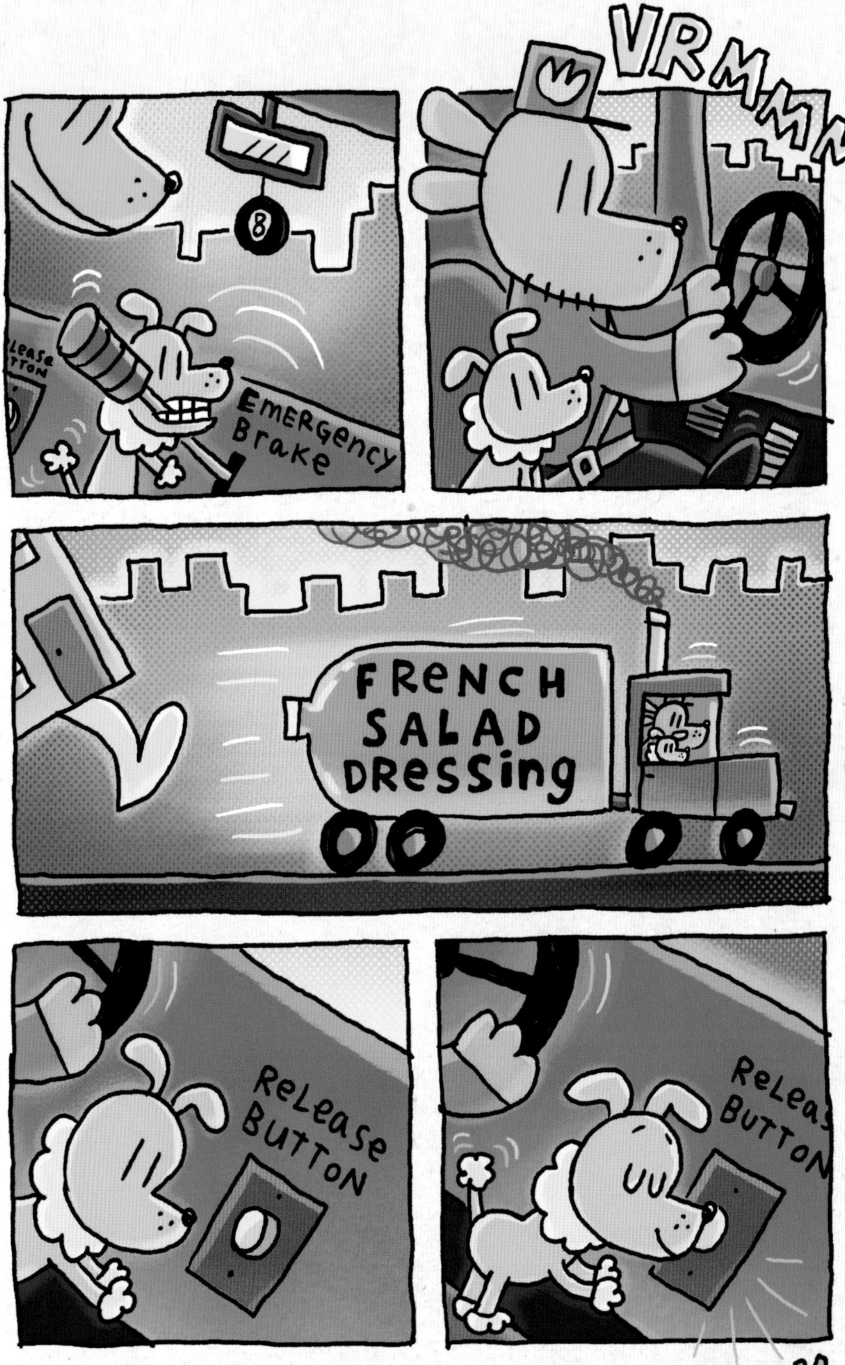
EMERGENCY Brake
VRMMMM
FRENCH SALAD DRESSING
RELEASE BUTTON
CLICK

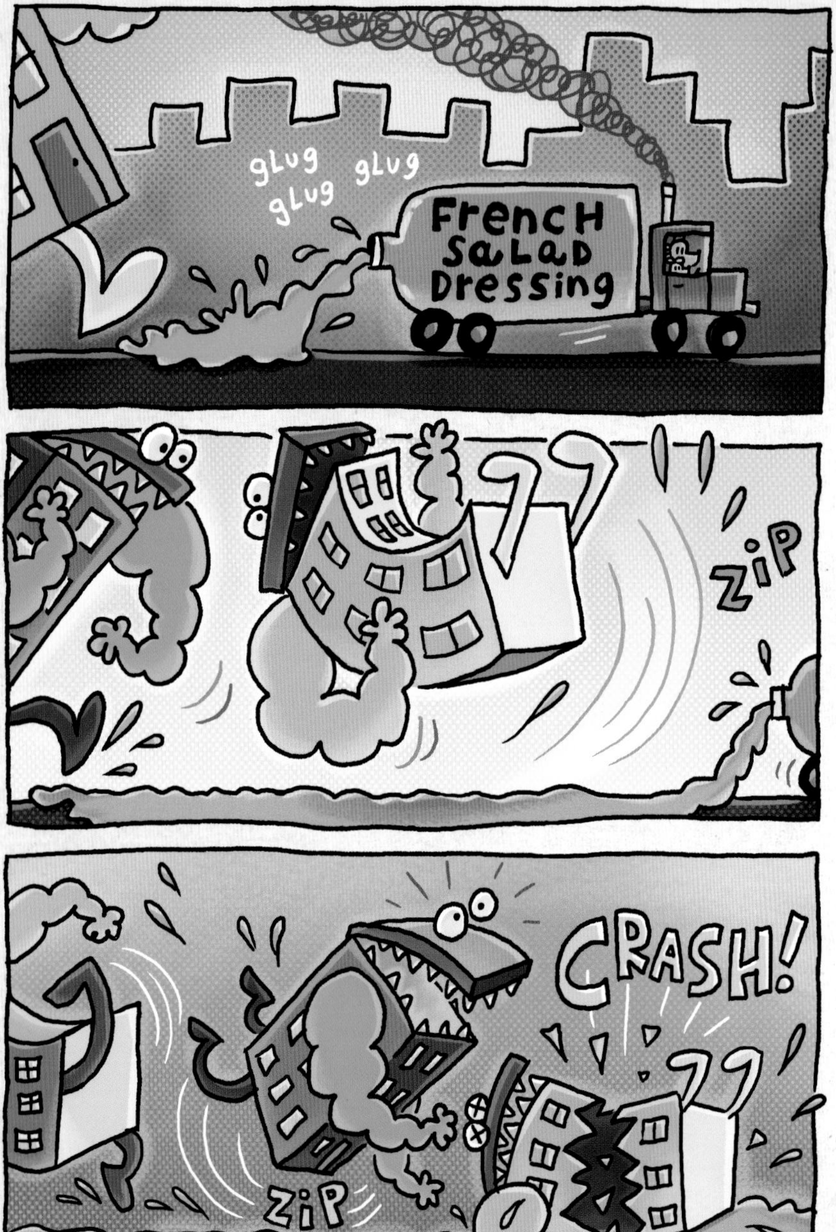
glug glug glug
French Salad Dressing
ZiP
CRASH!
ZiP

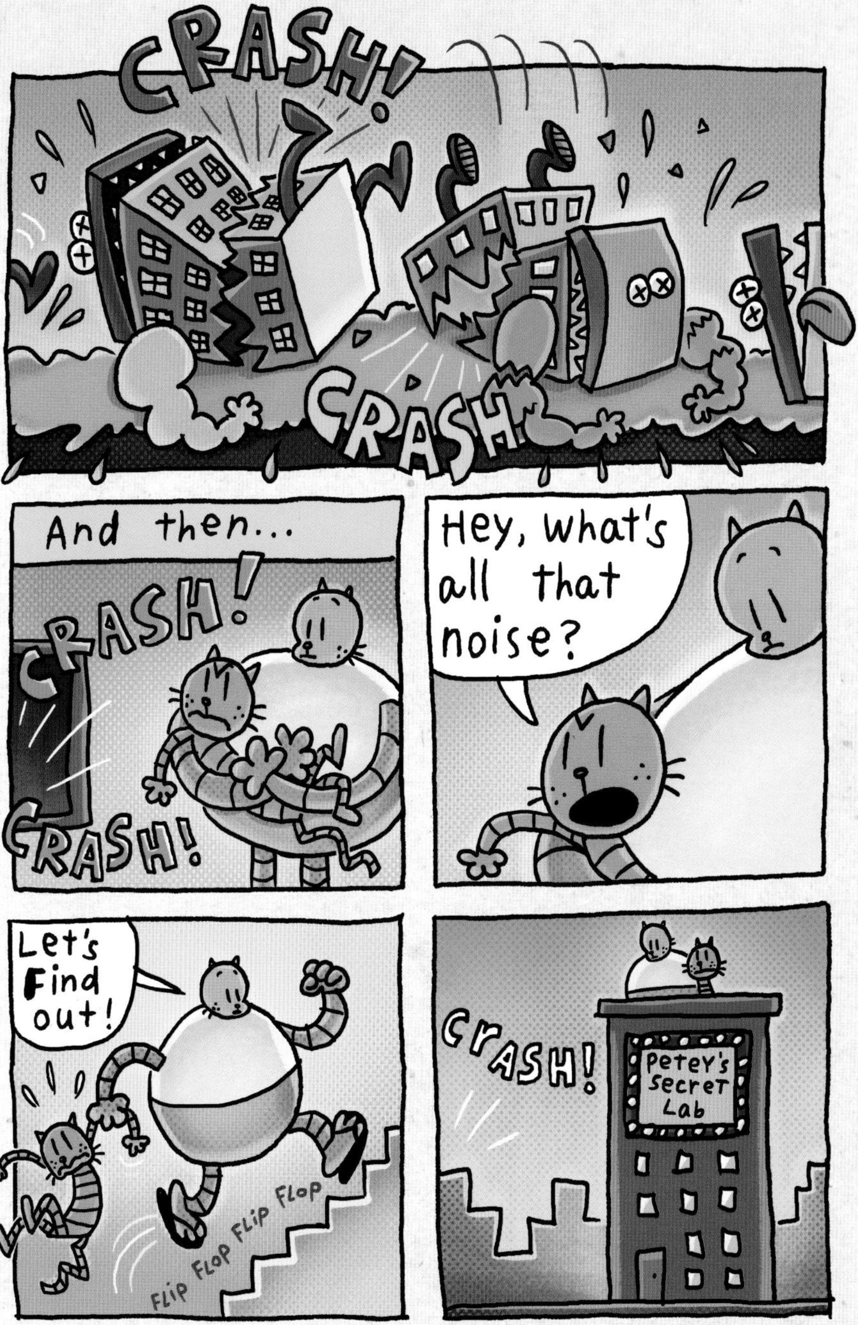
CRASH!
CRASH
And then...
CRASH!
CRASH!
Hey, what's all that noise?
Let's Find out!
FLIP FLOP FLIP FLOP
CRASH!
Petey's Secret Lab

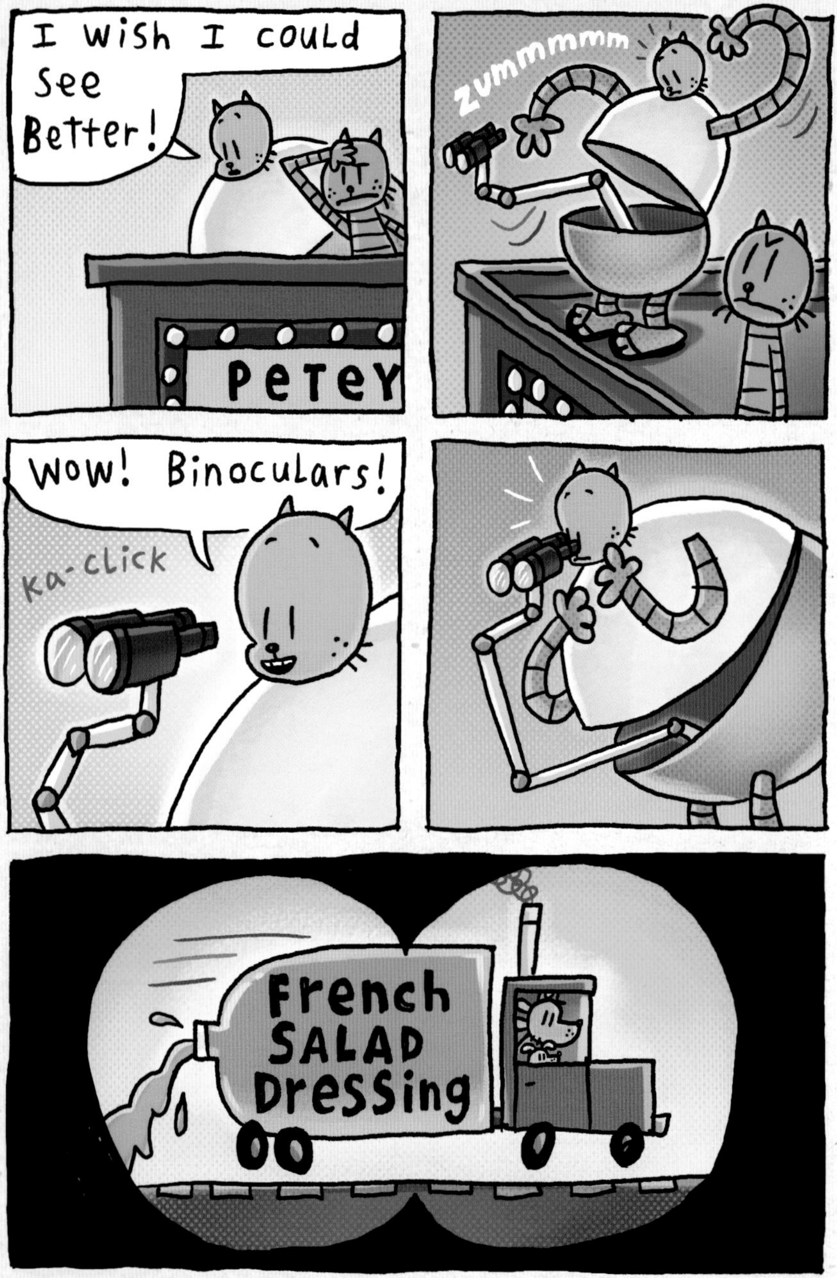
I wish I could see Better!
PETEY
ZUMMMMM
WOW! Binoculars!
KA-CLICK
French SALAD Dressing

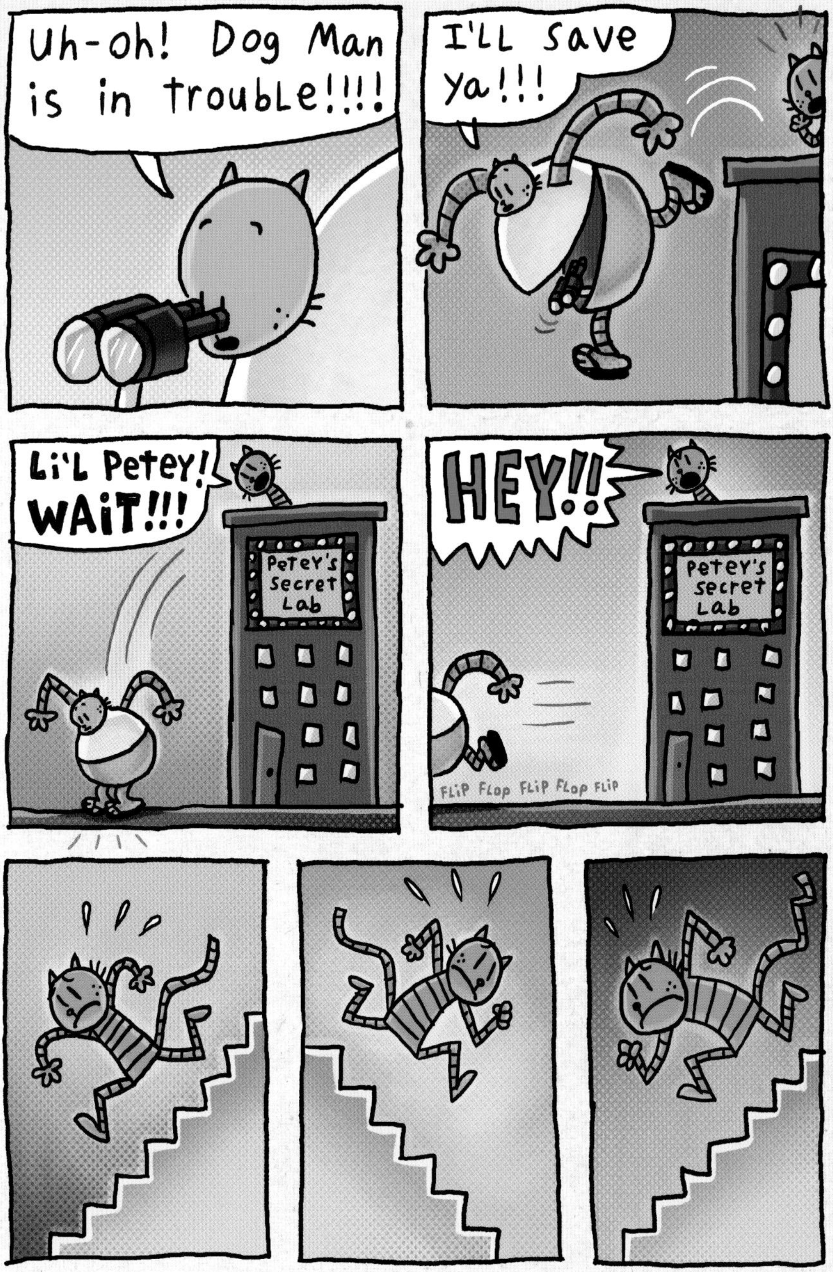

Uh-oh! Dog Man is in trouble!!!!
I'LL save ya!!!
Li'L Petey! WAIT!!!
Petey's Secret Lab
HEY!!
Petey's Secret Lab
FLIP FLOP FLIP FLOP FLIP

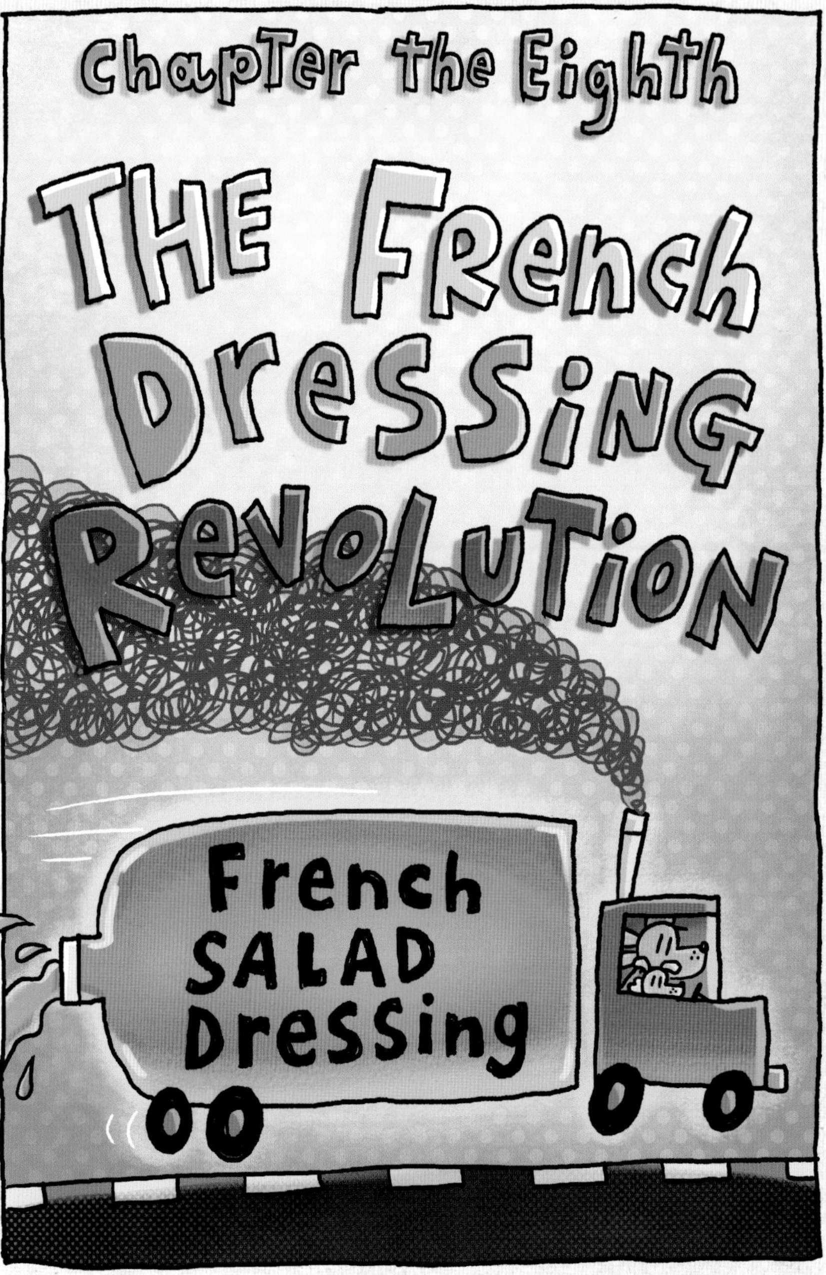
Chapter the Eighth
THE French Dressing Revolution
French SALAD Dressing

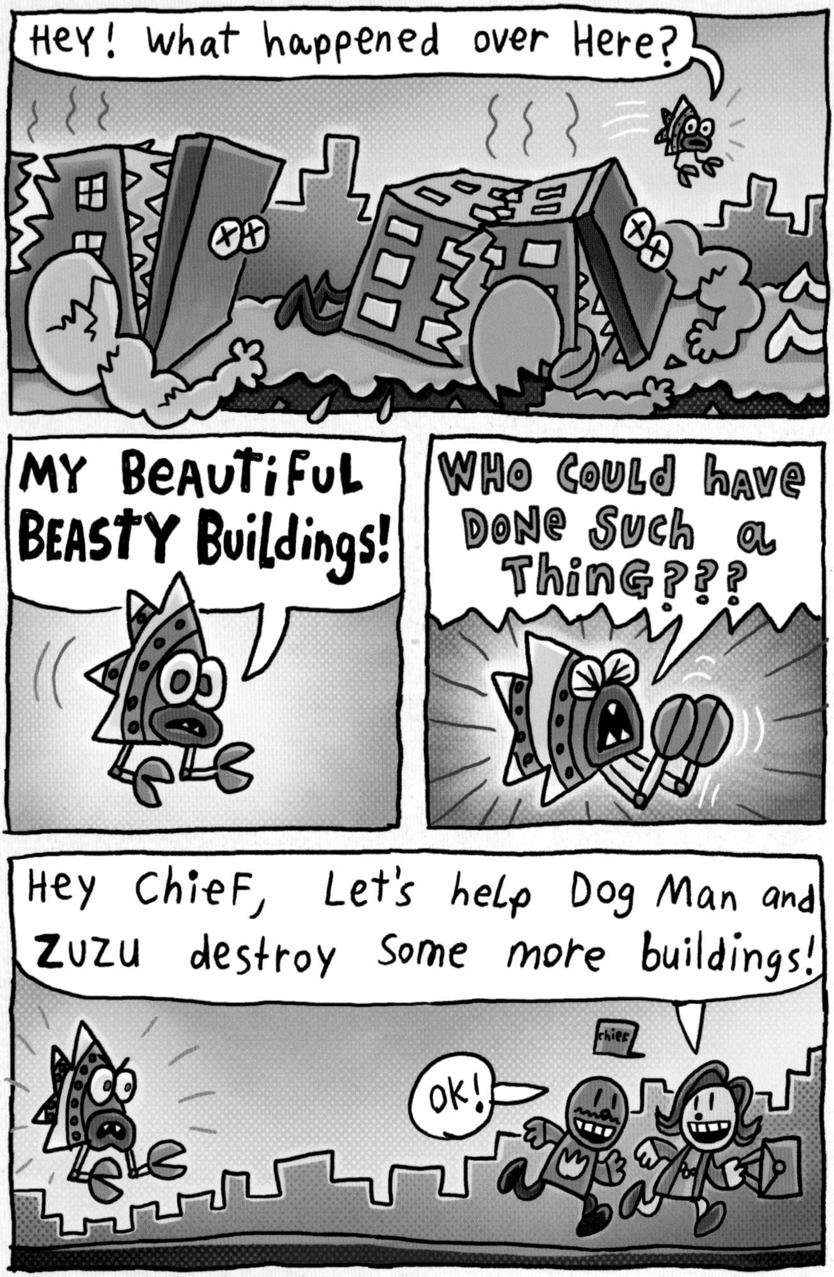
Hey! What happened over Here?
MY BeAUTiFUL BEASTY Buildings!
WHO COULD have DONe SUch a THinG???
Hey Chief, Let's help Dog Man and ZUZU destroy Some more buildings!
OK!
chief

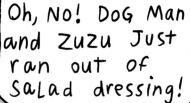

Oh, No! Dog Man and Zuzu just ran out of salad dressing!

But that's not the worst of their problems!

LOOK OUT, DOG MAN AND ZUZU!

FRENCH SALAD DRESSING

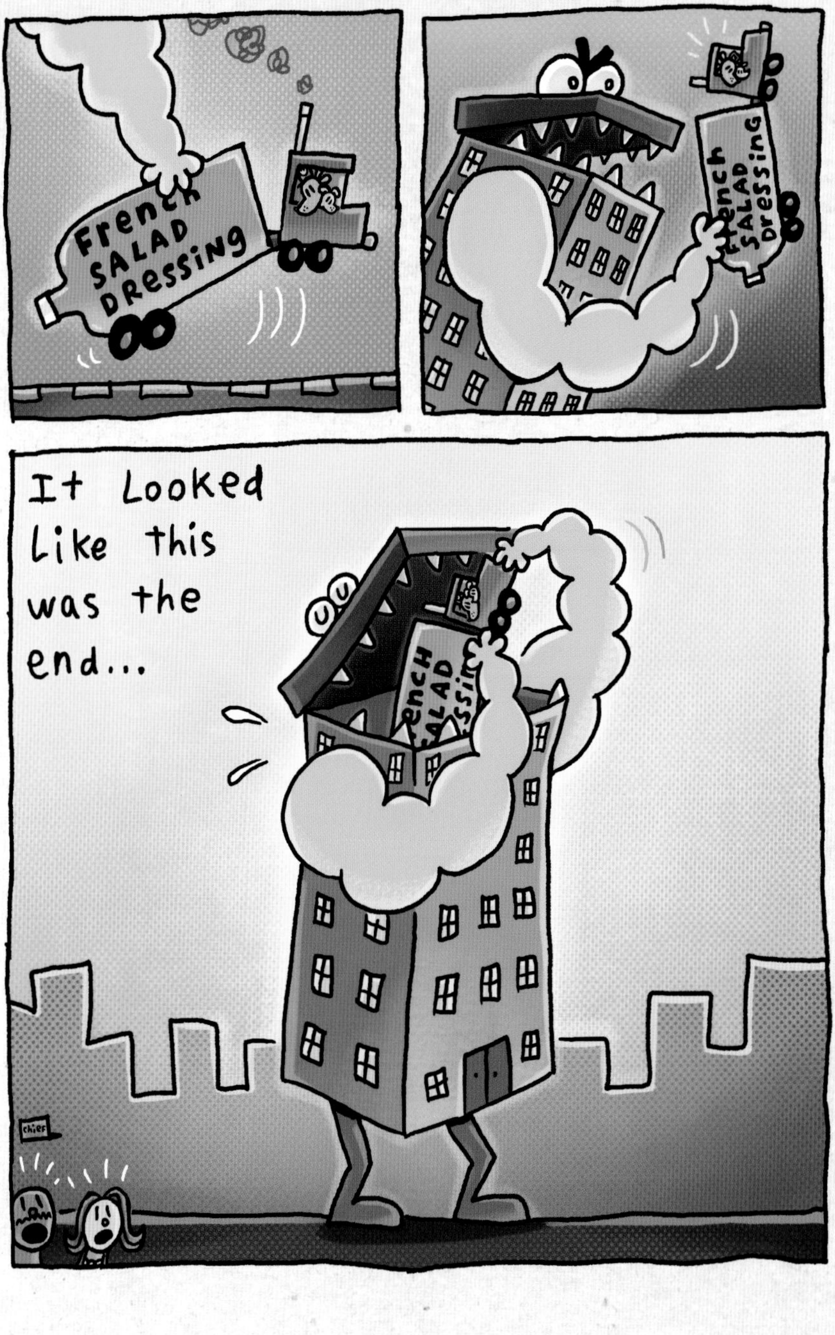
French SALAD DRESSING
French SALAD DRESSING
It Looked like this was the end...
chief

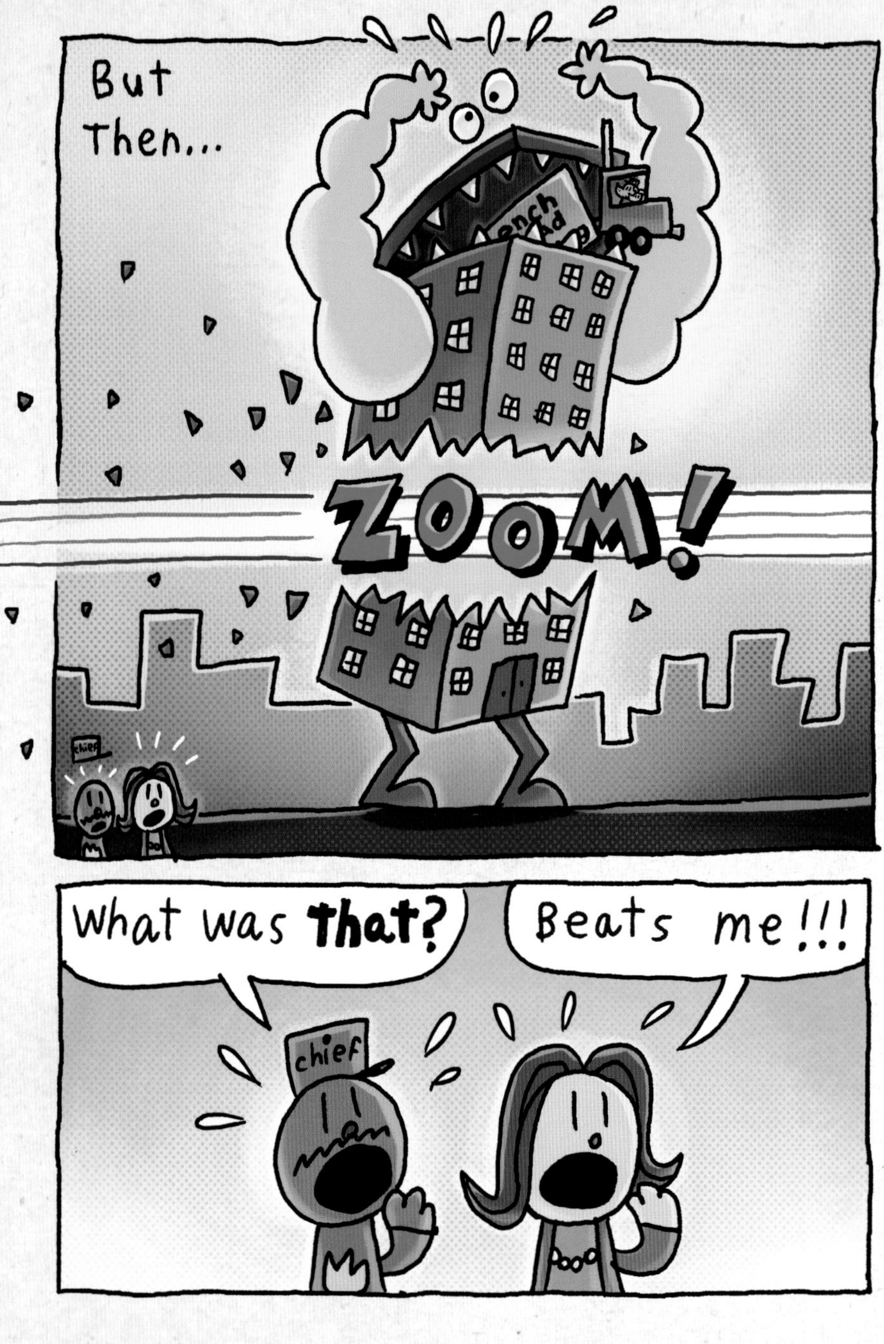
But Then...
ZOOM!
chief
What was **that?**
Beats me!!!

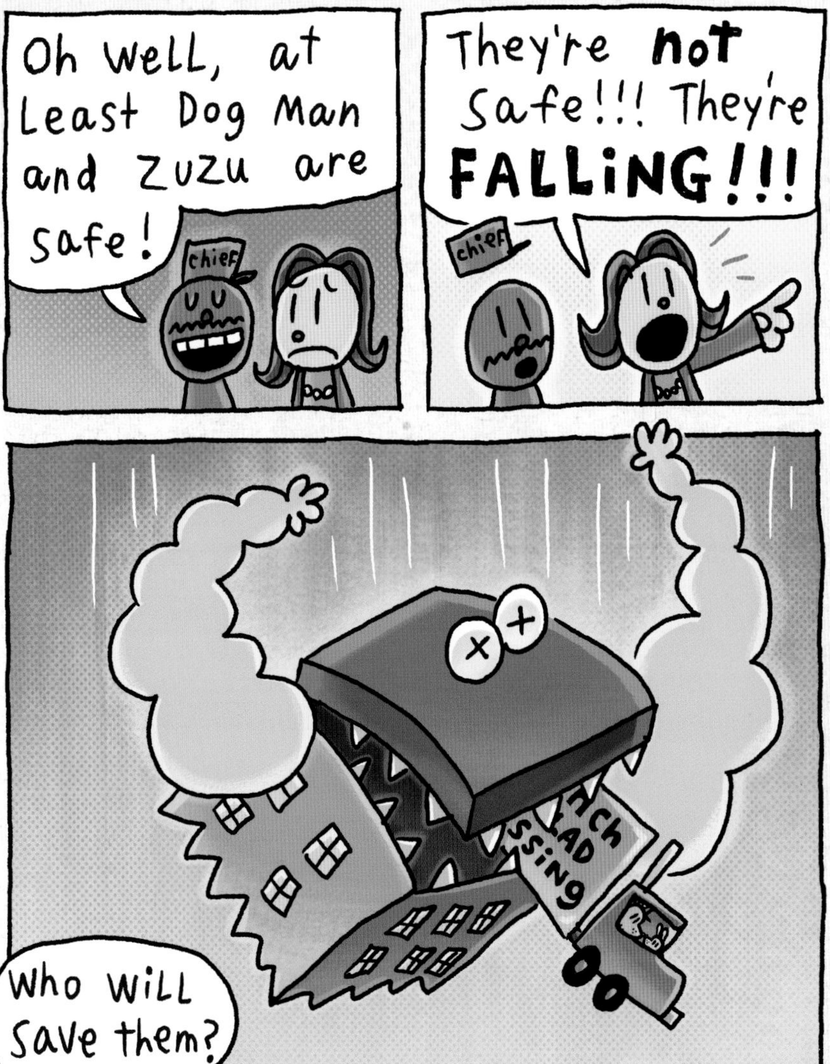
Oh WeLL, at Least Dog Man and ZUZU are safe!
They're **not** Safe!!! They're **FALLiNG!!!**
Who WiLL save them?

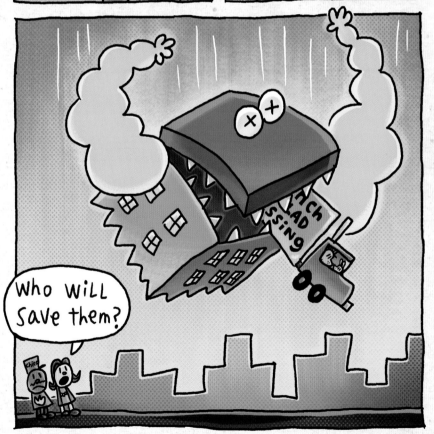

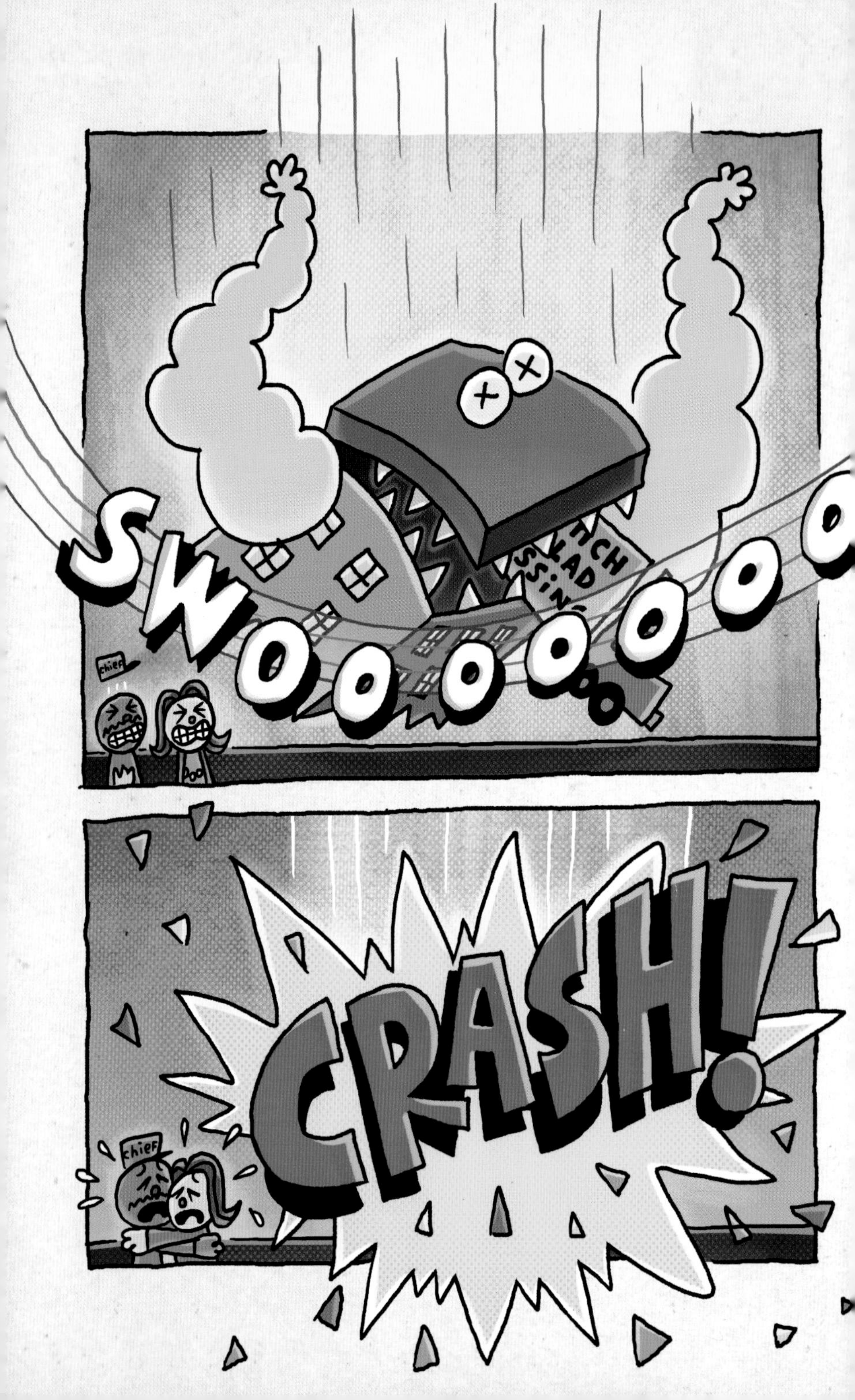

SWOOOOOOO
chief
CRASH!
chief

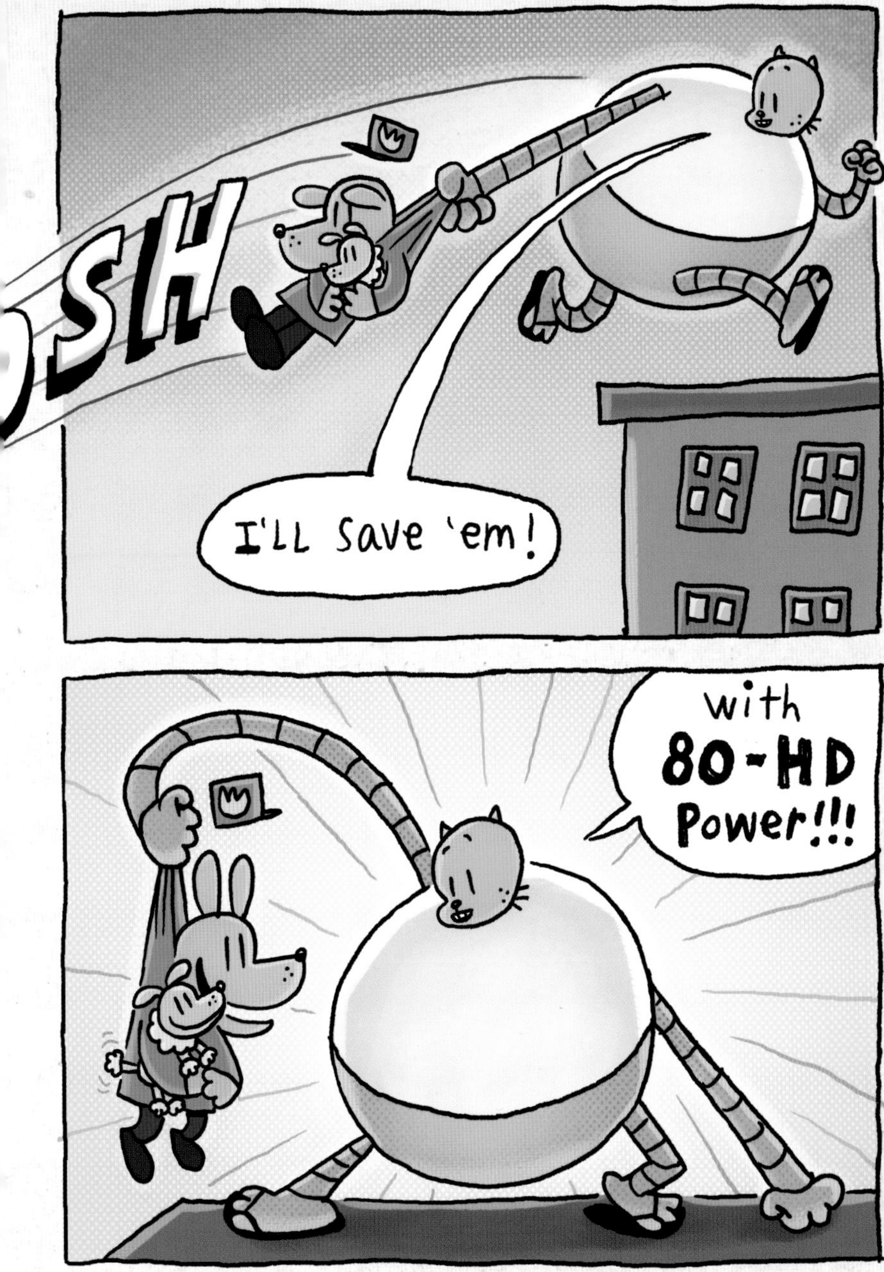
SH
I'LL Save 'em!
with
80-HD
Power!!!

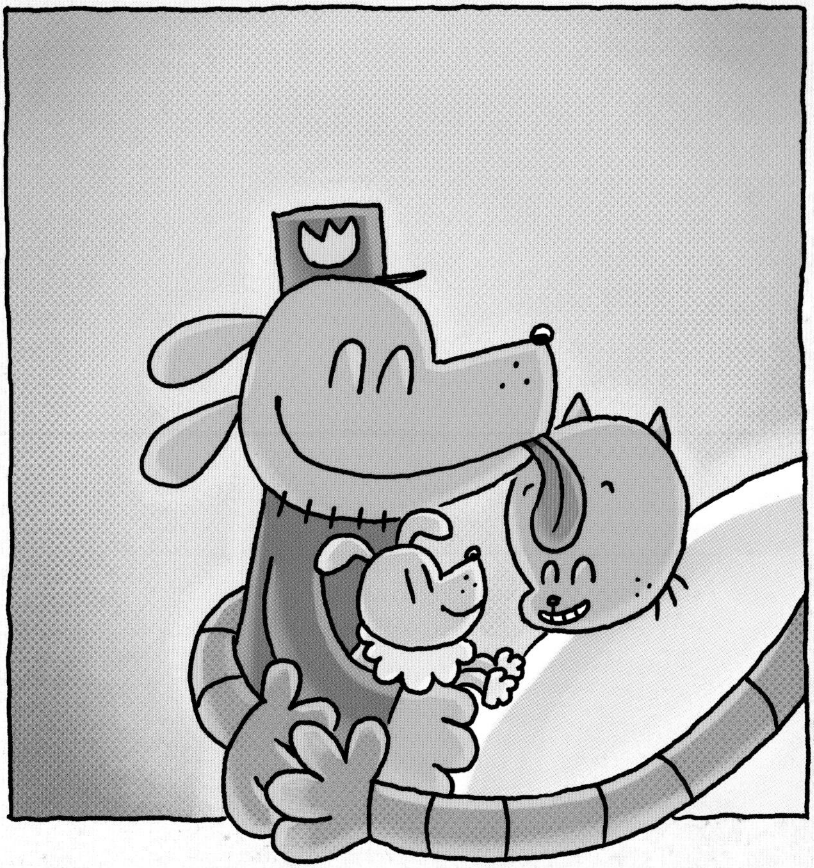

He takes a Lickin'
and keeps on Tickin'!!!

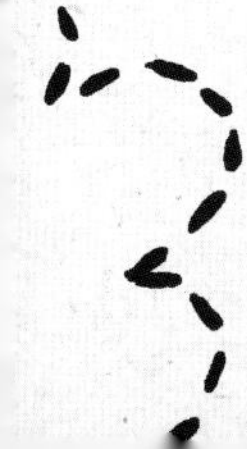

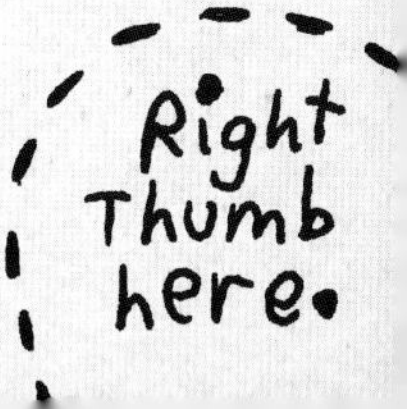
Right
Thumb
here.

He takes a Lickin'
and Keeps on Tickin'!!!

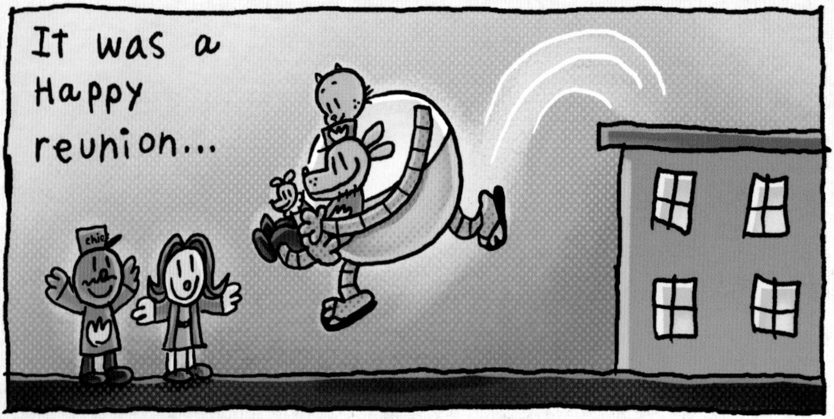
It was a Happy reunion...

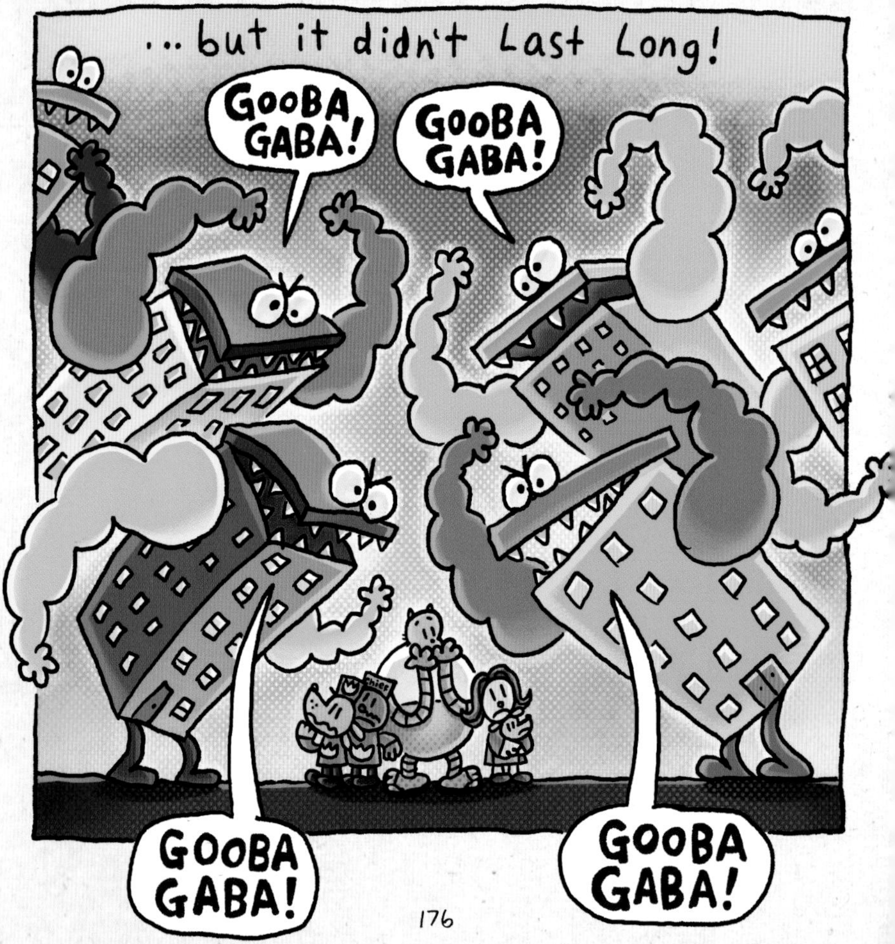
...but it didn't Last Long!
GOOBA GABA!
GOOBA GABA!
GOOBA GABA!
GOOBA GABA!

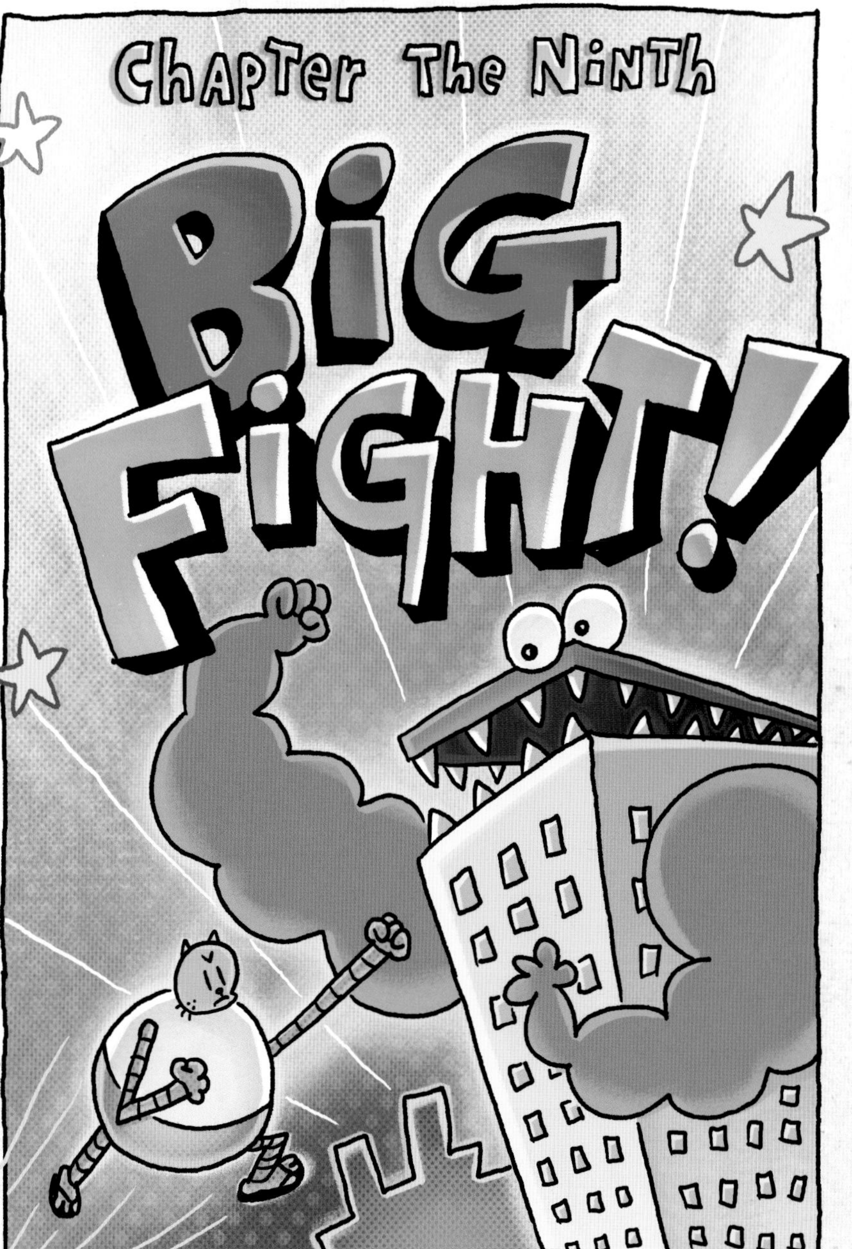
Chapter The Ninth
BIG FIGHT!

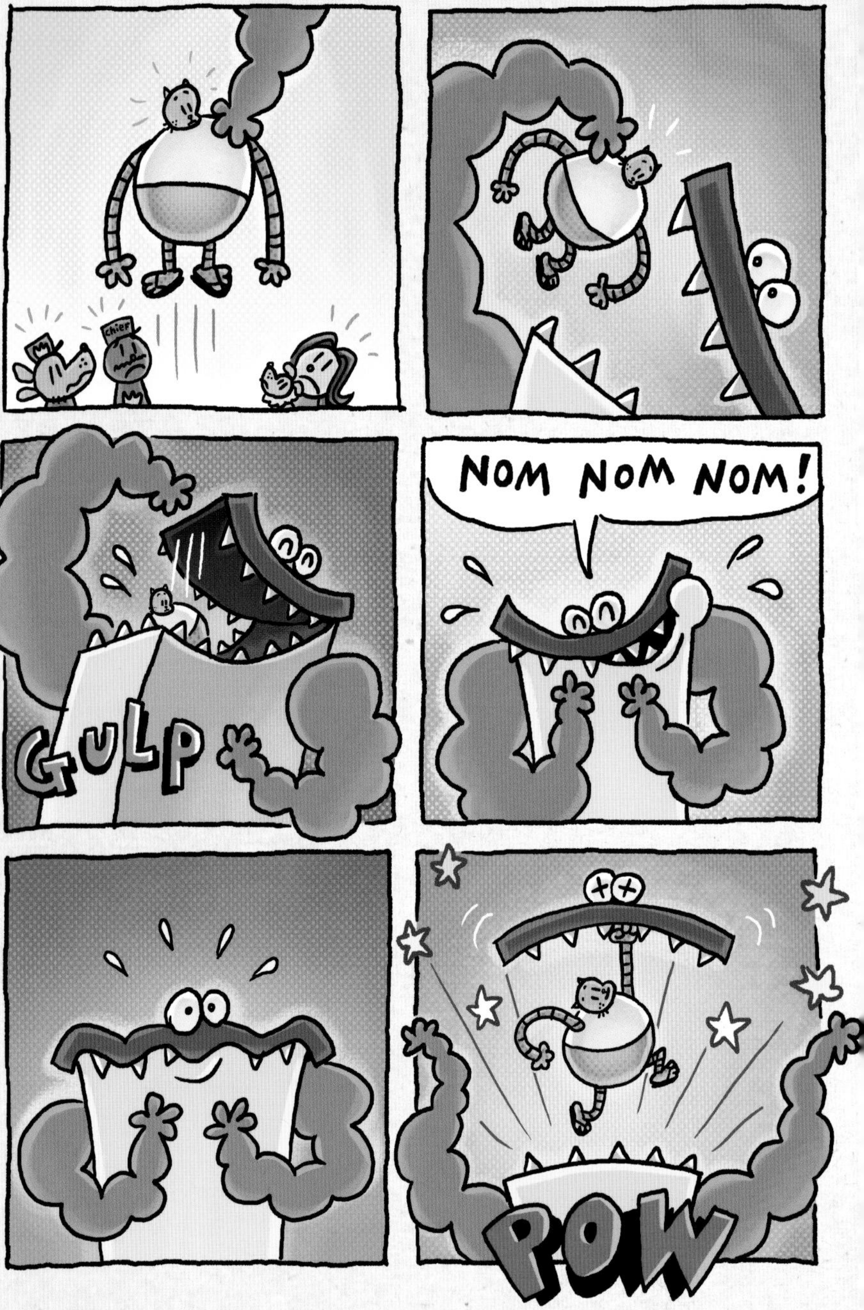
Chief
GULP
NOM NOM NOM!
POW

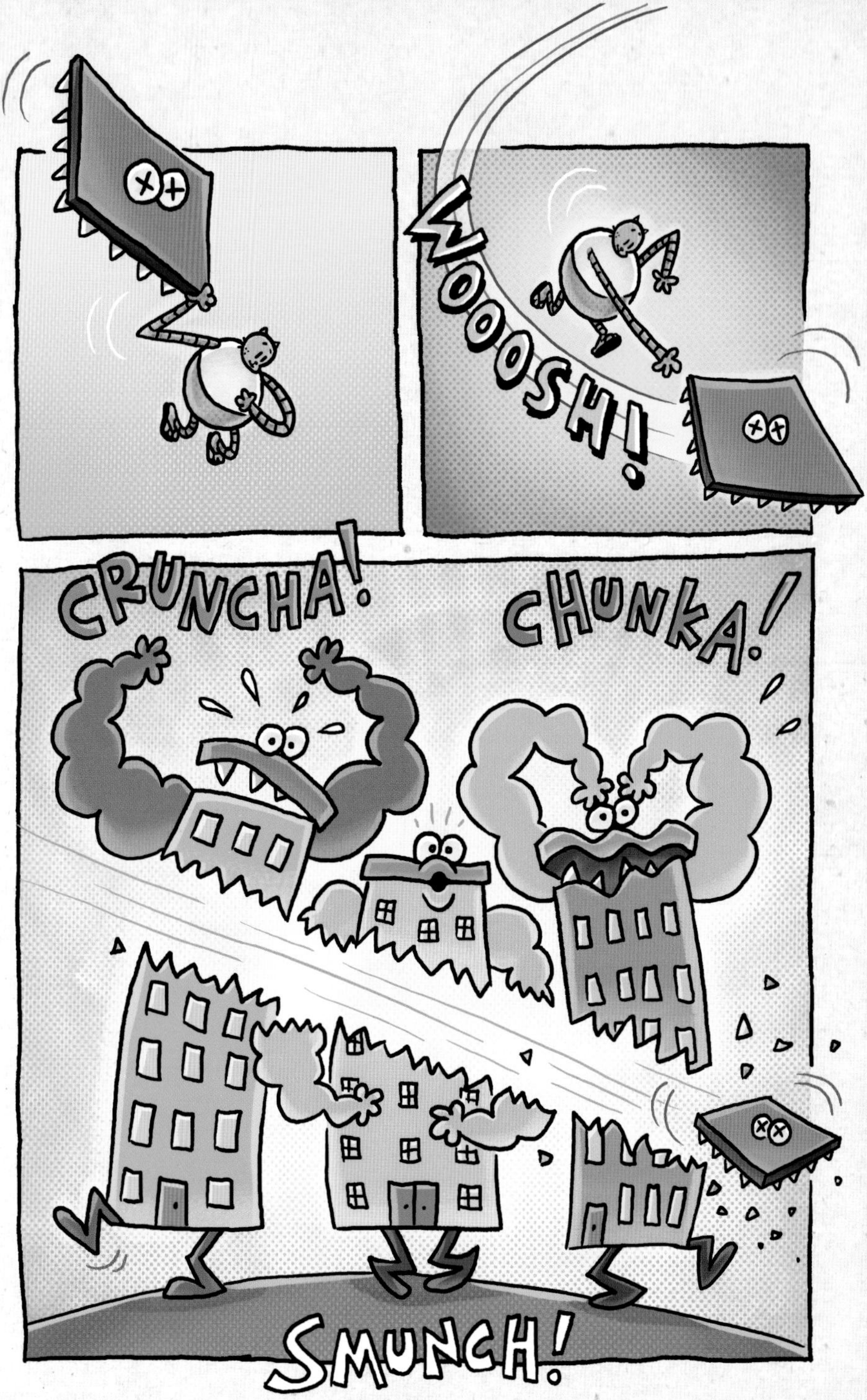
WOOOSH!
CRUNCHA!
CHUNKA!
SMUNCH!

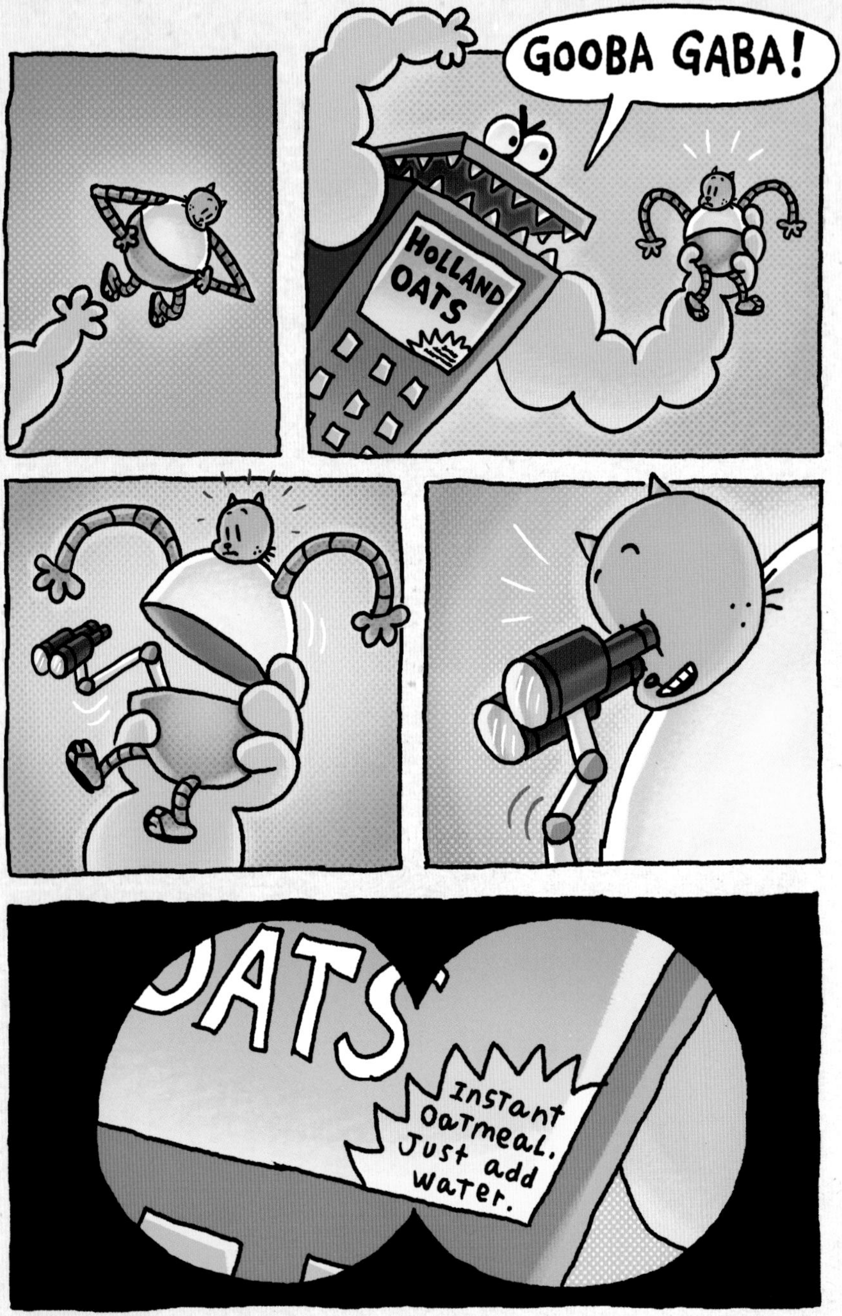
GOOBA GABA!
HOLLAND OATS
OATS
Instant Oatmeal. Just add water.

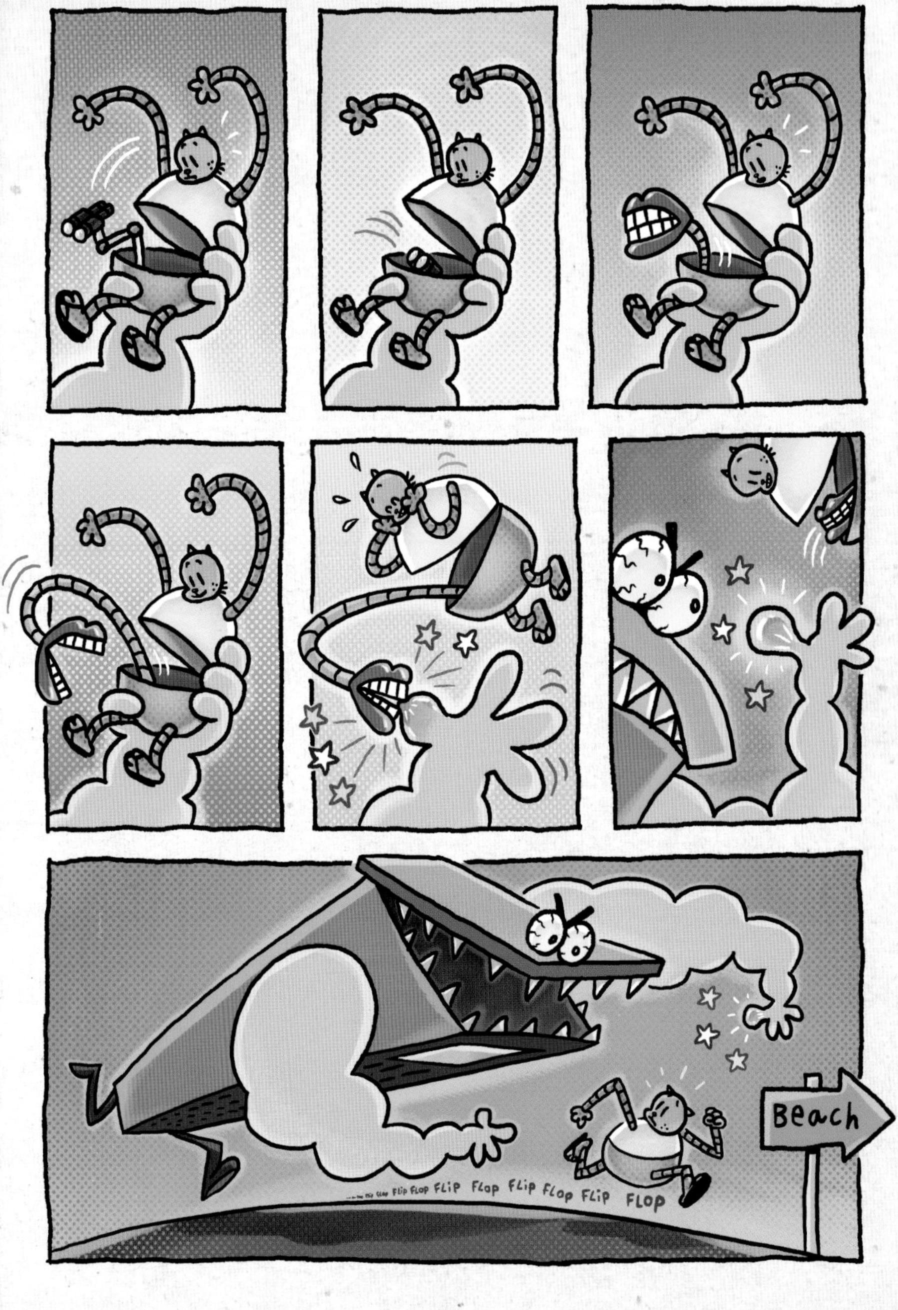
FLIP FLOP FLIP FLOP FLIP FLOP FLIP FLOP
Beach

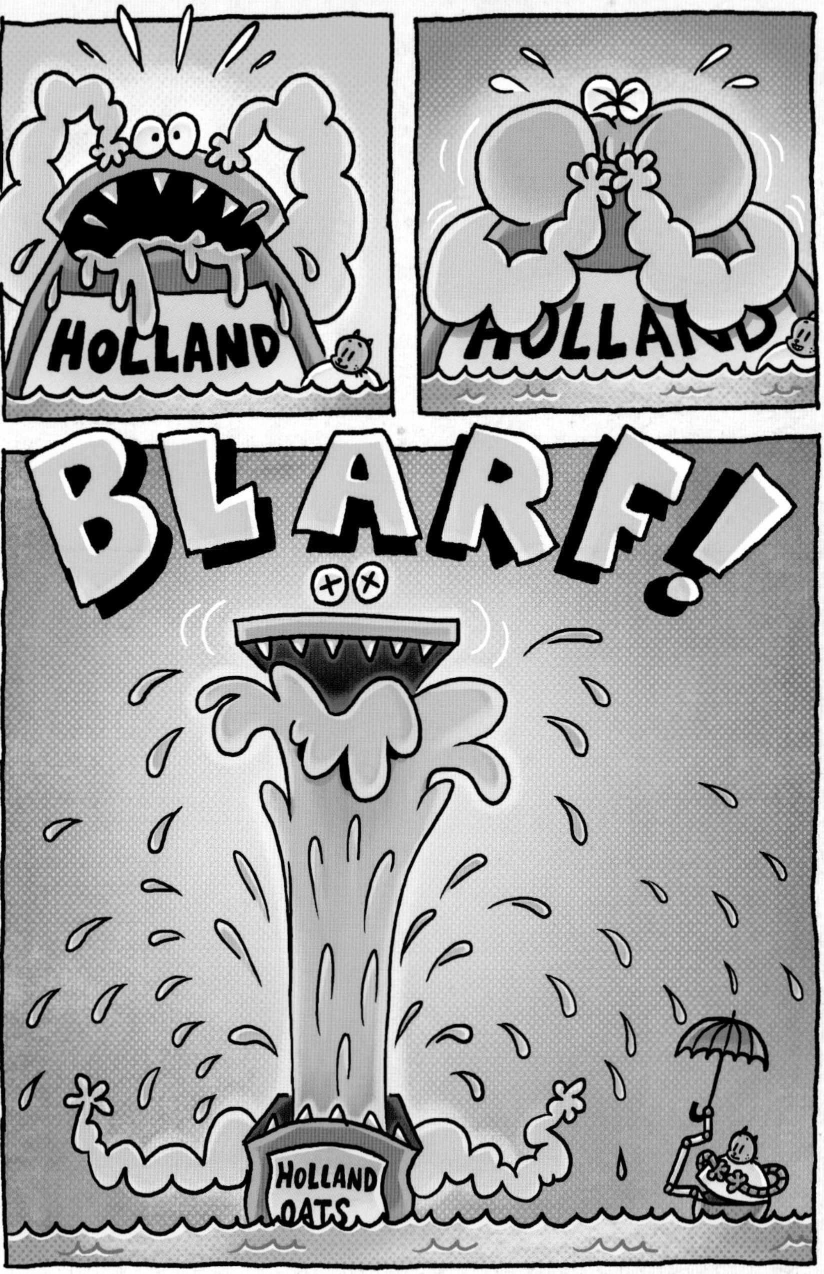
HOLLAND
HOLLAND
BLARF!
HOLLAND
OATS

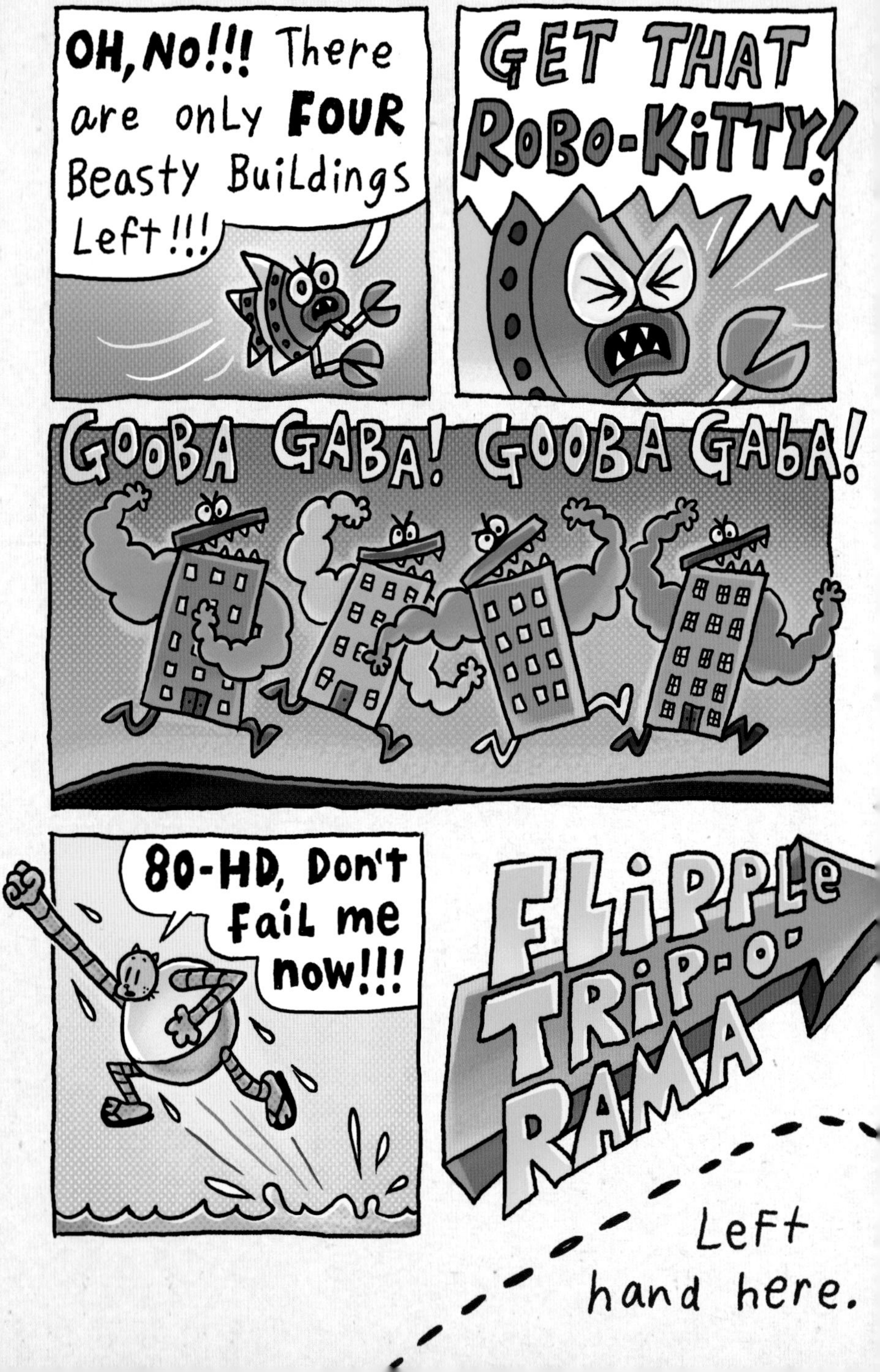

OH, NO!!! There are onLy FOUR Beasty BuiLdings Left!!!
GET THAT RoBo-KiTTY!
GooBA GABA! GooBA GABA!
80-HD, Don't FaiL me now!!!
FLiPPLe TRiP-o-RAMA
LeFt hand here.

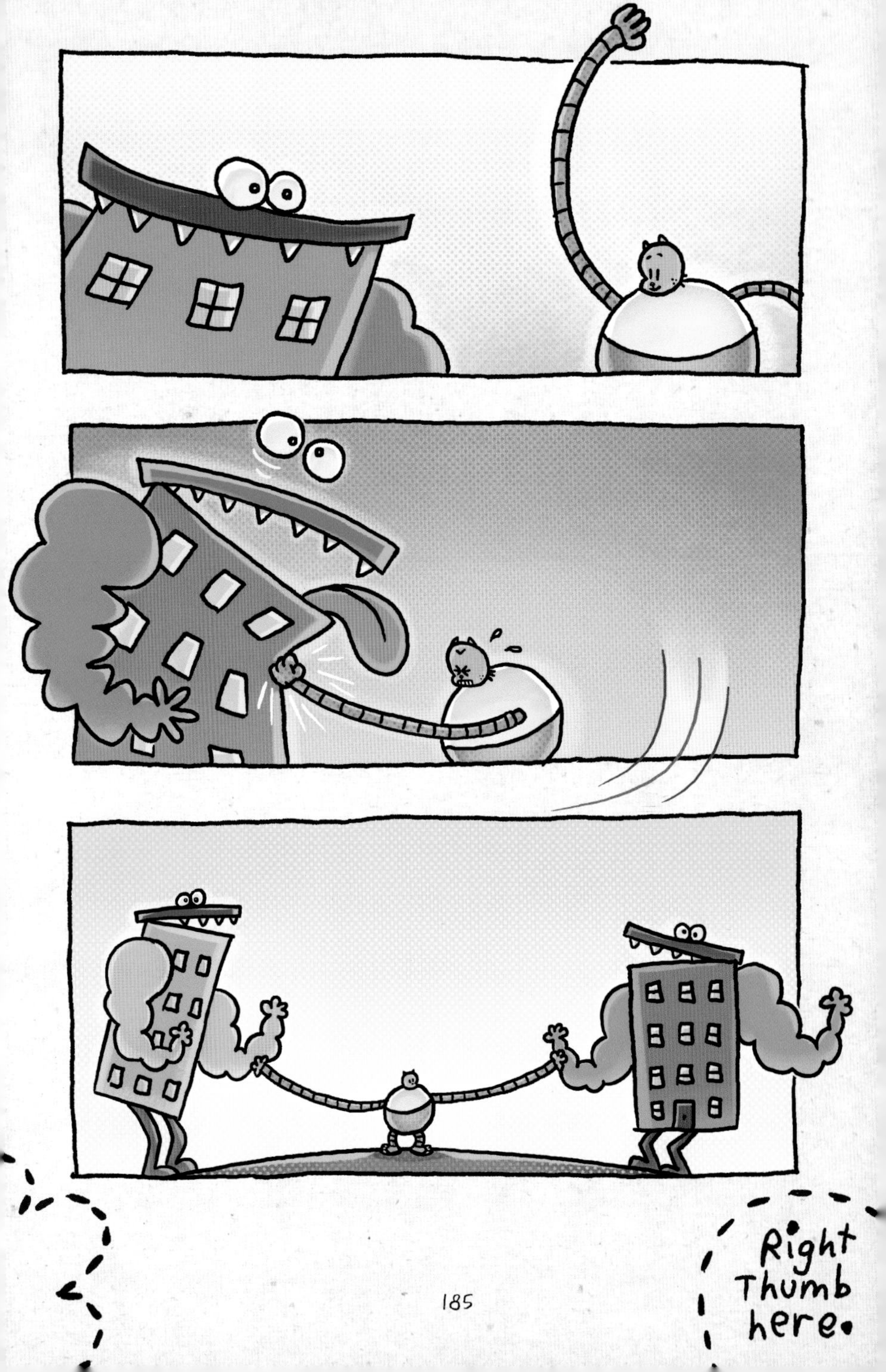

Right
Thumb
here.

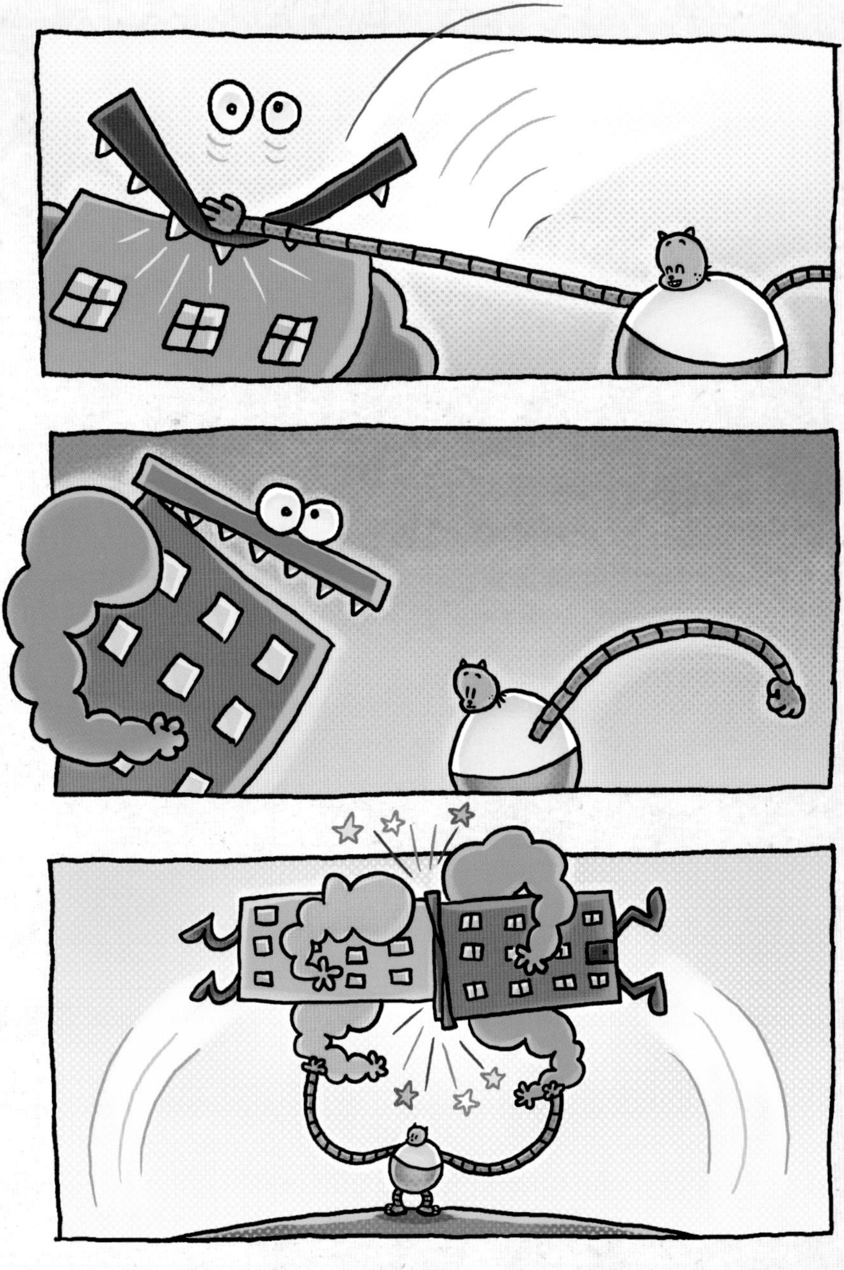

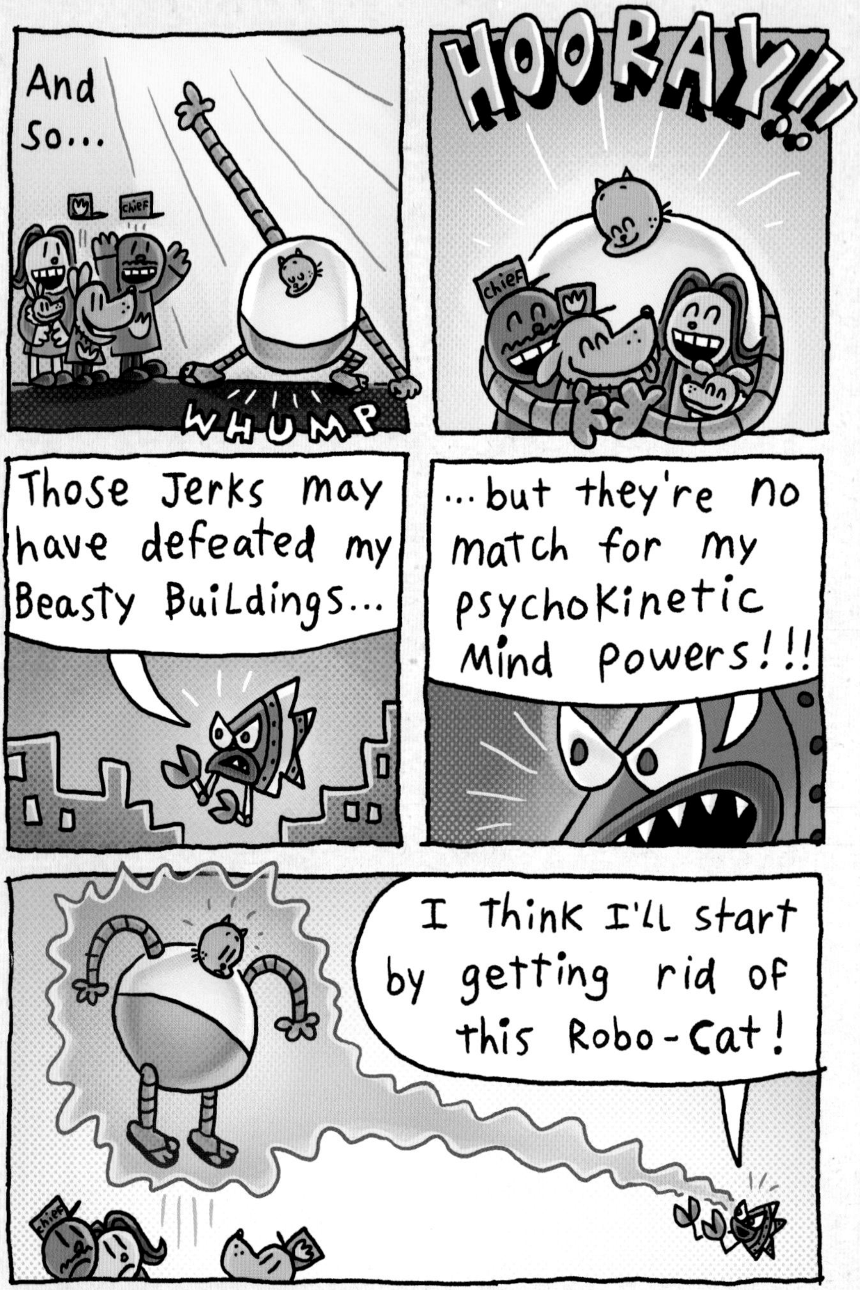
And so...
CHIEF
WHUMP
HOORAY!!!
CHIEF
Those Jerks may have defeated my Beasty Buildings...
...but they're no match for my psychoKinetic Mind powers!!!
I think I'll start by getting rid of this Robo-Cat!
CHIEF

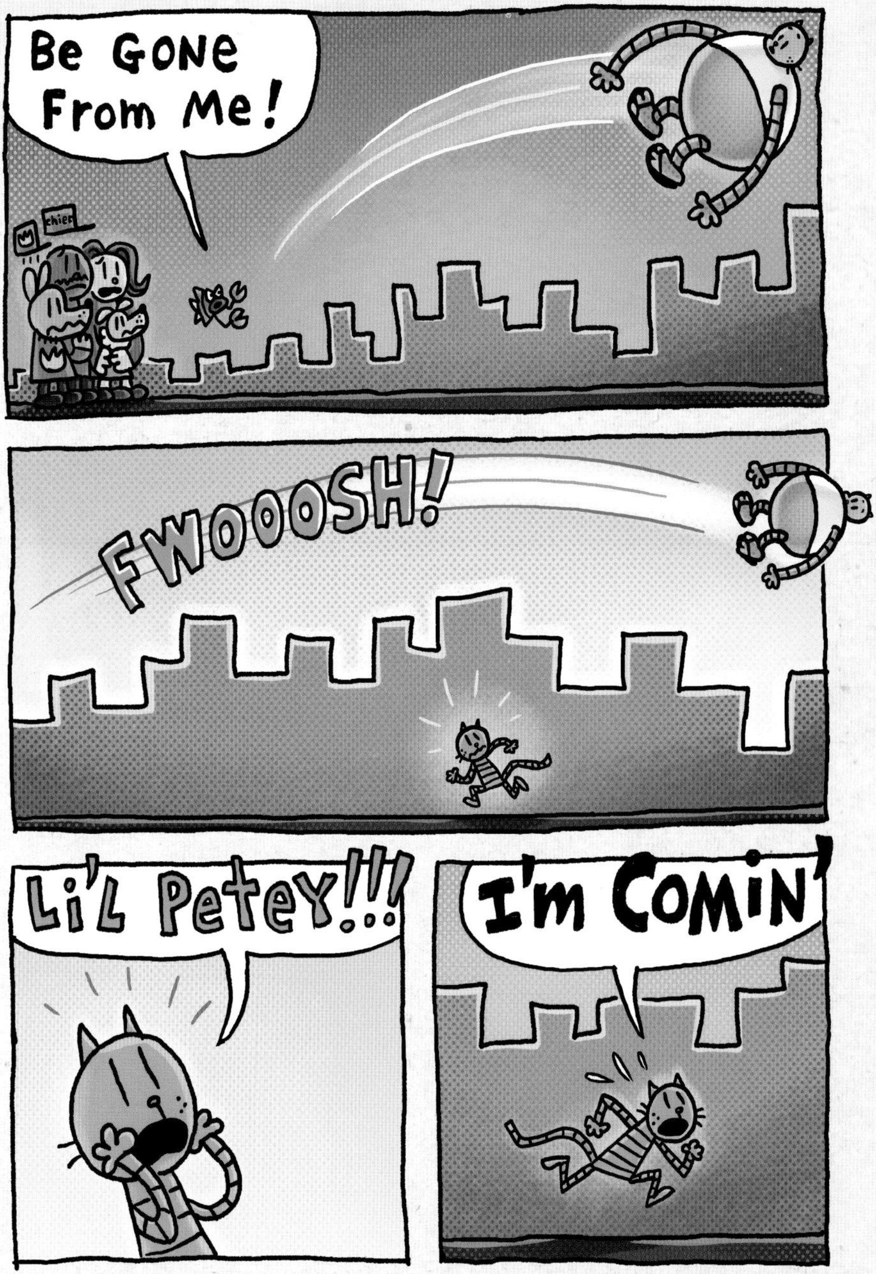
Be Gone From Me!
Chief
FWOOOSH!
Li'l Petey!!!
I'm Comin'

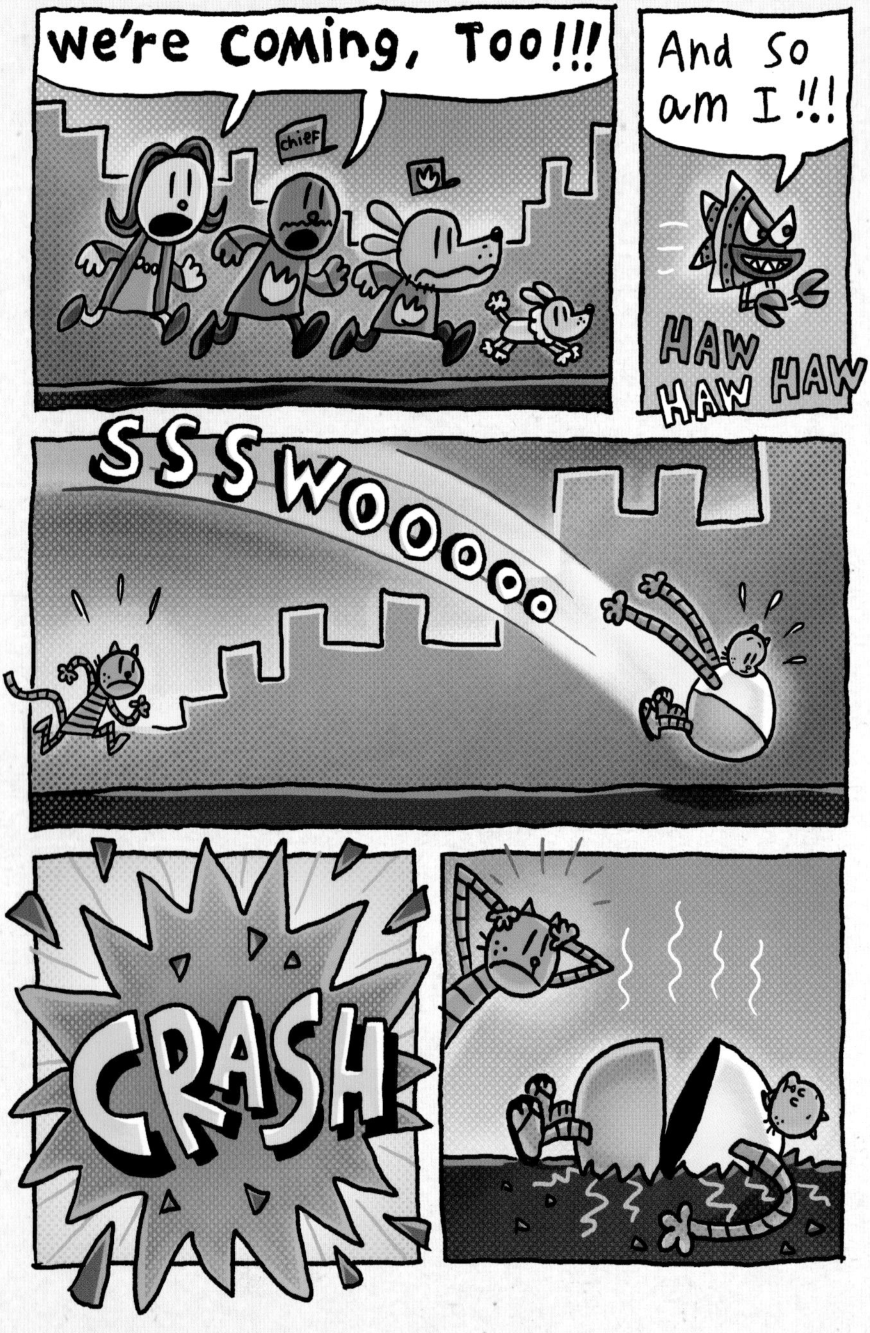
We're Coming, Too!!!
Chief
And So am I!!!
HAW HAW HAW HAW
SSSWOOOOOO
CRASH

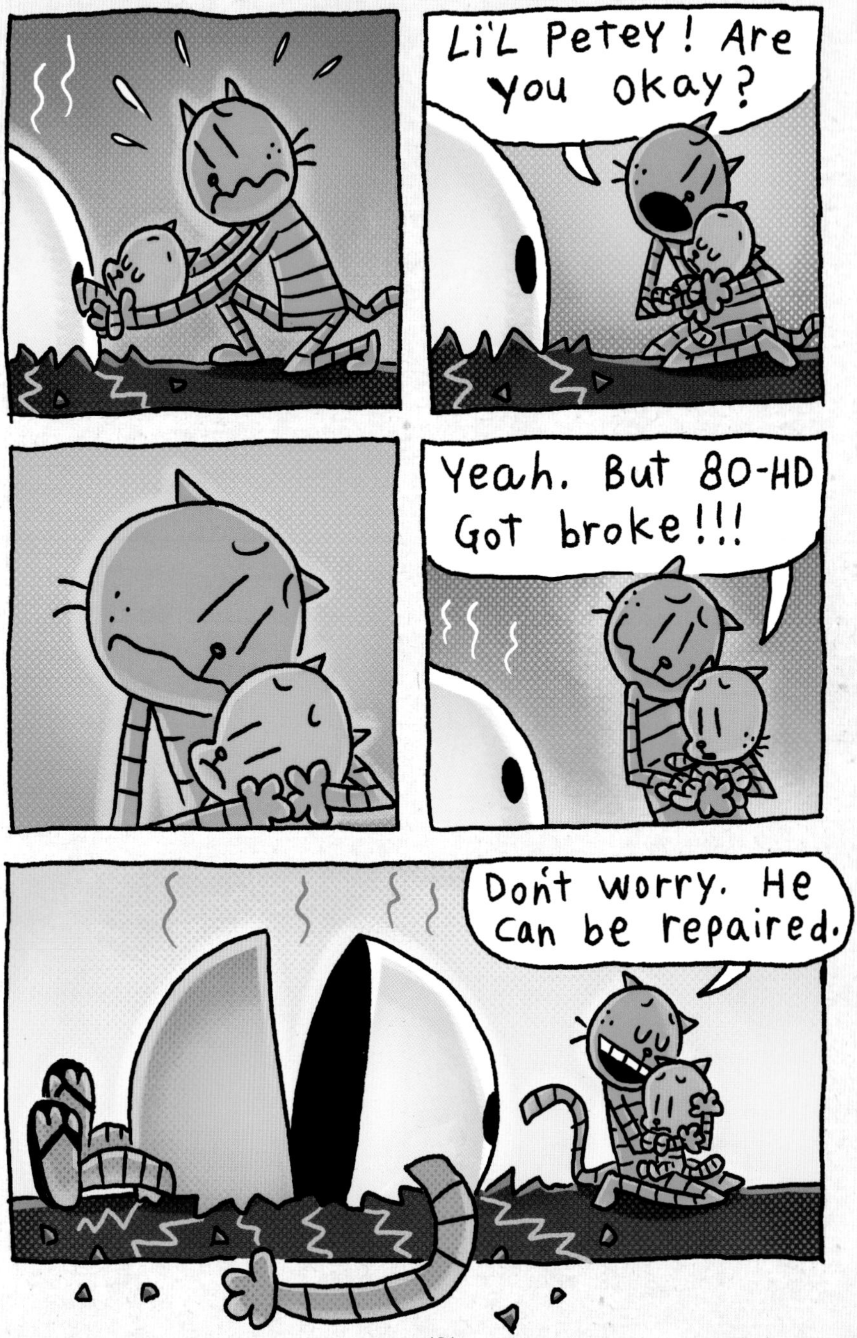
Li'L Petey! Are you okay?
Yeah. But 80-HD Got broke!!!
Don't worry. He can be repaired.

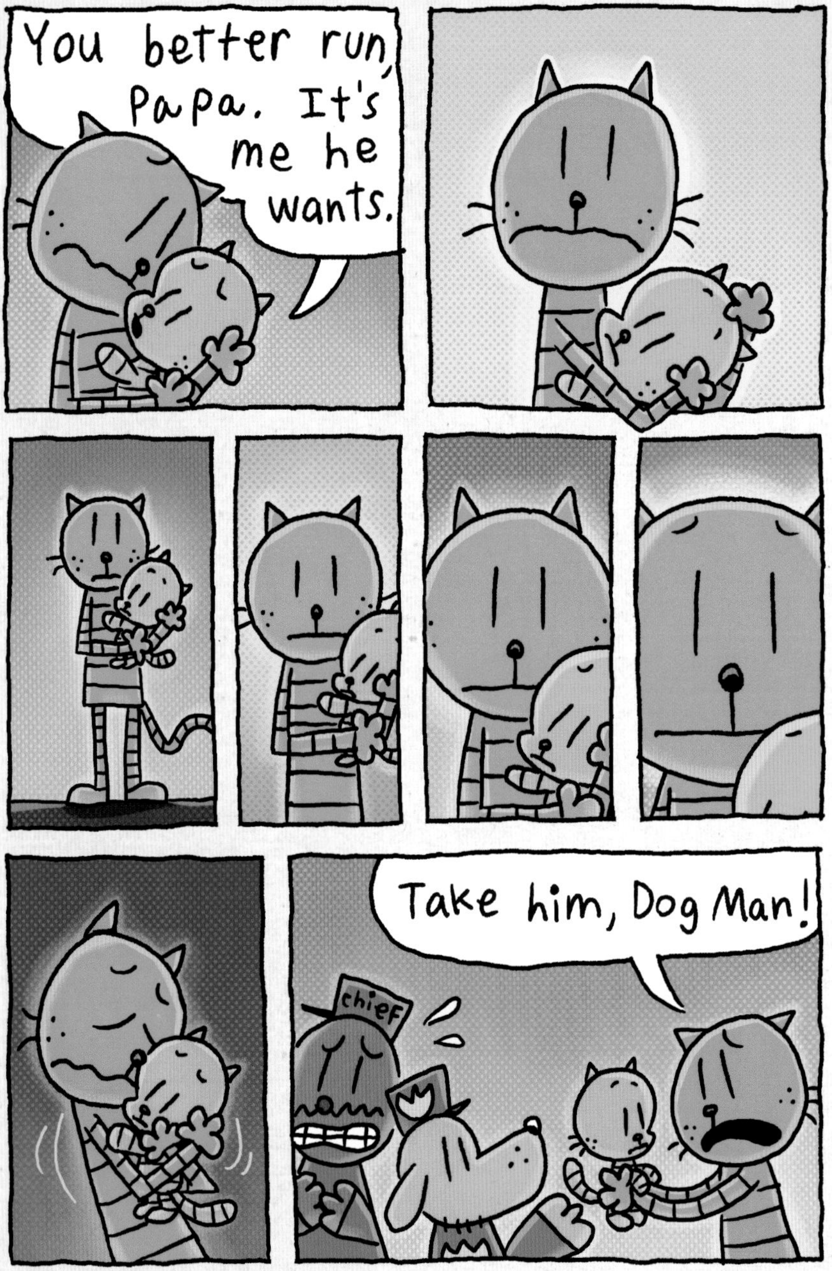
You better run, Papa. It's me he wants.
Take him, Dog Man!
chief

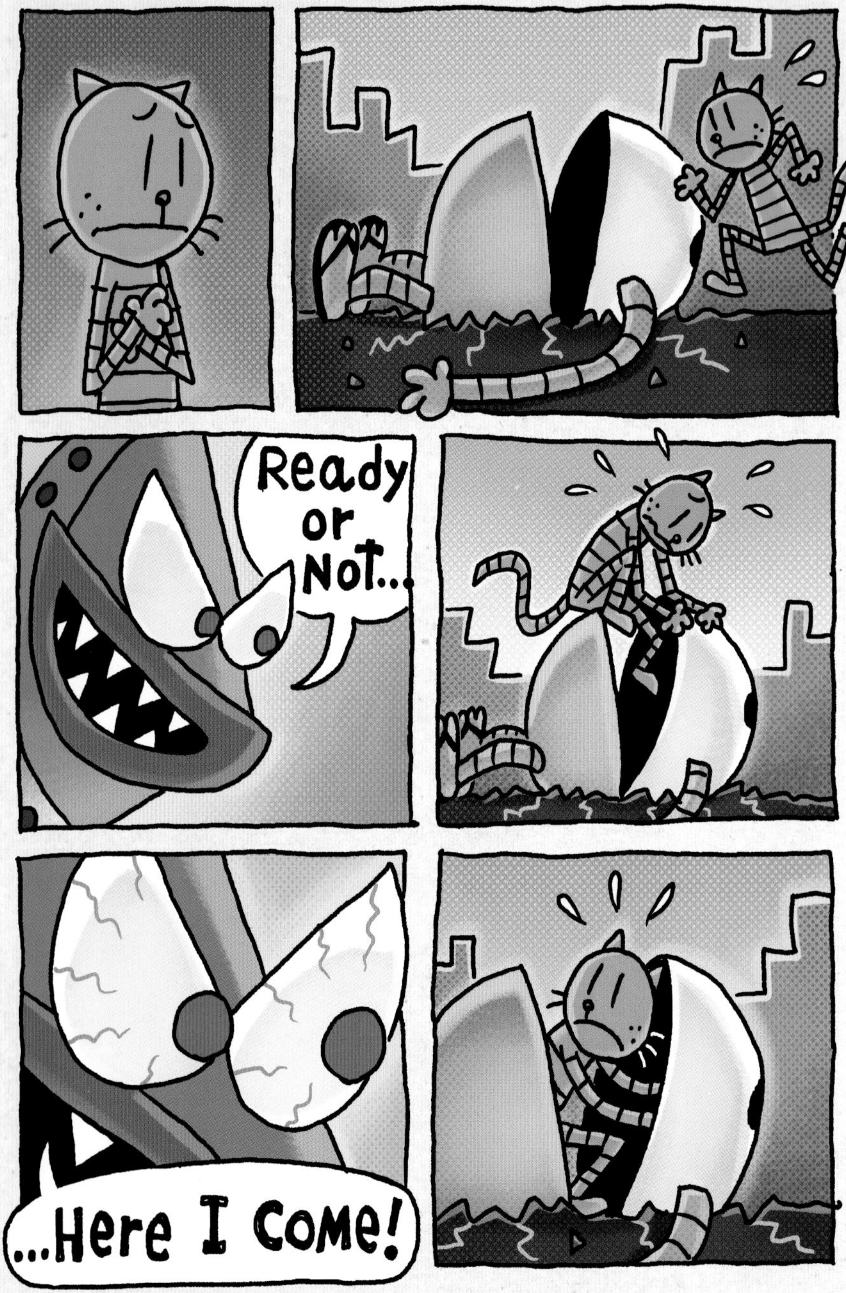
Ready or Not...
...Here I Come!

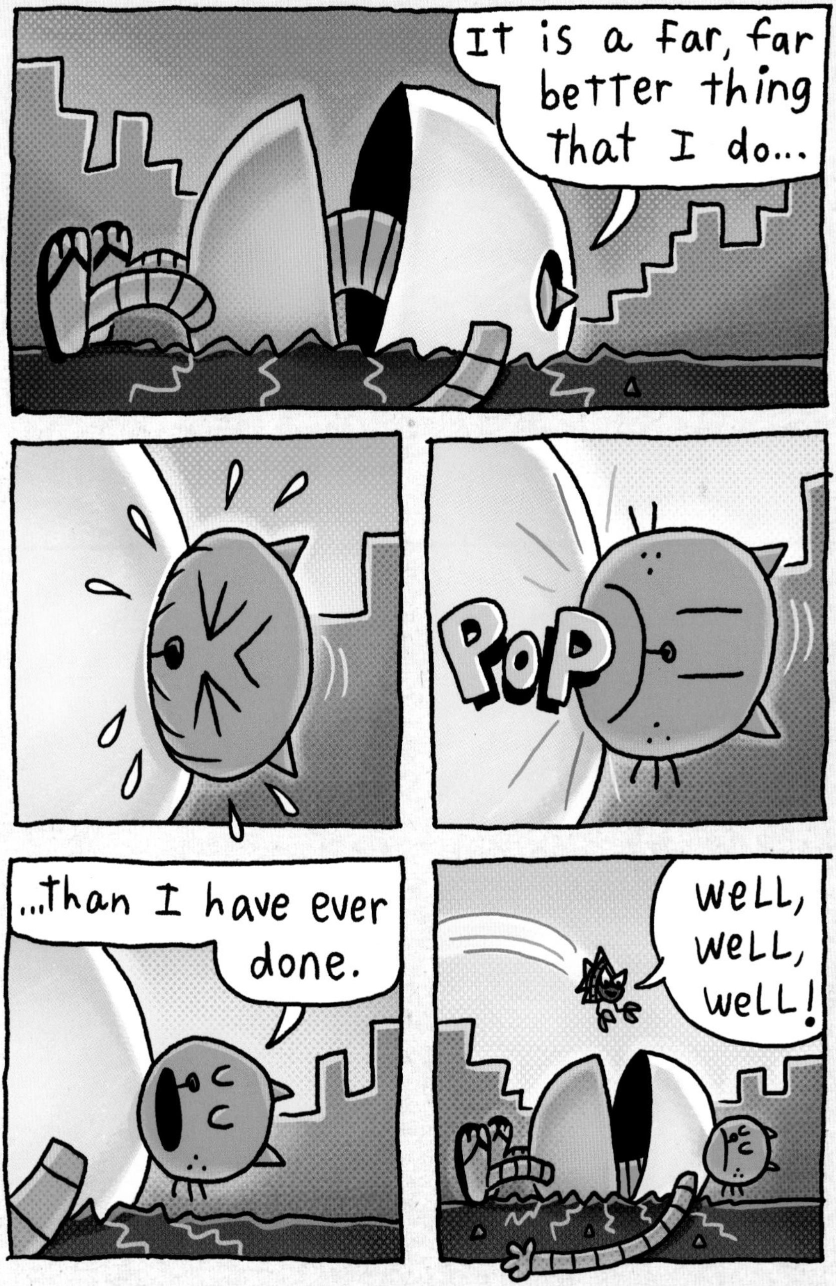
It is a far, far better thing that I do...
POP
...than I have ever done.
WELL, WELL, WELL!

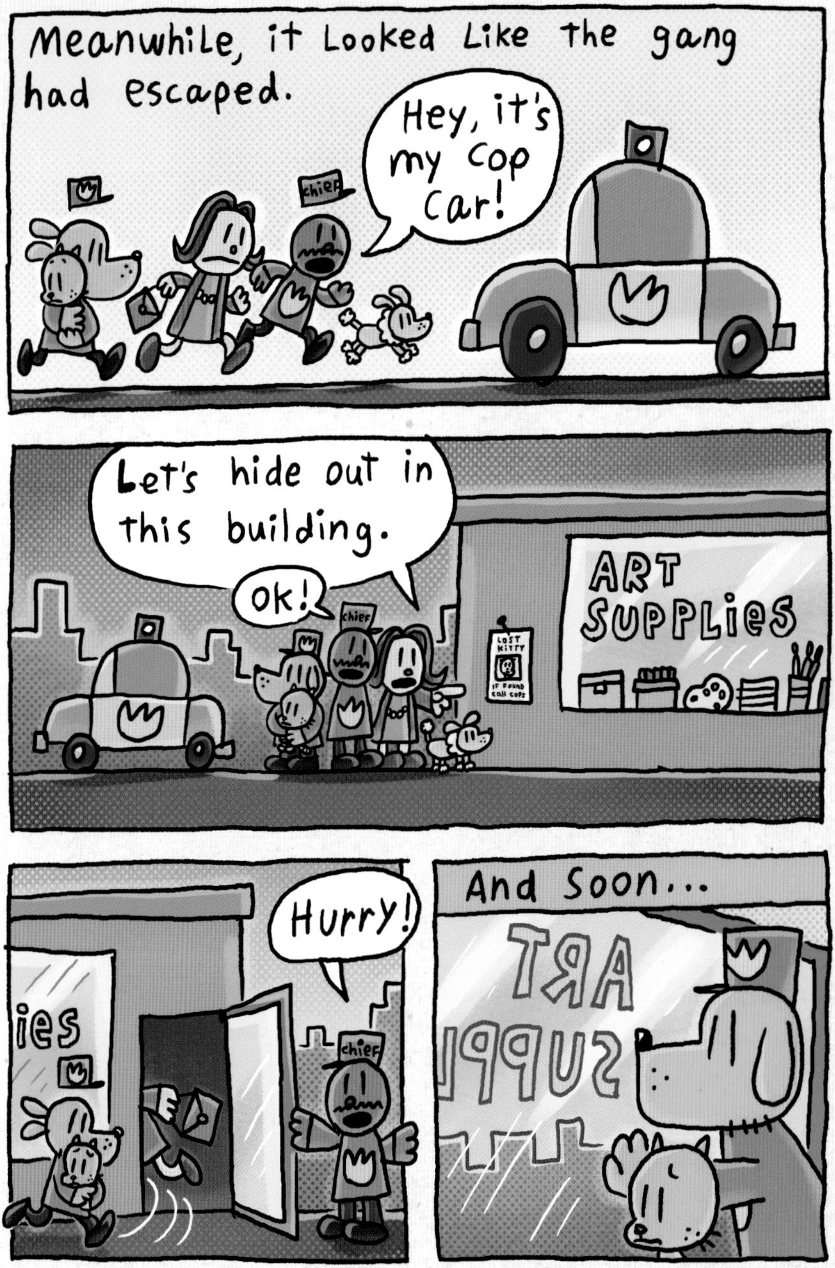

Meanwhile, it Looked Like the gang had escaped.
chief
Hey, it's my cop car!
Let's hide out in this building.
Ok!
chief
LOST KITTY
IF FOUND call cops
ART SUPPLies
Hurry!
chief
And Soon...

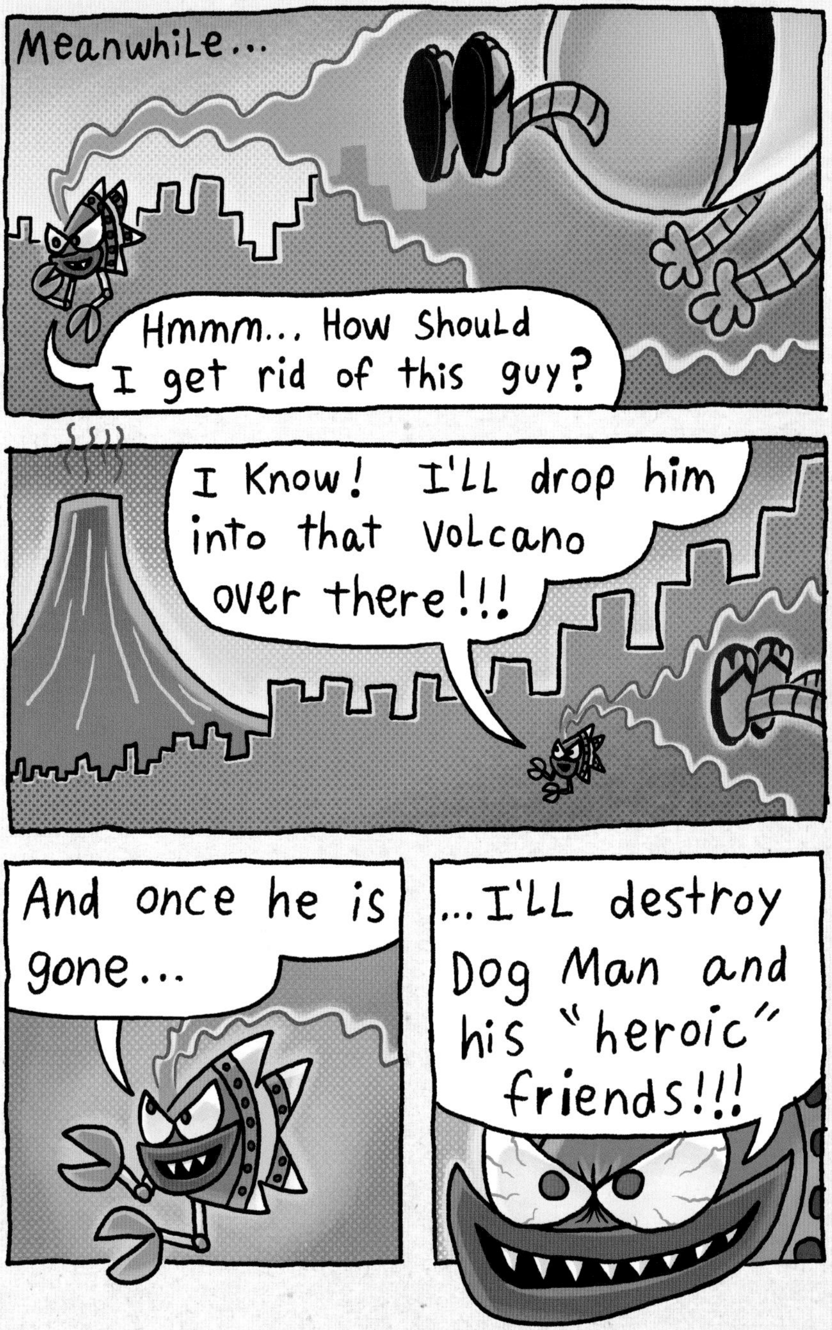
Meanwhile...
Hmmm... How should I get rid of this guy?
I Know! I'll drop him into that volcano over there!!!
And once he is gone...
...I'll destroy Dog Man and his "heroic" friends!!!

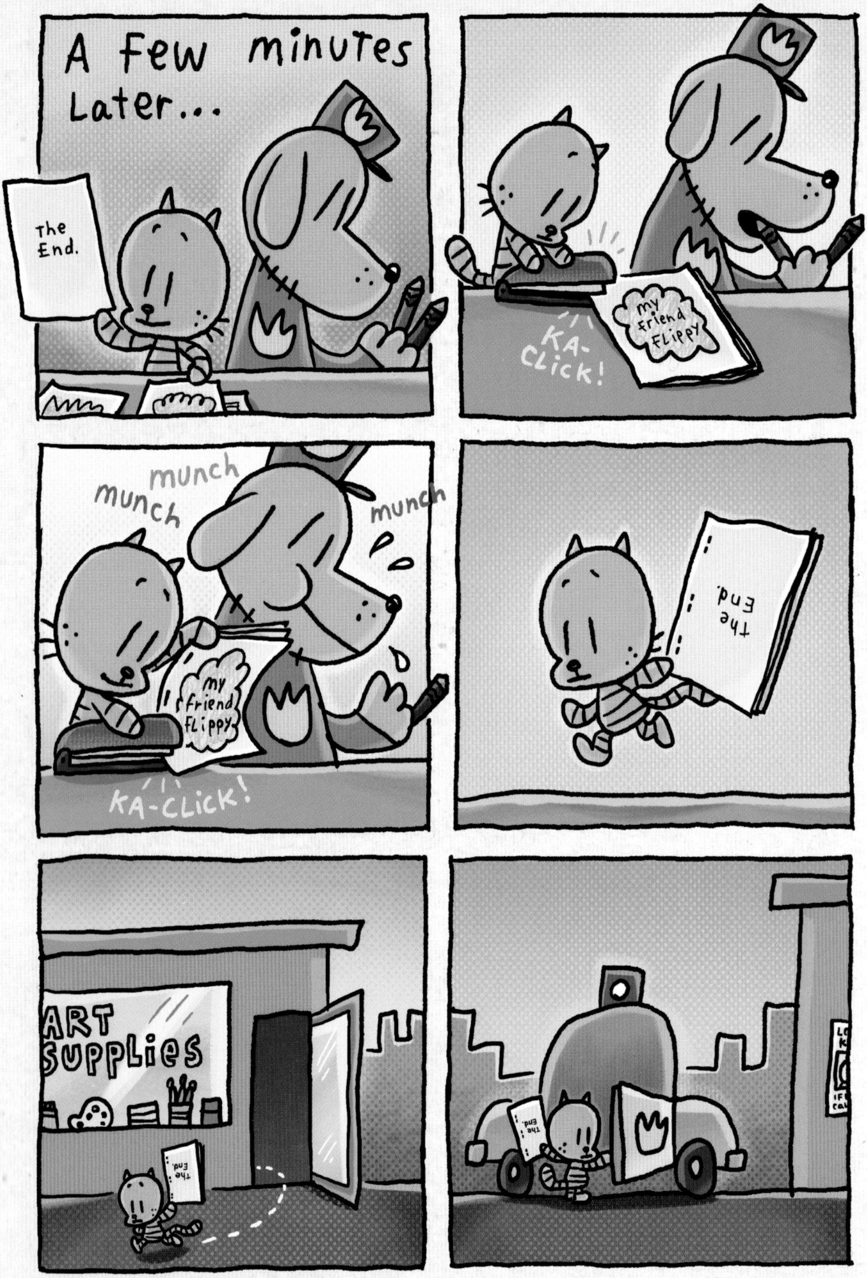
A few minutes Later...
The End.
KA-CLICK!
my friend Flippy
munch
munch
munch
my friend Flippy
KA-CLICK!
the End.
ART SUPPLIES
the End.
the End.

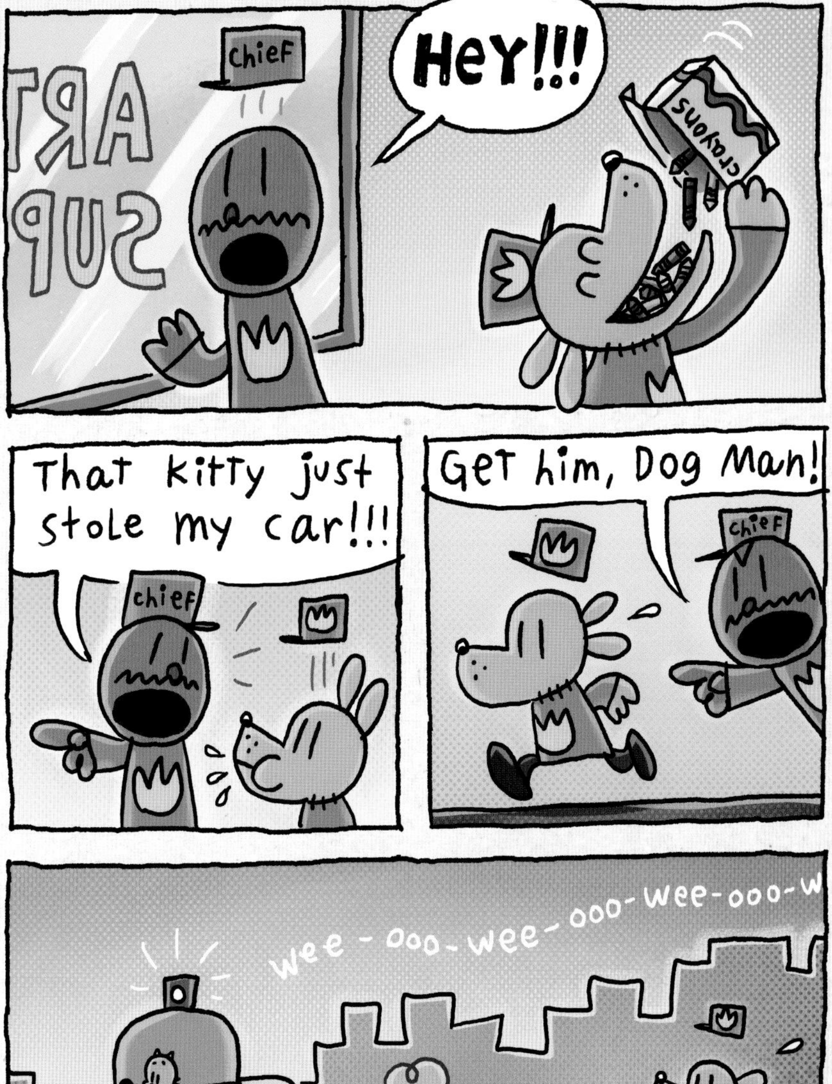
Chief
ART
SUP
HEY!!!
crayons
That kitty just stole my car!!!
chief
Get him, Dog Man!
chief
wee-ooo-wee-ooo-wee-ooo-w

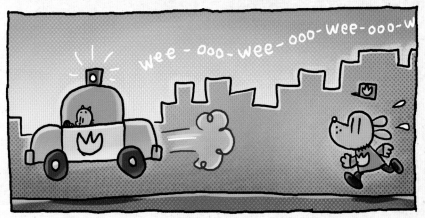

Hi, Dog Man!

Roof Roof Roof!

Oh, yes. I see you've noticed our **ROOF!** We have a new sign!

Please feel free to test drive any of our fine products!

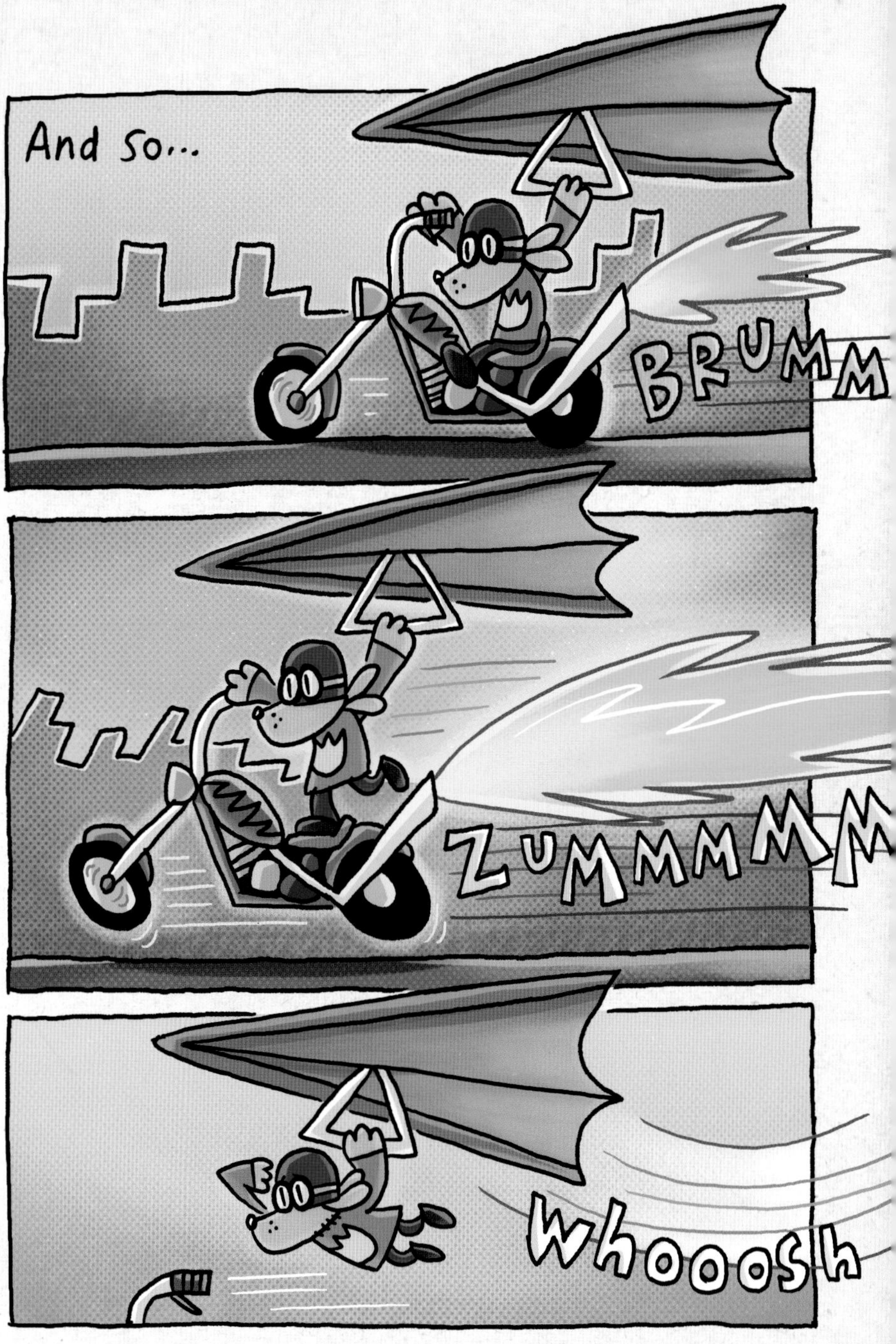
And so...
BRUMM
ZUMMMMMM
Whooosh

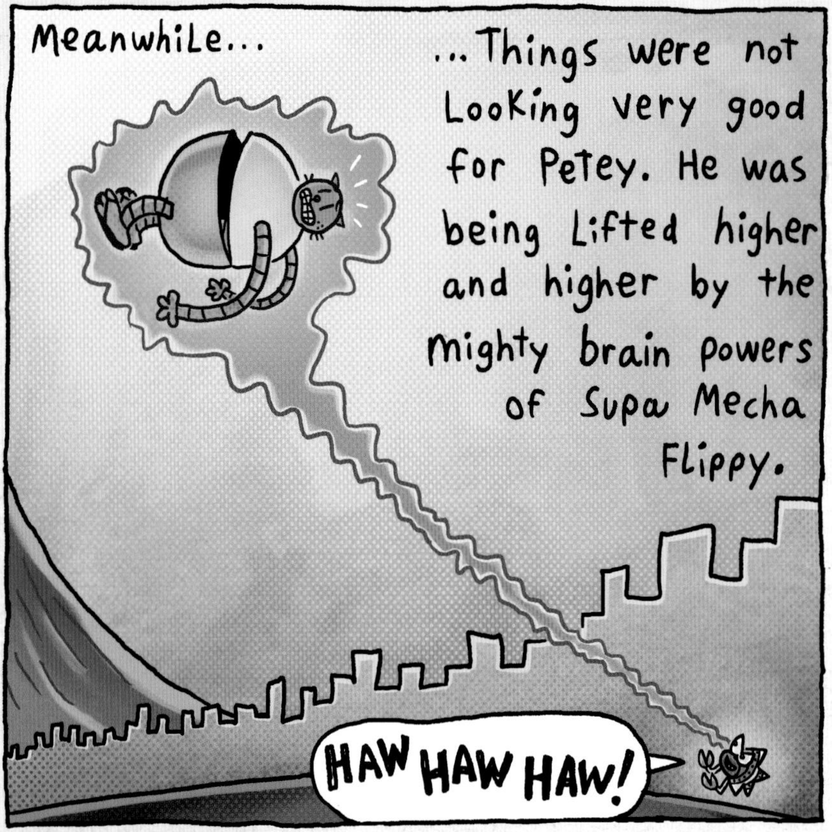
Meanwhile...
...Things were not Looking very good for Petey. He was being Lifted higher and higher by the mighty brain powers of Supa Mecha Flippy.
HAW HAW HAW!

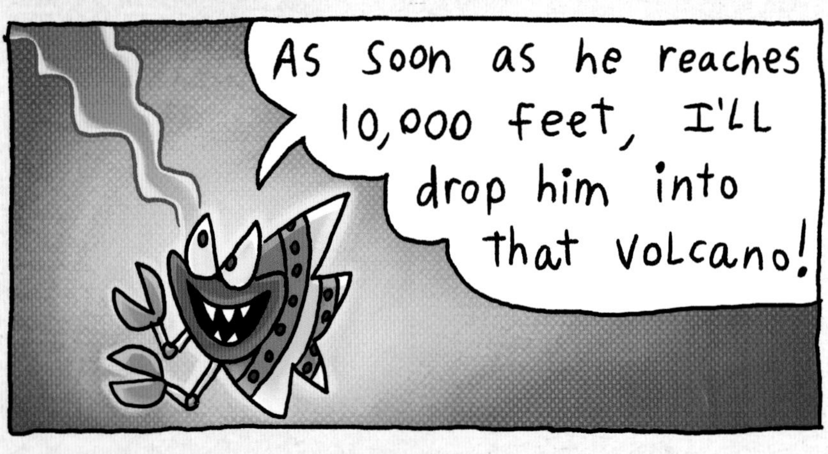
As soon as he reaches 10,000 feet, I'LL drop him into that volcano!

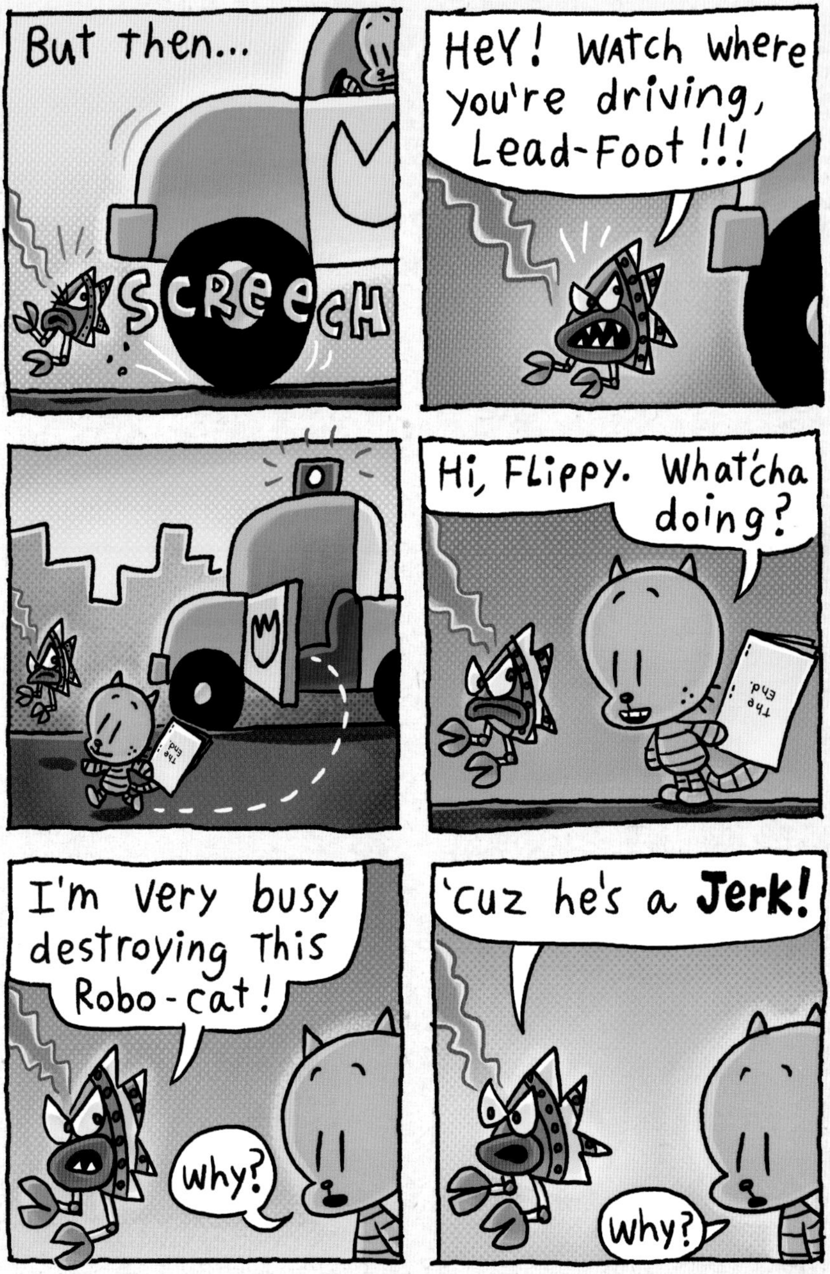
But then...
SCREECH
HEY! WATCH where you're driving, Lead-Foot!!!
Hi, FLippy. What'cha doing?
I'm very busy destroying this Robo-cat!
why?
'cuz he's a **Jerk!**
why?

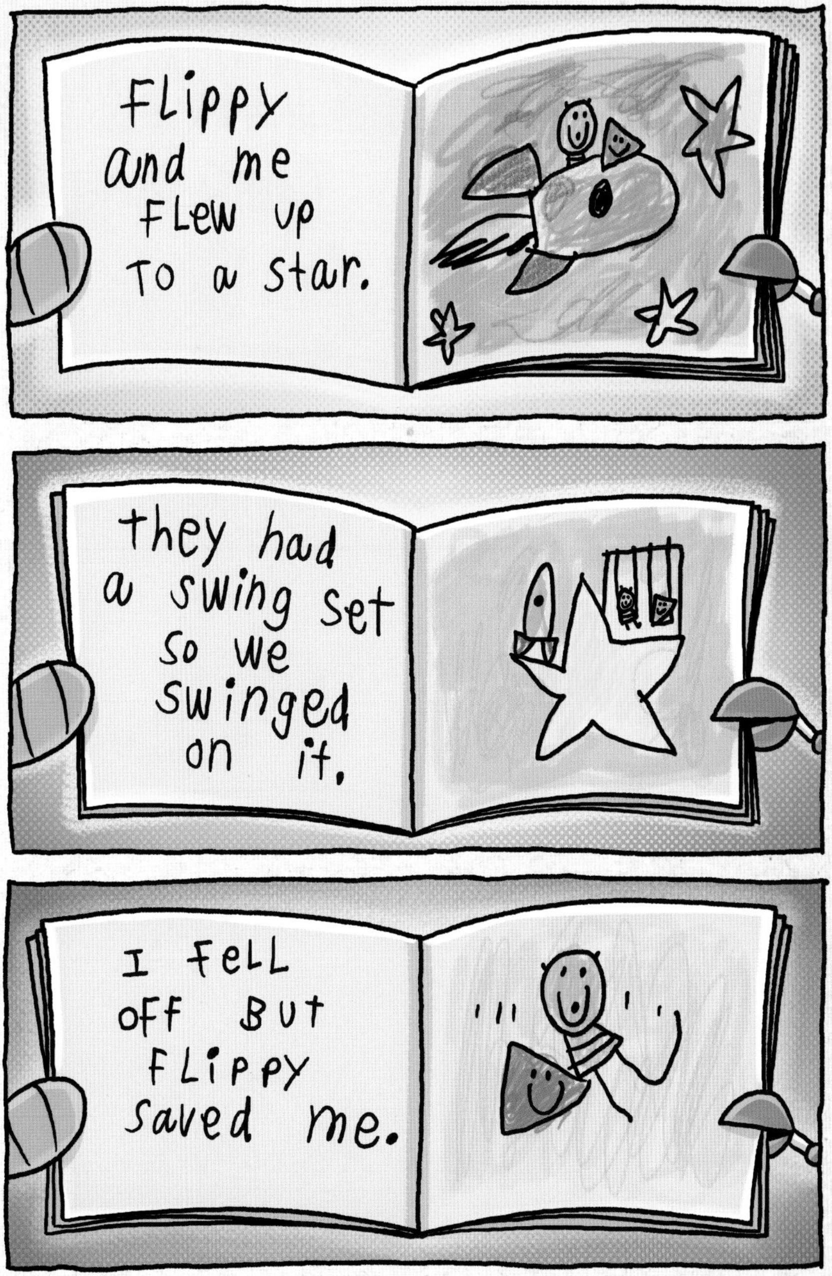
FLippy and me FLew up To a star.
they had a swing set so we swinged on it.
I FeLL off But FLippy saved me.

FLippy and me went under the sea

then we ate five soups.

The End.

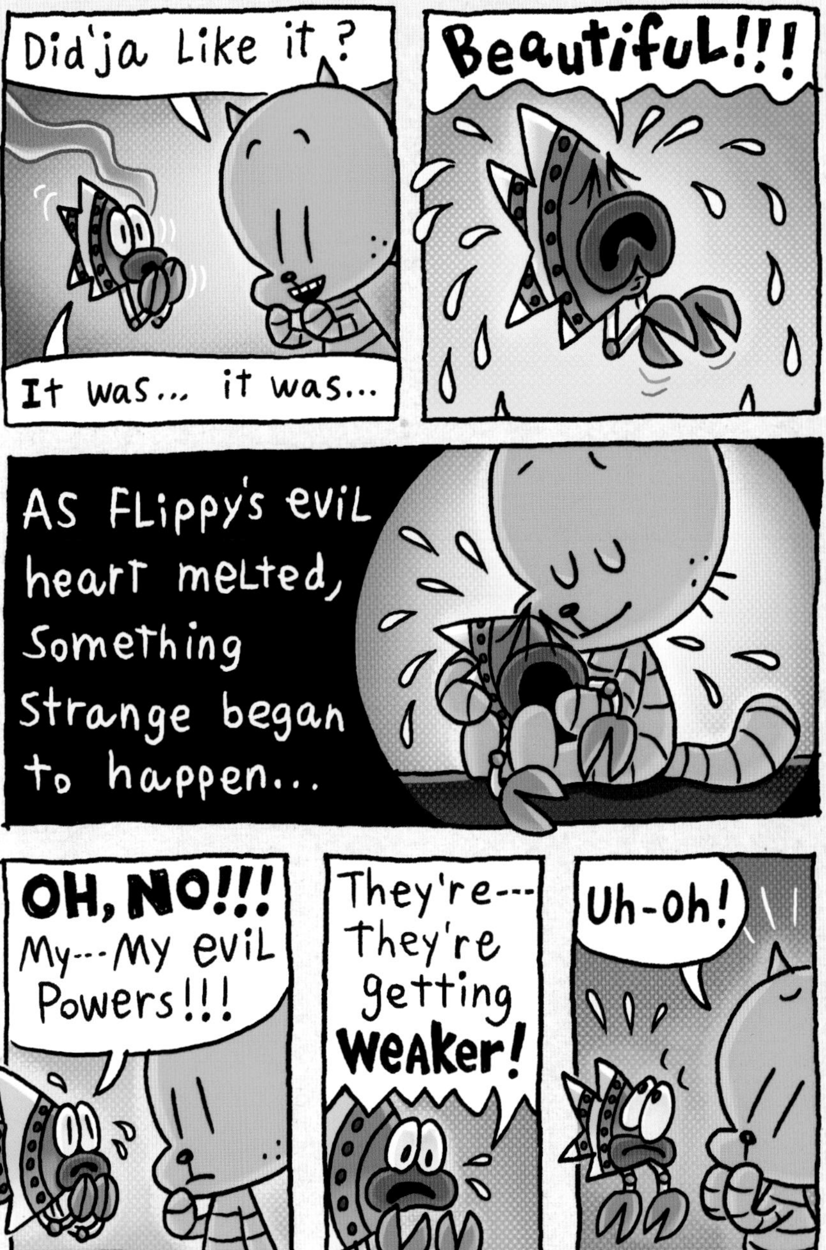
Did'ja Like it?
It was... it was...
Beautiful!!!
AS FLippy's eviL heart meLted, Something strange began to happen...
OH, NO!!! My---My eviL Powers!!!
They're--- they're getting WEAKER!
Uh-Oh!

This was not good news for Petey.

Uh-Oh!

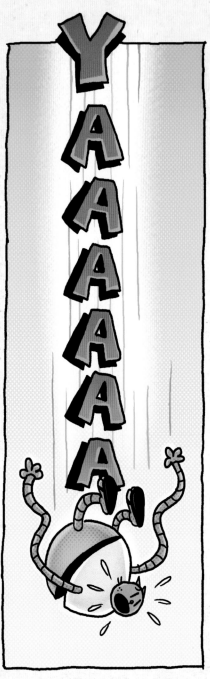

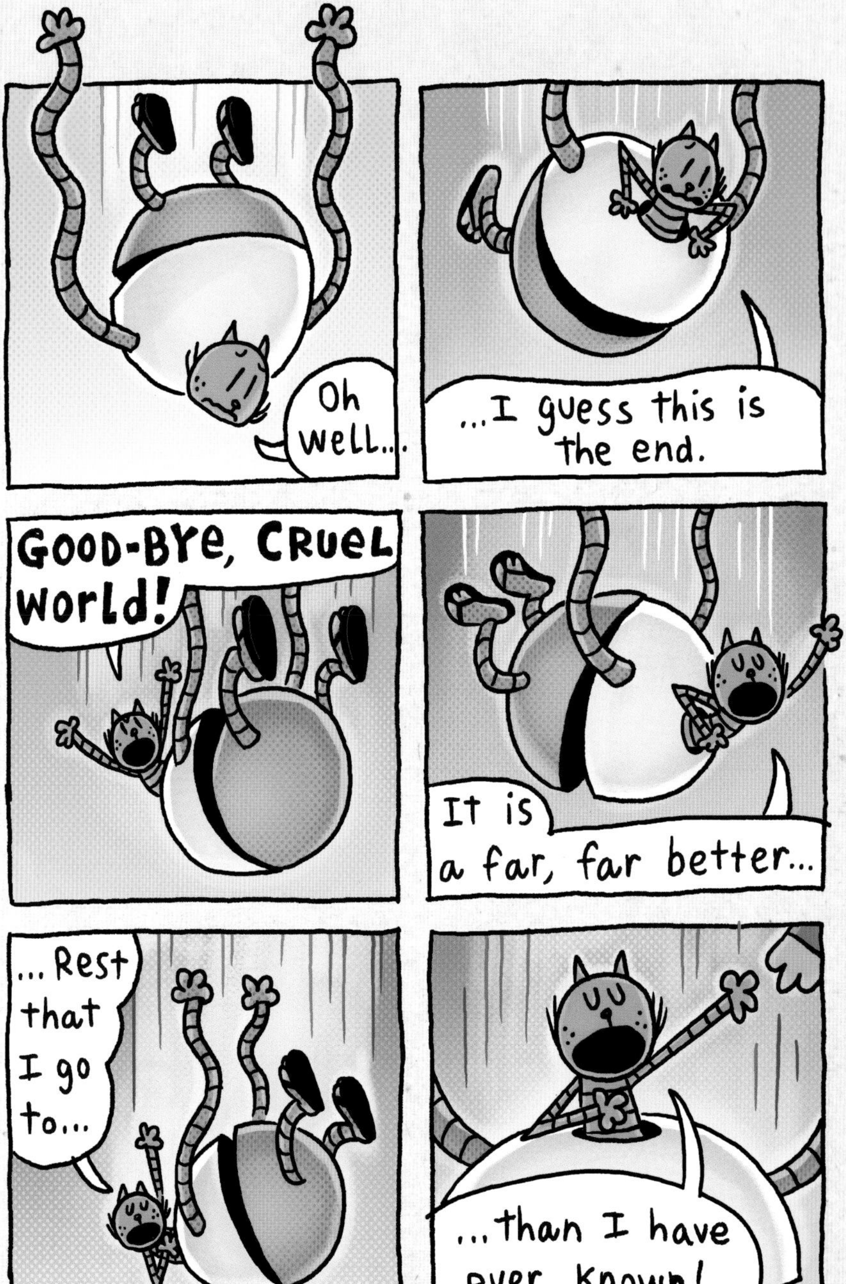
Oh well...
...I guess this is the end.
GOOD-BYE, CRUEL world!
It is a far, far better...
...Rest that I go to...
...than I have ever known!

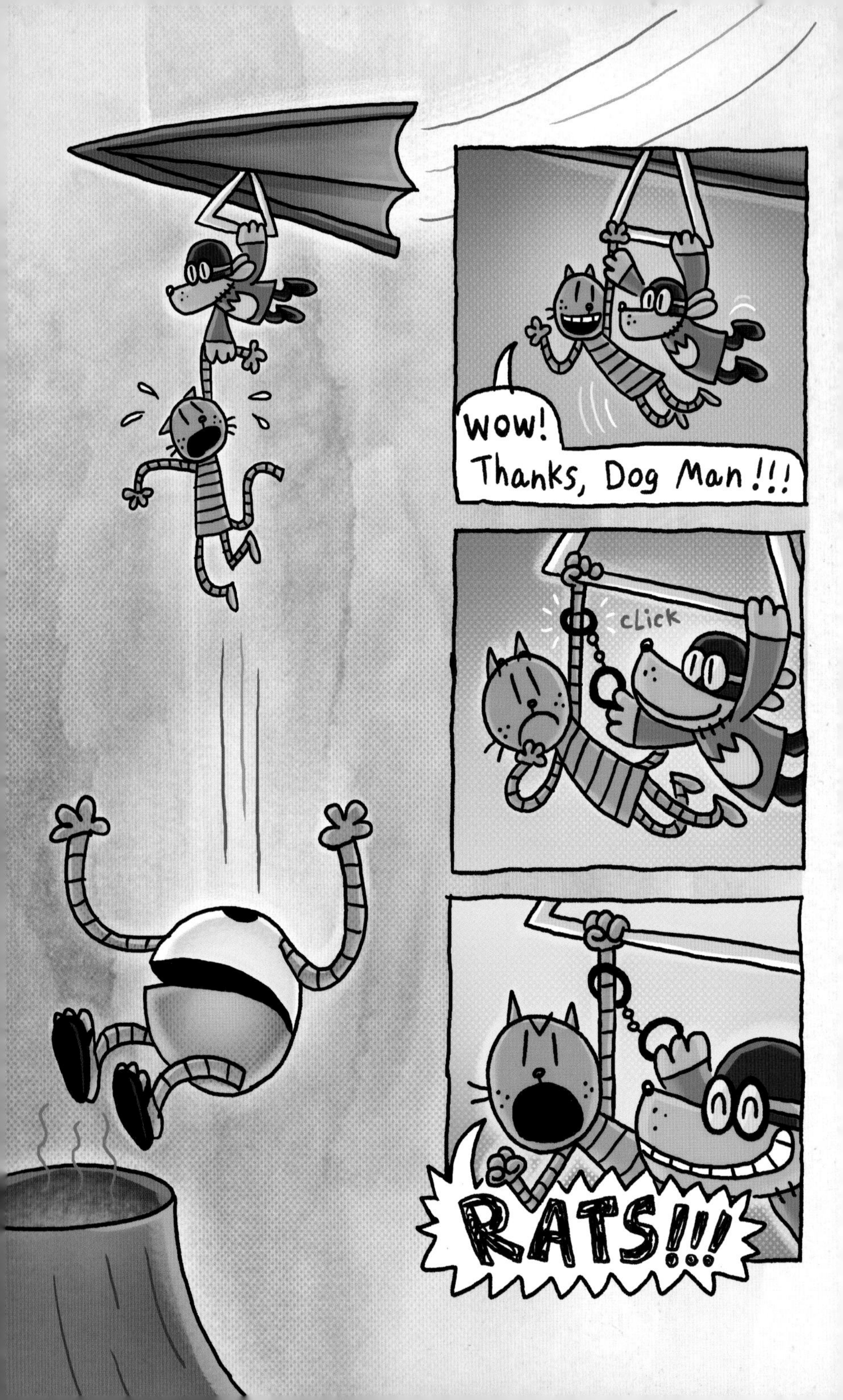

WOW!
Thanks, Dog Man!!!
CLICK
RATS!!!

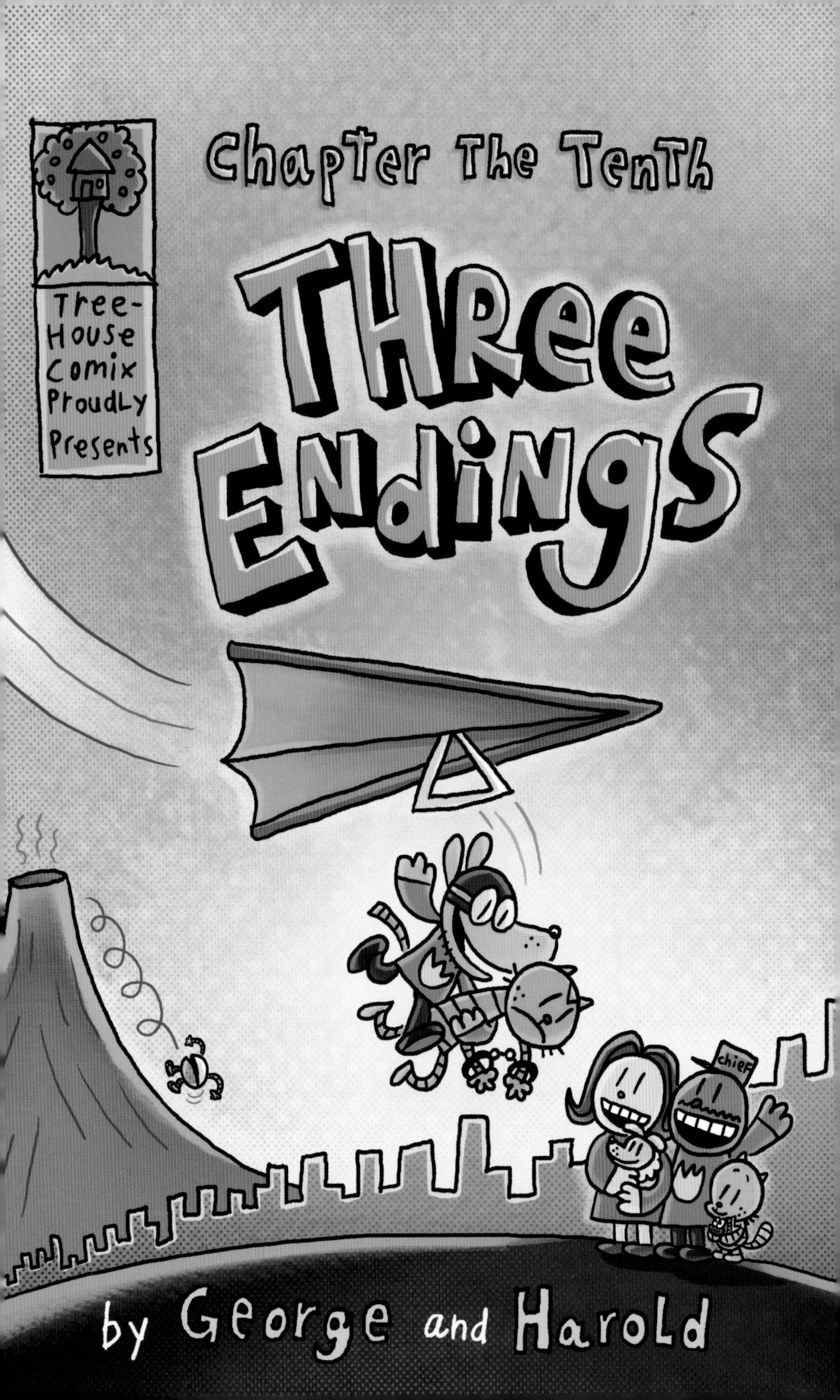
Tree-House Comix Proudly Presents
Chapter The Tenth
Three Endings
chief
by George and Harold

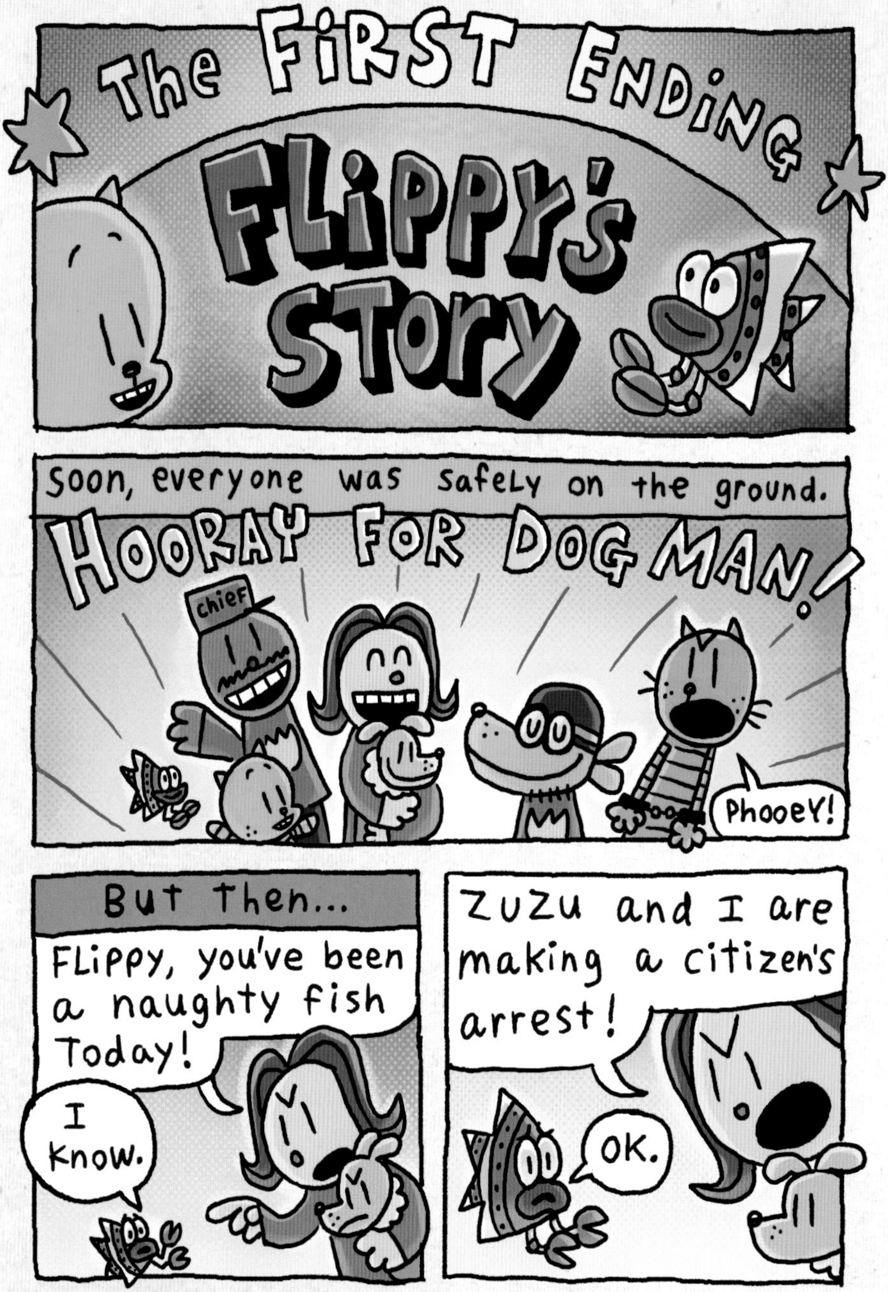
The FIRST ENDING
FLiPPY's Story
Soon, everyone was safely on the ground.
HOORAY FOR DOG MAN!
chief
PhooeY!
But Then...
FLippy, you've been a naughty fish Today!
I know.
ZUZU and I are making a citizen's arrest!
OK.

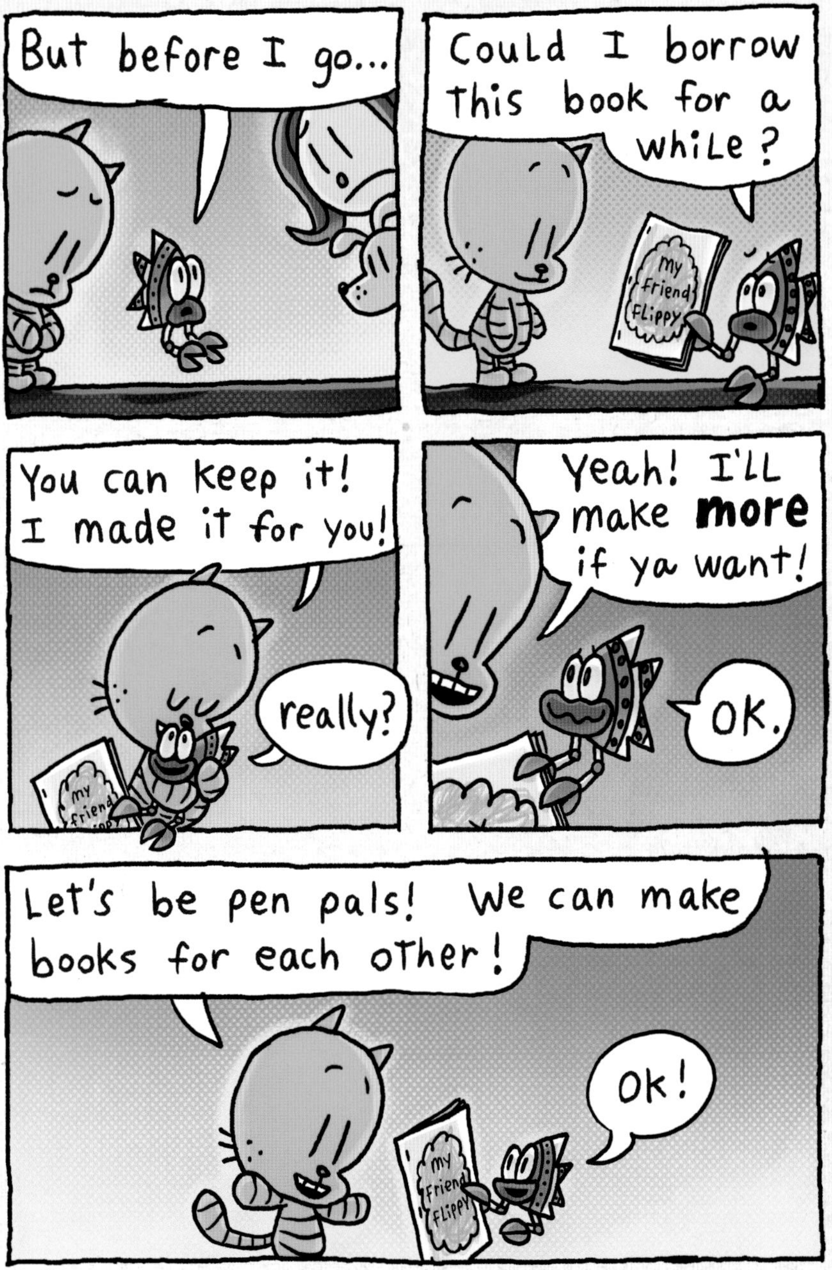
But before I go...
Could I borrow this book for a while?
My Friend Flippy
You can keep it! I made it for you!
really?
Yeah! I'll make **more** if ya want!
OK.
Let's be pen pals! We can make books for each other!
OK!
My Friend Flippy

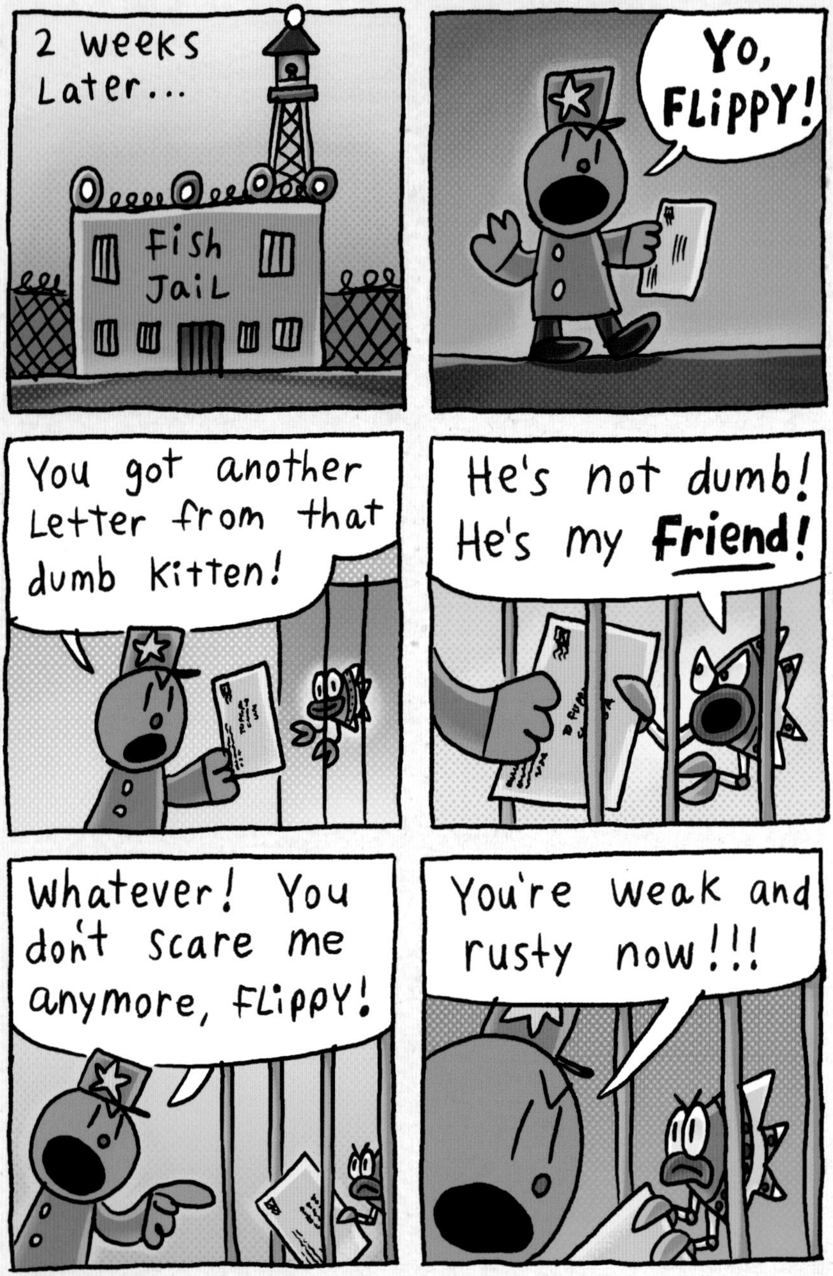
2 weeks Later...
Fish Jail
Yo, FLIPPY!
You got another Letter from that dumb Kitten!
He's not dumb! He's my **Friend**!
Whatever! You don't scare me anymore, FLIPPY!
You're weak and rusty now!!!

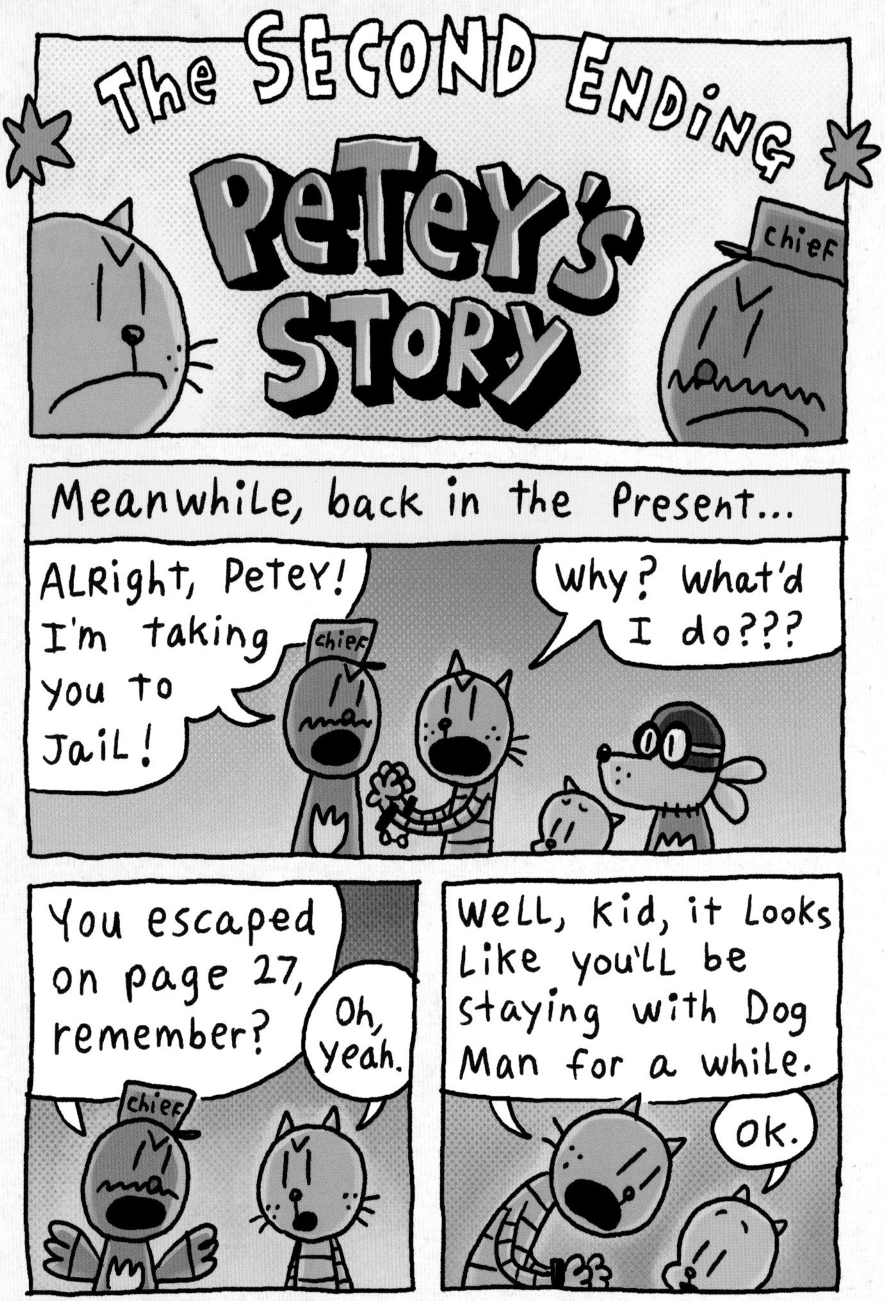
The SECOND ENDING
Petey's STORY
Chief
Meanwhile, back in the Present...
ALRight, Petey! I'm taking you to JaiL!
chief
Why? What'd I do???
You escaped on page 27, remember?
Oh, yeah.
chief
WeLL, kid, it Looks Like you'LL be staying with Dog Man for a whiLe.
OK.

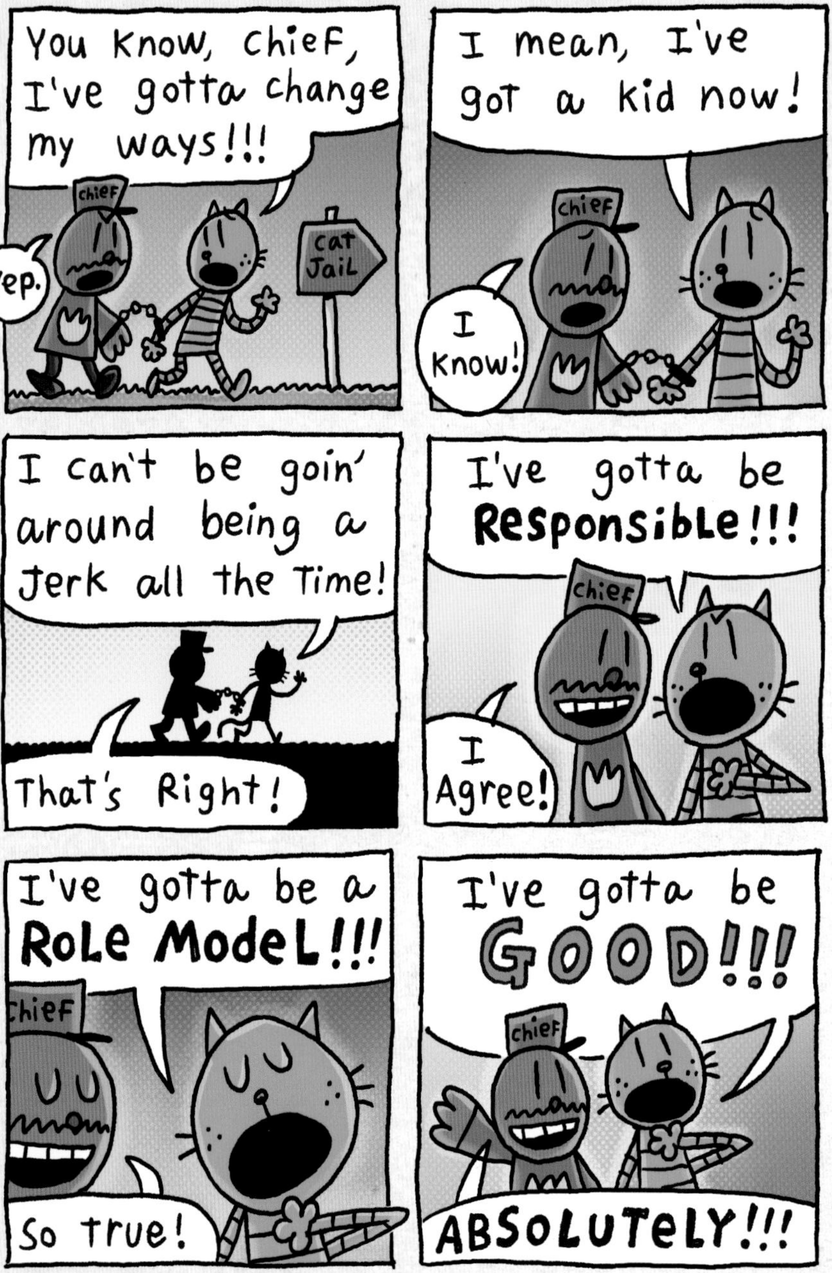

You know, chief, I've gotta change my ways!!!
Yep.
chief
Cat Jail
I mean, I've got a kid now!
I Know!
chief
I can't be goin' around being a Jerk all the Time!
That's Right!
I've gotta be RESPONSIBLE!!!
I Agree!
chief
I've gotta be a ROLE MODEL!!!
So true!
chief
I've gotta be GOOD!!!
ABSOLUTELY!!!
chief

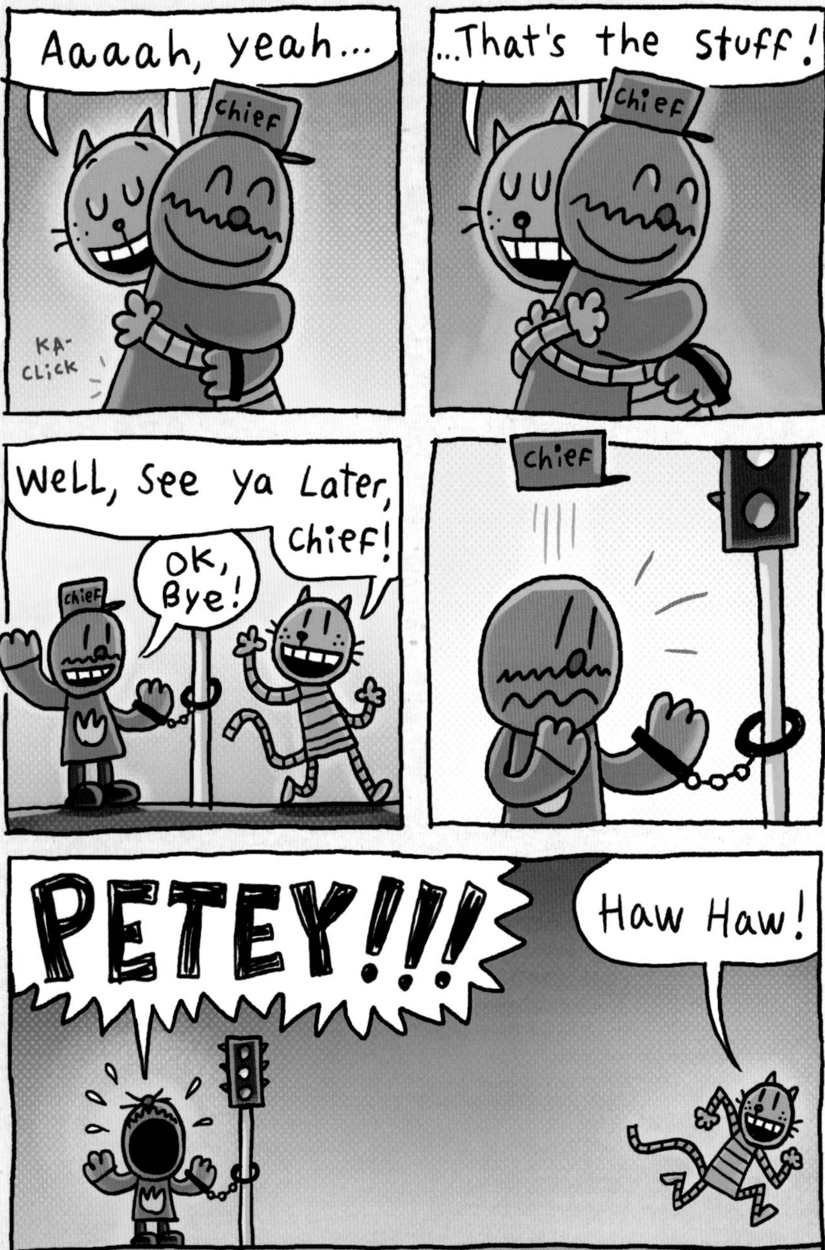
Aaaah, yeah...
Chief
KA-CLICK
...That's the stuff!
Chief
WeLL, see ya Later, chief!
Chief
OK, Bye!
Chief
PETEY!!!
Haw Haw!

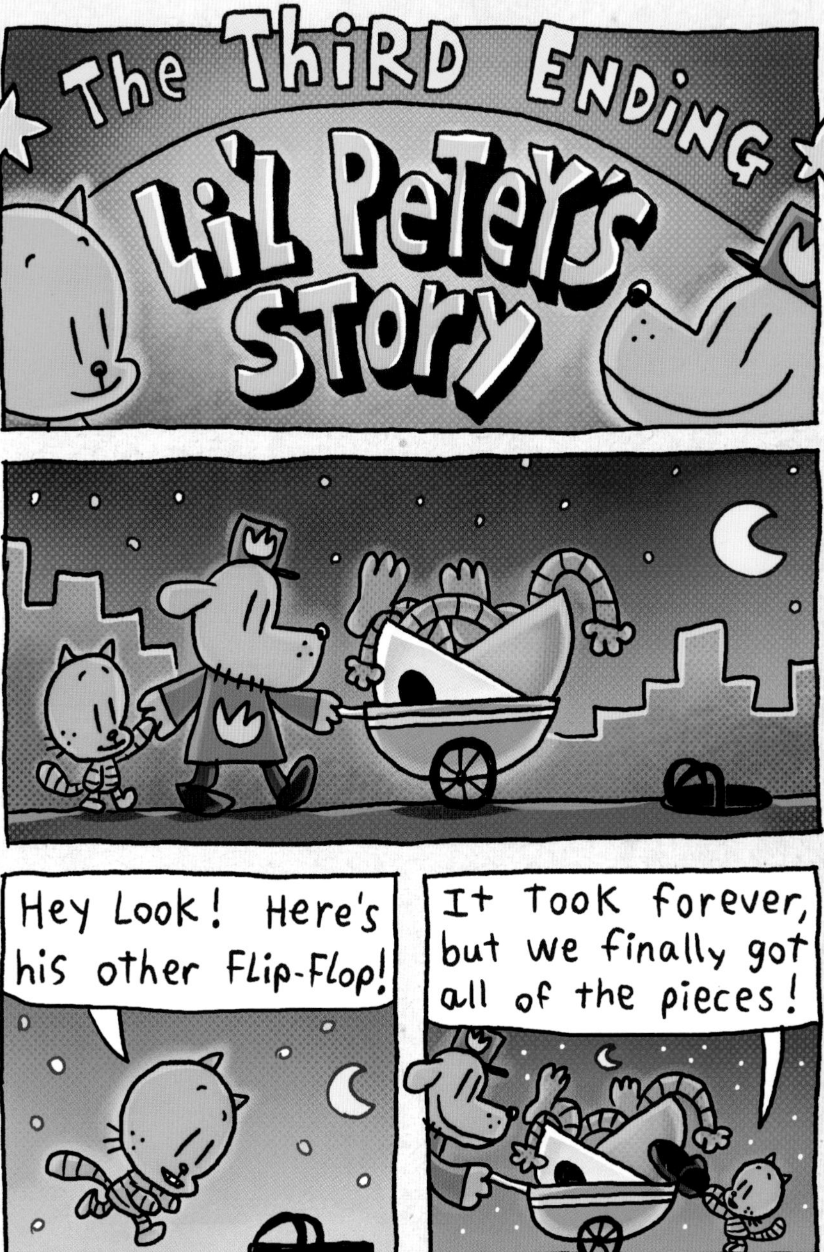

The Third Ending
Li'l Petey's Story
Hey Look! Here's his other Flip-Flop!
It took forever, but we finally got all of the pieces!

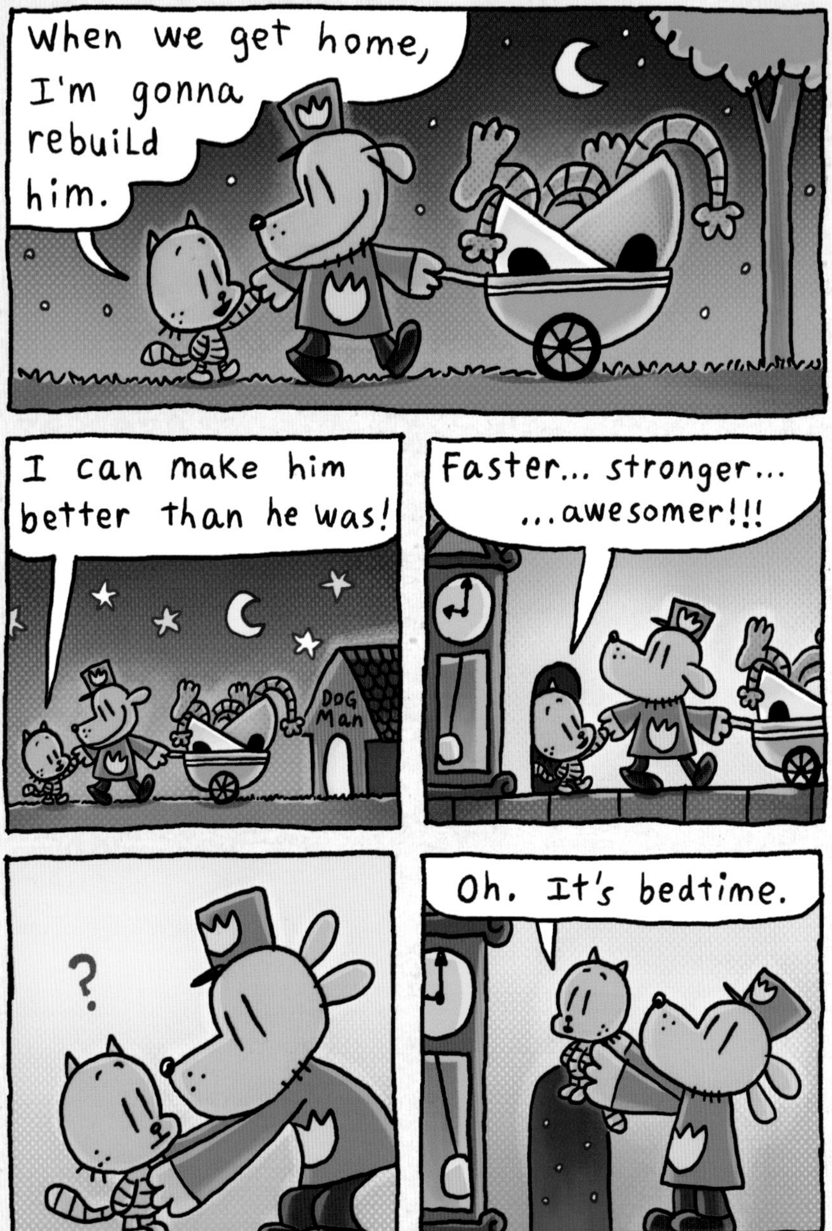
When we get home, I'm gonna rebuild him.
I can make him better than he was!
Faster... stronger... ...awesomer!!!
DOG Man
?
Oh. It's bedtime.

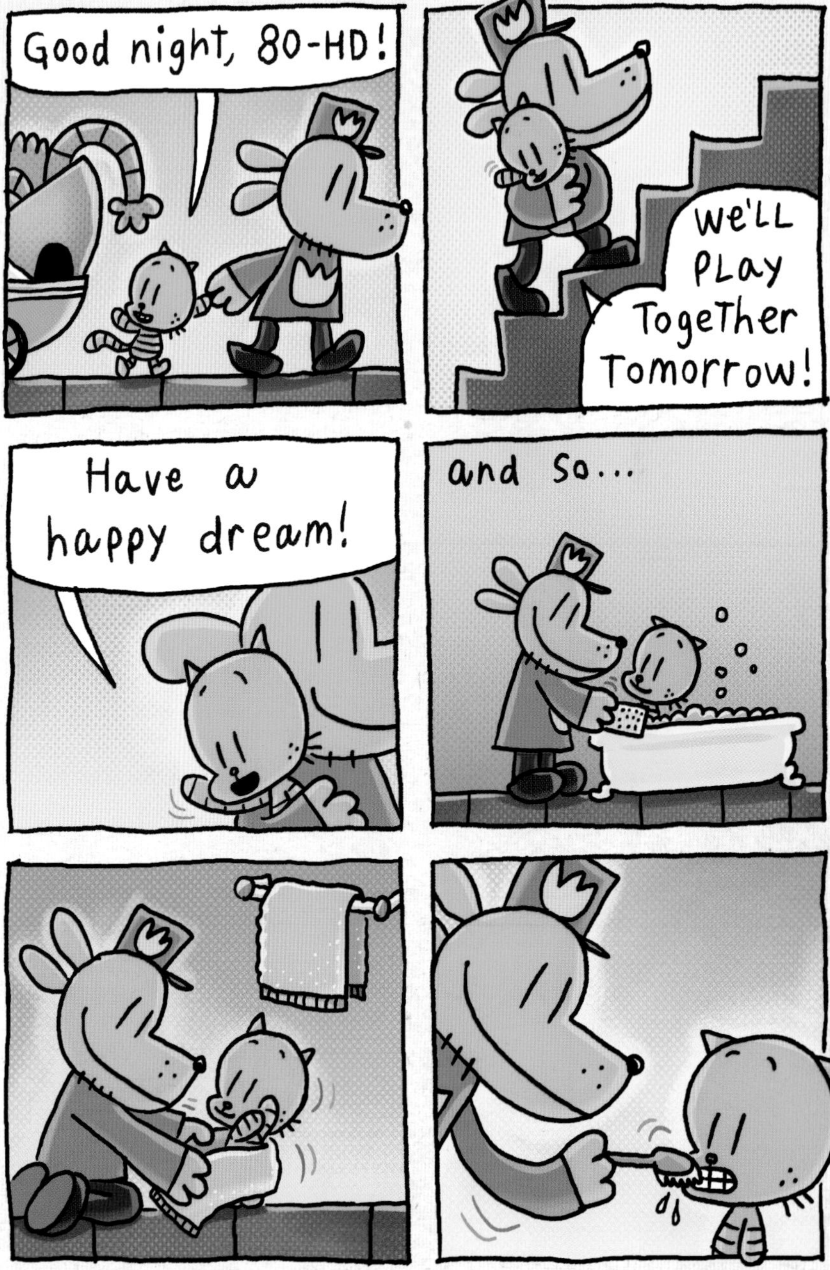
Good night, 80-HD!
We'LL PLay TogeTher Tomorrow!
Have a happy dream!
and so...

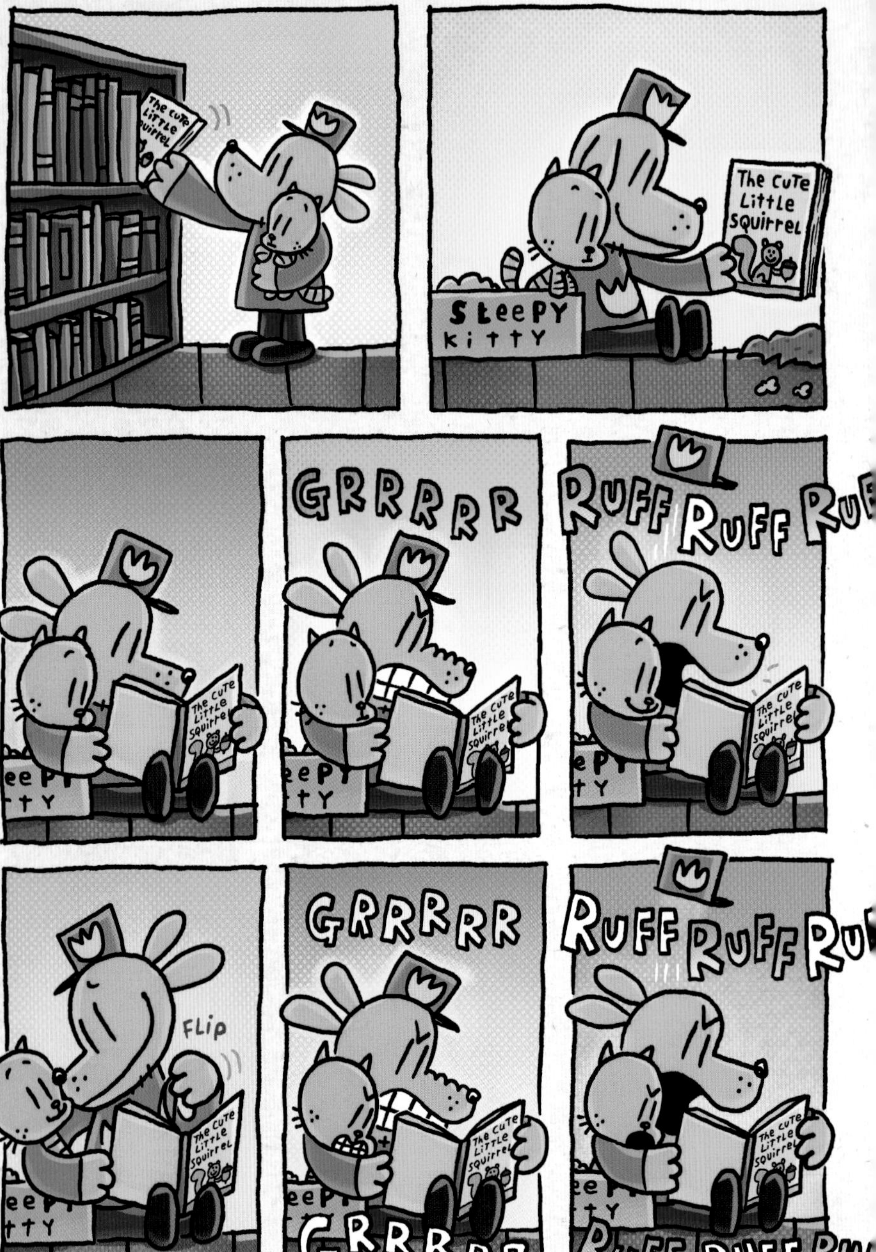

The Cute Little Squirrel
The Cute Little Squirrel
SLeepy Kitty
GRRRRRR
RUFF RUFF RU
FLip
GRRRRRR
RUFF RUFF RU
GRRRRRR
RUFF RUFF RU

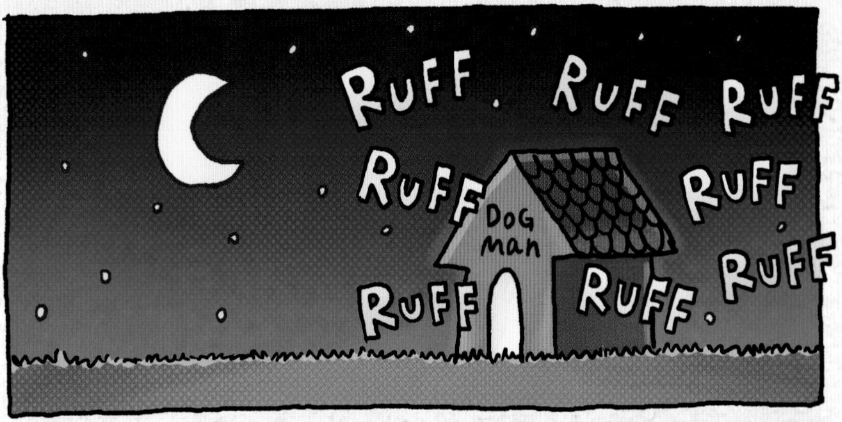
RUFF
RUFF
RUFF
RUFF
DOG man
RUFF
RUFF
RUFF
RUFF

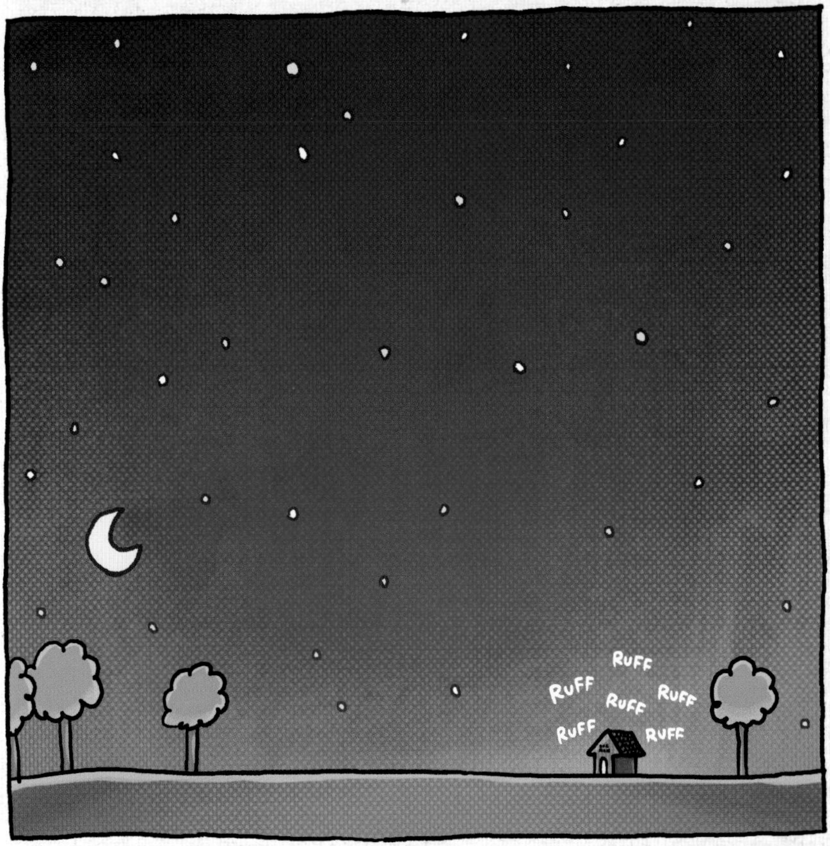
RUFF
RUFF
RUFF
RUFF
RUFF
RUFF

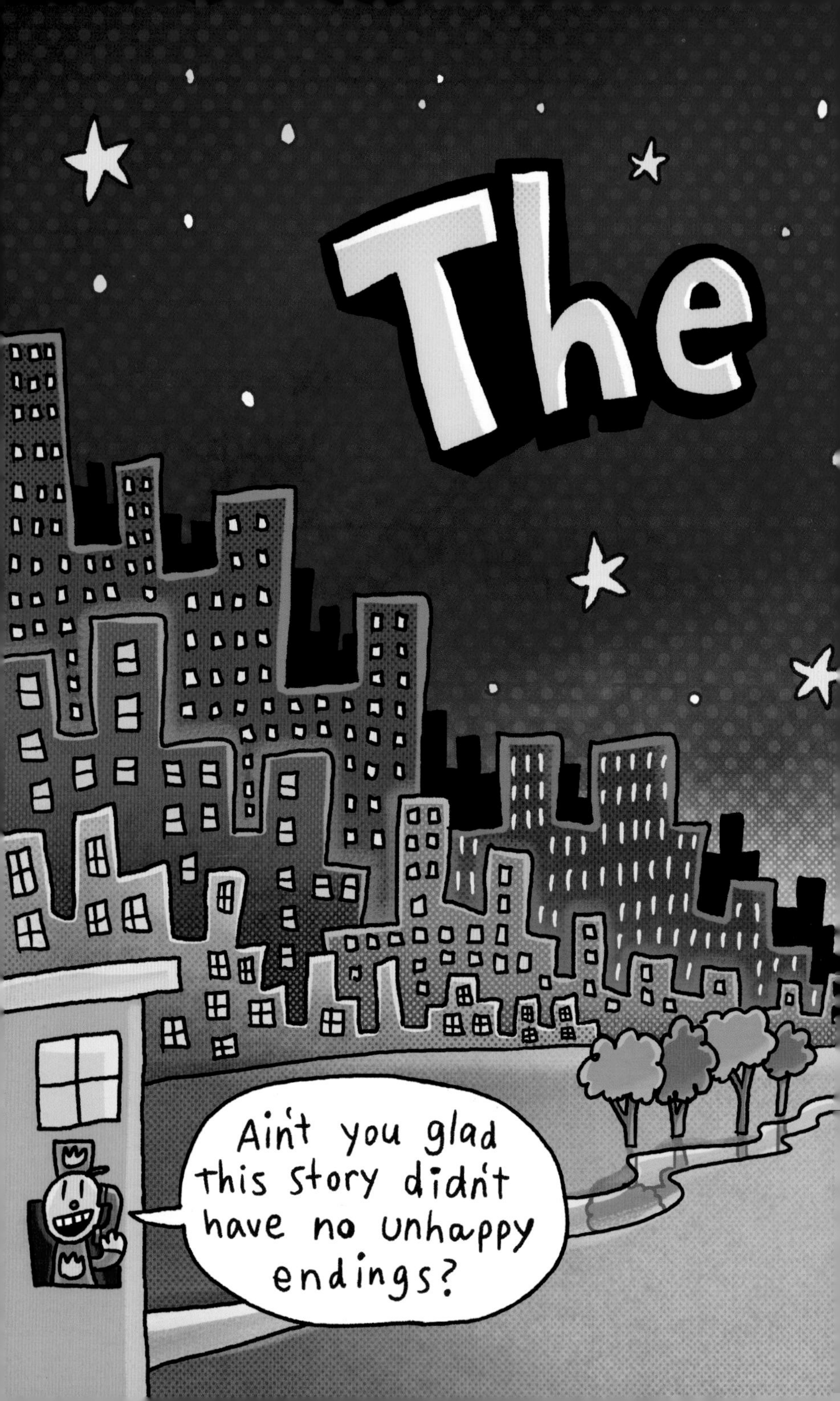
The
Ain't you glad this story didn't have no unhappy endings?

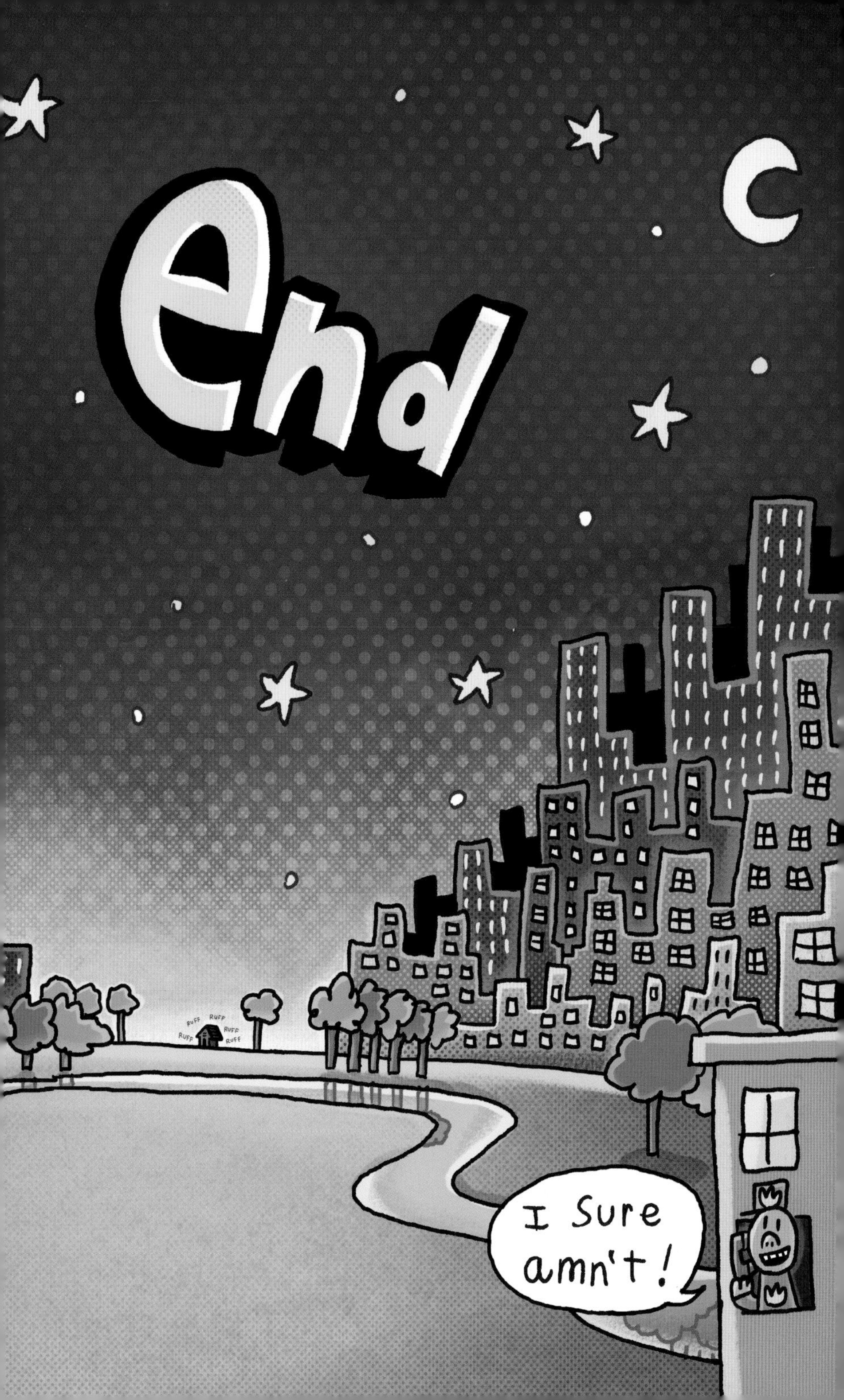
end
RUFF RUFF RUFF RUFF RUFF
I sure amn't!

...if you thought our adventure was over...

YOU Ain't ReaD <u>NOThin'</u> YeT!

AT this very moment, George and Harold are busy creating their **NEXT** work of depth and maturity.

Take a peep, my peeps!

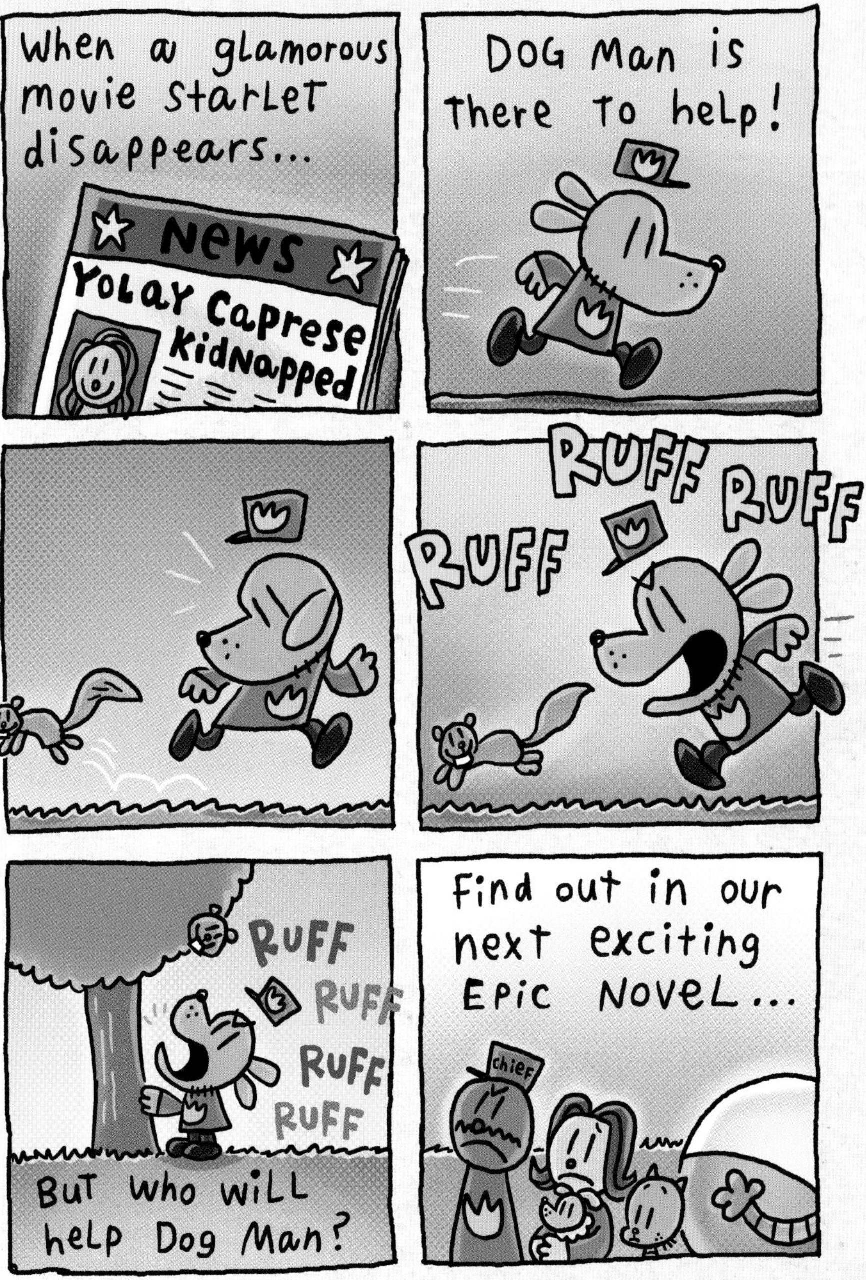
When a glamorous movie starlet disappears...
NEWS
Yolay Caprese Kidnapped
DOG Man is there to help!
RUFF
RUFF
RUFF
RUFF
RUFF
RUFF
RUFF
But who will help Dog Man?
Find out in our next exciting Epic Novel...
Chief

DOG MAN
AND CAT KID
DAV PILKEY

If You Like ACTION...

...AND You Like Suspense...

...And you Like LAFFS...

...Then DOG MAN is GO!

DOG Man is GO? That don't make no sense!
BUT we Like it!

HOW 2 DRAW LI'L PETEY

in 20 Ridiculously easy steps!

1
2
3
4
5
6
7
8
9
10
11

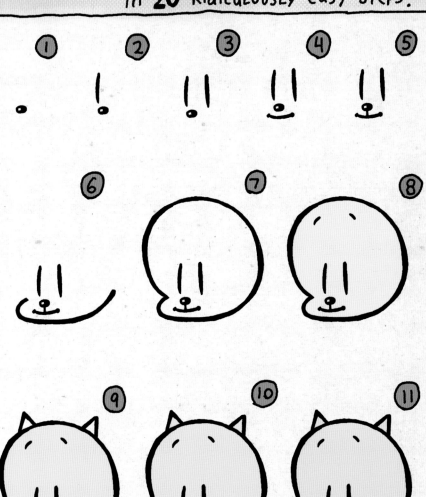

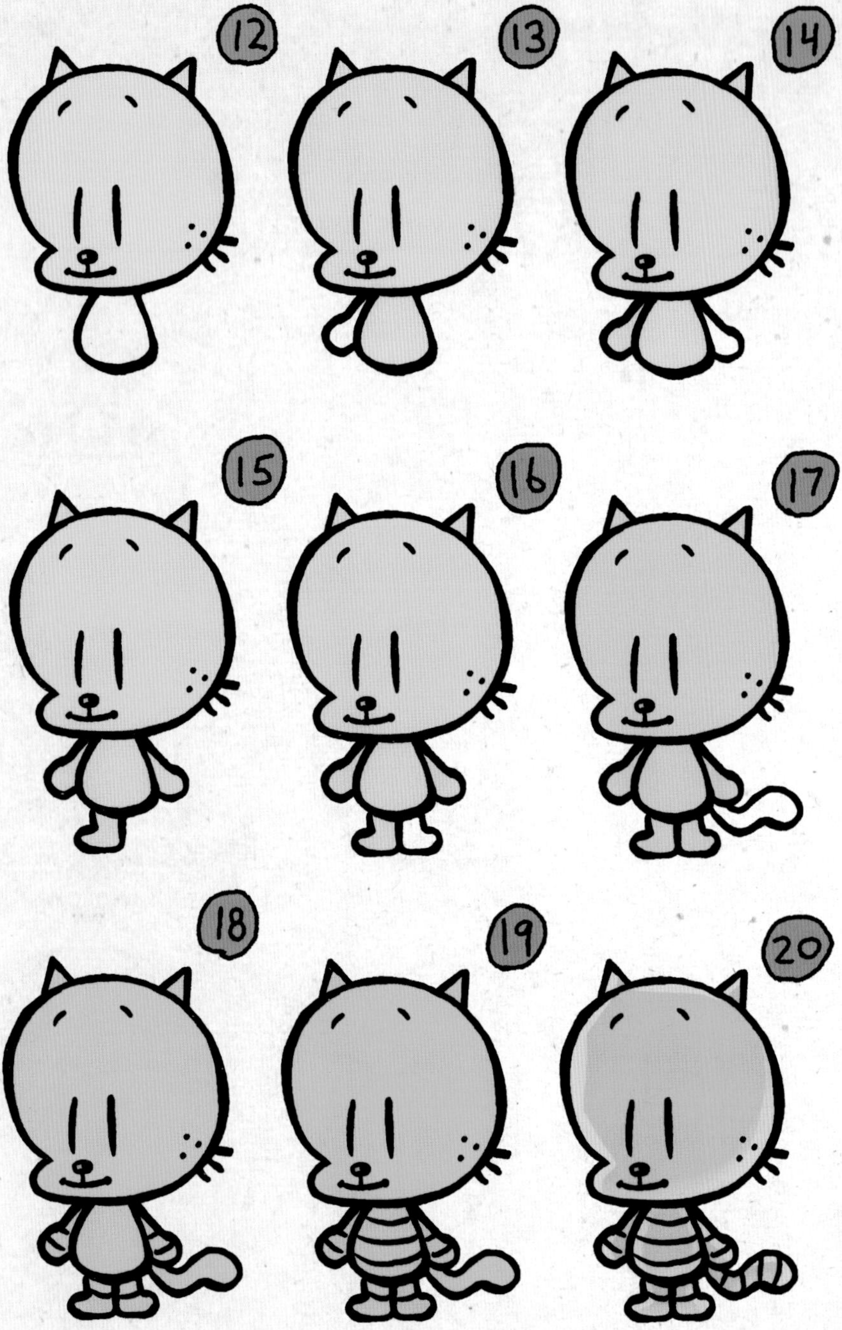
12
13
14
15
16
17
18
19
20

in 18 Ridiculously easy Steps!

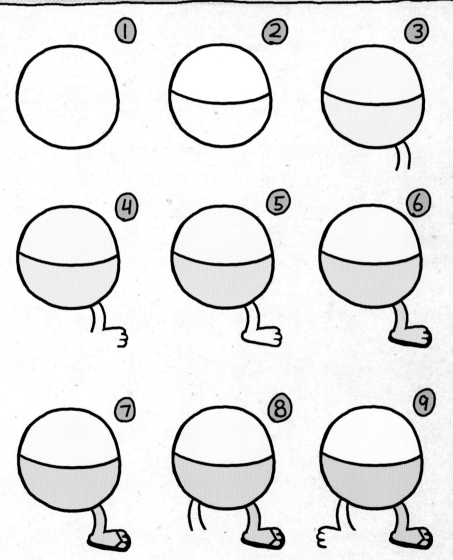

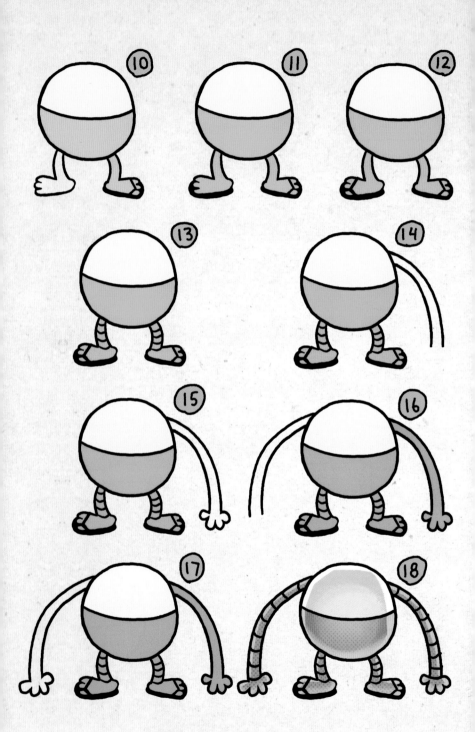

HOW 2 DRAW A BEASTY BUILDING

in **21** Ridiculously easy steps!

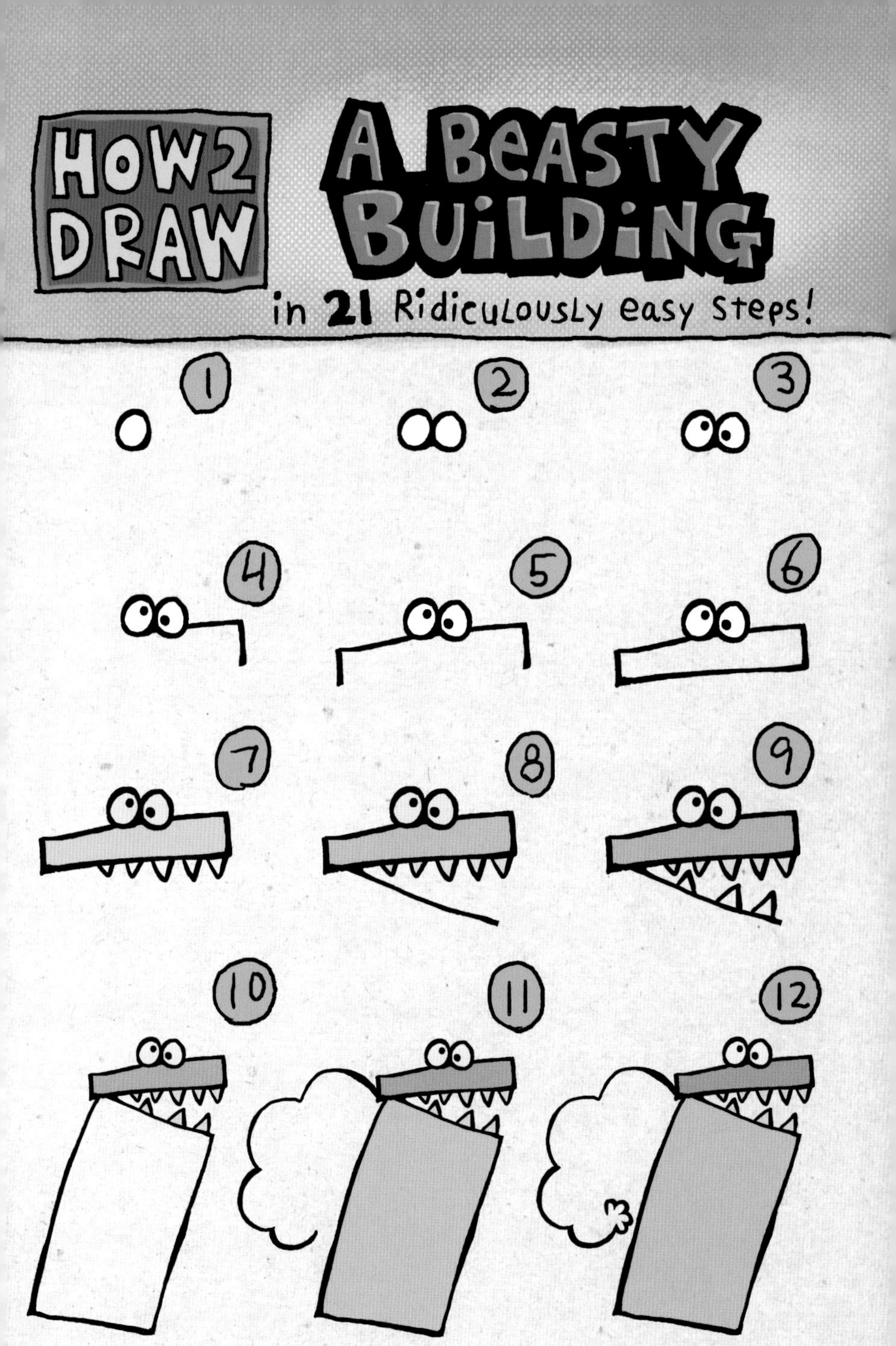
1
2
3
4
5
6
7
8
9
10
11
12

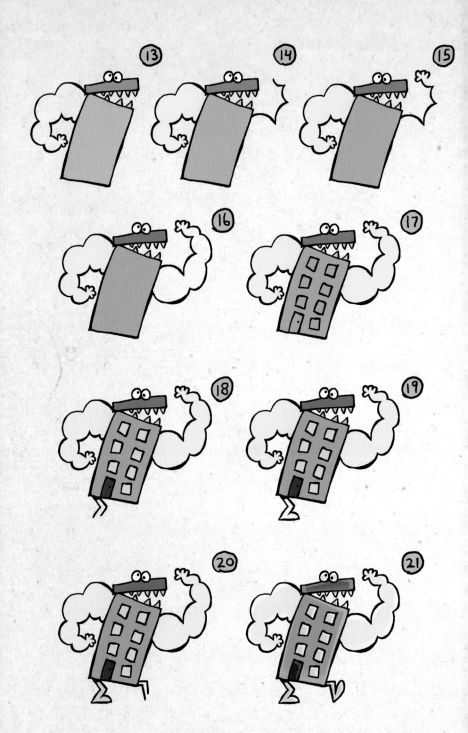

HOW 2 DRAW PETEY

in 27 RIDICULOUSLY easy steps!

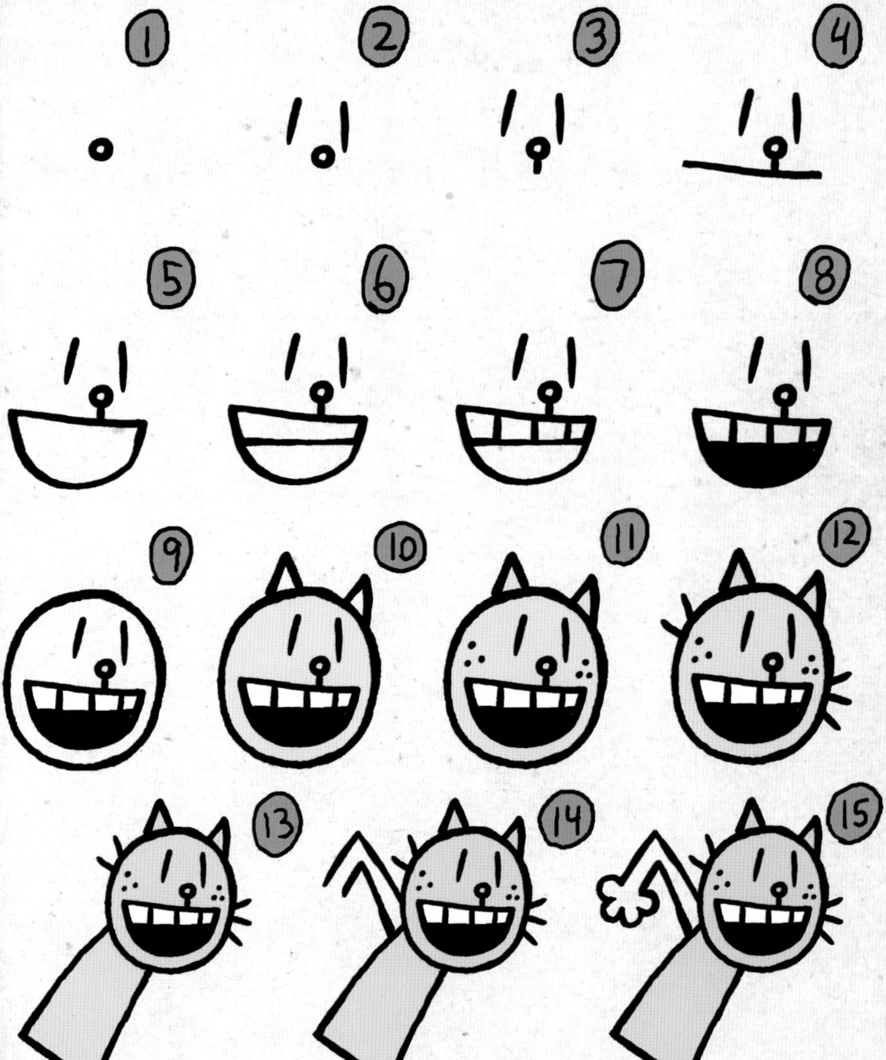
1
2
3
4
5
6
7
8
9
10
11
12
13
14
15

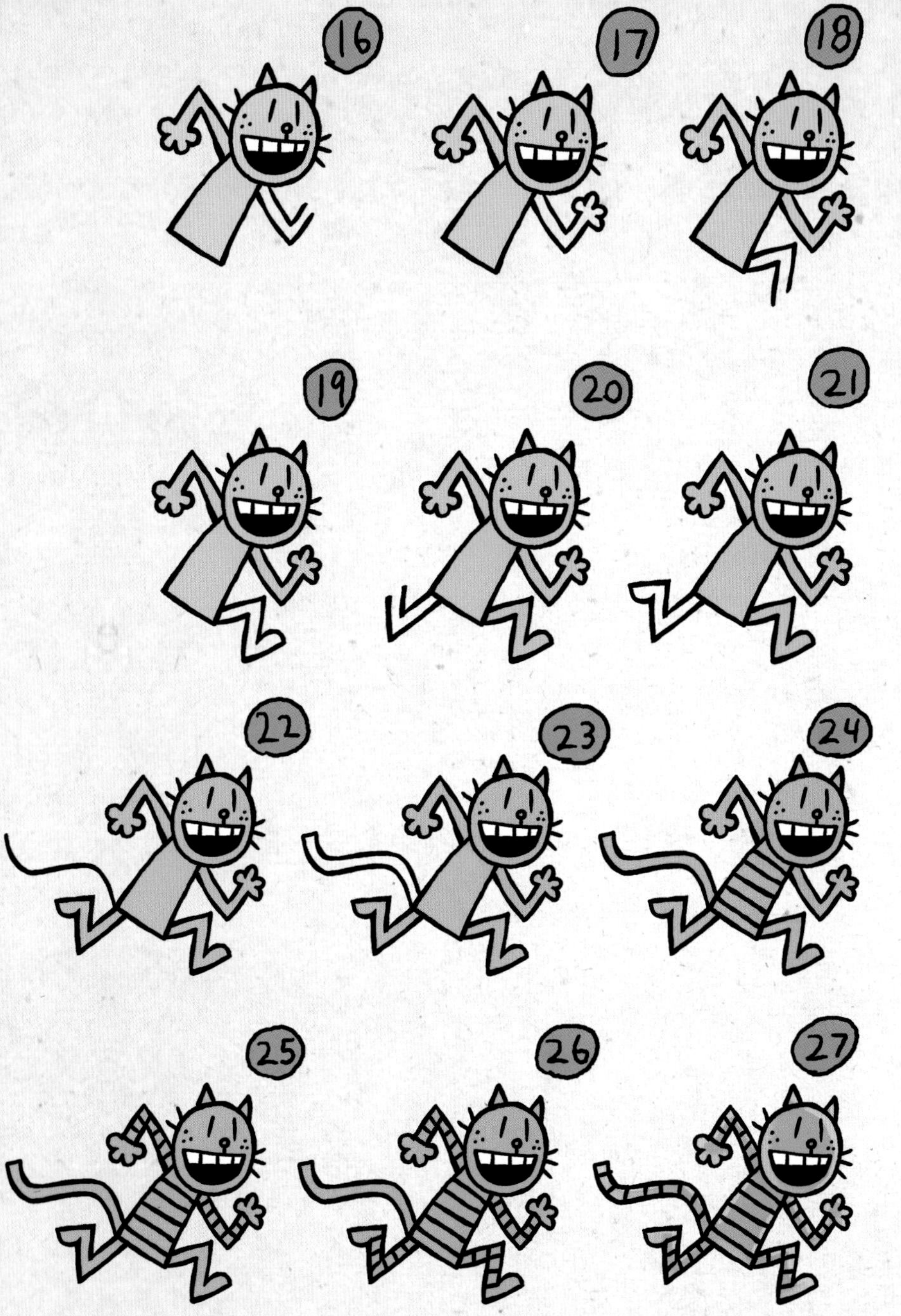
16
17
18
19
20
21
22
23
24
25
26
27

DOG MAN

in **34** Ridiculously easy Steps!

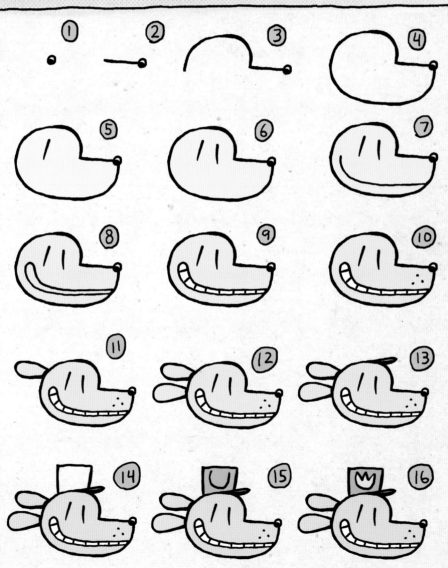

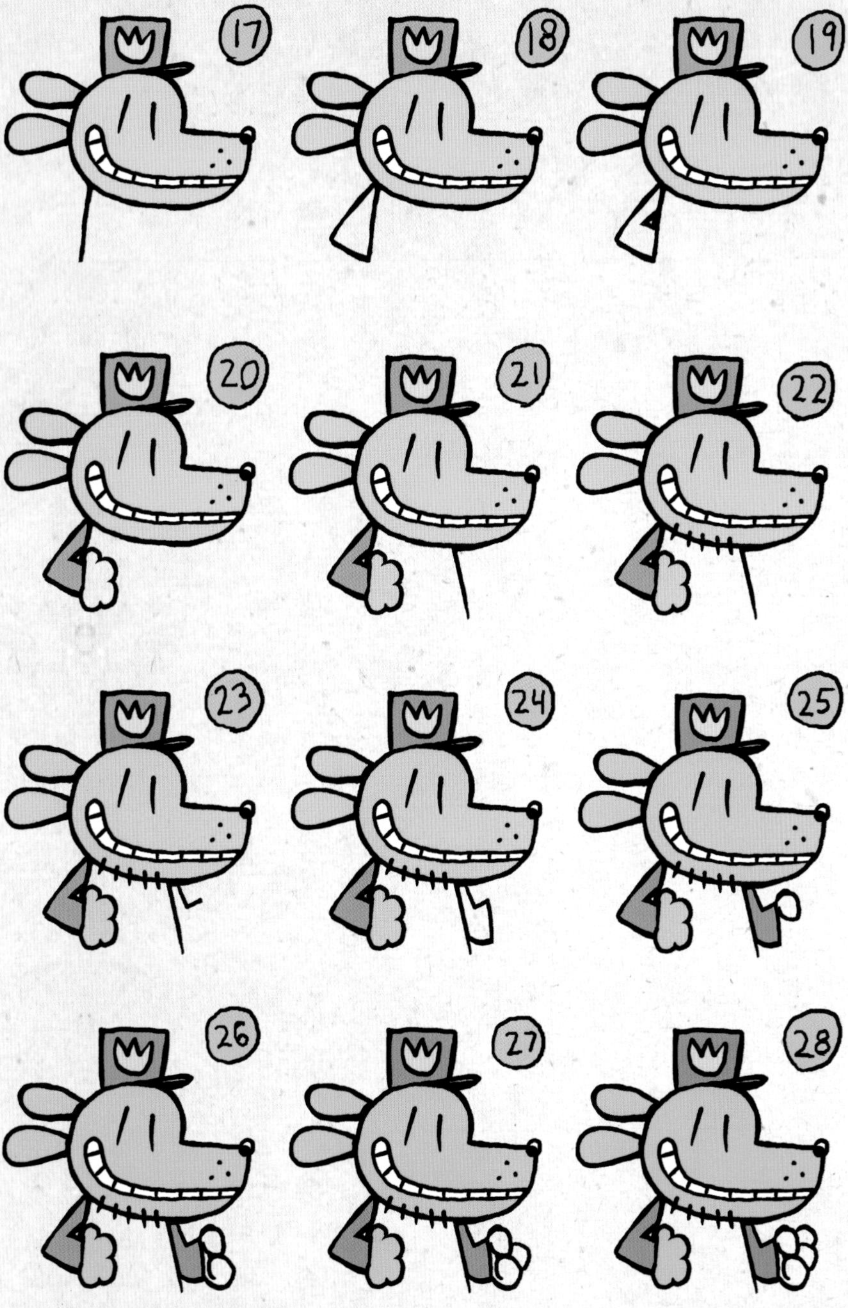
17
18
19
20
21
22
23
24
25
26
27
28

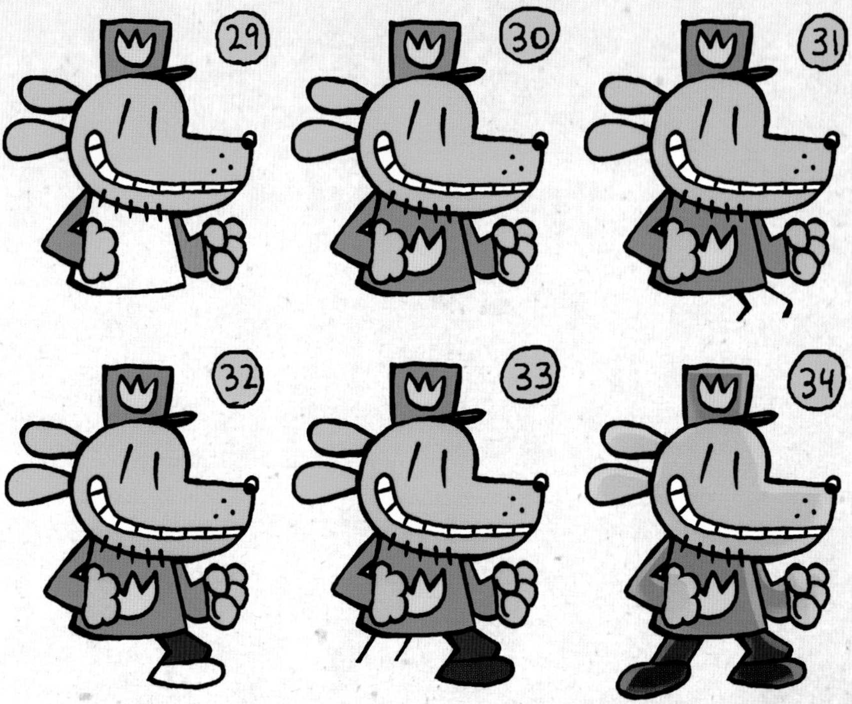
29
30
31
32
33
34

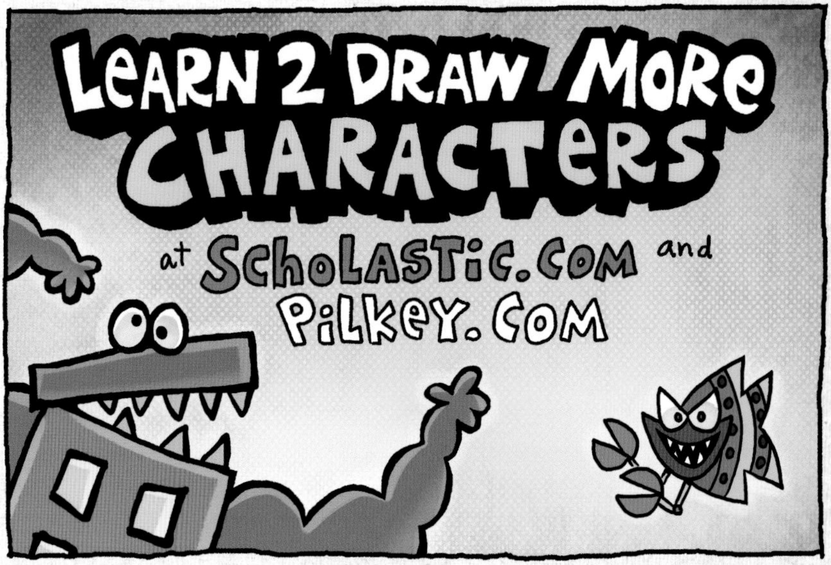
LEARN 2 DRAW MORE CHARACTERS
at SCHOLASTIC.COM and
PILKEY.COM

READ TO YOUR DOG, MAN!

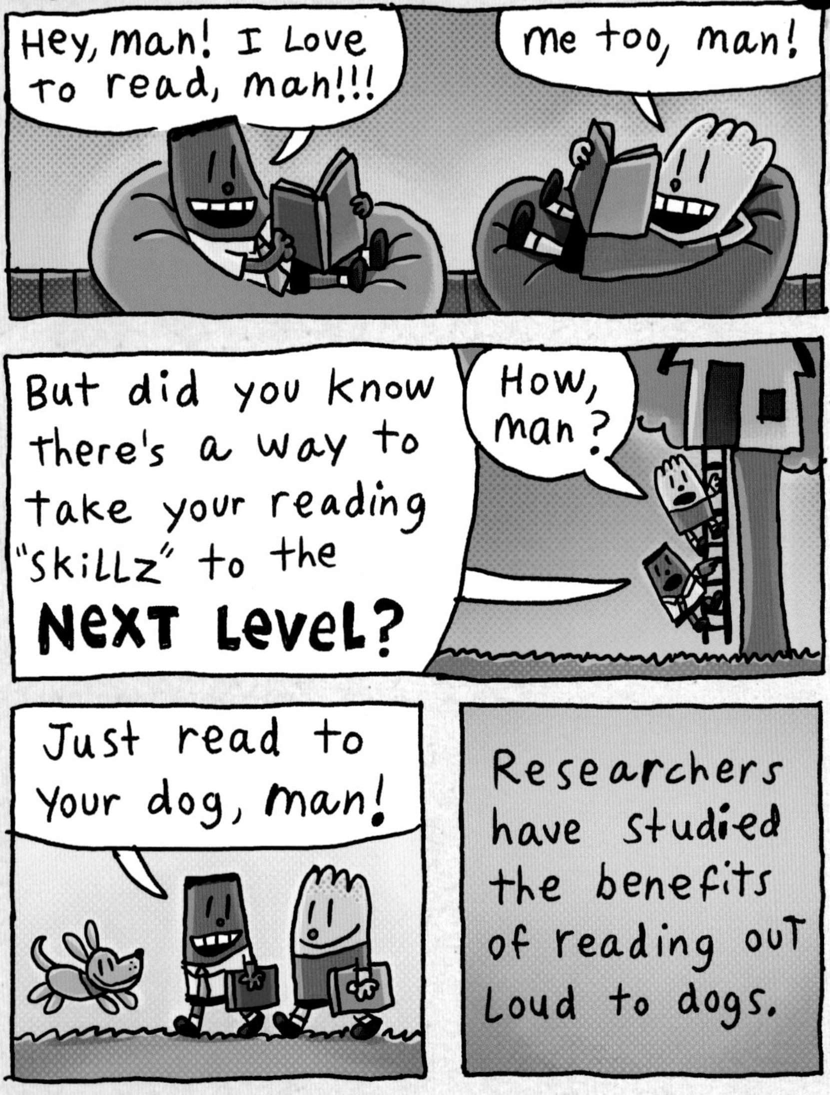
Hey, man! I Love to read, man!!!
me too, man!
But did you know there's a way to take your reading "SkiLLz" to the NEXT LeveL?
How, man?
Just read to your dog, man!
Researchers have studied the benefits of reading out Loud to dogs.

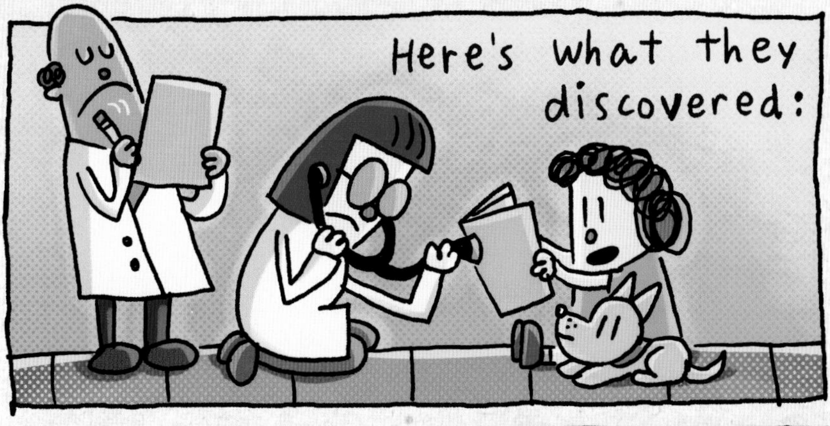
Here's what they discovered:

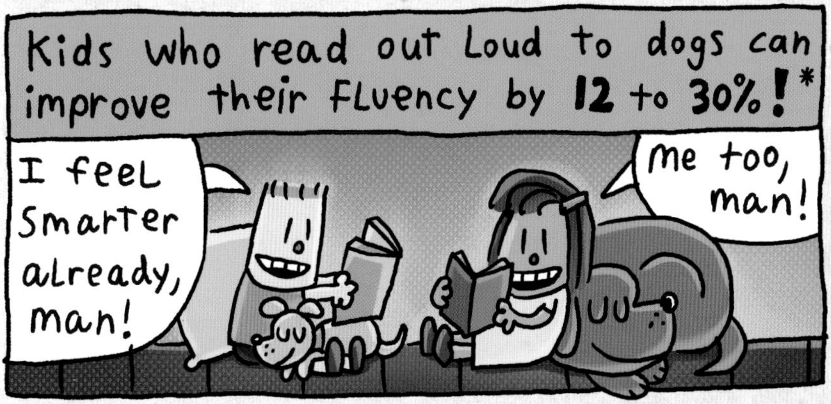
Kids who read out loud to dogs can improve their fluency by 12 to 30%!*
I feel smarter already, man!
me too, man!

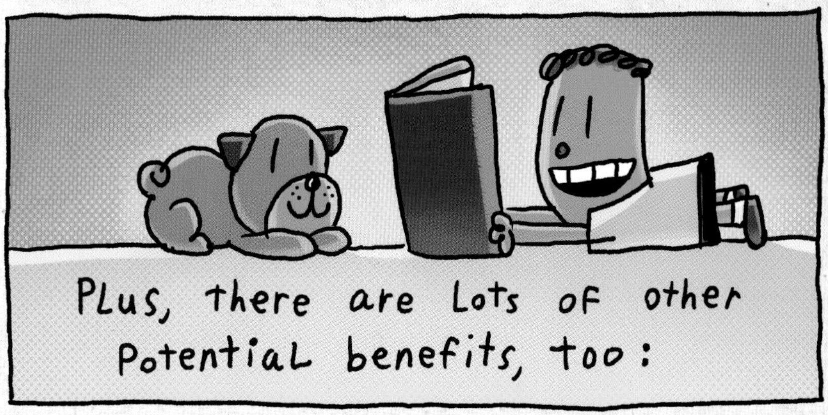
Plus, there are lots of other potential benefits, too:

* University of California-Davis: Reading to Rover, 2010

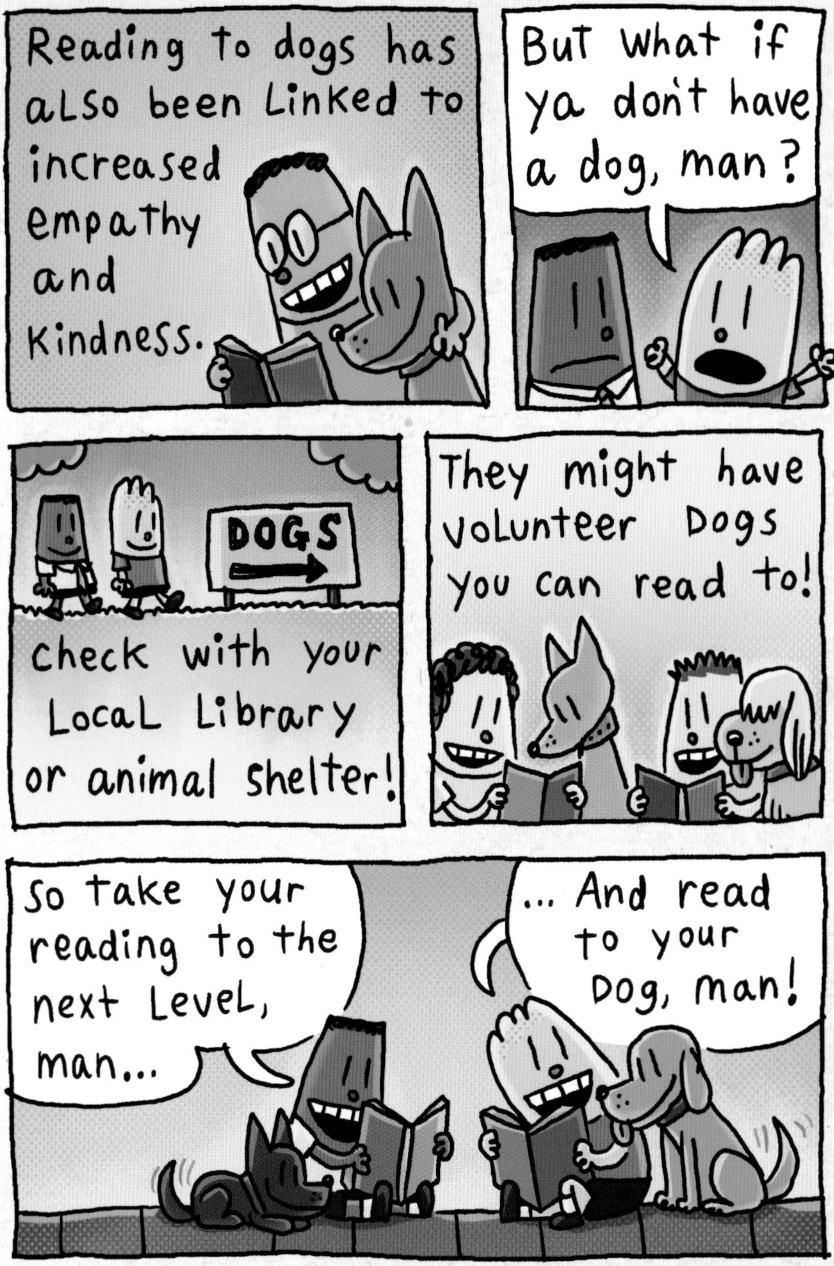
Reading to dogs has also been linked to increased empathy and kindness.
But what if ya don't have a dog, man?
DOGS
Check with your local library or animal shelter!
They might have volunteer dogs you can read to!
So take your reading to the next level, man...
... And read to your Dog, man!

READING TO YOUR DOG IS ALWAYS A PAWS-ITIVE EXPERIENCE!

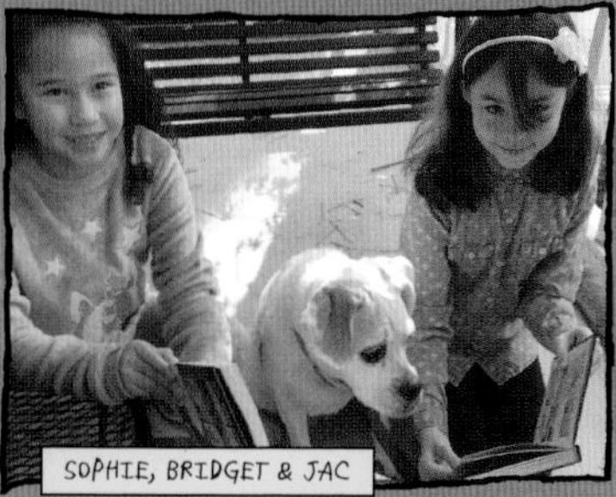
SOPHIE, BRIDGET & JAC

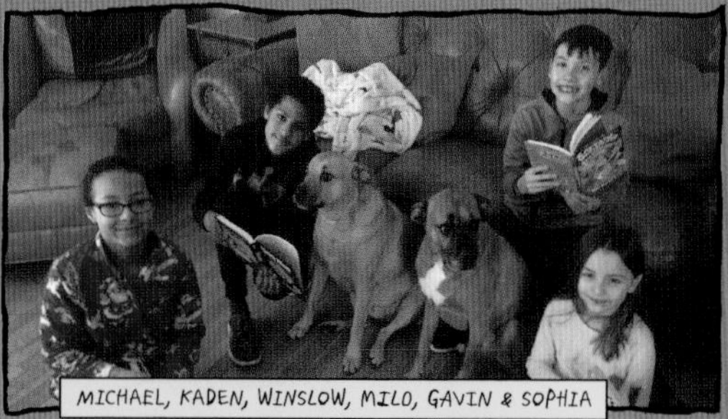
MICHAEL, KADEN, WINSLOW, MILO, GAVIN & SOPHIA

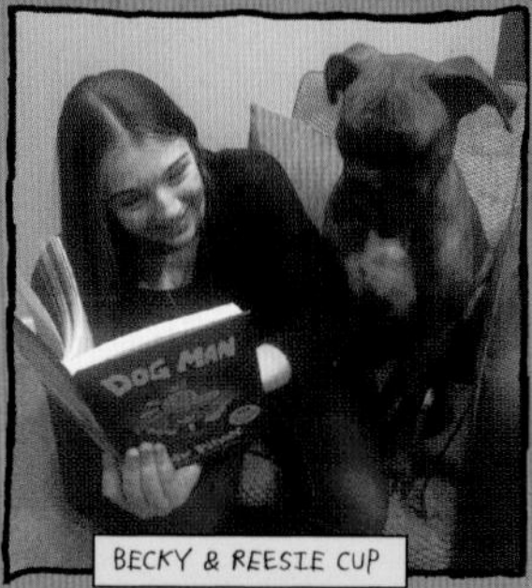
DOG MAN
BECKY & REESIE CUP

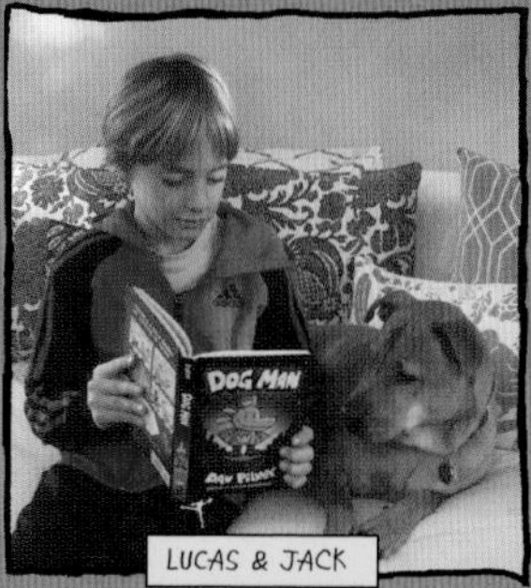
DOG MAN
LUCAS & JACK

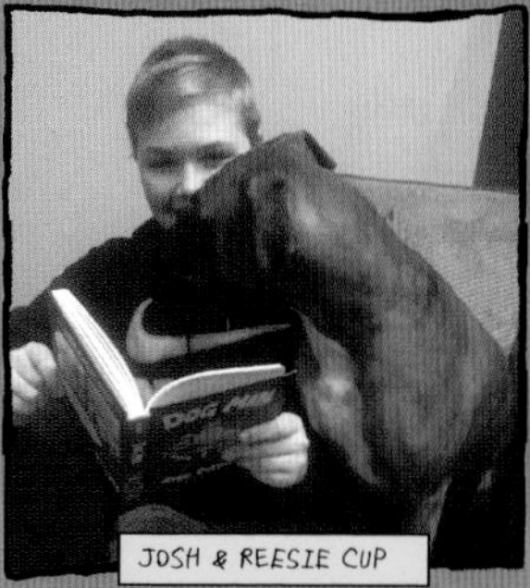
DOG MAN
JOSH & REESIE CUP

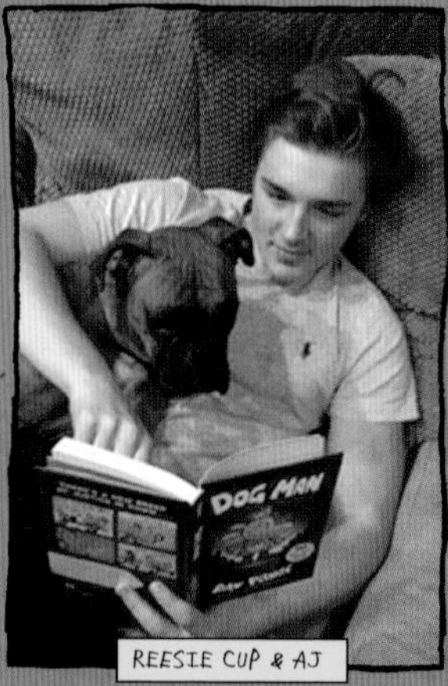
DOG MAN
REESIE CUP & AJ

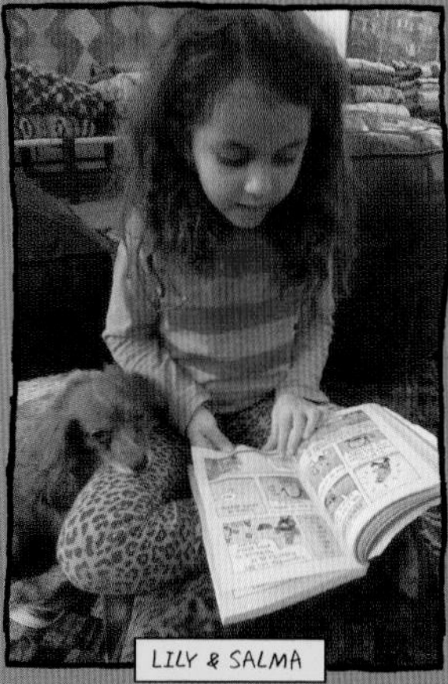
LILY & SALMA

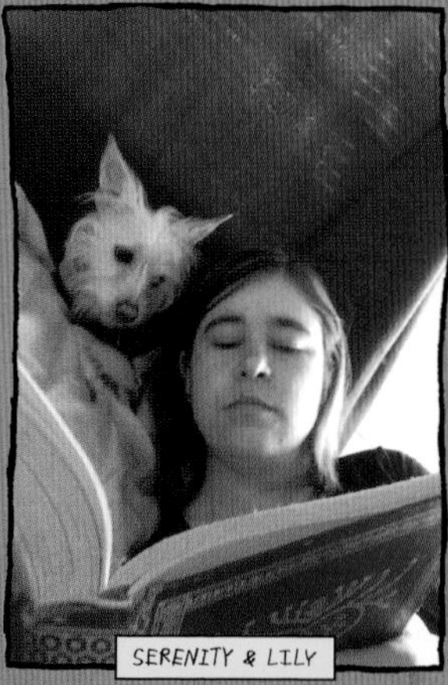
SERENITY & LILY

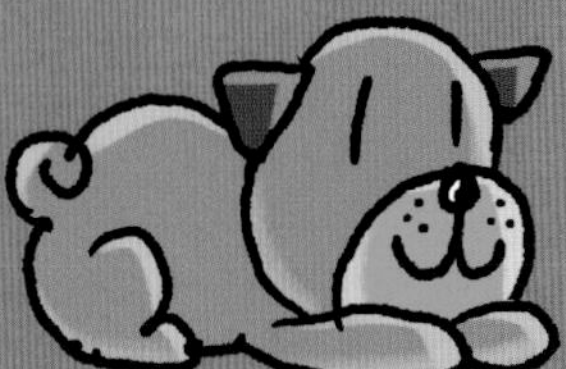

#Readtoyourdogman

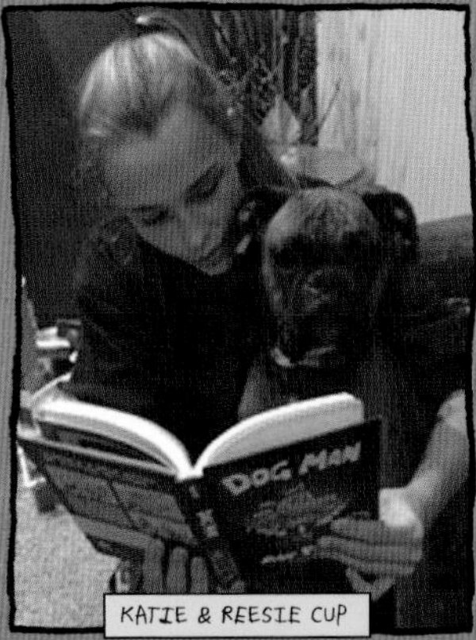
DOG MAN

KATIE & REESIE CUP

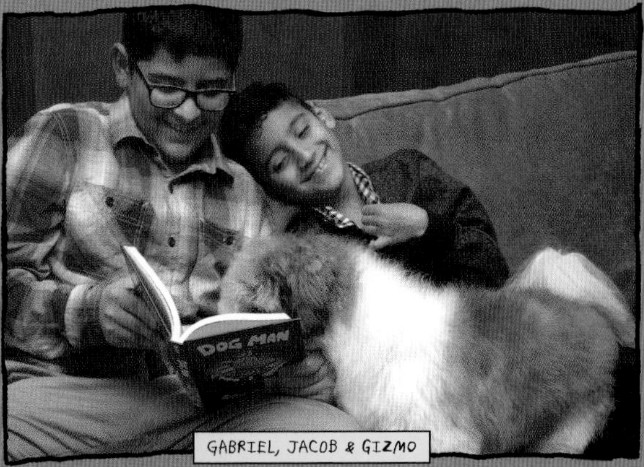
DOG MAN

GABRIEL, JACOB & GIZMO

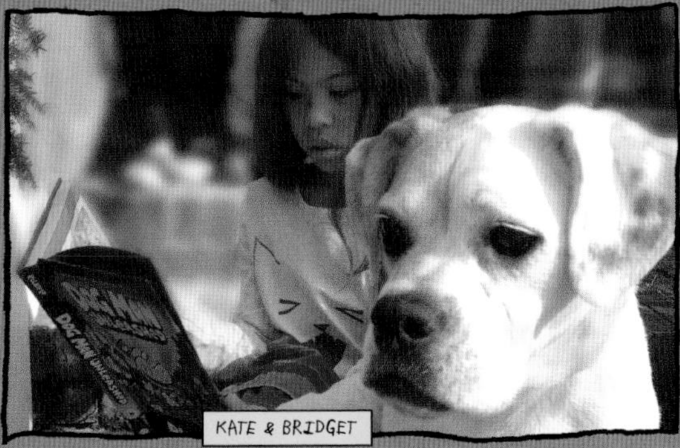

KATE & BRIDGET

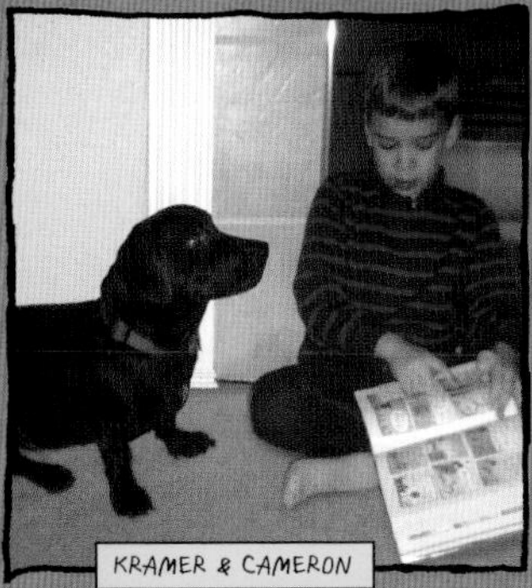

KRAMER & CAMERON

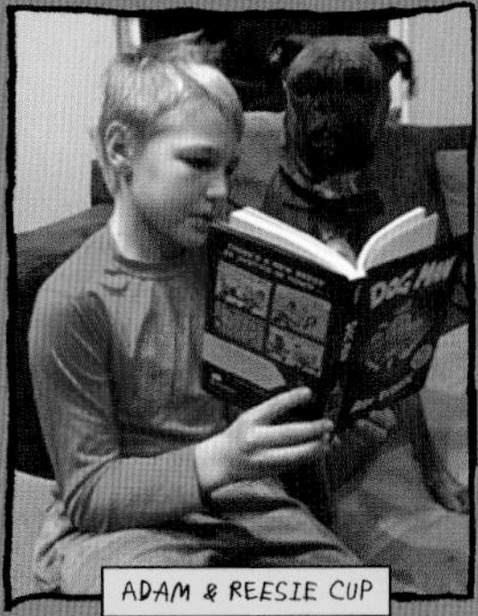
DOG MAN

ADAM & REESIE CUP

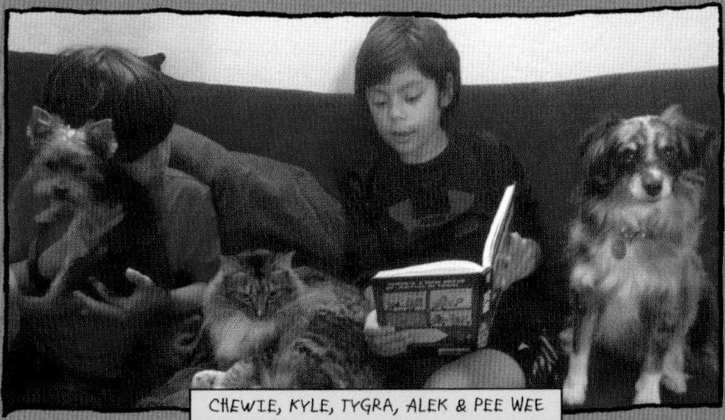

CHEWIE, KYLE, TYGRA, ALEK & PEE WEE

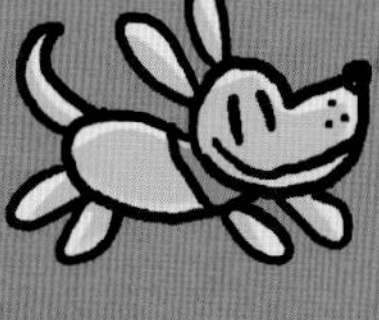

LEARN MORE AT PILKEY.COM!

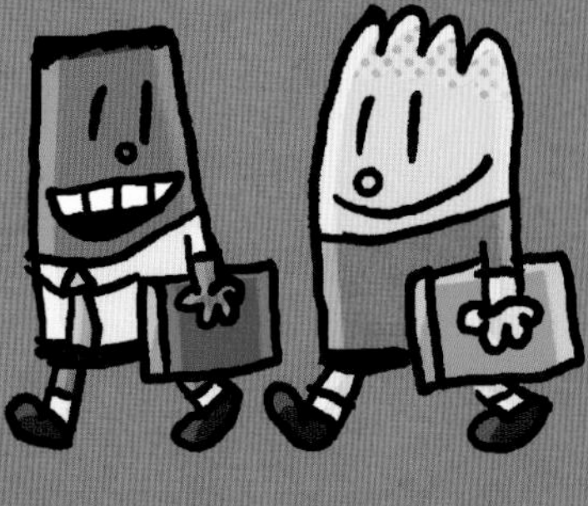

ABOUT THE AUTHOR-ILLUSTRATOR

When Dav Pilkey was a kid, he suffered from ADHD, dyslexia, and behavioral problems. Dav was so disruptive in class that his teachers made him sit out in the hall every day. Luckily, Dav loved to draw and make up stories. He spent his time in the hallway creating his own original comic books.

In the second grade, Dav Pilkey created a comic book about a superhero named Captain Underpants. His teacher ripped it up and told him he couldn't spend the rest of his life making silly books.

Fortunately, Dav was not a very good listener.

ABOUT THE COLORIST

Jose Garibaldi grew up on the South Side of Chicago. As a kid, he was a daydreamer and a doodler, and now it's his full-time job to do both. Jose is a professional illustrator, painter, and cartoonist who has created work for Dark Horse Comics, Disney, Nickelodeon, MAD Magazine, and many more. He lives in Los Angeles, California, with his wife and their cats.